"I saved the best f[...]
held out a straw cowboy hat. "It's the tree topper."

Clint laughed. "I might not know much about decorating, but isn't it supposed to be a star?"

"Not on a cowboy Christmas tree."

Clint smiled and sidled up next to her, gently taking the hat from her hand and placing it at the top of the tree.

They stepped back to survey their work. With the colored lights, cowboy ornaments and red bandannas tied here and there, it represented him and all he stood for. Something shifted inside him. Softened his heart.

It was his first Christmas tree, and it suited him perfectly. And it was all because of Lexi.

She turned to him, holding up her hand. "Nice work."

He high-fived her, wanting to express how much this day meant to him, but not knowing how.

"Come on. Pumpkin pie is waiting for us."

Pumpkin pie, Christmas decorating, laughter and music? He'd better not get used to this; it would be gone all too soon.

Jill Kemerer writes novels with love, humor and faith. Besides spoiling her minidachshund and keeping up with her busy kids, Jill reads stacks of books, lives for her morning coffee and gushes over fluffy animals. She resides in Ohio with her husband and two children. Jill loves connecting with readers, so please visit her website, jillkemerer.com, or contact her at PO Box 2802, Whitehouse, OH 43571.

Brenda Minton lives in the Ozarks with her husband, children, cats, dogs and strays. She is a pastor's wife, Sunday-school teacher, coffee addict and is sleep-deprived. Not in that order. Her dream to be an author for Harlequin started somewhere in the pages of a romance novel about a young American woman stranded in a Spanish castle. Her dreams came true, and twenty-plus books later, she is an author hoping to inspire young girls to dream.

A Bride for Christmas

Jill Kemerer

&

Brenda Minton

2 Uplifting Stories
The Rancher's Mistletoe Bride and
The Rancher's Christmas Bride

LOVE INSPIRED
INSPIRATIONAL ROMANCE

LOVE INSPIRED®
INSPIRATIONAL ROMANCE

Recycling programs
for this product may
not exist in your area.

ISBN-13: 978-1-335-42986-5

A Bride for Christmas

Copyright © 2022 by Harlequin Enterprises ULC

The Rancher's Mistletoe Bride
First published in 2017. This edition published in 2022.
Copyright © 2017 by Ripple Effect Press, LLC

The Rancher's Christmas Bride
First published in 2017. This edition published in 2022.
Copyright © 2017 by Brenda Minton

For questions and comments about the quality of this book, please contact us
at CustomerService@Harlequin.com.

Love Inspired
22 Adelaide St. West, 41st Floor
Toronto, Ontario M5H 4E3, Canada
www.LoveInspired.com

Printed in U.S.A.

CONTENTS

THE RANCHER'S
MISTLETOE BRIDE

Jill Kemerer

For Rachel Kent. This book wouldn't be here
without you. I'm thankful for you every day.

For Pen to Paper, the first writing group
I ever joined. Jan and Patricia, your gentleness
and knowledge were instrumental to my growth.
Thank you.

Do nothing out of selfish ambition or vain conceit.
Rather, in humility value others above yourselves,
not looking to your own interests but each of you
to the interests of the others.

—Philippians 2:3–4

Chapter One

He hadn't ranched in four years, but the tug of cowboy life always beckoned.

Clint Romine slowed his truck to study the magnificent property splayed before him. Well-maintained fences lined the perimeter and divided areas for rotating stock. Acres of grazing land, fields for hay production, barns, cabins, outbuildings, paddocks—all appeared neat and orderly and only a ten-minute drive from Sweet Dreams, Wyoming. Rock Step Ranch was everything a cattle ranch should be. And more. If Clint's interview went well, he'd be in charge of this entire outfit.

Unease slithered down his neck. Was he fit to manage it?

His mistake haunted him. A slip in his judgment. The death of a dream. But owning a ranch wasn't the same as being hired to manage one. Four years ago, he'd had everything to lose. And now? There was nothing left for him to lose. He'd already lost it all.

Clint drove into a gravel lot near the barn and paddocks, cut the engine, and stepped out. Mountains stood proudly in the distance, and the wind held the bite of early November. Cowboys shouted from the cutting pen. Looked like they were weaning calves. He longed to slap on his chaps and join them.

After watching for a few minutes, he checked the time and forced himself to stride toward the main house. A two-story log home with a covered porch, a pair of rocking chairs and a faded mat greeted him. Before he knocked, he paused to pray.

Lord, I've made mistakes. I don't deserve my own land. But if You'll give me the opportunity to manage this operation, I'll try not to let You or the ranch down.

Clint stretched himself to his full height and rapped twice on the door. It opened almost immediately, and he stared into light brown eyes the color of the pronghorns he often saw bounding across the land.

Alexandra Harrington had grown into a beautiful woman.

He wasn't in her league—had never been in her league. When he'd found out she was the one hiring, he'd been concerned about working for his former classmate. Attraction complicated the employer/employee relationship. When he'd worked on LFR Ranch, a cowboy had been fired for flirting with the owner's daughter. But now that he'd seen Alexandra, his fears disappeared. A smart, successful, stunning woman like her was out of reach for a working guy like him. Not that he needed to worry about it. Rumor had it you had to spend time with a woman, get to know her, to have a shot at dating her. He had no intention of spending time with her, let alone dating her.

"Thanks for coming, Clint." She ushered him inside, and once he'd taken off his outerwear, he followed her down a hallway to a large living room with views of the river. The hardwood floors were in bad shape. Scratched. Faded. Three rocks were missing from the stone fireplace climbing the wall to the ceiling. From somewhere nearby, the drip, drip of a faucet fought to override the sound of a ripped screen flapping against a window. Even the air had the stale tang of neglect.

Strange that the outbuildings, fences and property were in top-notch order, but this house had been allowed to fall apart.

He turned his attention to the woman he recognized from high school. Still slim in dark jeans and an oversize white sweater. Long, dark brown waves spilled over her shoulders. Her pale face held high cheekbones, full eyebrows and thin pink lips. But Alexandra wore sad the way he wore regret—it permeated her, surrounded her—and he had the strongest urge to take it from her. Which was a laugh, since he had no idea how. He'd never been around many women and probably never would be.

He *did* know what it was like to suddenly have no family, though. Her father had died three weeks ago. She had every right to be sad.

She took a seat on an old tan couch, motioning for him to sit opposite her, and he obliged, his cowboy hat in his hands.

"Dottie Lavert mentioned you might be interested in managing the ranch for me." Her words were quiet but firm. "As you know, Daddy died unexpectedly, and I need someone here sooner rather than later."

He nodded, not knowing what to think of the way she was fingering the bottom edge of her sweater. Was she nervous? No. This was Alexandra Harrington. Vice president of their senior class, organizer of proms and dances and who knew what else.

"I remember you from high school," she said. "You worked on a ranch then, too, didn't you?"

"Yes." He was surprised she remembered him at all. His one goal in high school had been to be as invisible as possible. As a teen, he'd poured all his energy into keeping his spot at Yearling Group Home for teen boys. The Laverts had been hired to run the group foster home. Back then, Big Bob Lavert kept the boys in line while his wife, Dottie, cooked their meals, made sure they did their homework and accompanied them to church. Too bad Yearling had shut down several years ago. It had helped a lot of kids like him who had nowhere else to go.

"From your résumé, I see you've been working for the oil company." She smiled, her expression open, expectant. "And before that you worked on LFR Ranch."

"Yes, ma'am."

"Call me Lexi."

Lexi? He couldn't call her Lexi. Couldn't even think of her as Lexi. Too familiar, too accessible. *Alexandra* had the right amount of remoteness for his liking.

"I learned about calving, grazing, hay production, keeping the books and maintaining the property from my years at LFR." He paused, unsure how much more to tell her. If he confessed how he'd left LFR and then been duped out of his own tiny piece of Wyoming, she'd boot him right out the door. And if he admitted he'd spent four years avoiding working on a ranch because it had hurt too much to be surrounded by what he'd lost, she'd think he was crazy. "I've been working for the oil company for four years now."

She picked up the top paper from a stack on the end table next to her. "Yes, I see you were promoted three times in as many years. Impressive."

Impressive? Him? If she only knew... He hoped she didn't ask about the six months between LFR Ranch and the oil company. If asked outright, he wouldn't lie to her. And he didn't want to return to his mind-numbing job.

"I need someone I can depend on to do all the things my father did. I own a wedding planning company in Denver. I've already told my employees I'll be living in Wyoming at least until Christmas. To put it simply, my business takes all of my time. If running my company from here proves too difficult, I'll have to move back to Colorado. In that case, I'd come to the ranch once a month or so. I need someone here who is self-motivated. Someone who can delegate work to the ranch hands. Someone I can trust."

Could she trust him? Did he trust himself?

She continued. "The next question might seem forward, but I have to know. Do you drink?"

"No."

She narrowed her eyes, her lips pursing, clearly unconvinced.

"I've seen what it does to people and have no desire to try it." He held her gaze. "I like to be in complete control of my faculties. At all times. I'll take a drug test if you'd like."

"I'll take your word for it." She massaged the back of her neck. She looked tired. More than tired. Exhausted. "You're not the first person to be considered for this position. I hired a man last week who had a problem with the hard stuff. What a disaster he turned out to be. Daddy's right-hand man, Jerry Cornell—you'll meet him in a little while—found him at noon on Saturday still lit out of his mind, sitting in the river in his drawers when he should have been working. When I called him into the office, he had the nerve to tell me not to worry my 'purdy' little head about it. Needless to say, I had to let him go." She got to her feet and started pacing. "He's fortunate he didn't get hypothermia."

Clint strangled the hat between his hands. He'd worked with plenty of cowboys who drank too much. The fact one of them would disrespect her made him want to rope the jerk up.

She spun to face him, chin high. "This is my home. The only thing left of my childhood and my parents. I have ranch hands and their families depending on me for their income. If keeping this operation profitable and in tip-top shape isn't your number-one priority, you will not work here. It's that simple. And, in case I didn't make it clear, I have the final say in all ranch decisions."

"Yes, ma'am." He could keep a ranch in tip-top shape. But profitable? He'd made a bad financial choice years ago. What if he made one again?

She sighed then, her body sagging as if someone had let the air out of her. "I'll take you out to meet Jerry. He'll show you around and feed you lunch. When you're done, come back up here and we'll talk."

Good. She was a take-charge woman unafraid to be his boss. The firmer the line between employee and employer, the better. As long as he made wise decisions concerning the cattle, he could spend his days doing what he loved best—living the cowboy life.

Working for the prettiest girl he'd ever laid eyes on.

Living the *single* cowboy life.

Pretty or not, no woman would want a man who'd

been stupid enough to get swindled out of the one thing he'd ever wanted—a ranch of his own.

"Well, Jerry, what do you think?" Lexi sat on a stool in the ranch manager's office adjoining the stables. The room smelled of dirt, large animals and burned coffee. Everywhere she looked, she found clutter of the male kind. Ropes, broken bridles, spray cans full of who knew what, stained papers and tools. Her office in Denver was painted the pale pink of a rose petal and smelled of magnolias. She missed it.

Which brought her back to the three-week-old question…why was she still here? After the funeral, she'd packed her suitcase with every intention of driving back to her life in Denver. She hadn't made it off the property before turning around, filled with the sensation she was deserting the place, the same way she'd deserted her father to focus on expanding her company.

Where did she belong? Here with her memories or back in the city with Weddings by Alexandra?

"Clint's a good 'un, Miss Lexi." The wire-thin man scratched his chin and scanned Clint's résumé. "His former bosses paint him as a fine man."

She thought as much, too, but it was reassuring to hear it from Jerry. She tapped a pen against her chin. "Any reason you can think of why I shouldn't hire him?"

"Nope." He rolled the paper and smacked it on the plywood counter.

Taking it from Jerry, she uncurled it. Perused it once more. "What about the gap between jobs? It was four years ago, but…"

Jerry shook his head. "A lot of cowboys have periods they can't account for."

"Really? Why?"

"Ah…well…these are lonely parts up here in this blessed country. You know those wild horses that run wild through the north property now and again?"

"Yes."

"Some cowboys are like those horses. They don't like to be fenced in. Something snaps, and they leave. Could be due to a lady. Could be a sense they need to move on."

Clint was the wild horse in this scenario, but he seemed quiet, steady. She bit her tongue. She'd been listening to Jerry's parables her entire life, and they tended to meander.

"Now some of the boys take their savings and go off and live awhile. Figure things out. Get close to the land and their maker…"

It made sense. Everyone needed time to figure life out now and then. Wasn't that what she herself was doing?

"…but the restlessness clears up, and they settle down right fine."

She hopped off the stool. "Okay, Jerry, I'll take your word for it. Send him up to the house when Logan brings him back."

"Will do." He gave her a nod. "Oh, and Miss Lexi?"

"Yes?"

"The Florida fella called again. Wants to know if he can count on us for hay next winter."

Lexi tucked her hair behind her ear. One of her father's pet projects had been to start growing high-quality hay to sell to horse farms and other large-animal breeders across the nation. He'd built the new storage barn in the spring and begun negotiations with various buyers. But the drought conditions coupled with low calf prices last year prevented him from purchasing the necessary equipment to produce the square bales. Putting up high-quality hay had been postponed until next summer.

"I don't know the answer. It will depend on the price we get for this year's calves."

"I'll call him and tell him we'll know more in a few months."

"Thanks, Jerry." She left the office, savoring the fresh air as she headed back to her house. Between the ranch and her business, there seemed to be an endless list of problems. For weeks, Lexi's assistant, Jolene Day, had been texting her every three minutes with an urgent crisis. Two clients had called earlier with major changes to their weddings, and the invitations Lexi had ordered two months ago were still on back order.

And then there was the ranch. Daddy had been the spine of this operation, and without him? If she didn't find a take-charge manager, she would have to sell Rock Step Ranch. She couldn't manage both, and she'd rather have someone else own it than let Daddy's legacy fade to ruins.

Just thinking about selling made her nauseous. This was her home. Her memories.

As she reached the path leading to her house, a gust of wind blew her scarf across her face, and she swept it back. Clint seemed to be the perfect candidate for manager, but if she were brutally honest with herself, he presented a new dilemma. One he couldn't help.

He was gorgeous.

And tall. Solid muscle. Quiet.

The gorgeous part was the problem.

She'd never expected to be attracted to him. She barely remembered him from high school. In fact, she couldn't recall having a single conversation with him back then. How had she overlooked him? He had thick, dark hair begging to be touched, and his midnight blue eyes seemed to notice everything. He was as fine a physical specimen as she'd ever seen.

A rugged, handsome cowboy.

Thankfully, he was all wrong for her. The strong, silent types were perfect for managing a ranch, but as far as dating? Not likely to sweep her off her feet any time soon.

She opened the front door and took off her coat and boots before heading to the living room and sitting on the couch. Her cell phone showed missed calls and texts, but she only checked the one from Jerry. Clint was on his way.

Even if she hadn't been overwhelmed trying to make double the business decisions as usual, she couldn't imagine dating anyone at this time and certainly not Clint. She wanted romance with a capital *R*, and after Doug, she'd decided under no circumstances was she settling for ho-hum. She wanted breathless kisses. Heart-pounding anticipation. A man who loved her enough to make a grand gesture or two. Someone who valued marriage and wanted kids.

She wanted more than any guy had offered her so far, and Clint, for all his curling eyelashes and silky, touchable hair, seemed too reserved to be that guy.

Besides, she *had* to hire him. She was out of options. She'd interviewed five men for the job, hired one, fired one. With the drought and extra expenses from the new barn, the ranch needed someone with experience who understood how to manage its resources wisely. And after losing Daddy, she couldn't bear to lose her home, too.

A knock on the door startled her. She opened it, once more struck by Clint's blue eyes. She waved for him to follow her into the living room.

"Well, what did you think?"

He perched on the edge of the chair, hat in hand. "It's a fine operation. Jerry's done a good job running it since…well…" His eyebrows drew together, and he cleared his throat.

"Yes." She clasped her hands tightly. Thinking about Daddy being gone formed an instant lump in her throat, one she'd gotten adept at ignoring. Somehow she needed to find a way to get over the pain of losing him that had taken up permanent residence in her heart. "Jerry's been a blessing. For many years."

"Why don't you have him manage it?" The question was simple, open, pure curiosity.

"He doesn't want to. His wife's been asking him to slow down. He's getting older. Said I needed a long-term solution. And Logan isn't interested, either. He's the most experienced full-time ranch hand, but he only plans on staying here a year or two more. He and his wife want to move back to Casper after they save enough money to buy a house."

Clint nodded, a lock of hair dipping across his forehead. She forced her attention to her raggedy fingernails. Flipping through the papers she'd left on the end table earlier, she found the list she'd typed.

"Jerry and I discussed it, and we think you're right for the position." After naming his salary and benefits, she went over his duties and wrapped it up with living arrangements. "We have a few empty cabins, a two-bedroom guest house and a three-bedroom manager's house. Logan lives in the manager's house with his wife, Sarah, and their children. She's the ranch cook. If you'd like, I'll ask them to move, but…"

"No." He shook his head. "One of the cabins will be fine."

"Does this mean you'll take the job?"

"I'll take it." His eyes glinted, reminding her of a wild storm on the prairie, all lightning flashes and black clouds rolling in the distance. Spectacular. Exciting.

Maybe Jerry was onto something with the whole wild horse analogy. And maybe Clint wasn't as reserved as she'd originally thought.

"When can you start?" she asked.

"When do you need me?"

"Yesterday." She sighed, waving her hand. "Sorry, it's just been hard on the crew. They've all had to step up and take on way too much responsibility here for weeks now. I know you need to give your employer notice and—"

"I'll move in this weekend and start Monday."

Just like that? She wanted to raise her fist and yell, "Yippee!" but she said a silent prayer of thanks instead. "Perfect. As for the living arrangements, I appreciate you allowing Logan and Sarah to stay in the larger house, but I insist you take the two-bedroom guest cabin. You're in a position of authority here, and your lodging should reflect it."

He nodded.

"Do you have any questions?" she asked. "Any concerns?"

"No, ma'am."

"Clint, we graduated high school together. *Ma'am* makes me feel like I'm a hundred and fifty years old. Call me Lexi."

"I don't know if I feel right doing that."

"Why not?"

"Well, if you're going to be my boss, I think it should be more formal."

"I will be your boss, but we're going to have to be comfortable enough with each other that you can come to me with any problems. We'll be meeting weekly on Thursday mornings to discuss the ranch. I might not be involved in the daily operations, but I am very invested in its future."

"I'm glad to hear that. This is your ranch. You should be invested."

"Exactly. Jerry has paperwork for you to fill out. I'll meet you down there in half an hour to show you to your new home." She held out her hand. "Thanks, Clint, for coming today. Welcome aboard."

The warm strength in his callused hand assured her she'd chosen wisely. He dipped his head and left. As soon as the front door clicked shut, she went to the kitchen to make a cup of tea. Her hand trembled as she filled the cup. She kept forgetting to eat. Maybe a piece of toast to go with the tea…

How had her life changed so drastically? One minute she was on top of the world, succeeding at her dream job. The next, plunged into the abyss of her father's death.

Six months. That's how long it had been since she'd visited Daddy. He'd appeared to be in fine health in May. They'd ridden on horseback around the ranch the way they always did. She'd had no idea he had cancer.

Had he known?

Of course not.

If he had known, he would have told her. She would have come back, gone to the doctor with him, made sure he got chemotherapy and radiation and anything that would have saved him. But they hadn't known. And now it was too late.

Why didn't I make more of an effort to come home this summer? He must have been sick. Must have had some symptoms. And I wasn't here to notice.

Her throat tightened the way it had repeatedly since she'd gotten the call from Jerry saying her father had died.

When she'd told Clint this ranch was the only thing left of her parents and her childhood, she'd meant it. And she wasn't about to lose it, too.

As Lexi gave him the tour of the two-bedroom log cabin, Clint mentally tallied a to-do list. It was dusty, but the open area with the kitchen, dining and living room was larger than his current apartment's, and the master bedroom had a nice view of the mountains. He planned to take his coffee first thing each day on the covered porch. Frankly, it was the nicest place he'd lived in and, even unfurnished, it felt like home.

Home. A sense of foreboding killed his good mood. Had he ever belonged anywhere? If he started identifying this place as home, he'd lose it, the way he'd been torn from every other place where he'd felt comfortable.

He needed to remain detached.

At least the main house was up the lane far enough for him to maintain a necessary distance from his boss.

Other than weekly meetings, he saw no reason why they would need to see each other.

"The river's great for fishing, and feel free to use the ATVs anytime. If you need help moving in, just holler. I'm sure one of the ranch hands would be happy to lend a hand."

"Yes, ma'a—" He caught himself. "Thank you, Miss Lexi."

She leaned against the kitchen counter and glared. "Clint, Jerry, who is seventy-five years old, calls me Miss Lexi. It's Lexi. Just Lexi."

He itched to smile, but she looked paler, more tired than she had earlier. He studied her more closely.

Thin. Too thin. Dark smudges under her eyes. Cheekbones jutting out. Her clothes hung on her. Was she eating enough? Or at all?

She had the look of someone who'd had to be strong for too long. It reminded him of moving into his first foster home after his grandfather died when Clint was six. Even though Grandpa had been mean as a rattler, when the man passed, Clint knew deep inside he was all alone in the world and his life would never be the same. Did Lexi feel alone, too? He wanted to tuck her under a blanket on the couch. Protect her.

He shook his head. Him protecting her? What a laugh. She didn't need someone like him.

She stepped forward and wobbled.

"Have you eaten lately?" He moved closer, ready to catch her if she fainted.

"What?" She blinked, shaking her head, and swayed. He reached for her, steadied her.

"Come on, I'll take you back. You need some food."

"I'm fine." Her protest sounded weak. "I had some toast a little bit ago."

"It's five thirty. You need a meal." He kept a loose hold on her arm and led her to the door. The wind had picked up, and the temperature had dropped. "Zip up. You don't want to catch cold."

To his relief, she didn't argue. She zipped her coat and fell in beside him. When they reached the house, he followed her inside. A napkin with a half-eaten piece of toast lay on the end table. Probably the only food she'd eaten today.

"Sit on the couch, and I'll make you something to eat."

"I couldn't ask you—"

"I'm not driving back to Cheyenne on an empty stomach. I'll make some supper and get out of here."

She sat on the couch, looking lost. "Okay."

He opened her fridge and pantry. Chicken broth, noodles, frozen carrots. "Are you saving the chicken in the freezer for anything?"

"There's chicken in the freezer?"

He chuckled under his breath. "I'm using it."

After opening cupboards and drawers, he had a good idea of where everything was stored. He chopped an onion, defrosted and diced the chicken, and heated oil in a frying pan. He filled a large pot with the chicken stock and set it on the stove to boil.

Lexi crept up and sat on one of the bar stools opposite him. "What are you making?"

"Chicken noodle soup."

"Really, you can cook?"

He nodded, suddenly uncomfortable. He shouldn't

be here, in her house, going through her kitchen. It was too intimate.

She wiped her fingers across her forehead. "I never really learned." Her cell phone rang. "Excuse me." She hurried to stand by the patio door as she answered the phone.

After stirring the chicken frying in the pan, he tracked her moves. Voice bright and confident, hand reaching for the pen and paper on the coffee table. Phone tucked between her ear and shoulder as she scribbled something. When the call ended, she seemed to deflate, and he quickly turned away.

"I forgot to mention I'll be out of town next Thursday through Sunday. It's the final wedding I'm in charge of for the year. My other planners are organizing the rest."

"Okay." He slid the cooked chicken into the boiling pot along with the noodles, onions and carrots. A pinch of salt and pepper, and he dialed the burner down to simmer for a while. "If you don't cook, what do you do for meals?"

"Well, in Denver, I order a lot of takeout. I'm usually working late, anyhow."

"But you're here. And there's no takeout."

"I manage."

Not very well, from the looks of it. He doubted she'd eaten more than a bowl of cereal all week. "Why don't you eat with the rest of the crew?"

She grimaced, shaking her head vehemently. "I wouldn't feel comfortable, and neither would they."

She had a point there. "You mentioned a cook— Sarah, right? She would probably fix you a plate."

Lexi shrugged, a wistful expression in her eyes. "I'm sure you're right."

He could tell she had no intention of asking Sarah for a meal. He'd stop over at the manager's house soon and have a quick chat with Logan and his wife. One of the hands could pick up a meal from them to drop off at the main house each night. Whether Lexi ate it or not wasn't his concern.

Her phone rang again. She smiled an apology and answered it, walking away. He couldn't imagine a job with constant phone calls. He stirred the soup, decided it was ready, and ladled out a bowl for her. She was sitting in a chair, saying something about bouquets and cost overages. He'd done his duty. Made her food. She wouldn't even notice if he left without eating. Sharing a meal with her seemed a little too cozy at this point.

But as he sneaked out to his truck, his mind kept returning to her and the bowl of soup he'd left. He didn't want her fainting. Didn't like that her clothes were hanging from her.

She's not my problem.

He'd been hired to manage the ranch, not the ranch owner. Sure, she was alone and grieving and not taking proper care of herself, but fixing it wasn't within his realm.

As he drove past the paddocks, he barely noticed the property that had so mesmerized him earlier. He'd better get his focus back on the cattle and the land where it belonged. He'd finally gotten the nerve to try working on a ranch again. He couldn't make another mistake and ruin this, too.

Chapter Two

Visions of weddings and twinkle lights and Clint filled Lexi's head. Well, not all three together. She sprayed glass cleaner on the new desk she'd installed in the front den. Clint was only on her mind because he was on his way over for their first official ranch meeting. She hoped it wouldn't be awkward. The weddings and twinkle lights were remnants from the weekend, when she'd organized her final wedding of the year.

Two weeks had passed since she'd hired Clint, and she hadn't seen him much, except in passing. They'd nod and exchange pleasantries before going their separate ways. Strictly business.

Strictly business was good. She could pour her energy into weddings, where it belonged. Except she kept thinking back to the night she'd hired him. He'd cooked her soup. Soup! And it had been the best chicken noodle soup she'd ever tasted. She'd indulged in two bowls that night. She'd slept well, too, which was saying something, considering her sleep had been spotty and elusive for a long time.

After wiping the desk clean, she straightened the

shelves and displayed the latest bridal magazines she'd brought back with her from Denver. She moved the floor lamp to the corner and studied it before picking it up once more.

"Can I help you with that?" Clint stood in the doorway. He wore a plaid navy-and-white Western shirt with jeans and boots, and a file was tucked under his arm.

"No, just finishing up." She plastered on her brightest smile. "Come in. Sit down. Would you like something to drink?"

"No, thanks."

"Well, have a seat." She sat in the swivel chair behind the desk and fired up her laptop. "How is your house? Are you settling in okay?"

"It's fine."

Didn't exactly answer her question, but she wasn't surprised. Something told her their weekly meetings weren't going to be as conversational as the ones she led in Denver. She was used to chatting about the latest trends in weddings in her chic conference room with her team of creative professionals. Talking about the ranch with Clint would most likely be brief and to the point.

Clint was currently eyeing her new office. She almost laughed at the frightened look on his face when his gaze landed on her vision board. Swatches of silks, photos of various flowers and motivational quotes in gold calligraphy adorned it.

She took pity on him and clicked through to the checklist she'd created. "Before we get started, I think you should know I've never been involved in ranch operations. Growing up, I helped Daddy move cattle, of course, but...well, you know more about this than I do." She scanned the notes she'd typed after asking

Jerry what to expect on the ranch each month. "Let's see... I'm assuming the calves have all been weaned?"

"Yes, they were actually weaned by the time I moved in. We're keeping a close eye on them. Getting ready to sell. I looked over your winter feed program. We'll continue your father's plan this year."

"As opposed to what plan?" She enjoyed watching him as he talked. Cattle seemed to loosen his tongue; animation lit his face.

"The calf sale date is on the books for the second week in December." He brought his hand to the back of his neck. "But prices will rise after the new year, and if we spent the money to feed the calves longer, they'd weigh more, and we'd get a bigger return on investment."

The words *bigger return on investment* were precisely what she loved to hear. "Do you have numbers?"

He opened his folder and handed her a sheet of paper. A spreadsheet held the number of cattle, the amount of feed needed through the winter and the estimated calf sale price for every month until March.

"But what about the drought? Will we have enough hay stored to feed them along with the rest of the cattle?"

"We would have to supplement with outside feed." He sounded gruff.

"Which, I'm assuming, would be expensive." She wasn't sure how to read him, so she studied the spreadsheet more carefully. "What you're suggesting—do you think it would be smarter to wait a few months to sell the calves?"

He didn't make eye contact. "I think you should do what's best for the ranch."

"Which is?"

"There are pros and cons to both."

Lexi tapped the desktop with her fingernails. He didn't seem the wishy-washy type, so why was he dithering? Maybe he'd taken her declaration about having the final say in all decisions personally.

Or maybe he wasn't the take-charge guy she needed for the ranch after all.

Jerry had assured her they had enough hay stored to feed the cattle this winter. But feeding additional calves? Not likely.

"We'll stay on Daddy's plan this year." Tipping her chin up, she asked, "What else do I need to know?"

He shifted his jaw before filling her in on the state of the fences, the repairs he and the hands were working on, and other winter preparations.

"Are you having any trouble with the employees?" She folded her hands and leaned forward across the desk.

"I'm keeping an eye on Jake."

"Jake?" She twisted her lips, trying to remember a Jake.

"The kid you recently hired. He's part-time."

"Has he done something?"

Clint shrugged. "A gut instinct. I have a zero-tolerance policy for breaking the rules."

"No three strikes you're out?" she teased.

"No." He didn't crack a smile.

Hmm… Hard to tell if he had a sense of humor hiding under all his toughness. She tried to picture a kid named Jake again. She made a point to interact with all the employees of Weddings by Alexandra, and she didn't even know all the people working on her land. It was time to change that.

"Where will you be this afternoon?"

"South pasture. Riding the fence line."

"I'll join you. It's been a while since I've ridden the property. You can introduce me to the crew when we saddle up."

He opened his mouth as if to protest, then nodded. "Meet me at the stables after dinner."

She'd lived in Denver long enough to think of the midday meal as lunch, but around here, she'd better get used to thinking of it as dinner again. She rose to see him out. On his way past the living room, Clint stopped and looked around. The muscle in his cheek flickered.

"Is something wrong?"

"No." Then he tipped his hat to her and left.

What was the tension in him all about?

Was he mad she'd decided to stick with her father's plan?

Her phone showed six missed calls and eight texts. She didn't have time to worry about his feelings. Back in her office, she opened her email account to twenty-six fresh messages. Looking over her schedule, she exhaled in relief. The video conference call wasn't until tomorrow. She'd squish everything in to take an hour or two off this afternoon. She hadn't ridden Nugget, her favorite horse, since May.

A vision of her and Daddy riding together filled her mind, and she willed away the knot in her throat. Had he been thinner the last time she saw him? Shouldn't there have been warning signs cancer was killing his body?

How many times had she thought she should call and check up on him? But she'd put it off. Too busy replying to texts and placing orders and calling clients.

And now it was too late.

She squeezed her eyes shut.

Lord, I don't know how to get through this. Every time I think of Daddy, I can't breathe.

She curled her fingers into her palms. Her father hadn't raised a coward. He'd always told her two things: "Keep your word good" and "Don't forget to close the gate."

She had a feeling she'd offended Clint earlier, and she couldn't afford to lose him, not when he'd taken the weight of worrying about the ranch off her back. She hoped riding the land where she'd spent so many hours with her father wouldn't be too difficult and the tears she'd suppressed for weeks stayed down under, where they belonged.

Clint ignored the harsh wind on his face and admired Nugget, the fifteen-hand palomino Lexi rode. A beauty of a horse. And the woman riding it? Could have been born in the saddle.

Lexi was intriguing. Sophisticated, yet completely at ease with all the ranch employees she'd shaken hands with before they'd ridden out. A shrewd businesswoman, yet utterly feminine. Sitting in her office earlier had felt like sitting in the center of a wedding bouquet. He'd never felt so out of place in his life. He preferred his ranch office with tools, rope, rags and the smells of earth and cattle.

Once again, the state of her house picked at his conscience. He'd noticed it all again when he'd left their meeting. The dripping faucet. The torn screen. The worn, neglected air of the place. The missing stones from the fireplace.

The fireplace flue probably hadn't been cleaned out

in years. What if she wanted to build a fire? It could be dangerous.

Not my problem. I'm her employee. And my place on this ranch will be secure as long as I keep my mouth shut and the operation running smoothly.

The longer he worked on the ranch, the more impressed he became. He hadn't felt this alive in a long time. But as remarkable as the ranch was, its income and expenses were precarious this year.

Jerry had told him all about RJ Harrington's plans to produce and store hay to sell throughout the country, but Clint didn't see how they could afford to buy the farm equipment this winter.

The prices of cattle lately were low. Too low.

Should he have urged her to wait to sell the calves? When Lexi had asked his opinion earlier, he'd blanked. The decision had felt as important as pressing the button to launch a nuclear bomb. He'd mentally gone back to the day when he'd lost his land, the day he'd stopped trusting himself. And instead of telling her what he really thought, he'd backed down.

Lexi deserved better than that.

He glanced at her again. She didn't trust him. He was used to it. As far as he could remember, no one had ever trusted him until they'd gotten to know him, and most never did. His grandfather had called him a worthless brat on a daily basis. Foster parents watched him with the eyes of a red-tailed hawk. Teachers referred to him as *that Romine kid*. Employers gave him the lowliest jobs before giving him the benefit of the doubt.

Trust had to be earned.

And Lexi was right not to trust him. He hadn't told her about losing his land. But if he had, would she have hired him? Doubtful. And anyhow, he was doing everything in his power to manage Rock Step Ranch wisely.

They approached the fence line.

"I haven't been to this pasture in a few years." Her voice was muffled, and he strained to hear her. She faced him then, her light brown eyes wide and watery. Was the wind ripping the moisture from them, or was she about to cry?

He stilled. This was his boss, and he didn't have much experience around tears.

She turned Nugget to the east. Ridges and gullies of windblown grass and sage surrounded them.

"Daddy and I used to ride out to check fences before I got so caught up in high school activities. I must have been eleven or twelve when we came out here on a day like this. Cold. But it hadn't snowed yet. I'd missed a sleepover party at my friend's house, so I was sulking. But coming out here with Daddy made my troubles disappear."

Clint hung on every word. He almost wanted to raise his hand, to tell her to stop, to not say anything more, because sharing memories, no matter how small, would bind them. Even if he didn't reply, he'd get more invested in Lexi as a person than he already was.

And he needed her to be Lexi, the nice lady he worked for, not Lexi, the woman he could care about.

She swept her arm across the land. "He noticed everything. An elk off in the distance, the remains of a snake near the fence where a hawk had made its meal. I remember thinking there was nothing better in the world than being out here with him. Daddy was smarter and kinder than anyone I knew. And we could just be quiet, be ourselves. You know what I mean?"

Clint did. It was how he felt about his best friends, three other foster kids from his days at Yearling Group Home. When he got together with Marshall, Wade and Nash, he didn't have to force a conversation. He could just be himself.

She lifted her face to the sky. "Every time we'd end a ride, I'd give him the biggest hug and say, 'I love you, Daddy.' And he would always tug on my braid or ponytail and reply, 'You, too, kiddo.'"

Clint's heart was doing funny things. He'd never experienced what she described, but it moved him just the same.

"I would do about anything to be able to give him another hug and say those words again," she said softly.

Clint moved his horse closer to her and reached over to take her hand. Her suede gloves didn't dull the connection, and she stared at him, a tear dropping from her eye. Without thinking, he swung off his horse and held his hands out to help her down. When she'd dismounted, he drew her close, sliding a clean handkerchief out of his pocket to give her. Her slender frame shook with tears, but she didn't wind her arms around him. She simply let him pat her back and murmur comfort.

How long they stood like that, Clint had no idea—could have been a minute or an hour—but at some point, Lexi wiped her eyes free of tears and blew her nose into the handkerchief.

"Sorry, I don't know what came over me. I have to get back." She set her foot in the stirrup and swung her leg over the saddle. "I won't keep you. You stay and check the fence."

He watched her urge Nugget into motion. Off to spend the rest of the day answering calls and doing whatever wedding planners did. And from what he could tell, she'd been doing it nonstop since she'd hired him. Which left no time for grieving...

It hit him then. No wonder she was as thin as a piece of licorice. She hadn't grieved her father's death.

There was no one here to look after her. No clients to meet with. No friends to force her to eat lunch. No father to ensure she lived in a safe, well-maintained house.

Nobody but him.

He slapped his thigh and mounted his horse. Miles of checking fence wouldn't be enough to pretend something hadn't shifted inside where Lexi Harrington was concerned, and he didn't like it. Not one bit.

Lexi pulled her favorite velvety blanket up to her chin and pressed the mute button on the remote. Ever since leaving Clint in the pasture earlier, she'd been unable to work. Tears kept erupting.

Because everything here, in this house and on the ranch, reminded her of her father.

Things she hadn't noticed for weeks—his favorite coffee mug, the faded hand towel with an embroidered cowboy boot she'd bought him for his birthday—unleashed her memories. Two hours ago she'd walked past the master bedroom's closed door, the one she hadn't opened since finding out he'd died, and her feet had backtracked until she stood face-to-face with the pine door. Without thought, she'd fallen to her knees, sobbing in front of it.

It was at that point she'd given up on getting anything done. She'd changed into sweatpants, brewed a pot of tea and flipped through the channels until she found one playing original romantic Christmas movies. They always made her feel better.

Not today, though.

Thanksgiving was a week away. She would be celebrating the holidays alone. Oh, she could drive to Denver, join friends with their families, but she wouldn't. Her heart couldn't take being surrounded by happy people, people who would want to cheer her up. She was in no state to fake pleasantries while choking on tears as she ate their turkey dinner.

And she couldn't believe she'd broken down in front of Clint. The man probably thought she'd lost her mind. Maybe she *had* lost her mind. What had possessed her to start telling him those personal things?

Unacceptable on her part. She wasn't paying Clint to be her therapist. The poor guy. Probably worried she was having a nervous breakdown. She'd apologize. Assure him it wouldn't happen again.

Her phone rang.

Clint.

Her palms grew moist. Oh, why had she dissolved into a weepy mess in front of him?

"Hi." His deep voice calmed her nerves. "One of the herding dogs is missing. Banjo, the older one. I didn't want to bother you, but I'm concerned and... Have you seen him?"

Banjo, Daddy's favorite border collie? "No, I haven't. Have you tried the barns?"

"Yeah, I'll keep looking." He sounded like he was going to hang up.

"Wait!" She threw off the blanket, tired of being alone. "I'll come with you."

"It's not necessary. I know you're busy—"

"I'm coming."

"Lexi," he said in his low, soothing tone. It was the first time she'd heard him use her name, and it did something funny to her pulse. "I don't want to upset you."

"Look, I know I was overly emotional earlier, but that's not me. I don't cry all the time."

"No, that's not what I mean." He sighed. "Dogs hide when they're sick or when it's their time."

His words hit her in the gut. It was true. Dogs were social animals, but when it was their time, they slunk away to die by themselves.

Not Banjo. Not on top of everything else.

"I can handle it, Clint." She couldn't handle it, but being the boss meant dealing with tough situations.

Three minutes later, she wrapped her scarf more tightly around her neck and shivered as Clint handed her a flashlight. Dusk had fallen, and shadows lurked.

"I've checked the stables, the barns, all the obvious places." Clint strode tall and confident toward the cabins. He had the air of a man in command, and right now, she needed someone else to be in charge. "Unless you can think of someplace the dog would have gone… I figure he might have followed one of the cowboys home."

"It's worth a shot." She kept pace with him. "When did you last see him?"

"He trailed in behind Logan and Mike when they returned from checking calves, but he didn't come in with the other dogs at feeding time."

Nothing but the sound of the wind and their feet against the hard dirt met her ears. The fact Banjo hadn't eaten was a bad sign. Where would the dog go if not with the other dogs in the barn? Coyotes were common in these parts. He couldn't have been attacked, could he? Banjo knew better than to tangle with one of them.

They rounded the bend where windows in three of the cabins glowed.

"Why don't you ask Logan and Sarah if they've seen him while I ask the other guys?"

She nodded. After knocking on the door, she rubbed her hands together. Felt like snow was on its way.

"Lexi, what a nice surprise!" Sarah, a pretty blonde in her late twenties, beckoned her to enter, but Lexi stayed on the porch.

"I don't mean to bother you, but Banjo's missing. Have you seen him around tonight?"

The smile slid off Sarah's face. "No, I haven't, and I've always been fond of that dog. Did you check all the barns? He might be trying to stay warm."

"Clint checked already, but we'll try again." Lexi turned to leave. "Oh, and thanks for supper every night, Sarah. You don't have to do that."

"Well, we're all sorry about RJ's passing. He was a good man. Treated us like family. Anything you need, just ask."

"Thank you." Lexi's throat tightened as she turned away. *Not again.* What was it with today? If she cried one more time, so help her…

Clint loped up. "Did they see him?"

Not trusting herself to speak, she shook her head, willing the emotions to pass. Clint rubbed his chin. He seemed nervous, upset.

"Are you okay?" She placed her hand on his arm. The muscles bunched, but she didn't pull away.

"Yeah." The sky grew darker. "I guess I'll check the barns again."

"Let's look behind the cabins. Maybe he wandered back there."

The glance he flashed her said it was a fool's errand, but she didn't care. They trained their flashlights behind the row of cabins. No sign of the dog. Clint's house stood at the end of the drive. The dark windows gave it a sad air, like it was waiting for him to come home.

"Clint, what's that on your front porch?"

He twisted to see and took off toward his house. She ran to catch up with him.

Banjo! Clint knelt next to the dog, massaging his ears. Banjo's tail thumped on the wood, and his tongue hung out. The dog was clearly thrilled to see Clint.

"I thought we'd lost you, old boy," he said.

"I guess he missed you." She leaned her shoulder against the rail, never imagining Clint could look this happy.

He continued lavishing Banjo with affection. "Probably looking for a treat or something."

"He can stay here with you, you know."

"It wouldn't be right." He rose.

"Why not? I can tell you like dogs."

"I've never owned one."

The man whose face lit up like the carnival rides at the rodeo when he saw Banjo had never owned a dog? Impossible.

"He's getting old," Lexi said. "If you don't want him here, that's fine, but if you like him, well…maybe he needs some TLC after long days with the cattle."

"He *is* getting old." Clint straightened, thinking about it. "I've been meaning to mention the ranch should add a few more dogs. I've trained cattle herders. It takes time for them to learn the ropes. If something happens to Banjo…"

"I'll check into it."

He looked as if he wanted to say something, then he shook his head. "I'll walk you home."

"It's not far." She waved the flashlight in the direction of her house. "The boogeyman won't get me."

"I'm walking you home." And there was serious Clint again. Only Banjo seemed to lighten him up. "I know you can take care of yourself. But I'd feel better if…"

Such a small thing, him caring about her safety, but it made her feel warm and toasty. And for the first time in hours, she didn't feel like crying in the slightest.

She'd been right to hire Clint. Nothing escaped his notice on the ranch, not even a sweet old dog.

Careful, Lexi. Start to romanticize him, and you'll end up like last time. In a dull relationship without the things you really want. The ring. The emotional connection. The once-in-a-lifetime love.

Whether she liked it or not, she was the boss, and she'd better not forget it.

Chapter Three

"Storm's coming tonight. I'm heading into town."
Clint shifted from one cowboy boot to the other Monday afternoon. "Do you need any supplies?"

"I'll come with you." The words were out of Lexi's mouth before she'd thought them through. She stood in the open doorway as a gust of wind swooshed inside.

She hadn't left the house in three days, and she was losing her mind. Natalie Allen, her vice president and top wedding planner, had taken more responsibilities off Lexi's shoulders, but details continued to slip through the cracks. Lexi was still reeling from the nasty phone call she'd received this morning from a very unhappy client. She couldn't help thinking if she'd been there, the situation could have been prevented.

In his Carhartt jacket, jeans and cowboy hat, Clint looked ready to bolt. "If you give me a list—"

"I want to tag along." She was already pulling on her faux fur–lined boots.

"I have errands to run first."

"Even better." She shrugged into her coat. "Just drop

me off downtown and text me when you're ready to go to the store."

His expression darkened, but he nodded. "I'll be in the truck."

He didn't have time to walk away, because she'd grabbed her purse and followed him outside. With Clint managing the ranch, maybe it was time for her to return to Denver. For good.

She bit the corner of her bottom lip, less than thrilled at the thought.

He opened the passenger door of his black truck for her, and she buckled herself in, thankful the cab was warm.

"So…what's on your agenda?" She watched him adjust the mirrors then back the truck up.

"Dottie will be mad if I don't stop in and say howdy, so I'm headed to her diner first. Then I'm meeting Art McFall about his hay supply. I have to stop in at the bank, and I'm due for a trim."

"Dottie. Hay. Bank. Barber. Got it. How long do you think it will take?"

"Two hours."

Two whole hours.

She watched the bare countryside pass by. It was part of her, the same way selecting complementary colors for a bouquet was part of her. After living in the city for years, she'd never thought she'd miss the raw emptiness of the land, but she did. Was that why the thought of returning to Denver wasn't lighting up her insides?

"I've looked over the ranch's books some more," Clint said. "We'll be selling the calves soon, even though the prices are low."

"Okay." She faced him, remembering the twinge of doubt she'd had at their meeting last week.

"The new barn is empty, and it cost a lot to build."

"I know."

"To fill the barn with square bales next summer, you need farm equipment."

She knew where he was going with this. Equipment cost money.

He concentrated on the road ahead. "If you want the equipment, you need to get a high price for your calves."

A dull ache formed behind her eyes. "You think we should wait a few months to sell, don't you?"

"Not if we can't feed them."

"Can we feed them?" She watched him carefully, trying to read his reaction.

"I think we can."

She weighed her options. If they couldn't feed the cattle, they'd lose even more money than if they sold them soon at a low price.

"Let me think about it more." She waited for him to argue, but his only reaction was a curt nod. Was he mad she hadn't instantly agreed with him?

Maybe these unresolved ranch issues were the reason she wasn't speeding back to her real life. It wouldn't be fair to Clint if she deserted him now. She'd told him she planned to stay until Christmas.

"I can't take chances with the ranch," she said. "Every decision I make is important."

"I understand."

He remained silent as the miles passed. She wished she could tell him to go ahead and do whatever he wanted with the calves, but she had to think about the big picture. Logan and Sarah and their little ones depended on her. As did the other ranch hands. Not to mention the cattle—she wouldn't risk harming them. Preserving the ranch itself loomed heaviest. Would Daddy have approved of Clint's plan?

The lingering silence set her on edge.

"Has Banjo been okay?" she asked.

"He's fine."

Not exactly forthcoming with information, that Clint Romine. What was a safe topic for small talk?

"What are you doing for Thanksgiving?" she asked. "Hard to believe it's only a few days away."

His hands tightened around the steering wheel. "I'll feed the cattle in the morning and later ride out to check on them."

"What about your family?"

"I don't have one."

"What do you mean?" It hadn't occurred to her he'd be spending his Thanksgiving alone, too.

He glanced her way and shrugged. "Dad died in a blizzard back when I was four. Multicar pileup. He drove trucks for a living. Never knew my mom. My grandfather took care of me until I turned six, then he died. I lived in foster homes from then on."

The full impact of his words didn't hit her for a few seconds. When it did, she didn't know what to say. Was he completely alone in life? "Who do you usually spend Thanksgiving with? And Christmas?"

"Thanksgiving isn't a big deal to me. Dottie always invites me to her place, but it's a little too crowded for my liking. As for Christmas, my best friends and I usually get together when we can, but we're all bachelors, all live a cowboy life to some degree…"

"So you spend the holidays alone."

"Yes."

She tapped her legs. He didn't sound bothered at the thought of being alone for Thanksgiving and Christmas. Unlike her.

"Here we are." Clint stopped in a parking spot in front of Dottie's Diner. "I'll text you when I'm done."

"Tell Dottie hello from me." She climbed out of the truck, shoved her hands in her coat pockets and headed toward the jewelry store. Clint's childhood must have been pretty bad for him to spend holidays alone. She'd been blessed to always have Daddy to come home to. Who knew how she'd spend the holidays from now on?

Sweet Dreams was all decked out for Christmas. Rows of buildings—some brick, some with awnings—lined both sides of Main Street, and all were trimmed in green-and-red decorations. White lights wrapped around light posts and store windows. Evergreen boughs and red ribbons abounded. Very Victorian Western. She imagined women in long dresses and bonnets singing carols back in the day. Throw in a cowboy or two, and the picture would be complete.

Lexi ducked into Sweet Dreams Jewelers and instantly felt at home. There was something about jewelry, soft lighting and gleaming glass displays that soothed her. She zoomed to the diamonds showcased on blue velvet. Lingering over the engagement rings, she sighed in delight. The one in the top right corner caught her eye. She'd pick it as her ideal ring. Oh, how she loved weddings.

The recent Anderson nuptials had been particularly moving. The bride and groom had stared into each other's eyes so deeply as they said their vows that Lexi had shed a few honest tears at their devotion. Those moments made her job worth the petty calls, ornery brides, making payroll and endless meetings. Yes, the *I do*s made it all worth it.

After browsing the store, she made her way to Amy's Quilt Shop. Lexi herself had never quilted, but the fabrics might give her ideas for any rustic weddings coming up. The bell clanged above her, and she stopped to take it all in. The aroma of spiced cider and the sounds of soft contemporary Christian Christmas music filled the room, pretty rag rugs in navy blues and brick reds covered the wood floors, and the displays—magnificent! She plunged forward, marveling at the combination of fabrics. The quilts hanging from the walls were works of art.

"Can I help you?"

Lexi turned and squealed. "Amy Deerson? You're Amy's Quilt Shop?"

"Lexi!" Amy embraced her, and they couldn't stop grinning at each other. "I can't believe it. I haven't seen you in years. I'm so sorry about your dad, and I feel terrible I missed the funeral. Stomach flu. If I'd known you were still in town, I would have come over."

"Thank you, Amy. That means a lot to me." Lexi couldn't get over how beautiful Amy had become. Luxurious dark hair tumbled down her back. Full red lips, a fit but curvy figure, and her smile, so inviting and kind. The way she'd always been. Amy had been a good friend during high school, but after Lexi left for college, they'd fallen out of touch.

"Are you busy right now?" Amy asked.

"No, why?"

"Let's catch up over a cup of coffee."

"Can you do that?"

"I sure can. It's my store." Amy laughed. "Give me a minute and we can go to The Beanery."

A short walk later, they sat across from each other at a café table in the adorable coffee shop. Exposed brick walls contrasted with distressed plank floors. The way the door opened every few minutes told Lexi it was a popular place indeed. And the smell was pure coffee, pure bliss.

"Fill me in on everything." Amy sipped her pumpkin spice latte and leaned forward.

Lexi obliged. She told her about earning her degree in public relations and getting her first gig as a wedding planner. She'd quickly made a name for herself, quit her job and started planning weddings full-time. Then a swanky Denver magazine featured her in their wedding issue, and the business exploded. "Your turn."

"There's not much to tell. I opened shop six years ago. Let's just say I was on the verge of getting engaged twice and both times got jilted. I'm finally coming to terms with the fact I might never marry or have children. I've been spending time working on my relationship with the Lord."

Lexi's heart twisted at Amy's tale. Her vibrant friend had always been nurturing. If anyone should be married with kids, Amy should. "I need to do some of that myself."

"Which part?" Amy teased.

"The last part. Losing Daddy…it's been hard." She sipped her coffee.

"I can't imagine," Amy said. "How long did you know about the cancer?"

"I didn't. None of us did." She blotted a napkin over

the drop she'd spilled. Something about the question bothered her. Had anyone else known?

Had Daddy known?

No. If he'd known, he would have told her. He'd been as in the dark as everyone else.

"Maybe that's a blessing. He didn't suffer."

Lexi didn't see how it was a blessing, but she wouldn't argue. If they'd had more time, they could have fought it.

Amy smiled warmly. "Looks like you're making big changes in your life. I'll pray for you."

"I need all the prayers I can get. I think God's mad at me." She half laughed.

Amy covered her hand and squeezed. "He's not mad at you, Lexi. You can go to Him with anything, big or small."

"Thanks, Amy," she whispered. Her phone dinged. Clint. "Well, it's been wonderful to catch up with you, but my ride is almost here. Let's get together soon."

"Here's my number. Let me know if you need anything."

They hugged, and Lexi left, wrapping her coat tightly around her waist against the cold air. Amy's words about going to God with anything filled her thoughts.

In the past, she'd trusted God with her plans. But she'd gotten busy with her company, and after her father died...

Was she being punished? She'd put her business first and lost him a month after planning her most prestigious wedding. She'd been named homecoming queen two weeks before her mother died. Whenever something wonderful happened to her, she paid a price too heavy to bear.

Could she take anything to God in prayer?

Lord, I want to believe You listen to my prayers. Am I foolish to stay here until Christmas? Should I go back to Denver? And what should we do about the calves?

She shook her head. Why would God care if she stayed or left or sold the calves now or later?

Do You really care? About things big and small?

Clint's truck drove into the spot directly in front of her. That man did everything he said he would do. He was reliable. A hard worker. And in her heart she knew he was right about them needing a higher price for the calves. Owning a business meant taking calculated risks.

She buckled into the passenger seat. "I think we should try it your way and wait to sell the calves."

He blinked. Then he nodded, a sheepish smile playing on his lips. "Okay."

One decision out of the way. Her business would not collapse if she stayed here until Christmas. One more month. Then she'd figure out the rest.

Clint hauled plastic bags full of groceries into Lexi's kitchen later that afternoon. Walking into this house was like getting a hearty slap to the face each and every time he came in. The dripping of the faucet pounded into his temples. The wind had picked up, flapping the broken screen. And how had he not noticed the bulb missing in the can light above him?

Here he was living in the lap of luxury in his cozy home down the lane, and Lexi was stuck in this run-down tomb of a house.

The minute he'd moved into his cabin, he'd scrubbed it and checked the windows, furnace and plumbing.

He'd tightened the place up good for winter, and every room sparkled like sunlight off the river.

If anyone but Lexi lived here, he probably would assume they'd fix it up themselves, but this was a woman who had lost both parents, held a demanding job and didn't have a boyfriend or husband to rely on.

Which left him responsible.

Repairs would put him in Lexi's direct vicinity far longer than he could handle. Even if he could admit— at least to himself—he didn't mind making chitchat with her. It wasn't conducive to keeping their relationship professional, though. And now that she'd actually trusted his decision about the calves, his palms wouldn't stop sweating.

What if he was wrong? What if they ran out of feed and had to sell them for a loss?

He closed his eyes and shook away the doubts. It was too late for regrets now. He'd show Lexi her faith in him wasn't misplaced. And he'd start today.

"Lexi?"

"Hmm?" She pushed a jar to the side and shoved a box of cereal onto the shelf.

"I've noticed there are some items around here that need fixing. I'm busy tonight—have to check the generators and equipment before the snow comes in—but tomorrow night, I'll come by and get a few of the more pressing problems repaired."

Lexi wiped her palms down her jeans. "What problems?"

Was she joking?

From the expression on her face, he'd say she wasn't. "I hear a faucet dripping somewhere. It might be an easy fix, or it might need a new gasket or have to be replaced altogether. The screen in the window—" he pointed to the living room "—is ripped and banging around in the wind. Your fireplace needs to be inspected." He turned in a slow circle, seeing cobwebs, a loose cabinet knob, an electrical outlet missing its cover.

With her hands on her hips, she scrunched her nose and studied the rooms. "It's needed a cleaning for a long time. I didn't realize there were so many other issues, though."

Understandable with her father dying and her business keeping her so busy.

"After my mother died when I was seventeen, I think Daddy gave up on the house. He lived here, but he poured all his time and energy into the ranch itself. Maybe he was afraid of moving on, or he could have thought changing the house would make him forget her." She bowed her head. "I haven't been blind to it being so dirty. I just haven't had the energy… You must think I'm a slob."

"No, I figured you've been busy."

She smiled up at him, and he held his breath. She had a knight-in-shining-armor glint in her eyes. "I would appreciate it very much if you'd stop by tomorrow night. I'll do my best to help."

He was no knight.

"I can manage fine."

She tilted her head, still smiling. "I know you can. But it's my house. And I'd feel like the worst sort of person if I let you do it all without lifting a finger."

An image of Lexi holding a wrench and him accidentally touching her hand made him squirm. She was too pretty to be near for long periods.

"I said I can manage."

"And I said I'll help."

He clamped his mouth shut. He couldn't argue with her without sounding like a grizzly bear. He hoped the faucet was an easy fix. The screen and fireplace, too. Because if she started helping, she'd start talking, and when she talked, he had a hard time remembering why he needed to keep his distance.

And he needed to keep his distance. For both their sakes.

Lexi paused in front of the master bedroom door the next evening. She'd made too big of a deal out of Daddy's room. She knew what she'd find—the double bed with a faded blue-and-yellow quilt, dusty dressers with her father's personal items on a tray. Why had she been avoiding it for so long?

Slowly, she opened the door. His presence hit her, the faintest smell of cologne lingering. The bed, the quilt, the dusty dresser were the same. She crept to the tray with her dad's belongings and gingerly picked up his watch. It had been a gift to him from her mother. He'd worn it every day Lexi could remember. It looked so out of place and lonely sitting here instead of wrapped around his wrist. Tears filled her eyes, and she gripped it tightly to her chest.

This was why she hadn't gone in. It reminded her too much of him.

Swallowing her emotions, she clutched the watch in one hand and trailed her finger over the rest of the surfaces, stopping at the framed picture of her parents on their honeymoon. Daddy's arm was slung over Mama's shoulders, and they looked so happy and young. *How I wish you were still here.*

She'd loved both of them so much. It didn't seem possible they were gone. Slowly, she turned, taking in the room, trying to hold on to the memory of his smile, the sound of his laugh, the feel of his arms pulling her into a hug. *Oh, Daddy, I miss you.*

The top drawer of her mother's dresser was slightly ajar. She pulled it open. A file had been placed on top of old scarves. She lifted it out, but a knocking sound from the front door made her jump. Quickly, she wiped her eyes, and with the file in hand, she hurried back to the living room and let Clint inside. Snowflakes flurried around him. He tapped his hat on his leg before entering.

"You look cold." Her spirits lifted now that he'd arrived. "And, wait, are you smiling?"

His teeth flashed in a grin as he set his tool belt on the floor to take off his coat and boots. "I love this weather. It's not blowing too hard, and the cows are munching away as the snow piles up on them. I hope you don't mind, I dallied a few minutes to take some pictures."

"You? Dallied?" She padded down the hall with him at her heels. "I'm shocked. And here I pegged you as all business all the time."

She stopped to face him, and he bumped into her. His hands shot to her biceps, his touch warming her down to the tips of her icicle toes.

"I pegged you as the same." His dark blue eyes flashed with intensity.

She felt aware of him in a way she hadn't previously. She wanted to lean into his muscular frame, let him take away the sorrow of losing her father. Instead, she stepped back, forcing a laugh. "You pegged me right, then. Let's see those photos."

His face blanked. "You want to see my pictures?"

"Well, yeah." She shook her head. "Why wouldn't I?"

Color flooded his cheeks, but he swiped his phone and held it out. Two cows stared at her, both munching on hay, an inch of snow on their backs. The sky was white behind them.

"This picture is really good, Clint." She pulled the phone closer to get a better look. "They seem content."

"That's what I thought." The moment stretched, and he cleared his throat. "Where is the bathroom? I suspect the dripping is coming from that sink."

She showed him to the room, and she stood in the doorway as he turned on the faucet and opened the cabinet to check the pipes. "What can I do?"

"Nothing."

"Clint…"

He glanced up at her. "Well, you can show me where the water main is."

"Oh, that might be a problem. I don't know where it is."

"I'll find it." His eyes danced with amusement.

He was easy to be with. Not much of a talker, but she liked him just the same. Her thoughts bounced to two days from now, Thanksgiving, and how they were both alone with nowhere to go.

Didn't it made sense to ask him to join her? Yes, it was taking a risk. Spending time together meant further developing a friendship. If something happened to end the friendship, he might quit. She had to keep the ranch's welfare number one in her priorities. But the loneliness of this upcoming holiday enveloped her.

They were both adults. Surely they could have a meal with each other without their working relationship blowing up.

Clint straightened and moved toward the door.

"Wait, I have a question for you." She touched his arm, all firm muscle, then snatched her hand back. "Why don't you have Thanksgiving dinner with me?"

"I have plans."

She cocked her head to the side. "You told me you were feeding the cattle."

"Yes. Those are my plans."

"You can't feed cattle all day."

He didn't look at her.

"Come on." She sighed. "Neither of us has family, and I don't want to go to a well-meaning friend's house, if you know what I mean."

He met her eyes, understanding connecting them before he moved past her into the hall. "I thought you don't cook."

"I don't. I can buy a premade dinner from the supermarket."

"Where's the utility room?"

She tried not to let her disappointment show as she gestured for him to follow her past the living room and kitchen to the door next to the garage. Clint gravitated toward the pipes against the wall. His lack of interest in her offer was apparent. And that was fine. She'd been thinking of him as a friend when she should be thinking of him as the ranch manager.

She'd spend Thanksgiving alone. Maybe she'd drive somewhere, eat Chinese food or something. She didn't *have* to spend it here.

"If I eat Thanksgiving dinner with you," he said over

his shoulder, "we're not having supermarket food. We're going to cook it. I'll show you the basics."

"Really?" Had the sun suddenly appeared? Were rainbows arching over the house? "Thank you! But cooking isn't my strong suit. The basics might be beyond me."

He cranked a lever on a copper pipe. "Something tells me you'll pick it up quickly. Now, stay in here while I turn on the faucet. If I yell to turn it off, pull this lever up, okay?"

She nodded, admiring his broad back as he left the room. Only then did she realize she was still holding the file she'd found in her mother's drawer. Absentmindedly, she opened it, scanning the sheet.

Her mouth dropped open. Heart stopped beating. Vision blurred.

Clint ran back into the utility room, yanking the lever up. "Didn't you hear me calling?"

She lifted her face, the file and its contents dropping to the floor, each sheet gliding in a different direction.

"He lied to me, Clint. He lied. He knew." Everything she'd thought to be true since the funeral suddenly came into question. And the betrayal almost buckled her knees.

He placed his hands on her shoulders and peered into her eyes. "Who? What are you talking about?"

"Daddy knew he had cancer, and he didn't tell me."

Chapter Four

Clint had no idea what to do, so he bent and picked up the papers that had scattered across the floor. He scanned the top sheet. Pathology report. Dated October 1 of this year. A handwritten note about getting a second opinion was scrawled in the margin.

"He must not have known for long. A month, tops." Clint handed her the papers, but she kept her arms by her sides, her hands balled into fists.

"He kept this from me." Her words were tight, cold, hard. "He robbed me of helping him."

"I'm sorry—"

"The faucet will have to wait. I need to be alone."

Clint nodded, set the documents on a shelf and left. His thoughts were jumbled as he strode under the dark sky back to his cabin. Lexi had so many dimensions. He'd seen her exhausted, mourning, professional, playful and now this. Whatever this was. Upset didn't quite explain it.

Betrayed, most likely. It was the lying part she'd focused on.

And the lying part was something he knew a little too well.

A pit formed in his stomach. He'd been keeping something from her, too. But what could he do about it now? She was already reeling from her father's death. Finding out RJ had known about the cancer had put her over the edge. If Clint came clean and told her about how he lost his property, it would add to her burdens. She'd fire him and be left without a manager. She'd work night and day to save this ranch as well as her company, and she'd be as hollowed out as she'd been when she hired him.

It wouldn't be right to add to her problems to self-ishly clear his conscience.

He ducked his chin against the snow pellets. Why was she so upset about her dad not telling her, any-how? A month seemed pretty quick to go from diag-nosis to death. Maybe RJ had planned on filling her in at Thanksgiving. Or maybe he thought he was invinci-ble. From all accounts, he sounded like the kind of guy Clint had been surrounded by his entire adult life—a tough Wyoming rancher who never admitted defeat, not even to cancer.

Regardless, Clint and Lexi weren't close. They'd only known each other a short time. Not telling her about his past wasn't a betrayal. He was doing what she'd hired him to do—managing the ranch.

Speaking of which… He hadn't secured additional feed for the winter. If he didn't find any in the next week or so, they would have to sell the calves at the scheduled date or risk losing valuable cattle in the frigid months ahead.

Was he making the best decisions for the ranch?

Maybe he'd been lying to himself and his past *was* affecting his work performance.

His porch light glowed, and he muttered under his breath at the sight of Banjo curled up on the welcome mat the same way he'd been every night since Clint had found him there last Thursday. Each night he'd tried to take the dog back to the barn, but Banjo wouldn't budge from the porch.

"We've got to stop meeting like this." Clint bent to stroke Banjo's black-and-white fur, and the dog got to his feet, wagging his tail and adoring Clint with his big brown eyes. "This isn't your home. You can't stay here."

Banjo cocked his head.

"Fine. I can't have you freezing. You can sleep on the floor. Just this once." He unlocked the door. He'd said those same words every night, and *just this once* had turned into *Banjo, you own me.* "Okay, I'll admit I'm a pushover. But you are sleeping on the floor."

The idea of Banjo sleeping on the end of his bed appealed to him, but he couldn't allow it. He didn't want the dog living with him. Banjo was old, arthritic, and Clint doubted he would make it through the next year. Growing attached to the dog would not be smart. He'd lose him, too.

Clint took off his coat and boots and stretched out on the couch. Banjo lay on the rug.

It felt as if every hour brought a new set of issues to deal with. Banjo. The faucet still not repaired. And Thanksgiving with his boss.

She was probably too upset to celebrate Thanksgiving now. He should be relieved, but part of him hoped otherwise.

His cell phone dinged, showing a text from Lexi.

I'm sorry I flipped out. Please send me the list of ingredients I need to buy for our Thanksgiving dinner.

Had she read his mind? "Guess Thanksgiving is still on."

He texted her back.

I'll buy everything tomorrow. See you Thursday.

Leaning back, he tried to relax. He hadn't had this much excitement in years. He tried to avoid drama. But the anticipation kicking up his pulse didn't lie. He kind of liked drama of the Lexi variety. Maybe a little excitement wasn't such a bad thing after all.

She would be on her best behavior with Clint today. This Thanksgiving would be difficult enough without Daddy. If she scared Clint off, she'd be alone with only her thoughts to keep her company. They kept circling like buzzards over roadkill. Why hadn't Daddy told her about the cancer? She deserved to know. Hadn't he understood she would want to rush home and be with him?

Stop fixating on it. It's over.

She slid a dusty platter into the soapy dishwater. Her mother's fine china stayed in the hutch most of the year. Lexi had always loved the blue-and-white set. Rinsing the platter, she could almost smell her mother's perfume and hear her laughter. Mama had been such a joyful, optimistic person, and Lexi had been close to her until she died from complications due to pneumonia.

And now Daddy was gone, too.

Tuesday night after she'd basically kicked Clint out, she'd stood in the utility room, trying to make sense of the pathology report, hearing Clint's words about not knowing for long. But the report had made her paranoid. Who else wasn't telling her vital information? Had Daddy confided in someone other than her? The mere thought sliced her heart open.

Had she been the only one *not* to know?

While her father had had many acquaintances, the one person she could imagine him confiding in besides her was Jerry. Yesterday morning, she'd asked Jerry if he'd known about the cancer, and from the expression on his face, she'd believed his hearty no. Who else would Daddy tell? His brother had died five years ago, and he didn't have any other close friends.

Clint arrived carrying several bags of groceries.

"Happy Thanksgiving." She hurried to the hallway and reached for one of the bags.

"Here, take this one. It's not as heavy."

She peeked inside. A Dottie's Diner box labeled pumpkin pie. Her mouth began watering. As they unpacked the groceries in the kitchen, a charged silence filled the air. She had to say something, but she didn't want to discuss her dad or her reaction to the pathology report.

"What should I do?" she asked.

"Do you have a roasting pan?" All business, Clint washed his hands. "I bought a turkey breast instead of an entire bird. We'll rub butter on it and sprinkle it with salt and pepper. It will cook pretty quick."

Some of her tension leaked out. "What does a roasting pan look like?"

"Rectangular with a wire rack inside." He rinsed the turkey breast and patted it dry with a paper towel.

She searched through the cupboards and finally found a pan fitting the description. "Is this it?"

"Yes." He smiled then, and she couldn't help but stare. He wasn't a man who smiled often. Catching a glimpse of it felt like being let in on a spectacular secret. It made her want to find out more of his secrets. Who was this man? Why was he single? Had he ever been in love? Married? And why had he been working at an oil company for years when he clearly loved ranching?

"Put this in the microwave for twenty seconds." He handed her half a stick of butter.

Her questions were too personal. If she asked him the real stuff, she might not like the answers.

"How did you learn to cook?" She pushed the microwave button and leaned against the counter, watching him pull out cutting boards, knives and salt and pepper as if he lived there.

"Food Network."

She laughed, trying to picture him watching cooking shows. The image didn't mesh with the outdoorsy cowboy in front of her. He drew near, standing inches from her. What was he doing? Her heart pounded. But he simply reached around her to turn on the oven.

"I can't see you glued to the TV and taking notes."

Was a blush creeping up his cheeks? She didn't even try to conceal her glee.

"I don't. I got snowed in for a week. I was bored. Nothing was on television, and one of the cooking shows made me hungry. I decided to try my hand at the recipe. I got hooked."

"Well, I'm glad you did. The soup you made for me was delicious."

"Bring the butter over." He brandished a pastry brush

and demonstrated how to paint the butter on the meat. "You want to cover the entire thing."

She swiped the melted butter on the skin, and Clint sprinkled salt and pepper over it before sliding the pan into the oven.

"Easy enough, right?" He pointed to the items she'd grouped together on the counter. "You peel potatoes, and I'll chop the herbs and vegetables for the stuffing."

The sound of the knife hitting the board in precise thuds filled the air. She took her time peeling each potato and rinsing them. Now that Clint was here, her mind wasn't racing in tangled circles about her father. But other problems loomed. Yesterday, she'd called Natalie Allen, vice president of her company, and the conversation had left her perplexed. Something wasn't right in Denver.

"Do you ever question people's motives?" She lined the potatoes up on the board and turned to face him.

"Why do you ask?" The muscles in his shoulders flexed as he chopped celery.

"I talked to my vice president yesterday afternoon. She's been meeting with the other wedding planners, and she told me they think I should hire a purchaser to keep up with ordering the invitations, flowers, decorations and such."

"Who orders the stuff now?"

"The planners are responsible for their weddings. They rely on their assistants for most of the ordering."

"Can your company afford another full-time employee?"

The company could, but keeping up with the orders hadn't been a problem until she'd moved to Wyoming. "Yes, but it's never been an issue before. In the past

I've trusted Natalie had the best interests of the company in mind with her decisions. But I'm wondering if something more is going on. Something she isn't telling me."

"Why would you think that?"

The missed orders, the complaints. Lexi had always checked in with the wedding planners once a week. But since living at the ranch, she wasn't able to spend time with the individual employees the way she used to. Natalie had taken on the responsibility. Strange that no one had ever brought up needing a purchaser before. Was she overreacting?

"I guess finding the pathology report made me a little paranoid. Just because my father kept something important from me doesn't mean everyone else is, too."

Clint swept all of the tiny bits of onion, celery and sage into a large bowl. "What would you do if she *was* hiding something?"

"My company comes first. If Natalie doesn't know that by now… Forget it. It doesn't matter, because she's honest with me. Like I said, the other night messed with my head." She wiped her hands on a paper towel. "What do I do now?"

His eyes met hers, and for a brief moment she wondered if he was hiding something, too.

Don't look for the worst in everyone.

"Cut them into small pieces and put them in here." He pointed to a large pot.

Lexi cut the potatoes up in chunks, mentally chastising herself. He was a hard worker, a great ranch manager. He'd gone to the trouble of buying this food, and he was teaching her how to cook it. The idea Clint was hiding something from her was laughable.

She'd nip this suspiciousness in the bud. It wasn't her style. If she couldn't trust the people she worked closely with, she didn't know what she would do.

He couldn't remember a Thanksgiving dinner he'd enjoyed more. Even the delicious feasts Dottie Lavert used to cook at Yearling Group Home didn't compare to this. It wasn't that the food tasted better, although it was delicious. Today was the first time he'd felt like he belonged somewhere on Thanksgiving.

"Dinner was yummy." Lexi closed the door to the dishwasher and pressed the start button. "I'm stuffed. As much as I want pumpkin pie, I think I need to wait awhile for dessert."

"Same here." Now what? Dinner was over, so should he leave? Then he remembered the faucet. "I'll finish fixing the leak in your faucet, then I'll get out of your hair."

"Oh, don't worry about the faucet." She waved dismissively. "And you're not in my hair."

She didn't seem in a rush to get rid of him, but now that she'd mentioned hair, he found himself mesmerized by her silky dark waves. His thoughts detoured to a less professional place than he'd prefer. "It's no trouble. I'll fix it now."

Fifteen minutes later, after tightening the faucet's adjusting ring, he returned to the living room, where Christmas music played.

He cleared his throat. "You're all set. Thanks for having me."

"Wait." She sprang to her feet, her eyes darting back and forth. "I have another favor to ask, but you don't have to say yes."

"What is it?" He wanted to stay. Liked being here with her. The Christmas music reminded him of movies he used to watch with happy families celebrating the holidays. Hanging out with her, listening to the music, almost made him believe he could experience a taste of the happy Christmas feeling, too.

"Would you help me bring down our Christmas tree? It's in the garage attic with the other decorations. I can pull the bins out myself, but the tree is heavy."

"I'll bring it down." A surge of masculine pride filled his chest. It was nice to be needed for something.

On the way to the garage, Lexi chattered about old decorations and the pink lights she'd ordered for her tree in Denver. Pink lights? Sounded like Lexi. He climbed the attic ladder first, tugging on the lightbulb string when he reached the top. Lexi bumped into him on her way up, and he moved to the side, steadying her.

Standing so close to her messed with his head. Warm, feminine, smelling fantastic—she was special, all right.

"I think the decorations are over here. It's been years since I helped decorate, and I never had to bring them down. Daddy might have moved them." Carefully, she made her way to the corner, where shelves held bins and boxes. "Wow, I can't believe all this is here. My mom used to plan themed trees. She got such a kick out of picking the perfect ornaments and color schemes. These boxes—" she turned to him, her eyes shining "—they're all her Christmas tree themes. Daddy must have saved them. Oh, there's what I was looking for!"

"Which one?" He saw four long boxes clearly marked as artificial trees.

"On the top. It's prelit. He bought it a few years ago. Why he hung on to the old trees is a mystery."

Clint took the long box by the handles and effortlessly brought it down the ladder and back to the living room. Lexi followed with a plastic bin. Back and forth, they brought down all the boxes she wanted.

"Thank you so much." She wiped dust off her sweater. "When do you usually decorate? Thanksgiving weekend is my favorite time."

"I, uh—" he massaged the back of his neck "—I don't decorate."

She gaped at him. "What do you mean you don't decorate?"

"Well, I don't see much point." Why did he feel like a high school freshman about to fail an important math test? "I don't entertain."

"But it's not just for entertaining. It's for you to enjoy. To capture the glorious spirit of Christmas."

Glorious? Christmas had never been very good for him.

"I have a great idea. Let's go decorate your cabin." She gestured to the garage. "We have extra trees. And I know the perfect decorations for you. Mom went through a cowboy Christmas stage when I was in middle school. I saw the boxes up there."

"What? No. What are you doing?" She had already disappeared down the hall. He tried again. "I don't see the point—"

"This is what I do. I love to decorate. You're going to be thrilled with the results!" She looked back over her shoulder at him and winked.

The wink shut him up. He never knew what he was in for when he spent time with Lexi Harrington. One thing he'd learned? If she got something in her head, he might as well play along, because she did not let go of an idea easily.

They spent the next half hour piling the boxes on the bed of the truck. The wind was blowing, and it was cold out, but it wasn't snowing. As he drove them to his cabin, he kept glancing over at her. She wore a red stocking hat with a pom-pom on top, matching red scarf and a black jacket. Her cheeks were flushed.

When they arrived at his cabin, he hauled two boxes into the living room.

"First, let's get some music cranking." She set a small speaker on the counter and found a Christmas playlist on her phone. Then she unwound her scarf, brought her palms together and pointed to the living room with them. "Okay, think about where you want the tree."

"You decide. I'll get the boxes." He had to escape. Having her in his cabin made the atmosphere too cozy. Outside he breathed in the crisp, cold air and yanked two boxes from the truck. Then he set them next to the fireplace and repeated the process with the artificial tree.

Lexi stood behind the couch, facing the window and holding her hands up as if creating a picture frame. "Is that everything?"

He nodded, stripping off his gloves and coat.

"The tree would look really good right in front of the window here, and you'll be able to see the lights from outside."

"Whatever." He didn't mean to sound uninterested or gruff, but he wasn't used to this. Wasn't used to having a woman in his space or someone caring enough to help him decorate his home. He wasn't used to trimming Christmas trees or listening to merry music with a pretty girl. He couldn't think straight.

He was ready to tell her he could decorate it himself, but she was already on her knees, digging through one of the boxes.

"This is the one time I'm actually glad my dad wouldn't get rid of anything." She held an extension cord up triumphantly. "There's a timer for the lights in here, too." She pulled out colored lights and other odds and ends. "Why don't you start putting the tree together—over there—and I'll organize all the decorations."

Clint scratched his chin. He'd never put a tree together, but it couldn't be too hard. With a shrug, he opened the box and began to stack individual branches of fake balsam on the floor. "Where are the directions?"

"There should be colors painted on the ends of each branch. Put the poles together, then stick the branches in the colored sections. It's easier if you start from the bottom. And fluff the branches as you go."

He sighed and did as he was told. As the tree took shape, he stopped telling himself having Lexi here was a big mistake. Maybe it was the upbeat country version of "Rudolph the Red-Nosed Reindeer" or the seven-foot tree before him. Whatever it was, he wanted the festive feeling to last.

"Nice job." Lexi stood next to him, and he was aware of her in a way he hadn't allowed himself to be previously. She wasn't short, but she was shorter than him. Slender, too. And everything about her seemed to sparkle—from her shiny hair to her red-and-white-striped socks. "Let's wrap a few strands of lights around this. Then we can do the fun part."

The fun part? Having her here was fun. He doubted it could get better.

They draped and tucked the lights around the branches of the tree, getting tangled a few times in the process, but before long, the tree was lit. Lexi set the timer to go on at five every night and to turn off at midnight. Then she plugged it in.

"Ooh…it's pretty." Her hands were on her hips, and a soft smile played on her lips.

"It sure is." He hoped she didn't know he was talking about her. She was the prettiest thing he'd ever seen.

"Let's get the horseshoes and lassos on here." She clapped her hands and grabbed a pile of miniature lassos with red bows on top.

He squinted at the other piles. Horseshoe ornaments, mini cowboy hats and— "What are the red bandannas for?"

"We'll tie them to the ends of some of the branches." She peeked from around the tree, where she was on her tiptoes hooking an ornament.

"Here, let me." He sidled up next to her, gently taking the ornament from her hand and placing it near the top of the tree. Sensing her sharp intake of breath, he stepped back quickly. Didn't want to crowd her or make her uncomfortable. Plus, he had a prickly feeling, as if he might do something weird, like touch her hair. "I'll put the horseshoes up."

He kept his distance as they continued decorating.

"I've saved the best for last." Lexi plucked something out of a bin and hid it behind her back. "Are you ready for this?"

"What is it?" What was she up to now?

She held out a straw cowboy hat. "It's the tree topper. Go ahead, put it on top."

He laughed. "I might not know much about decorating, but I've never heard of a cowboy hat on top. Isn't it supposed to be a star?"

"Not on a cowboy Christmas tree. The hat is the finishing touch." She grinned, holding it out to him.

Smiling, he shook his head and set it up top.

They stepped back to survey their work. He never would have thought of decorating a tree with lassos and horseshoes. With the colored lights, cowboy ornaments and red bandannas tied here and there, it represented him and all he stood for. Something shifted inside him. Softened his heart.

It was his first Christmas tree, and it suited him perfectly. And it was all because of Lexi.

She turned to him, holding up her hand. "Nice work, Romine."

He high-fived her, wanting to express how much this day meant to him but not knowing how. "Wouldn't have happened without you, boss."

"Come on. Pumpkin pie is waiting for us."

Pumpkin pie, Christmas decorating, laughter and music? He'd better not get used to this. The illusion of home had devastated him too many times in the past. He couldn't handle losing another one.

Chapter Five

Lexi craved a good sermon and familiar hymns. She couldn't face her problems alone anymore, and that meant spending more time with God. The good sermon and hymns were easy to find in the postcard-worthy church just outside Sweet Dreams. The spending more time with God, on the other hand, couldn't be rushed.

She made her way up the church aisle. Glancing to her left, she caught sight of Clint. In a button-down shirt and dark jeans, he looked right at home. Her spirits lifted. Whenever he was around, her loneliness eased. She scooted down the pew and sat next to him. He smelled masculine, like aftershave. "I didn't know you went to church here."

"Doesn't everyone?" He craned his neck to take in the people behind them.

"Good point." She opened the service bulletin, ridiculously grateful he was here. The thought of attending church with him every week appealed. "There's no sense in both of us driving. Next time, we should carpool."

A frown was his reply.

"I merely mentioned it to save gas," she whispered. It wasn't as if she was asking him to donate a kidney. She didn't like driving on icy roads, nor did she enjoy trying to control her car when the high winds blew. It wasn't because she craved his company or anything. "It's silly to take two vehicles."

Again, he didn't make a peep. The man was very independent, which was a nice way to say stubborn. She pursed her lips. Okay, maybe she did crave his company, but she wouldn't beg.

The service started, and she forced her attention away from Clint to sing the opening hymn.

The pastor rose. "Today's sermon text comes from the Gospel according to John, chapter fourteen. The night before He was crucified, Jesus comforted His disciples, telling them, 'Do not let your hearts be troubled. You believe in God; believe also in Me. My Father's house has many rooms…'"

Lexi straightened. Her heart *was* troubled. The past two months had brought a lot of anxiety into her life. Just because she believed in Jesus didn't mean she'd never worry, did it?

"He wanted the disciples to understand that this world and its problems are fleeting. We have an eternal home waiting for us. A room prepared in our Father's house."

Daddy was in one of those rooms. Her throat tightened, and she closed her eyes, wishing she could talk to him. What would she say? *Why didn't you tell me the instant you found out about the cancer? Why did you keep it from me? I had no idea you were sick and going to die. We would have gone to specialists and gotten you treatment.*

Even her imaginary conversations with Daddy were full of judgment and finger-pointing. If she had another chance to talk to him, would she really waste it reprimanding him?

"Are you okay?" Clint whispered.

Only then did she realize she'd rolled her bulletin into a tight scroll and her knuckles had turned white as she gripped it.

"I'm fine."

The service continued, and she kept hearing the words *Do not let your hearts be troubled.* Her heart was a tangled mess. How could it not be?

She tried to concentrate on the service. By the time the collection plate was being passed around, she realized her dreams were changing. What used to be her passion—Weddings by Alexandra—felt more like a burden. She lowered her head, her heart shrinking. Who was she without her company? Without her father?

Lord, I don't know who I am anymore.

The congregation rose. "Our Father..."

Lexi recited the prayer, the words hitting her. She was God's child. She braced her hands against the top of the pew. *Lord, thank You for reminding me I'm Yours. I'll always be Yours. Everything else can be taken from me, but no one can take You from me.*

After another hymn, everyone filed out. Clint took her by the elbow as they emerged into the winter air. His simple touch almost undid her.

"I'll drive next week." He tipped his hat to her and strode away.

With her hands in her coat pockets, she watched him until he got into his truck. He'd been exactly what she'd needed ever since she hired him. *Thank You, God, for sending Clint when I needed someone to depend on.*

"I thought I saw you inside." Amy Deerson approached. "Are you busy? Want to have breakfast with me?"

"I would love to have breakfast with you." Lexi unzipped her purse to find her keys. "Just what I need right now."

Amy beamed. "We can eat out or have scones and coffee at my place."

"Scones would be amazing."

"I live above the store. Come to the back entrance. I'll meet you there."

After letting her car warm up, Lexi drove to Amy's Quilt Shop. She entered the back of the building, climbed the steps and knocked on the wooden door, which Amy opened wide.

"Come in." Dark hardwood floors, tall windows and strings of Edison-style lightbulbs gave the large space a warm, modern feel. Fabrics were stacked by colors in wooden cubbies, and two sewing machines stood side by side on a long table against the wall. A large quilting frame displayed a partially finished quilt in traditional Christmas colors. Lexi had to forcibly refrain herself from touching the exquisite design.

"Amy, this is stunning. Do you make all the quilts you sell?"

"Most of them. I consign three other local quilters' pieces, too." She took plates out of a cupboard in the kitchen area opposite the work space. A round table with four chairs anchored the kitchen, and nearby a couch and love seat faced an entertainment center filled with books and a television. "Have a seat. The coffee won't take long."

"How do you find the time to make quilts on top of running the store?" Lexi sat on the couch, admiring the eclectic decor. A colorful photo of horses grazing in the sunset filled an empty wall space, and unlit candles dotted the room.

"Find time? I make time. I love quilting. Designing brings me joy."

What brings me joy? Lexi thought of Clint's face after they decorated his tree. He'd seemed pleased. More than pleased—touched. Making him happy for a little while had brought her joy.

She noticed an open sketchbook on the coffee table. "What's this?"

"Oh, nothing." Amy closed it. "Just doodles. I can't always find the fabric design I envision."

"So you create your own?" An uncomfortable blend of admiration and envy swirled in Lexi's core. Amy made time to do the things she loved. Lexi's life had devolved into an endless checklist of necessary tasks for her company, ones that brought little happiness.

"No, no." Amy waved. "I was sketching. I don't have the credentials to design fabrics."

"You sure could have fooled me."

The coffeemaker beeped, and Amy set a plate of scones on the ottoman and handed Lexi a mug.

"How are you holding up?" Amy bit into a pastry, her big brown eyes watchful, compassionate.

Lexi held the cup between her hands, letting it warm her. "Some days are better than others."

"That's to be expected."

"It is, isn't it?" Lexi wanted to confide in her, but was

it too much, too soon? "I'm tired of bitterness keeping me up at night."

"Oh, honey. I'm sorry. Losing your dad—I can't imagine."

"It's not just the fact he's gone." Sitting here in Amy's cozy world felt safe. "Earlier this week, I found out he knew he had cancer and didn't tell me."

"That's terrible!"

"I know." Lexi nodded. "And the sermon this morning is eating at me. 'Do not let your hearts be troubled'? Like I can control it. If Daddy had told me he had cancer, I would have come home. He would have gotten treatment."

Amy crossed one leg over the other as she sipped her coffee. "How long did he know?"

"About a month."

"Hmm..."

"What?" Lexi broke off a piece of scone and popped it in her mouth. Buttery, slightly sweet—the ideal comfort food on a winter morning.

"Well, I totally get why you're mad and all, but a month isn't much. The cancer must have been aggressive. Even with treatment, he might not have had long to live."

"I know. Chemo and radiation might not have cured him. But why didn't he tell me?"

"I wish I had the answer. I know he loved you, and you can be sure he is in Heaven, in one of those rooms prepared just for him."

I don't want him in Heaven. I want him here.

She missed him. Plain and simple. And maybe that's why she couldn't let it go. She changed the subject, and soon they were laughing about old times. But underneath it all, dissatisfaction lingered. She'd lost her dad. She could very well lose her business. And she didn't know what brought her joy anymore.

The one bright spot was Clint. She didn't have to worry about losing the ranch, too. Not with him running it.

Clint sat in a red vinyl booth at Dottie's Diner, the muffled conversations around him easing the raw edges of his solitude. Being around people, even when he wasn't interacting with them, sometimes made him feel less lonely. Other times, it punctuated how alone he was. Today was a less lonely day. Lexi had a lot to do with it.

"Missed you at Thanksgiving, tiger." Dottie filled his mug with coffee, then set the pot, nearly empty, on the table and slid into the booth opposite him. Her silver hair had poufy bangs in front and was twisted and clipped up in the back. She was a round, kind woman with a sassy tongue and a heart as wide-open as the state of Wyoming. "Every year I ask. Every year you refuse. I hate to think of you alone all the time. It's not natural."

Dottie and Big Bob hosted between thirty and fifty people every holiday. Clint had gone to Thanksgiving there once and had felt out of place. Making small talk with strangers was worse than dealing with an angry bull.

"I wasn't alone." He cautiously sipped the hot coffee, instantly regretting his words. The way her blue eyes started sparkling, he knew he would be forced to give an explanation.

"No?" Her voice climbed an octave. "Who were you with?"

He took another drink, scalding his tongue in the process. Dottie didn't need to know who he'd been with.

"Don't you go getting a burr under your saddle, Clint Romine. I've known you since you were thirteen. Now fess up."

If she blew this out of proportion, he was standing up and leaving, rude or not.

"Lexi Harrington." He quickly added, "She didn't have anyone else."

Her face cleared like the sky after a hard rain. "That's kind of you. I worry about the girl. Losing her daddy and not having her mama around anymore. Plus she's been stuck in the city for years. I don't know how anyone can live like that. People everywhere." She visibly shivered. "You takin' good care of her, hon?"

Was he taking good care of Lexi? He could have asked her if she needed a ride to church this morning. Never mind he hadn't known she was going. And if he had known? He still wouldn't have asked. Decorating his Christmas tree with her had left him wound up tighter than a rope around a wayward calf.

He'd rarely been the center of someone's attention, and Lexi treated him as if he mattered. Thanksgiving— cooking with her and decorating his tree—had shaken him, left him wanting more. More time with her, more of her attention. But if he gave in to the feeling?

She'd change her mind. Realize she'd been vulnerable and spending time with him had been a mistake. She didn't understand he'd always been *that Romine kid*, a worthless brat. If he didn't distance himself, she'd see the truth of who he was, and he didn't want her to think less of him.

Dottie covered his hand with hers. "Where do you

go in that handsome head of yours, tiger? You've been doing it ever since I've known you. It's as if you retreat somewhere none of us can find you."

"Sorry." He shook his head. "I'm doing my best at the ranch. I'm still searching for winter feed to buy. If you hear of anyone willing to sell, give me a call."

"I've been keeping my ears open, but all I hear is the same predicament you're in. Ranchers are looking to buy feed, not sell. Big Bob is at home. Why don't you stop by on your way back? Maybe he's heard something different."

He hoped Big Bob had a lead. If not, Clint would have to sell the calves as soon as possible, take the profit and hope it would be enough to keep the ranch going until next year without having to dip into its cash reserves. The calf sale would be another challenge. It had been years since he'd sold calves, and he'd never done the negotiating.

Why was he worrying? He wouldn't be doing it alone. Jerry would help.

"Thanks, Dottie. I'll do that." He clung to the hope Big Bob had good news for him. He really didn't want to let Lexi down, and not securing additional feed felt like a major failure. He wanted to be more than the worthless Romine kid for once.

Two hours later, Clint marched into the stables, ready to stomp something—anything—in frustration. His chances at feeding the calves along with the cows through the winter were dwindling by the second. Big Bob hadn't known any locals with extra feed for sale. Jerry had no other names to call, and Clint's friends didn't have any leads, either. He'd contacted a ranch in

Montana and left three messages, but they'd never returned his calls. It looked like he would have to stick to the original calf sale date in mid-December.

Although it was technically not his duty today, checking on the cattle would take his mind off the fact the ranch wouldn't be buying the farm equipment RJ had wanted to purchase. Clint had a feeling RJ would have secured extra feed, one way or another.

He saddled up his horse and rode into the cold wind. To his surprise, Lexi was atop Nugget and heading toward the gate.

"Where you going?" Clint called.

Lexi expertly turned Nugget to face him. Her lips looked pinched, and even with her winter gear on, she seemed tense. "There's an old cabin northeast of here. Thought I'd check on it."

A cabin? He hadn't seen any cabins. He hadn't explored the property in depth, though. "You're not going by yourself, are you?"

"Why not?"

Why not? Because it's Wyoming and snowstorms kick up at will. Because I don't have the first clue where this cabin is, and I'll worry about you getting dropped by your horse, attacked by an animal or worse, and I'll have no way to find you. "It's not wise to be alone in this weather. I don't want you stranded."

"Well, I can't stay here right now. I'm going. I'll be fine." Under her stocking cap, her hair rippled like silky ribbons, framing her pretty—if agitated—face. Yep, she was ornery. Was she mad he hadn't asked her to come to church with him earlier?

"I'll come with you."

"It's not necessary," she said in crisp syllables.

His first reaction was to retreat, to let her go on her merry way since she obviously didn't want him around, but she'd been kind to him in a way that made him want to protect her. He couldn't let her go off by herself, not if it would put her at risk.

"If you don't want my company, I'll have one of the other hands ride out with you. I don't know where this cabin is, and cell reception is unreliable the farther out you get."

"I'll be fine. See the tree line? There's a winding river beyond it, and trails lead up to the mountains. The cabin is half a mile up on the nearest trail."

"You said trails. If it started to snow and you didn't come back, how would I know which one to take?"

She looked at the ground, considering, and met his gaze. "If you feel compelled to come, then come. It will take a couple of hours, so if you have someplace else to be, then don't bother."

"I don't have any place to be." Clint urged his horse beside hers, and they settled into a steady pace. They rode toward the lodgepole pines in the distance. The clip-clop of the hooves and sound of the wind kept them company for half an hour. He glanced at her often. Why was she mad? Why did she need to get away? Her pink cheeks jutted high as she rode tall and proud. They reached the river she had mentioned, and she gestured for him to follow her. She and Nugget hugged the river until it bent sharply and changed direction.

"The trail is up ahead," she announced, glowering.

"Did I do something to make you mad?"

She didn't reply, and a trail wide enough for both horses appeared as if out of nowhere. With trees breaking the wind, the air felt warmer, and they slowed their pace.

"No," she finally said. "It's not you. I have all these dilemmas in my head, and I don't know what to do with them. I thought getting out of the house, away from the million things on my list, would help."

"And is it helping?"

"Not really. I can't escape from myself."

Strangely, he understood exactly what she meant. He'd tried to escape from himself so many times over the past four years.

"It's been a long time since I thought about what makes me happy," she said. "Riding makes me happy. So that's what I'm doing today."

"But…you're not happy."

"No."

"Why not?" He dreaded her reply. What if he was the reason?

"Let's put it this way—bitter doesn't look good on me."

"Oh." He nodded. "You're still upset about your dad."

"I'm going to call his doctor. Get some answers." She met Clint's gaze, and he nodded, but he wondered if it would help. What answers could the doctor give her?

A small, ancient log cabin came into view. They dismounted and tied the horses to the hitching post nearby. Clint's senses alerted. Last week's snow had melted, and the weather had warmed for two days, but the temperature dropped since then, leaving the ground solid. Lexi reached for the door.

"Wait." He hurried to her side. "Let me go in first."

"Why?"

"Someone's been here recently."

"How can you tell?"

"Footprints." He crouched, pointing to the indentations around the entrance. "These were made during the thaw. The fact they're still here tells me someone stopped by before the temperatures dropped again." He back-tracked to the horses and inspected the area. "No signs of horses, though. I don't know how whoever it was got out here. A four-wheeler would have left tracks, too."

"People use the cabin from time to time. Daddy said an old mountain man must have built it in the late 1800s. It's a haven if someone is hunting and needs a rest. It's never locked."

"Regardless, I'll go in first." He opened the door. It creaked as it swayed inward. Misshapen wood floors, three windows, an old army cot, a cupboard, two wooden chairs, a table and a stone fireplace greeted him. The dust on the floor and table was patchy, as if someone had been there recently. He poked through the cupboard. Two empty liquor bottles were tucked behind a few plates and mugs.

Lexi stood behind him. "Why would there be empty bottles here?"

"I don't know." Clint shifted his jaw. "But I'm going to find out. Looks like someone thinks your cabin is their party house."

She inspected one corner while he mentally added up possible explanations.

"Looks like whoever was here did more than drink-ing." She pointed to the butt of a marijuana cigarette.

"Unacceptable. For anyone to be coming out here and doing this on your property…" He couldn't finish the thought. "I'll get to the bottom of this."

"It was probably some hunters. I doubt it's the first time someone has done this. As long as they don't bother us."

"You don't deserve this."

She placed her hand on his arm, and he pivoted to face her. Her expression, like her words, was soft, soothing. "Don't be so upset."

"But—"

"As Jerry likes to remind me, cowboys are like wild horses. You never know when one needs to get away, blow off steam, or whatever else Jerry claims. This was probably a one-time thing."

Clint collected the bottles. Lexi claimed it wasn't a big deal, but he wasn't so sure. She walked out of the cabin.

"What if it's someone from the ranch?"

Surprise then distrust flashed in her eyes. "Wouldn't be the first time I was left in the dark. I don't mind someone using the cabin as a refuge or to hunt, but I won't put up with anyone in my employ getting high or drunk on my property."

"I'll look into it." He ground his teeth together as her words singed his raw conscience. How self-righteous could he be? He, too, was keeping her in the dark. And more and more, he wanted to rid himself of the burden. But how could he? She'd fire him and be left alone, vulnerable, with possible drunkards about.

"I went to see my friend after church. You might know her—Amy Deerson. She owns Amy's Quilt Shop. She has the most incredible studio, and I think that's one of the reasons I've been in such a bad mood." Lexi strode to where they'd tied the horses.

He shook his head. His mind was still 100 percent focused on the person using her cabin for illegal activities, and she wanted to talk about old friends?

"She's making time for her joy. My job used to be my greatest joy." Lexi mounted Nugget. Clint made one more quick sweep of the area, didn't see anything out of the ordinary and got back in the saddle.

"You said 'used to be.'" Clint signaled his horse to move forward. Lexi did the same.

"For the past two years, I've been knee-deep in business details. I've had to cut way back on how many weddings I plan. I never set out to be a manager, but I'm afraid that's what I've become."

He frowned. She didn't like managing her business?

"I'm going to have to make some changes, and I might have to go back to Denver sooner than I'd planned. I've worked too hard to build this company to let it fall apart. Maybe I'm expecting too much from my vice president. I don't know."

His mind raced. She…was leaving?

He didn't want her to leave. He liked her here. Liked their weekly meetings and fixing her faucet and listening to her talk.

He liked being near her.

"I'm so glad I can depend on you, Clint. I can't tell you what a relief it is I don't have to worry about the ranch."

How could she say that when they'd just found evidence that he wasn't on top of the ranch? He hadn't even known this cabin existed. What if whoever had used it knew Lexi was alone up at the main house? He'd seen mild-mannered cowboys get aggressive when they'd had too much to drink.

They emerged from the tree-lined path, and he wanted to shout, *Sorry, but you're putting your faith in the wrong guy.*

"When will you go?"

She prodded Nugget to follow the river. "Tonight. I'm

getting to the bottom of whatever's going on at Weddings by Alexandra. Let's plan on our usual Thursday morning meeting this week, okay? I should have the answers I need by then."

It would give him a few more days to make a decision about the calf sale. He might not like it, but Denver was the best place for her. He'd have to get used to her not being around eventually. Besides, he'd never be more than a hired hand, and he'd better not forget it.

Chapter Six

Thursday morning, Lexi unpacked linen samples and draped them around her office at the ranch. Odd that driving into the garage last night had filled her with a sense of home she'd lost during the six years she'd lived in Denver. The past three days had been spent talking to her planners and their assistants, and she was no closer to knowing why so many business details were slipping through the cracks, but she knew for certain something bigger was wrong.

When she'd entered the Weddings by Alexandra headquarters, the front desk's fresh flowers—always the palest of pinks—had been replaced with red roses. Three years ago, she'd hired a professional team to help brand Weddings by Alexandra. They'd emphasized the importance of creating a distinctive identity for her business. The color of the flowers, the music playlist in the waiting area, even the stationery had been selected with care. These details set her apart from other wedding planning companies.

She'd also noticed that two of the planners had unopened boxes stacked in their offices when company policy was to check each delivery as it came in, then move the packages to the storage room. When she confronted them, they quickly moved the boxes, but it didn't change the fact the standards she'd put in place were not being met.

Natalie hadn't been in the office, and her phone had gone directly to voice mail. Last night she'd returned Lexi's calls, assuring her she would handle everything. But why had Natalie let things slide in the first place?

Lexi plunged a box cutter through the packing tape of another box. Daddy's doctor still hadn't called her back. She'd called Monday and yesterday. Left messages, too.

Didn't anyone respect her anymore?

She unpacked the linens and folded a dove-gray napkin before placing it on her desk. After spreading a tablecloth over the folding table she'd brought in, she set it with sample plates and flatware. She stepped back, finger on chin, taking it in. Maybe the table would look better with the classic silverware. Every time she put a wedding together, she couldn't help stashing ideas for her own. Blush bridesmaids' dresses. Tons of flowers—white peonies and pale pink roses—everywhere. The most delicate of stemware. Hand calligraphy on the invitations. And a handsome groom who only had eyes for her.

Clint stood in the doorway.

The fork in her hand clattered to the floor. Her cheeks warmed. One of the reasons she'd anticipated coming home last night was the thought of talking to Clint today.

She was living in an alternate reality, one with a gorgeous cowboy who took care of her problems, a reality as flimsy and fleeting as the bubbles wedding guests blew for fun at receptions. And the man before her *was* her employee. An important detail she dared not forget.

Last night she'd prayed about the situation, hoping she'd feel led to keep things light and professional with Clint. Instead, here she was, dropping forks and blushing like a flighty middle schooler the instant he appeared.

"How did the trip go?" He took off his hat and held it between his hands.

She took a moment to get her equilibrium. "It was eye-opening. I'm disappointed. When I'm not around, the standards seem to slip. My vice president assured me she'd take care of it, but it's frustrating. Plus, one of my couples—a March wedding—canceled."

He frowned. "Why?"

"They broke up. The wedding's off."

"I'm sorry to hear that."

"Me, too." Boy, she was all gloom and doom today. *Look at the bright side, Lexi.* "But, hey, a senator's daughter set up a call with me next Wednesday to discuss the possibility of me planning her wedding. Madeline Roth is a high-profile client, good publicity, so I'm glad."

"Next Wednesday, huh." Clint frowned. "That reminds me. The calf sale is scheduled the same day, and I've got some bad news."

Her stomach clenched. She braced herself for whatever was coming.

"The only feed I can find is three times the price it should be. No one else has a surplus to get us through the winter."

The implications were clear, and she didn't like them. "So we have to sell?"

He nodded, regret all over his face. "I have one more

lead, but he's not answering my calls, and we're out of time. If we're going to sell the calves, we need to keep our sale date."

It was as if another ten pounds had been added to her already too-full load. Instead of slumping, though, she kept her back straight.

"That's too bad." She tucked her hair behind her ear. "After looking at your spreadsheet, I'd hoped we wouldn't have to sell right away." The sudden emotion in her chest crushed her. She was letting Daddy down. He'd been excited about producing and selling the hay, and she wouldn't be able to make it happen. Not this year, anyway. "I guess we'll have to wait on the farm equipment."

"I'm sorry. I tried everywhere."

"I know you did. Don't worry. That's life on a cattle ranch. Unpredictable." She rounded the desk, took a seat and gestured for him to also. "What else is going on?"

"Still looking for the cabin crasher." He lowered his frame into the chair opposite her desk.

"No leads?"

"No, and I've ridden back twice. No one has been there again that I can tell." He looked like he was going to say more, and she tilted her head slightly to encourage him. "I've put feelers out about it around the ranch. The only two cowboys I'm not sure of are Jake and Ryder. They're young."

"Youth isn't a crime."

"No, but I know the type."

"Do you? From personal experience?" She couldn't imagine straitlaced Clint as a troublemaker.

"I guess you could say that."

"Were you trouble with a capital *T*?" she teased.

"My grandfather thought so."

"But you only lived with him as a small child, right? Or did I remember that wrong?"

"Until I was six. I'm sure I was a pest."

"You, a pest?" She propped her elbows on the desk and rested her chin on her fist. Thinking about him as a child made her worries disappear. She tried to picture him as a little boy. "No way. I'm guessing you were adorable with those big blue eyes. You must have been a quiet kid."

"Um, I guess." He ran his fingers through his hair. "What about you? I don't see you as being quiet."

She chuckled. "I wasn't quiet, but I was very girlie."

"I'm not surprised."

"I wore dresses and pretended I was a princess. My mom and I had tea parties and baked cookies and planned special parties for my friends." She let the sweet memories seep inside. "I had a really great childhood."

The things he'd told her about his dad and grandfather came back. She suppressed a groan. She'd been insensitive. "I'm sorry. I forgot you didn't have a home like mine growing up. Do you have good memories? Who raised you after your grandfather?"

"Sure, I have good memories." The starkness in his eyes convinced her he was lying. "I had a real nice foster mom right after my grandfather died."

"Why did you end up at Yearling, then?"

"Miss Joanne got sick when I was eight, and I lived in a couple other homes after hers."

"Define a couple." A sinking feeling in her chest made her want to take back the question.

He glanced up at the ceiling, his lips twisting. "Hmm. Four, I guess."

"Four? But that would mean moving almost every year."

"Yes."

"Why so many?"

He shrugged. "Crowding. Funding. Babies. I didn't mind leaving most of them."

She rubbed her temples. "You didn't mind? But they were your families."

"No, they weren't." His dry laugh held no pleasure. "There are a lot of great foster parents out there, but besides Miss Joanne, I wouldn't call any of the people I lived with before Yearling my family. The guys I met there? They're my brothers. And Dottie and Big Bob have always looked out for me."

"How did you meet the Laverts?"

"They ran Yearling while I was there. Dottie still watches out for me. Listen, I'm not complaining. I had a roof over my head and food to eat my entire life."

"There's more to life than food and shelter."

"Miss Joanne taught me that."

"Tell me about her."

Clint shifted in his seat. "I went to live with her— she had two other foster kids, too—after my grandfather died. She taught us Bible stories and played board games with us. I was pretty broken up when she got sick and had to move back in with her folks in Idaho."

"And you said you were eight when she left? Where did you go next?"

He shrugged. "A lot of places. Some good. Some bad. None lasted."

The picture he painted sounded bleak. No mother to comfort him. No father to ride around a ranch with. No childhood home. Just random people he had no choice but to live with. She'd been fortunate to have had two parents raising her.

"We should probably discuss the sale next week," Clint said, clearly wanting to change the subject. "The vaccinations are done. Jerry and I will..." He filled her in on all the sale details, but she had a hard time concentrating. She found herself wanting to know more about the man in front of her. And wanting to give him some of his lost childhood back.

When they'd discussed the sale and other items on the agenda, Clint stood to leave.

"I've been meaning to ask—how is Banjo?" Lexi followed him out of her office through the hall.

"Fine. I've been letting him sleep on my floor at night. He won't take no for an answer."

"You're a good man, Clint." They stopped in the living room.

He looked ready to argue. With a glance at the far wall and the fireplace, he shifted his jaw. "Don't start a fire in the fireplace until I get a chance to inspect it. I'll get to it after we sell the calves."

A good man? If she only knew the memories she'd kicked up with her innocent questions, she wouldn't be so quick to brand him. Unexpected emotion had hit him hard in her office, and at first he couldn't define the feeling. But then he'd realized it was sadness. Long ago he'd stopped hoping to experience the things she described. He'd never known his mother or had the sense of belonging to parents the way most kids did. How many times had adults given up on him? How many adults had he given up on?

Lord, I know who I am. Lexi acts as if we're from the

same world, but we aren't. I want to live up to her ex-
pectations, but I'm not going to fool myself into think-
ing I can.

Clint trudged through the snow on his way to the
ranch office. He was her employee. Nothing more. And
now that he had her approval, he could call the auction
house and confirm next Wednesday's sale date.

As he strode past outbuildings, he saw someone duck
into the horse barn. Logan? No, Logan had told him
earlier he was checking calves. Clint detoured to the
barn, his eyes adjusting to the dimmer light, his nose
trained to smell anything beyond manure and hay. Nothing seemed out of the ordinary. He inspected the empty
stalls as he walked past them then heard rustling in a
stall in the opposite aisle.

"Who's there?"

Jake's head appeared, and he held a pitchfork in one
hand. His face was flushed. The kid had *guilty* written
all over him. "Just cleaning out stalls, boss."

"It's Thursday. You're supposed to be in school." Jake
and Ryder were seniors in high school and only came in
on weekends or in the afternoon during the occasional
busy times throughout the year.

"I don't have class right now."

Somehow Clint doubted it. He made his way over
to the stall Jake was supposedly cleaning out. "So you
decided to muck stalls between classes?"

"Yep." Jake's brown eyes darkened. He wore old
jeans, a stained work coat and gloves. A stocking cap
covered his overgrown brown hair. With the exception
of not wearing his winter overalls, the kid was dressed
to work, but Clint wasn't buying his story.

"Didn't see your car out front. How'd you get here?"

"A buddy dropped me off." He shifted as if to block Clint's view of the straw bales behind him.

"Hmm." He tried to see around Jake without being obvious. "How are you getting back to school?"

"He'll pick me up later." Jake wrapped both hands around the pitchfork and leaned on it.

Whatever he was up to, it wasn't cleaning horse stalls. A dozen possibilities came to mind. He could have run away from home for a day or two. Maybe he'd stashed a bag with some clothes behind the straw. Or the kid could be playing hooky for whatever reason.

He should command Jake to move out of the way, but compassion stopped him. Clint had told Lexi the condensed version of his years in foster care. What he hadn't told her was the abusive foster home he'd been assigned to right after he turned thirteen. He'd stuck it out for a month, but the family's eighteen-year-old son kept using him as a punching bag. Clint had called his caseworker. A week later she still hadn't come out to visit, so he ran away, staying with a school buddy for a night or two then moving to another friend's house. When he'd overstayed his welcome, he contacted his caseworker again, and she told him to return to the foster family until she found him a new place.

He'd refused.

She'd tried to get him to tell her where he was staying, but he knew she'd just take him back. She asked him to call her the following week while she worked on finding a new home for him. He didn't tell her he'd been hiding out in a barn. The weather had been mild that June, and the situation suited him fine. A couple jars of peanut butter and cheap bread kept the hunger pains at bay. True to her promise, his caseworker had secured him a spot at the Yearling Group Home, and he'd moved in the following week.

Those two weeks in the barn had changed him, though. And if Jake was dealing with similar issues, Clint wanted to help.

"How are things at home?" Clint leaned against the wood post, crossing one foot over the other.

"Fine. Why wouldn't they be?"

"I don't know. You live with your folks?"

"My dad and stepmom." His shoulders braced defiantly.

"Do you get along with them okay?"

Jake averted his eyes. "I guess."

"If something's going on—"

"Nothing's going on. I just came in to work. That's all."

Clint regarded him a moment and decided to drop the subject. "Call your buddy and have him pick you up now. We'll see you Saturday morning." He turned to leave.

"Whatever, dude," he muttered.

"What did you say?" Clint pivoted back. This kid was really pushing it with him.

"Nothing." He propped the pitchfork against the stall and pulled out an old cell phone from his pocket.

Clint began walking away, then paused. "Oh, and from now on, I don't expect to see you here unless it's your scheduled shift. Got it?"

Jake nodded before texting his friend.

Out in the fresh air once more, Clint's cell phone rang. He wanted to ignore it, but maybe it was the Montana ranch with news about selling him feed.

He answered, not slowing his pace.

"How is life working on a ranch again, man?"

Clint grinned. Nash Bolton was one of his best

friends from his days at Yearling. It had been a while since they'd talked. Clint hadn't been specific about where he was working, because Nash had left Sweet Dreams under mysterious circumstances. Clint wasn't sure how he'd react to him being back.

"It's good." He checked his watch. Lunchtime. He needed a break. He could inspect the stall Jake had been in later. Changing course, he headed back to his cabin. "How are you? Haven't seen your name in the papers lately."

"Yeah, got bucked hard two weeks ago. Broke a couple ribs and my ankle. I'm mending fine." Nash had risen to bull-riding stardom right after high school. He'd won the Professional Bull Riders world championship seven years ago, and he still competed on the circuit despite the never-ending injuries plaguing him. "I've been off my feet, and I couldn't be more bored. Figured it was time for you, Wade, Marshall and me to plan a get-together. Haven't seen you since, what, September?"

"Yeah, September sounds about right. Where are you staying?"

"I'm holed up in one of Wade's empty cabins. He remodeled them all. Must have sunk a lot of cash into them, too, because I'm telling you what, I'm living in style. I'll hate to leave this luxury next month."

Their friend Wade Croft owned property all over the state, but his ranch was only a thirty-minute drive from Sweet Dreams. With Nash staying at Wade's, Clint had even more incentive to visit soon.

"Another month, huh? What next?"

"Doc wants me to retire."

Clint stopped in his tracks. Nash had never talked about retiring. Every season it was broken bones, sprains and bruises, but he kept on riding, laughing off any suggestion of quitting. "Are your injuries more serious than you're letting on?"

"No, of course, not. The wear and tear is getting to me. Maybe I'll come visit you before I decide."

"Yeah, about that… The ranch isn't in Cheyenne. I moved back to Sweet Dreams. Rock Step Ranch. I'm working for Lexi—Alexandra Harrington." His cabin came into view, and he loped the rest of the way.

"What? Why didn't you tell me?" Nash sounded angry.

"I didn't know if it would work out."

"Why wouldn't it work out?"

Clint hadn't told anyone all the details of losing his property. He'd simply told them he made a mistake and lost it. While Marshall accepted his words at face value, Wade and Nash had pressed for the full story. Regardless, Clint had remained silent. Wade and Nash had both become successful beyond any of their wildest dreams, and Clint didn't want them thinking less of him. He also knew they would have offered him money. Money he never dared take. He couldn't think of anything sadder than borrowing from them and losing their cash, too.

"Have you seen… Never mind."

Clint knew exactly whom Nash was referring to. Amy Deerson. "In church. In passing. Lexi's friends with her." He let himself into the cabin, peeling off a layer of outerwear in the process. "I should have told you this was where I was working. Dottie was the one who convinced me to try it."

"How is Dottie? I haven't seen her in years. And don't apologize—I'm glad you finally realized you were meant to work on a ranch. The job with the oil company was killing you."

"It feels good spending my day in the saddle again."

"Boy, don't I know that. When are you free? You should come up to Wade's. I'll call Marshall. It's past time we got together."

"Call Marshall and get back to me. I can't get away next week, but after that I'll find time to drive up."

"Will do. I miss you. Talk to you later." He hung up.

Clint tossed the phone on the table and stalked to the fridge. What was going on? Nash never said things like *I miss you.* First he'd mentioned retiring, and then he said he missed him? Maybe the bull had tossed him on his head.

The day they met flashed in Clint's mind. Nash had been sitting on one of the top bunks in the room they shared with Marshall and Wade. His legs dangled over the edge of the mattress, his feet in dirty athletic shoes with a hole in one toe. Nash had taken one look at Clint and said, "You got a problem with the bottom bunk?"

Clint had tossed his bag on the floor and replied, "No. Do you?"

And Nash's million-dollar smile had spread across his face. He'd hopped off the bunk, stood in front of Clint and grinned. "We're going to be good friends, you and I."

Clint had never had anyone accept him like that. And Nash had been right. They were good friends. The closest thing to a family he had.

He had a good life here. He had enough. So why couldn't he stop wanting more?

"Thank you for calling me back, Dr. Lotusmeyer. I have some questions regarding my father's health." Lexi twirled a pen between her fingers. Since Clint left, she'd spent her time trying different napkin and flatware options until choosing three potential combinations for the wedding she was planning for June. She'd taken pictures and emailed them to her assistant, Jolene, for feedback right as the doctor called.

"I'm sorry about your loss, Ms. Harrington."

"Thank you. Unfortunately, my father's death came as a complete surprise to me. He hadn't told me about his cancer diagnosis, and until recently, I assumed he hadn't known, either. But I found his pathology report. It's dated back in October. Is it normal to go from diagnosis to…well…death in such a short period of time?"

"Cancer isn't always predictable. Some people go into remission for years."

Had her father been in remission for years and she hadn't known about that, either?

"Was this the first time he'd been diagnosed with cancer?" She held her breath, not knowing what she wanted to hear, just certain the doctor could make this gnawing question mark in her heart go away.

"Yes, this was the first time he was diagnosed. It's important you mention your father's disease to your primary physician so he or she can make sure you get the recommended health screenings."

A surge of relief rushed through her body at hearing this was his first diagnosis, but the information brought new questions.

"Are you saying this could have been prevented?"

"Not at all. But early treatment can make a big difference."

"Treatment. Like chemotherapy and radiation."

"Yes. But they don't always work. Some patients die while being treated. Other patients live for years without treatment. It depends on the type of cancer and the overall health of the individual."

She really wanted to know one thing. "Was my father open to getting treatment?"

"I can't answer that."

She closed her eyes, tightening her grip around the pen. How hard could it be for him to give her a simple yes or no?

He continued. "I can tell you he had a follow-up appointment scheduled for the day after he died. I would have discussed his treatment options at that time."

Hope unfurled her fingers, and the pen fell to the desk. "Thank you for telling me. It... It's a relief."

"It's difficult losing someone suddenly. You'll have to excuse me, but I have an appointment. You take care, and have a Merry Christmas."

"Thank you. Same to you."

She hung up the phone and padded out of the office to the living room. Standing before the large windows, she took in the view of the winter countryside and shivered. Her father hadn't known about the cancer for long, and he'd made the follow-up appointment. That had to mean something, right?

She curled her fingers around her forearms, barely noticing the softness of the cashmere sweater. Maybe he'd planned on getting treatment.

Maybe he had planned on telling her. In his own time.

She'd never know.

She wished he would have trusted her enough to tell her right away.

Lord, I'm trying to get some closure. I don't know

how. Everyone dies. I know it. But I'm struggling with all these questions. What do I do?

The Bible on the mantel caught her eye. She took it from its spot, caressing the hard cover. Daddy had told her to read a psalm when life got tough. She flipped through, skimming until she landed on Psalm 119:76. "May Your unfailing love be my comfort, according to Your promise to Your servant."

Unfailing love?

How many times had she skipped church, failed to pray, relied on herself, ignored the needs of those around her and brushed her own dad off? Too many to count.

She dropped onto the couch as regret and shame flowed thicker than sludge through her veins. *Lord, I'm sorry. I always put myself first.*

Visions of the weddings she planned flitted to her mind. Decorating Clint's Christmas tree did, too. Okay, she didn't *always* put herself first. But her motives were still selfish. She liked planning weddings and made a very good income at it. And the Christmas tree was more about having fun with Clint than anything else.

Lord, can You really love me with an unfailing love? I don't deserve it. Well, I guess no one does. That's the whole reason why You came down, lived a perfect life, died and rose again. Why do I conveniently forget that part?

Maybe she didn't need all the answers to move forward. She couldn't change the past, but she could pray about the future.

Chapter Seven

"Do you want Logan to go with you?"

At Lexi's innocent question, Clint pressed the accelerator. The wind was picking up, but the roads weren't icy. They'd make it to church early, so there was no reason for him to speed up. He was just frustrated. He eased his boot from the gas pedal to slow down.

"No, with Jerry sick, I need Logan to stay and take care of the remaining herd." Why had Jerry come down with pneumonia at this critical time? Clint dreaded not having the older man's expertise at the auction. Decisions would have to be made. He didn't want the responsibility of making them.

"Do you want me to come with you?"

Yes. He glanced over at her. "I thought you had a call with the senator."

"The senator's daughter." Her light brown eyes couldn't hide the truth from him. She needed to take the call. "I don't normally cancel, but if it would help, I'll reschedule."

"No need. I've got this. I've researched current prices. I'll check again tomorrow to see if they change, and I'll print them out for you to review. I'm not going to sugarcoat it—prices are low."

Being responsible for the ranch's future weighed on his shoulders, reminded him of his past.

"I know. We'll manage."

The white church came into view. He wished he shared Lexi's faith that they'd manage, but he had a lot of doubts. It cost a large amount of money to run an operation the size of Rock Step Ranch, and no matter how many times he added the numbers, the bottom line looked inadequate.

He turned into the parking lot, found a spot and cut the engine. "What if the calves don't bring enough in to cover expenses?"

"The ranch has reserves, and I have a nest egg, Clint. I'll use both if I have to."

His mind blanked.

A nest egg.

He'd lost one once. He could not be responsible for losing hers, too. How could she trust him like this with her future?

Clenching his jaw, he knew what he had to do. He had to come clean and warn her that she was putting her faith in the wrong guy.

"Lexi, I have to tell you something."

"What is it?"

"I owned property a while back. Almost five years ago. And I made a bad decision and lost it."

She scooted closer and touched his hand. "I wondered about the time between jobs."

"I don't know if I'm the best person to make these financial decisions."

"But you don't." Her voice was soothing. "I make them."

"Yes, but—"

"Look, whatever happened is in the past. Ranching is a tough business, especially for anyone just starting out. I trust you."

The words gripped him, made him want to believe she had reason to trust him. But she didn't know the circumstances of how he lost his land, and he debated telling her the rest. There were three things he'd never told a living soul. One was that his grandfather had called him a worthless brat every day for the two years he'd lived with him. Another was he'd cried every night for a month after Miss Joanne moved, and he'd hated his new foster family although they were nice people. And the third was he'd known better than to make a business deal with a virtual stranger, but he'd been too greedy to say no.

If he told his friends or Lexi any of these things, they'd see him in a different light. He'd once more become the worthless, lonely kid who didn't deserve a home or family. The day he'd taken his last punch from the kid at the foster home was the day he'd said goodbye to his former self. He'd promised himself he'd stop hoping for the family everyone else seemed to have. He'd accepted he was alone, and he'd set out to make a life for himself no one could take away.

But it had been taken away.

And he'd spent four years in penance, punishing himself for becoming the worthless, undeserving kid again. Maybe that was his problem. Once more he'd found something he wanted that could be taken away, and it scared him.

"Can we go in now?" Lexi asked.

Her lips were glossy, her skin smooth, and she looked more rested than when they first met. He shook away his thoughts. *You're not that kid anymore, so stop acting like it.*

"Yeah, let's go." He'd taken some of the weight off her slender shoulders. She needed him to be strong, to get the best price for the calves, and he would do that for her. Even if his best wasn't good enough.

"What is your favorite Christmas hymn?" Lexi turned slightly to face Clint after church. He was dead silent as he drove them home. The wind from earlier had grown more intense, and Lexi tried to ignore it, but the way it shook the truck made her doubly glad Clint was the one driving.

Church had been uplifting, and her mood was buoyant ever since Clint had confided in her. He hoarded personal details of his life. She had no doubt it had been difficult for him to admit he'd lost his property. She relished the fact he'd opened up to her. While she was curious about the details, she hadn't pressed. If he wanted her to know, he'd tell her in his own time.

"Christmas hymn? I don't know."

"Come on. You must like one."

"Haven't thought about it." The words were clipped. He didn't bother looking at her.

Refusing to take his curtness personally, she debated how far to push him. Now that he'd opened up a little, she wanted to know more about his past. She'd assumed he'd always been single, but he never talked about it. Maybe he'd lost his land in a divorce.

"Have you ever been married?" She held her breath, hoping he'd say no.

He shot her a horrified glance. "No."

Good. "Serious girlfriend?"

"'Away in a Manger.'"

She burst out laughing. "Okay, but what about my other question?"

"You first." His eyes gleamed with interest and… vulnerability.

"'Joy to the World.'"

"And the other question?" He returned his focus to the road.

Fair enough. If she wanted the real stuff from him, she'd have to pony it up herself.

"No to marriage, yes to serious relationship." She waited for the regret and sadness that flashed whenever thoughts of previous boyfriends came to mind, but they didn't bother her today. "I dated a few guys in college. Very serious types. One was determined to be a lawyer. I got in the way of his studies, so he broke it off. The other was in the engineering program."

"What happened with him?"

"Let's just say circuits and electrical waves interested him way more than I did. Our breakup was mutual. After I graduated, I got busy with planning weddings."

"And you didn't have time to date." His matter-of-fact tone had her shaking her head.

"I didn't say that. I met Doug. He was an accountant. We got along well. We did things like visiting the art museum and going out for brunch. We would join mutual friends for dinner. I thought he might be the one."

Clint's hands twisted around the steering wheel, and his jaw shifted.

"But you know what? I was wrong. He wasn't the one at all. I've always wanted more, and I think I was willing to settle for less."

"Did he ask you to marry him or something?"

She'd thought she'd known Doug, but she'd put him on a pedestal. She'd assumed he wanted the same things she did—marriage, kids—but he hadn't. And worst of all, she'd overlooked the fact he didn't have a romantic bone in his body. She wanted a love like her parents had—affectionate and loyal and lasting—but she also wanted someone to sweep her off her feet.

"Not quite. We were at a restaurant. He asked me to move in with him. I told him I had no intention of living with anyone without being married. He seemed surprised, told me that a wedding would be too big of a distraction while he was working toward his CPA license. I understood. But then he grew agitated, said he really didn't see marriage in his future and claimed I only wanted his money. I threw a dinner roll at his chest. Never saw him again."

Clint's laugh was loud and unexpected. She started laughing, too, as they rumbled up the long road leading to the house.

"He was stupid." Clint parked the truck and turned to her. "Even I know a wedding planner doesn't want to just live with a guy. You deserve more."

And just like that, something changed inside her. The switch she'd been manning with an iron hand flipped, allowing her to view him as an eligible man. A dangerous thing, indeed. She couldn't fall for Clint. It would be awkward and end badly. He was her employee.

"What do you look for in a girl?"

"Nothing. I don't… I'm not looking for a relation-ship."

"Why? Did someone break your heart?"

"I never had a heart to break."

She pushed down her disappointment. She should be happy. He'd said the exact the words she needed to hear. She always fell for the reserved ones, ignoring the fact they were emotionally unavailable. She *did* have a heart to break. And Clint wouldn't be the one to break it, not if she kept her head on straight.

Thursday morning Clint sat on his couch, mindlessly petting Banjo, who had curled up next to him. He'd made a habit out of sitting for a while in front of the Christmas tree. He liked the peaceful feeling it gave him. After helping Logan feed the cattle this morning, he'd come back here to get his thoughts straight before his weekly meeting with Lexi. Yesterday's sale had gone as expected. Low prices.

Had he missed something? Was there anything he could have done to sell the calves for more money? After the meeting, he was going to ride out and check as many pregnant cows as possible. He would do his best to make sure next year's calves were born healthy.

He bundled up and headed to Lexi's with Banjo on his heels. For the fifteenth time this week, his conver-sation with Lexi on the way home from church came to mind. The fact she'd had serious boyfriends hadn't sur-prised him, but his reaction at hearing about them had.

He'd been jealous.

Worse, he'd gotten mad at this Doug character, and he hadn't even met him. Boy, he would have liked to have seen the look on the guy's face when Lexi beaned him with a dinner roll. He chuckled.

When she'd asked him if someone had broken his heart, he'd answered truthfully. But the more he thought about it, the more he realized it wasn't actually true. His heart had been broken, but not by a woman. By Devon Fields, the man who stole his land and money. From the time he was thirteen, Clint had only ever allowed himself to want one thing, and when it was taken from him, he'd fenced in his heart, the way he fenced in pastures. It was better for him not to want too much. For his own protection.

But Lexi… How did she do it? Give her heart out freely? Wear optimism and faith in mankind on her sleeve even when she had reasons not to? Her dad's betrayal could have shut her down, made her paranoid and petty. The ex-boyfriends could have made her doubt love.

Somehow, he knew she still was open to love.

And she should be. She should have a wedding with pink silk and gobs of flowers and fancy tables and whatever else she put together for all those other couples.

He reached the path to her house. "Banjo, go to the barn." He pointed to the barn, and Banjo loped away.

Two minutes later Clint approached Lexi's office. The room was more girlie than it had ever been, and that was saying something. Weird netting stuff was draped over the bookcases. A table had been set up with a white tablecloth, fine china, silverware, fancy glasses, note cards and a vase full of light pink flowers. Lexi's back was to him, and she was tucking a black ribbon in place. She stood back, surveyed the bow, and nudged it a fraction. Her hair was pulled back in a low ponytail, and she wore a dark purple sweater over tight black pants.

"What do you think?" She tapped her chin.

You're the most beautiful woman I've ever seen. He cleared his throat. "It's nice."

"Nice?" She frowned. "You don't like it?"

"I like it."

"No, you don't. It's the white tablecloth, isn't it? Ivory would be more elegant."

"Aren't white and ivory the same thing?"

"Oh, you!" She laughed, waving as if he'd made a joke. "That's good. Ivory and white. The same." Still chuckling, she sat at her desk.

He wasn't sure why she was laughing, but he dropped into the chair opposite her and slid the folder with the sale papers her way. "Here's all the documentation from the sale."

She skimmed the top sheet, licked her finger and flipped to the next one, perusing each until closing the folder and setting it down.

"I know I've expected a lot from you and you haven't been here long, but I'm really grateful for all you do. Thank you for handling the sale."

"I wish I could have gotten more money for you."

Her smile revealed white teeth. "Don't worry about it. You did your best."

His best wasn't good enough.

"Your father might have gotten more."

"I doubt it. The market is what it is. He had many years when he fretted about the sale."

Was she trying to make him feel better, or was she telling the truth? Looking in her eyes, he saw honesty. They were open, trusting. The kind of expression he wanted to live up to but doubted he could. It wasn't only his performance as ranch manager he wanted to impress her with. He wouldn't mind if she saw more in him as a man.

Averting his eyes, he felt heat climb his neck. Where had that thought come from?

He could no longer deny it.

He'd gone way beyond thinking of her as his boss.

"How did the call go yesterday?" He shifted in his seat, hoping she hadn't somehow picked up on his train of thought. He could *not* afford to let her know he was getting feelings for her or that just the thought of seeing her made his heart beat faster. Schoolboy stuff. A couple days out in frozen pastures would get him back to normal.

"It went really well. Madeline knows what she wants and asked me to send her pictures with my vision. That's why I'm staging the table. I'll have to wait until the other linens I ordered arrive to finish it." She gestured to the table. "This tablecloth won't do at all. I'm going to send three possibilities. Hopefully, she'll like one enough to get started. What else is going on?"

They discussed ranch details for the next half hour.

"I'm heading out to check all the pregnant cows." He stood. His gaze fell to her lips, and he snapped his eyes shut. *God, give me strength to walk out of here and get her off my mind.* "I'll leave you to your decorating."

She strolled next to him down the hallway. "I don't mean to be a pain, but I've been thinking it's not the Christmas season without a fire in the fireplace."

An excuse to see her again. Soon. Adrenaline rushed through his veins. Even though he knew it wasn't smart, he said, "I'll come by Saturday afternoon and check your fireplace. But you have to promise me you won't start a fire before then."

She smiled, biting her lower lip. That did it. He had to get out of here before he did something really stupid, like tell her she looked like a cowboy's dream in that cute little sweater of hers.

"See you Saturday," he said gruffly. Then he gave her a nod and hurried out the door.

Only when he was striding to the stables did he begin to breathe normally again. What was wrong with him? Thinking of Lexi as a woman? He knew better. If he didn't rein these feelings in, he would lose his job. This ranch wasn't his, but it was all he had. Without it, he didn't know what he would do.

Chapter Eight

"Come on in!" Lexi opened the door wide and ushered Clint inside late Saturday afternoon. The sky was already growing dark and it was only four o'clock. A gentle snow had been falling for the past hour. All morning she'd cleaned the house, ridiculously excited not to be alone on another Saturday night. And while spending it with Clint wasn't the wisest choice, she'd prayed about it and was reasonably confident she could keep her feelings under control if she reminded herself they could only be friends.

Clint set his tool belt on the floor and shrugged out of his coat and boots. His gray T-shirt left nothing to the imagination where his muscles were concerned, and his dark jeans fit him just right. *He works for you. And he's not looking for a relationship.* She forced herself to return to the living room.

Her Christmas tree sparkled with white lights, purple and silver ornaments, and violet garland winding around the tree. Daddy would have liked this one. He would have teased her and called it the lilac tree. Lately she'd been able to think about him without wanting to cry.

Clint entered and knelt by the fireplace.

She put her hand on her hip. "I hope you like pizza."

He opened the glass doors and poked his head under the fireplace opening.

"Do I take your silence to mean you don't like pizza?" She moved closer to the hearth.

He sat up, his sheepish smile making her chest flutter. Clint smiling brought his attractiveness to a whole new level. "I like pizza."

"Good. Because I bought one from the Pizza Factory earlier. I figure we can heat it up later."

"That would be fine. I hope I didn't bother you this morning. I went up on the roof to inspect the chimney. The chimney cap is in good shape. I'm guessing your father had it replaced recently."

"I wouldn't know." For several years, she really hadn't known what Daddy was doing on a daily basis. When they would talk on the phone, they'd catch up on ranch news, the weddings she was planning and things like that. Mundane items hadn't been discussed. And for once, she kind of wished they'd talked about it all. What else had she missed while she was building her empire in Denver?

"I'll give this a look." He beamed the flashlight around and slid a lever back and forth. Then he moved the light across the entire interior of the fireplace. "The damper is working fine. I don't see any signs of moisture or cracking in here, either. I think you're okay. Let me grab some wood and newspaper, and I'll get a fire started to make sure it's safe."

He left the room. The inspection had taken all of ten minutes. Knowing Clint, he'd find an excuse to leave as soon as the fire got going and they'd eaten. And she'd be alone. As usual.

She'd assumed he'd want to hang out with her. Maybe she'd been wrong. Couldn't hurt to ask. He'd fight her—he usually did—but she wanted him to stay.

Holding an armful of logs, he came back into the room. "I'll be right back with newspaper. Do you have matches?"

"I do." She went to the kitchen and searched the junk drawer until she found a box. Taking her time, she returned to the living room and held the box out to Clint. "Are you busy tonight?"

"No, why?"

"I was going to watch a Christmas movie after dinner. You're welcome to stay."

He took the box, his fingers brushing hers, and his eyes darkened, gleaming. "Okay."

Okay? Just like that? "I mean, you don't have to, but I… Well, it's been kind of lonely here, and I wouldn't mind the company."

"Yeah. I'll stay." His matter-of-fact tone surprised her. He wasn't one to answer quickly. And he usually had to be convinced. What was going on with him?

"Are you sure?" She crossed her arms over her chest.

"I wouldn't mind watching a movie." He began to stack the wood inside the fireplace. Then he tucked wadded newspaper rolls underneath the logs. "Come here a minute."

Her pulse took off. Why did he want her over there? She bent next to him, inhaling the clean scent of soap and aftershave on his skin.

Maybe she shouldn't have asked him to stay. His nearness gave her a jittery sensation.

"See this hook?" He pointed to the lever inside the fireplace.

"Yes."

"It's the damper. Move it like this to open it before you start a fire. If it's not open, smoke will fill the house." He took her hand and moved the damper with it. His fingers were warm, strong. She could feel his breath on her cheek.

She didn't blink. Didn't move. If she did she feared she'd turn her head and...

"Why don't I heat up the pizza?" She stood abruptly and backed up two steps.

"And I'll get the fire started." His voice sounded coarse.

They didn't need a fire. Ten seconds near Clint and she was warmer than she'd thought possible. As she made her way to the kitchen, she mentally kicked herself. She was too attracted to him.

No, she was lonely. That was it. This empty Wyoming land combined with the big house and no daily interaction with her Denver employees had warped her. Made her desperate for company.

She turned on the oven. Who was she kidding? The days she'd spent in Denver last week had been just as lonely, just as desperate.

Ever since Daddy died, an unwelcome solitude had descended that she couldn't shake.

After popping the pizza into the oven, she set the timer and joined Clint in the living room. A small fire had come to life, and he was inspecting one of the spots where a stone was missing.

"I see rocks like these near the river all the time.

If you'd like, I'll try to find some to fit these empty spaces."

"That would be great. The fireplace was built with stones found on the property." She sat on the couch, tucking her legs under her bottom. "Clint?"

"Hmm?" He stuck a screwdriver into the mortar.

"You've been an orphan a long time."

"Yeah."

"Do you ever feel lonely? Like you don't belong anywhere in the world?"

He faced her, his expression serious. "Lonely? Sure, sometimes. Like I don't belong? Always."

That's what she'd been afraid of. She pressed her palms to her cheeks and whispered, "I'm scared."

He put the screwdriver down and joined her on the couch. Sitting next to her, he reached to take her hand.

"You don't have to be scared, Lexi. It was different for me. I never had a place like this. A home. You belong here. You'll always belong here."

"But I feel displaced without my father." She fought the emotion tightening her throat. "I took him for granted. I didn't come home enough. I didn't—"

Clint wrapped his arm around her shoulders, and she leaned her cheek against his chest. She could feel his heartbeat through his shirt.

"Don't," he said softly. "Don't do this to yourself."

"I can't help it." Her voice sounded small. "I was so busy, so happy, so selfish. All the time working on my business, planning the weddings—I didn't see… And now I can't."

"That's not true. You're not selfish." His hand caressed her upper arm in soothing circles. "You told me yourself when you came home you always rode the property with your dad."

"But I should have done it more often. What if I'm being punished?"

He brought his arm back, turning his head to stare at her, his blue eyes shining with compassion. "For what?"

"For wanting too much."

"We all want too much." He leaned forward, his elbows resting on knees. "You aren't being punished. You deserve good things."

The timer went off, startling her. She had to get herself together. What was her problem, anyway? One minute she was asking him to stay for a movie, and the next she revealed her deepest fears?

And what in the world happened to her decision to keep their relationship professional? Hadn't she warned herself to be careful? Lonely or not, she had a lot to lose if Clint quit.

She'd lose her manager, but worse, she'd lose his friendship.

Are you really trying to tell yourself he's just a friend?

The smell of oregano and mozzarella reminded her the pizza was probably burning. She hurried to the kitchen. After taking the pizza out, she brought two plates with slices to the living room. "Okay, I promise I won't be weird anymore. What movie should we watch? *Elf* or *It's a Wonderful Life*?"

"*Elf.*"

She kept her promise. Didn't act weird or sappy or reveal any more secrets the rest of the evening. Instead, she found herself watching Clint's reaction to the movie, memorizing the way his lips curved when he laughed.

Telling herself she'd go back to all business tomorrow, but tonight she'd enjoy sitting by him in front of a cozy fire with her pretty Christmas tree twinkling nearby.

Tomorrow, she'd be his boss. Tonight, she'd enjoy his company.

The following morning, Clint shifted in his seat next to Lexi at church. The pastor was midway through the sermon, but no matter how hard Clint tried, he couldn't process a word the preacher said. Last night had surprised him. He'd taken one look at Lexi's fuzzy red sweater and her big eyes, and he'd agreed to pizza and a movie without putting up a fight.

Because he didn't want to fight it.

But he had to.

Had to.

He felt like an insect being spun in a spider's web, except Lexi wasn't the spider. His past was. And when she'd opened up about being lonely and feeling like she was being punished, he'd wanted to yell, *Yes, I get it, I understand. I've been punished my whole life for wanting too much.* But how could he? She actually deserved the things she thought she was being punished for, and he didn't. He'd been greedy, in a hurry and sloppy with his trust. Lexi would never be any of those things.

Clint sneaked a peek her way. She looked pale today, and her cheeks were drawn. He hoped she hadn't stayed up thinking about their conversation after he left. Frankly, he hoped she'd put those thoughts out of her head forever. He didn't want her beating herself up.

As soon as the service ended, he was riding out to inspect the cows. Jerry was still recovering from pneumonia, and his wife, who Jerry referred to as the missus, wouldn't let him come back to work until his cough was gone for good. Although Ryder and Jake were checking the herd this morning, Clint wanted to be sure none of the pregnant cows were acting off. The ranch was important to Lexi, and he wouldn't let anything jeopardize her home, including him. It was time to distance himself from his beautiful boss.

The congregation sang "Amazing Grace," and Clint found himself enthusiastically singing along. The lyrics went straight to his heart.

Thank You, Lord, for saving a wretch like me. Please let Lexi see she has nothing to feel guilty about. Fill her with the sense of belonging she's missing right now. And give me the good sense and fortitude to leave her alone.

The service ended, and they greeted other members on their way out. After helping Lexi into her coat, he took her arm to steady her over the icy sidewalk on the way back to his truck.

She didn't say a word the entire time. Unusual for her.

"Something wrong?" He opened the passenger door and boosted her up.

She shook her head.

He started the truck, knowing he should drive home and check the cows, but his conscience poked at him.

"Want to get some breakfast?" As soon as the words were out of his mouth, he held his breath, wanting her to say no. Hoping she'd say yes.

"I could eat."

"Dottie's Diner?"

"Sure."

Now why had he gone and done that? He'd told himself he needed to stay away from her. Hard to do if he kept finding excuses to prolong being near. He drove the short distance to the restaurant, and they stood inside the breezeway for several minutes as they waited for a table.

Finally, a booth opened, and Dottie stopped by with coffee as soon as they'd settled in.

"Lexi, so good to see you, sugar. How are you doing? You getting enough to eat?"

"I'm good, Dottie. Thank you for the casseroles you dropped off after the funeral. They were delicious."

"My pleasure, hon. We all loved RJ. He was a good man. And he was right proud of you, sugar. If you need anything, say the word." She turned to Clint, her face all sunshine. "I sure love having you back in Sweet Dreams, tiger."

"I like being back." It was true. He'd moved two hours away after high school and hadn't lived here in over a decade, but it was the closest thing to home he had. He didn't even mind that Dottie called him tiger.

Maybe he did belong somewhere. Sweet Dreams had been good to him.

"What can I get you two?" She untucked a pen from behind her ear and flipped a sheet on her small notepad. After Lexi ordered the Sunrise Special, he asked for the same, ignoring Dottie's wink before she left. The diner was crowded and loud and put him in a good mood.

"I didn't know you went by tiger." Lexi's eyes twinkled.

He knew his cheeks were flaming. "You're not one to talk, sugar."

She laughed. "I guess not. I know Dottie treats everyone like family, but she clearly has a soft spot for you. When you were at Yearling, did you live with them?"

"No, we lived in a bunkhouse on the ranch with a youth care worker, and the Laverts had a small house next to us."

She twirled a straw in her glass of water. "Why were you sent there?"

He took a drink of coffee before answering. "Yearling was different than many group foster homes. They only accepted teen boys who had no chance of being placed with their parents. In my case, my parents were dead, but the other guys had parents who were abusive, addicted or imprisoned, and it limited their foster options. As long as we followed the rules—and there were many—we lived there until we aged out."

"Aged out? What does that mean?"

"When I turned eighteen, I legally had to leave the foster home because I was an adult."

"That's awful." Wrinkles appeared in her forehead. "I couldn't have lived on my own at eighteen. I was still in high school."

"So was I."

The way she stilled and stared at him made him squirm. Guffaws came from the booth behind him, and the smell of bacon filled the air. He hoped Dottie would bring their breakfasts soon so he could avoid talking about his childhood anymore.

"What in the world did you do?" She leaned in, lowering her voice. "Where did you go?"

Looked like the childhood conversation wasn't over yet.

"Big Bob helped me get hired at LFR Ranch. The Laverts always looked out for us as best they could."

"But isn't LFR Ranch a couple of hours away?" She wrapped her hands around her mug.

"I was still able to graduate. My guidance counselor helped me the two months I was gone. I was blessed. A lot of kids have nowhere to go. They're literally homeless."

"Oh, my, I had no idea."

"Eat up, kids." Dottie placed two steaming platters of eggs, bacon, hash browns and toast in front of them. "I'll be back in a flash with more coffee."

He dug into his eggs. As much as he'd missed living with Miss Joanne, he'd been fortunate to end up at Yearling. Throughout high school he'd been in a stable environment instead of on edge about possibly being moved to another home. The one thing he'd really feared was getting kicked out, so he'd followed the rules and never bent them. Plus, he'd learned the cowboy life and gotten his first taste of ranching.

"Big Bob taught me to ride." He shook salt and pepper on his hash browns. "We all had ranch chores. I loved it. God was looking out for me there."

Lexi bit into her toast, a thoughtful expression on her face. "I guess it's all how we look at things, isn't it?"

"What do you mean?"

"You see your placement there as God looking out for you, and all I can do is feel sad that you didn't grow up under the care of your parents."

"I try not to think about it. Doesn't change things." He used to think about it. A lot. He'd wanted Miss Joanne to be his mom. He'd resented the homes he'd been shuffled to. In the deepest part of him, he'd wondered what was wrong with him. Why was he worthless? Why did no one ever even come close to wanting to adopt him? Why didn't he have parents? As the years progressed, he'd come to terms with the fact he wasn't meant to be part of a loving family.

"Well, at least when you have babies, you'll be able to give them all the things you missed." She sipped her coffee before taking another bite of bacon.

Babies? He'd never thought about having babies. Sure, he liked kids, but families were for other people. Weren't they?

His chest tightened, and he was finding it hard to breathe. *Great.* The thought of kids was giving him a heart attack.

"I have to admit," she said. "I thought I'd be married and starting a family by now."

He could easily see her holding a baby or two. "You'll be a great mother."

Her face fell. "Well, it's kind of a moot point. I'm not starting the family until I get married." She raised her left hand and pointed to the ring finger. "And it hasn't happened yet. I'm not sure it ever will."

"Any single guy in this town would drop to a knee and propose in a minute." As the words left his mouth, the tightness in his chest amplified. Why would he tell her that? It was true, but he didn't want a bunch of guys sniffing around the ranch to date her.

She shook her head, a big smile on her face. "Oh, Clint, you crack me up. No one in Sweet Dreams is beating down the door to date me."

Yet. Frowning, he attacked the food on his plate. He didn't see what was so funny. He'd spoken the truth. If any of these guys thought they had even the slimmest of chances with her, they'd be wooing her.

Wooing? Now he sounded like Jerry with his old-timer sayings. And anyhow, it wasn't any of Clint's business if someone wanted to date Lexi or if she got married. He was only there to do a job.

And what would happen when she did get married? Any guy in his right mind would want to run Rock Step Ranch. Clint wouldn't be needed there anymore. Or if she married someone without ranch experience, Clint would have to take orders from him.

He lost his appetite.

"Can we walk around town a little after breakfast? I'd like to see the storefront decorations. I usually stroll around downtown Denver to get in the Christmas spirit, but this year..." She shrugged.

The cows needed to be checked, but they would have to wait. If he didn't walk her around town, someone else might, and he wasn't ready to think about getting another job or worry about her getting married. The bottom line? He couldn't afford a heart attack this close to Christmas. Guess he was strolling around Sweet Dreams.

What had possessed her to talk about babies with Clint? Lexi huddled under her scarf as she strolled next to him along Main Street. One minute they'd been talking about his childhood—which was about as depressing as it could get—and the next she'd tried to make the situation better by telling him he'd be a good dad. But the whole thing had backfired. As soon as she'd mentioned babies, she'd pictured him holding one.

And Clint was gorgeous enough without adding an adorable baby to the mix.

"Well, the wind isn't so crazy now." She stopped in front of the window of the secondhand shop. Plush stuffed penguins were sitting on nests made of white lights, and children's books with penguins were propped up next to them. The longing in her heart surprised her. She hadn't thought about having babies in a long time. Her company *was* her baby. But it felt more like a rebellious teenager lately, and she couldn't snuggle it in her arms or sing lullabies to it.

"Isn't that a cute display?" Would she ever buy little books and stuffed animals for her own children for Christmas? Life hadn't turned out the way she'd dreamed it would. What if she never got married? Never had babies to cradle in her arms?

"Uh-huh." Clint barely glanced at the window. Not a shock where he was concerned.

She'd been around him too much, and she was forgetting the things that were important to her. Maybe she was destined to be single the rest of her life. She wanted more than mutual affection, more than discussing ranch operations, more than a pleasant afternoon together.

She wanted love.

Love was intense, unpredictable. It was knowing each other's secrets. She'd seen it firsthand with friends in Denver. Her own parents had been affectionate, with eyes only for each other. She wanted the same.

"Do you want to turn around?" Her mood had slipped to melancholy. What was the point in window shopping with someone if they weren't into it?

"Whatever you want."

She almost rolled her eyes. She wanted… It didn't matter. What had Clint said at breakfast when she'd been sad he didn't have parents? *Doesn't change things.* He was right. She could want love and marriage and babies, but it didn't change things.

She needed clarity. Because living between her two

worlds was getting too hard. Either she moved back to Denver and fixed her company, or she lived here permanently. She didn't see how she could continue to live here and effectively run Weddings by Alexandra. But what about her feelings for Clint?

"Let's keep going," she said brusquely. "There's not much left to see."

They passed a barber shop and a real estate agent's office with a wreath on the door and red lights shaped like cowboy boots in the window. At the end of the block, she prepared to go back, but the corner building across the street caught her eye.

"Why is the old chamber of commerce building all boarded up?" She started forward, but Clint caught her arm. Just then a vehicle turned directly in front of them.

"Whoa, there." He kept hold of her arm. "Didn't you see that truck?"

"No, I— Come on!" She checked for traffic this time and ran across the street, gazing up at the two-story brick building. It had been there forever, but she'd never paid it much attention. It had housed several businesses over the years, but the only one she could remember was the chamber of commerce, and she'd never been inside. "I wonder why it's empty. I can't believe I never really noticed it before. Whatever it was originally used for must have been important for them to put all this architectural detail into it."

Clint walked to the front, where plywood covered the large picture windows and a faded For Sale sign hung lopsided from the door. "Looks like it was a department store."

"How can you tell?"

He pointed to the bricks above the window. Engraved stones of a lighter shade spelled out Department Store.

She tossed her head back and laughed. A grin spread across his face.

The recessed entry held an old-fashioned door with peeling black paint. It had a narrow window near the top, and, standing on her tiptoes, she rubbed the dirt off with a tissue and tried to peek inside. It was hard to tell from her view, but it appeared to be a large empty space.

Perfect for a wedding reception.

"I wonder how long it's been boarded up."

He shoved his hands into his coat pockets. "Why are you excited about this place? Looks like it hasn't been used in years."

A ticker tape of things to research spun through her mind, and she craned her neck to try to see more of the interior.

"You're taller than me." She pulled him next to her and practically shoved him to the narrow window. "Can you look in there and tell me what you see?"

He peered into it. "A counter. Looks like some left-over scaffolding. I think there's a staircase."

"Is it wooden?"

He shaded his eyes to see better. "I can't tell."

"Boost me up."

"What?" With a deer-caught-in-headlights expression, he pressed his back to the alcove wall. She popped her fist on her hip and gave him her most withering glare.

"I need to know if it has hardwood floors and how the space flows."

"I'll check again."

"I won't be able to see it through your eyes."

He exhaled. Loudly. "Fine."

"Crouch down a little. I'll step onto your thigh." She couldn't wait to see what the room looked like. Clint obeyed, and as she put her foot above his knee he hoisted her up, his hands around her waist. Even through her wool coat, she was aware of his touch.

She gasped. "It's better than I imagined! I can't really see the floors, but I can tell they're hardwood. And there *is* a staircase—I think it's original. Oh! This is the right size."

She slid down with his arms still at her waist, and spun to face him.

"The right size for what?" His voice was husky.

"A wedding reception."

The words hovered above them like the Christmas lights strung across the town, and as she met Clint's eyes, she forgot the ticker tape of things to research. Forgot the hardwood floors and breathtaking staircase. Forgot everything.

He leaned in, his blue eyes as bright as she'd ever seen them. Was he going to kiss her?

At the last second, he brushed her cheek with his lips. At his simple touch, she melted into his arms. All the burdens and guilt and worries she'd been carrying for the past two months no longer mattered. For the first time since burying her father, she belonged somewhere. In his embrace.

She didn't have to be the boss of anything—not her company, not the ranch—not with his arms locked around her and her cheek pressed against his shoulder.

Please don't let this moment end.

Clint stepped back and rubbed his neck, not looking at her.

"Don't say anything." She blinked, shaking her head. "Don't say a word. Just…thank you."

"Lexi—"

"Don't." She couldn't bear it if he announced this moment was a mistake or any other lame thing men came up with when they were afraid of getting in too deep. This had been too real, too precious to let anything ruin it.

"I'm going to find out about this building. It's the perfect place for wedding receptions. Think of all the themes I could do with it. And parties! I don't think there are any upscale reception halls in the area. Sweet Dreams has a VFW hall outside town, but frankly, it was always on the dumpy side. Don't brides in Wyoming deserve a special place to celebrate close to home? I think they do." She hooked her arm in his and told him all the ideas running through her head on the way back to the truck. He didn't say a word, and she tried not to read anything into his silence.

All she knew was she'd found two vital things in under thirty minutes: a sense she belonged and something that brought her joy.

She couldn't wait to get home and start researching.

Chapter Nine

What kind of a cotton-pickin' fool was he?

He'd almost kissed her. Sure, he'd brushed her cheek in the nick of time, but it had been a close call. Too close.

The cold air bit at his exposed cheeks as he rode around the pasture that afternoon checking pregnant cows. His insulated coveralls kept his body warm, but his heart had been chilled ever since Lexi thanked him.

She'd *thanked* him.

For what? For being inappropriate? Because he had been. At breakfast she'd been talking about babies, and then she'd been so over the moon about the abandoned building. When she'd uttered the words *wedding reception*, he'd taken one look at her face—sparkling and beautiful and good—and he'd lost his mind. And when she'd burrowed into his embrace with her cheek against his shoulder? He'd actually allowed himself a peek at the dreams he'd buried long ago.

He couldn't seem to put the dreams back. He hadn't simply held her. He'd kissed her cheek. Thought about kissing her lips. He'd taken their relationship beyond employer/employee, way past friendship…to risky.

He couldn't go any farther. Not where she was concerned.

His horse trotted through the frozen pasture around the grazing herd as snow fell. The air pinched Clint's lungs, made him feel alive. This—riding a horse on a winter day, checking pregnant cows, making sure their drinking water hadn't iced over—this was what he'd been made to do. The good Lord had blessed him with a love of ranching. And he was working on one of the finest ranches in Wyoming, so how could he jeopardize it by wanting more?

He was Lexi's employee, and his status wasn't going to change unless she fired him. He'd spent his entire life as no one's choice. There was something flawed inside him. It was why his dad had abandoned him, why his grandfather couldn't stand him, why none of the foster families considered making him a permanent part of their lives. Other kids had gotten adopted. Not him.

He belonged to nobody, and no one belonged to him. And that's the way it would stay.

Wishful thinking would only bring disappointment, the way it always had.

Lexi was nice to him because she was nice to everyone. She was lonely, needed a friend, and he was nearby.

And when she finds out the reason you lost your land?

She wouldn't want him around at all. She'd made it clear she hated being lied to. And he hadn't told her the whole truth.

Lexi made people's dreams come true. It was who she was, what she did. And she deserved someone who would make her dreams come true.

Every dream he'd had, he'd found a way to mess up.

She might not know him as a worthless brat or that Romine kid, but he did. He'd never been enough. Never would be enough for someone like her. When she got her life figured out, she'd find someone who belonged in her world. Someone with a family who would treat her like their daughter. And she'd be happy.

With a clicking sound, he urged his horse to keep moving. A snow-covered lump caught his eye. He made his way around the cattle grazing contentedly on the prairie grass and headed toward the lump, which he could now make out beyond the ridge.

A knot formed in his gut as he realized what it was. He dismounted and lowered to one knee to make sure. A cold, unmoving heifer. He checked the tag and stood so abruptly the blood rushed from his head.

No! He bent over, bracing his hands against his thighs as the heifer's death hit him. This animal had seemed fine. How had he missed the signs? Had she been off by herself? Where had he gone wrong?

Carefully, he brushed the snow off her, looking for signs of attack or trauma, but he didn't see any. He and Logan had selected this heifer to keep based on her overall health and her mama's calving record. They'd fully expected her to be a top producer in the future.

And now she was dead.

He hadn't wanted to cry in a long time, but emotion strangled his throat. He coughed to dislodge it, but the knot forming only grew bigger.

While he'd been off with Lexi, this precious animal had died.

He got back on his horse and rode hard back to the barns. After he put the horse away, he strode to Logan's cabin, dreading the conversation he was about to have.

"Hey, Clint, what are you doing here?" Logan stood back to let him inside.

"I need you to come out to the east pasture with me."

"Why? What's wrong?" Logan shoved his feet into the boots next to the door and grabbed his heavy coat off the hook. He called over his shoulder, "I'll be back later, Sarah."

As they strode toward the stable, Clint said, "It's the thirty-six yellow-tag heifer."

Logan paused and let out a sigh. "I knew I should have checked on her this morning. I noticed she looked poorly yesterday and gave her antibiotics. How is she?"

"Dead."

Logan looked stricken. "This is all my fault."

"It's not your fault. I planned on riding out after church, but I didn't come home right away."

"It's your day off. I told Jake and Ryder to keep an eye out as they rode, but I forgot about the heifer. I should have had them check the water tanks instead of me. Man, this stinks." He slapped his thigh. "I'll tell Lexi. The heifer was my responsibility, and I let her down."

"You gave her antibiotics yesterday, so there wasn't anything more you could do. I'll tell Lexi, but for now, let's get the animal back here and try to figure out what killed her. I can't have any more cattle dying, and I want to make sure this isn't something that might spread."

If Clint had any wishful hopes about a future with Lexi, this put an end to them. He'd placed his personal life ahead of the ranch, and a heifer was dead because of it.

If he didn't get his head out of the temptation Lexi

presented, he'd mess up her life as much as he'd messed up his own. He would not let that happen.

"Thanks for coming with me, Amy." Lexi rubbed her hands together as they waited for Shawn Lesly, an old family friend and local real estate agent, to open the door to the empty building. Although it was late Tuesday afternoon, she'd stopped into Amy's Quilt Shop on the off chance Amy would join her. Thankfully, Amy had agreed.

"I'm glad you asked. I can't wait to see inside!"

Lexi had spent Sunday night and all day yesterday jotting ideas and researching the surrounding area for the feasibility of opening a hall for receptions and events. She'd set up the appointment with Shawn and had wanted to ask Clint to join her today, but he'd been so down when he stopped by Sunday evening to let her know the heifer died, she hadn't had the heart to drag him from the ranch. Jerry had finally been well enough to come to work yesterday, and he'd told her Clint had been out from dawn to dusk checking fences and the herd. She had a feeling he'd be doing the same today.

Shawn, a balding man with a gray mustache, let them inside. Lexi's eyes had to adjust to the dark room.

"I talked to the listing agent, Lexi. The electricity has been off for a couple of years." He opened a folder. "Water's been shut off as well to make sure the pipes don't freeze."

Amy crossed her arms and shivered. "What's the scoop behind this building, Shawn? Didn't I hear a rumor the dollar store considered buying it a while back?"

"Yes, and that was four years ago. The dollar store

found it more cost-effective to rent space in the strip mall. The heating system might need to be replaced, but the plumbing and electrical have been updated."

"Why do you think it's been empty? It's a large space and full of character." Lexi touched the beautiful wood trim. She'd preserve it, the crown molding and the staircase. She envisioned the room all polished and glowing. Brides sweeping down the staircase to meet their new grooms. People lined up on either side to cheer and welcome them.

"The owner held onto it for two years. There was interest, but he wanted top dollar for it. I was his agent at the time. Then he died and a distant relative inherited it. The woman has turned down several offers since."

"Why?" Lexi bent to check out the floor. Scratched and in need of refinishing, but it appeared to be oak. "Did she give a reason?"

"Rumor has it she's a bit particular about the type of business that goes in here. Seems she had dreams of opening a tea shop."

"Hmm... I wonder what stopped her," Amy said.

"Probably the fact she's in her late eighties." Shawn took a sheet of paper out of the folder and handed it to Lexi. "Here you go. The list price, comps and square footage."

"Thank you." She scanned the sheet, raising her eyebrows at the price. "Do you think the building is worth this much?"

"No." He tapped his chin. "But the owner might work with you on the price. Why don't you look around? I'll be down here if you have any questions."

"Let's go upstairs." Amy linked arms with Lexi, and

they strode to the grand staircase off to the side. "What do you think is up there?"

"Dead mice. And hopefully more gorgeous floors and space for a smaller party. It would be nice to have a dedicated area for bridal showers, Christmas parties, anniversary parties and similar events."

They climbed the stairs, and Lexi couldn't help but pause midway to take in the main floor. With some TLC, this building could be stunning. A real gem in Sweet Dreams.

"Would you really move back, Lexi? For good?" They reached the top.

The question sent swirls of uncertainty through her stomach. Clint's eyes before he kissed her cheek came to mind. If moving back for good included exploring what could happen beyond friendship with Clint, then yes, she could easily imagine moving back. But if not? She bit the corner of her bottom lip. She wasn't sure.

"I'm not making decisions right now." She turned to view the second floor, which appeared to be split into offices with a side room perfect for entertaining a large group of people. "Just looking and seeing what my options are, but so far, this building feels as if it was built just for me. It's perfect!"

Amy glanced out of the window overlooking the side street. "What will you do with your wedding business in Denver?"

"That's the problem. I don't know. My wedding planners work on commission, and they could easily branch out on their own. But right now I take care of the business issues like insurance and meeting rooms for clients and such. Plus, they have expense accounts for up-front costs. I'd hate to put any of them in financial jeopardy by closing the business." Lexi pulled a tape measure out of her purse and measured the length of the larger room. "I thought about it a lot yesterday, and if I'm serious about moving back, then I would offer to sell the business to my vice president, Natalie."

"Would she be in a position to buy it?"

Lexi straightened, the tape measure recoiling with a snap. "I don't know. But I have to make a decision one way or the other. I can't divide my time between Wyoming and Denver forever. Both the ranch and the business demand my attention."

Amy opened a cabinet built into the wall. "I'm surprised you're considering giving it all up to move back."

"The longer I'm here, the more I feel I'm ready for a new adventure. I'm taking your advice, though, and praying about it."

"I'm glad. Keep praying, and I will, too. Does this mean you're getting some closure about your dad?"

The permanent lump in her throat had dissolved at some point over the past few weeks. "I think so. Honestly, having Clint around has helped."

Amy's smile fell. "I didn't realize you were getting close to him."

"I hadn't realized it, either."

"I didn't know him well in school... I wonder..." Amy's eyebrows drew together, then she shook her head. "Never mind."

"Don't you like him?"

"I was close to one of his friends years ago, and he turned out to be unreliable."

"I'm sorry. I didn't realize. Clint is very reliable, though, so don't worry about that." Lexi strode toward the offices. "I'd like to get him something nice for Christmas. Any ideas?"

"Well, what does he like?" Amy followed her, leaning against the doorjamb of the room Lexi was inspecting.

What *did* Clint like? "Ranching and riding and cattle."

"What about something along those lines? A gift card to the Western store would let him pick out exactly what he wants."

"I could do that." She peeked into the closet and noted the electrical sockets on the walls looked modern. "But it's impersonal. After all the work he's done to take over managing the ranch, I'd like it to be a little more special."

"Hmm…wish I could help you out, but I don't know him very well."

Lexi frowned. Clint was used to spending holidays alone. He had no family. Grew up in foster homes. He'd mentioned close friends. Besides them, did anyone really know Clint? Sympathy squeezed her heart at the loneliness of his upbringing. The adult Clint seemed secure in himself but just as alone.

She thought about his cabin with the cowboy Christmas tree. And Banjo. He'd mentioned how he enjoyed training herding dogs. He lit up whenever Banjo was around. And he'd never had a dog of his own.

What if she bought him a border collie puppy? His own herding dog to train and love? But how could she find one this close to Christmas?

"Do you know anyone who breeds border collies? Or good herding dogs?"

"Of course I do. This is Sweet Dreams." Amy smiled, waving her hand. "Dan and Lola Smith are known for their purebreds. They usually have a litter in time for Christmas, but they might all be sold."

"Thanks, Amy! I'll give them a call."

"If they don't have any, my mom will know who does," Amy said. "And I'm adding you to my prayer list. For guidance with your career."

It had been a long time since Lexi had had someone praying for her. She crossed the room and hugged Amy. "Thank you. I'm so glad we reconnected."

"I am, too."

They went back downstairs, inspecting all the nooks and crannies on the first floor, before joining Shawn once more. Lexi peppered him with questions about the building's history and if the historical society would be an issue if she wanted to add a kitchen. Finally, they locked the building up, and Lexi and Amy headed to The Beanery to discuss it.

A future back home in Sweet Dreams was looking more promising by the minute.

A knock on his door Tuesday night startled Clint. He'd been mulling over the email he'd opened earlier. The ranch in Montana had finally gotten back to him that yes, they had additional feed and could sell it to him. The price they quoted would have allowed Rock Step Ranch to hold off on selling the calves.

Too late now.

He moved Banjo's head off his lap and yelled, "Who is it?" as he got up.

"Lexi."

Fear and longing slammed into his chest. She rarely came to his cabin. Had she gotten the same email and was here to confront him about it? Or had she thought about his kiss and decided to fire him? He'd only spoken a few words with her since, and those words were merely to let her know the heifer had died.

She stood in the doorway with snow swirling around her, the glow of the porch light surrounding her. He'd never tire of seeing her pretty face.

"Are you busy?"

"No." He stepped backward. "Come in."

She unwound the scarf from her neck and took off her coat. Banjo loped over to her, and she petted him. "Hey, there, buddy. You look pretty content here."

"What's going on?" Clint led her to the living room, turning down the volume on the reality show he'd been watching.

"Amy and I toured the building downtown, and it's even better than I thought. Besides adding a kitchen and updating the bathrooms, I wouldn't have to do any major redesign of the floor space. It does need a lot of TLC and possibly a new heating system, though."

"I don't understand." The building had been a lark, hadn't it? Why would she check it out if her wedding business was in Denver?

"I'm toying with a few options, and buying the building is one of them. When I think of all the women in the area and how they could have special wedding receptions there, it fills me with energy." She took a seat in the chair next to the lit Christmas tree. "I've been having so much fun."

"I'll trust you on that."

She grinned, eyes twinkling. "Oh, come on, one of your girlfriends must have been a romantic. You never did tell me about them."

He'd avoided this topic with her in the past, but maybe

it would be best if she knew the truth. Then they could go back to being boss and employee, and his heart would stop jolting every time he saw her face.

"I've never had a serious girlfriend."

"Yeah, right." She rolled her eyes.

"I had a few dates in high school, but when I moved to LFR Ranch, there weren't many women around."

"Okay, but you went into town and attended church, right? There were women there."

"Yeah, but I was focusing on my future. Saving my paychecks. I wasn't thinking about anything serious with a woman."

She sank into the chair, her glow dimming.

"I'm not like other guys. I don't have parents. There will be no doting grandparents for a woman to hope for. No one to throw her a bridal shower. And I'm not exactly the relationship expert."

"Neither am I. I have none of those things to offer a man, either."

"No bridal shower for a groom to be?" He couldn't help trying to make her smile. She had so much more to offer than he did.

"You know what I mean." She reached over and straightened one of the lassos on the tree. "And I always thought Daddy would be around to give me away, but… Well, it doesn't matter. It has nothing to do with the building downtown. It will be for me to plan other people's weddings."

He met her eyes and didn't miss the longing in them.

"You'll plan your own wedding, too. I can tell you're starting to heal from losing your dad. You'll be back to yourself, and…" He couldn't finish his sentence.

Couldn't lead her on, but the thought of her eventually marrying someone else made him nauseous.

The way she was looking at him was doing strange stuff to his heart. He wanted to kiss her. Well, lately he wanted to kiss her every time he saw her or thought of her or...

"I need some help, and it's kind of late notice, so if you're busy, I'll ask someone else."

"What is it?" *Please don't let it be anything that gets me within three feet of you.*

"I'm wondering if you would come to the building with me tomorrow. You're so handy, I thought you'd be able to tell me if anything major seems wrong."

A rush of pride spread through his chest. She thought he was handy. Wanted his opinion.

"Sure thing."

"Thanks, Clint. Can you get away for lunch tomorrow and a few hours after?"

"I can." Banjo sat in front of Clint, setting a paw on his knee. He picked the dog up and settled him on the couch. Banjo laid his head on his lap, and Clint stroked his soft fur, massaging his fingers along the dog's spine.

"He's getting worse, isn't he?" Lexi crossed to the couch, petting Banjo's back. His tail thumped a few times.

"He is. I'm trying to keep him comfortable. The vet gave him steroids, but I'm afraid we'll have to say goodbye sooner rather than later."

"He's a good dog. Thank you for taking care of him." She put her coat and boots back on. Wound the scarf around her neck.

"It's been an honor."

And it had been an honor getting to know her, spending these hours alone with her, but the time was drawing short. He could feel it. And he had no idea what the new year would bring, but he knew it couldn't be cozy evenings with Lexi.

While it was for the best, it pained him just the same.

Chapter Ten

"Christmas is in a week and a half." Nash's voice came through Clint's cell phone loud and clear. "Pick a time and get up here. Marshall can't get away any time soon, so it'll just be the three of us."

Clint tucked the phone between his shoulder and ear as he unlocked and opened the side door to the old equipment shed Wednesday morning. He and Logan had finished feeding the cattle, and Clint had noticed footprints in the fresh snow leading to the shed. Without a reason to inspect the building, he'd never entered it before. He doubted anyone had a need to be in here. The keys to the outbuildings hung on a ring in his office, which stayed unlocked during the day, so any of the employees could have accessed this shed.

"You still up at Wade's ranch?" Clint felt along the wall for a light switch, came up with cobwebs and finally found one. The fluorescent bulbs fizzed to life, and dust motes hung in the air. He checked the floor for signs of a recent visitor, but the hard dirt was packed too much to see anything out of the ordinary. Peering to his left then his right, he tried to find anything that shouldn't be there, but nothing stood out.

"Yeah." Nash sounded disgusted. "I'm stuck here another month on doctor's orders. That's why you need to pack a bag for a few days."

"Do you mind waiting until after Christmas? I'll talk with Lexi and try to get away midweek. We should have enough hands to take care of everything."

"All right. Text me when you have a plan."

They caught up for a few more minutes before saying goodbye. Clint surveyed the shed. A trailer, an old tractor, tools that had seen better days and a plow all came into view. Tarps covered bulky items in the back. He squeezed between a rusty vintage tractor and a hay wagon. He still didn't see anything out of the ordinary—not that he knew what he was looking for—but he was curious about what lay under the tarps.

"Clint? Is that you?"

Clint almost jumped, and his heart began racing. "Yeah, Jerry. It's me."

"Thought I saw you come in here. You looking for something?" Jerry stood in the doorway before closing the door and picking his way toward him.

"Footprints through the snow led here. Seemed suspicious."

"Ain't no reason for anyone to be in here. Maybe they stopped in the doorway to get a break from the wind."

"Can't say for sure. Have you been keeping an eye out for Jake?" Since Jerry had returned to work after recovering from pneumonia, Clint had filled him in on the odd circumstances with the cabin and with Jake showing up on his day off. He'd asked Jerry to pay attention to Jake more, to make sure the kid wasn't bringing trouble to the ranch.

"Haven't seen him all week."

"Which is the way it should be. He's scheduled for Saturday and Sunday." Clint hitched his thumb in the direction of the tarps. "What's back there?"

Jerry pulled his jeans up by the belt loops. "I reckon one of them's the sled RJ used to take the girls out on. Let's have a look."

They peeled the tarp back from the first item.

"Well, I haven't seen this gal in a while. Old Betsy was a trouper." Jerry saluted the red-and-white Ford truck. "This F-100 was the purdiest truck I'd seen when RJ bought her, and she did everything we asked of her until it got too much for the old girl. Boy, she brings back memories."

Clint chuckled. "My first car was Shirley. I bonded with the old rust bucket."

"Help me with this here tarp." Jerry moved to the next big tarp, and together they folded it back, revealing a wooden sleigh.

Clint ran his hand along the curves. The sleigh had been painted black with glossy red trim and had a bench large enough to seat two or three people. He circled it, imagining hooking it up to Coco and Charger, the pair of Belgians they relied on to pull the hay sled when the snow got too deep. "When's the last time this was out?"

"Not since RJ's wife passed. He used to hook it up every Christmas Eve and take Lexi and her mama on a sleigh ride. We'd polish it and pile it with blankets. I used to get a kick out of watching them take off. When she was real little, Lexi would take her gloved hand out of her fancy muff and wave at me. So much joy in her darlin' face." Jerry spat on the dirt floor. "Hadn't seen that particular smile in a long time."

Clint could picture her, a little girl with long brown hair and sparkly eyes, sitting under a pile of blankets on this sleigh. If he had a little girl, he'd want to do the same for her. Drive her around the ranch and listen to the swish of the snow.

"Then you came along. Girls are like Christmas trimmings. They're easy on the eyes, and the right one is sweet as a candy cane. I reckon I've seen Lexi light up a few times when we've discussed you."

"You sure your eyes aren't going bad?" Clint teased, but his balance shifted at the thought of Lexi thinking of him as special. "She's lonely. Anybody would make her light up."

"Is that what you're telling yourself?" Jerry propped a cowboy boot on the sleigh runner. "She brought a man back a while ago. I think his name was Doug, but I called him Dud. She didn't light up for him, no sirree."

Good. He didn't like thinking of Lexi with another guy, even one she'd told him about.

"Miss Lexi sure loves planning weddings, but now she's back, well, I'd like to see her stay. I didn't think it was a possibility. With you here...well, maybe she'll change her mind. But you'd better hurry up. Denver won't wait forever."

A weight of cold dread landed in his gut. The mention of Denver should bring relief, but it didn't. Not one bit. And then there was this false impression—first Lexi, now Jerry—they both seemed to think he was someone he wasn't. *And why's that, Romine?*

He should have told them both about his past from the get-go.

"I know what you're hinting at—"

"Who said anything about hinting?"

"You can get that out of your head." Clint dragged the tarp back over the sleigh. "I'm the ranch manager. Nothing more."

"I just think it might be time to get this sleigh out again. Take Miss Lexi for a sleigh ride. Would do her a world of good."

"I'm not the guy you think I am. I've made mistakes."

"Well, who hasn't, boy?"

He leveled a stare at Jerry. "Not like this."

"You murder someone?"

"No."

"Thief? Jail time?"

"No."

"You one of those predators?"

"You know me better than that." Clint glared at him and edged around the sleigh to check for signs anything was amiss. "I lost some property."

Not just any property. *His* property. His dream.

"Is that so?" Jerry was following so close Clint could have given him a piggyback ride. "I know a bit about it myself."

Clint stilled, iced to the core. Had Jerry found out about his deal with the investor?

"Yeah, I guess it was going on forty years ago now, I decided it was time to make something of my life. I was going to take over a small sheep operation near the Montana border. The missus is a smart one. She told me she'd crunched the numbers and didn't see how we could make a profit. Back then my head was harder than a rock. I knew I'd succeed, and I told her so. Bless her heart, she went along with me, and we tried our hand at those sheep."

"It didn't work out?" Nothing seemed odd in the shed, so he gestured for Jerry to follow him to the door.

"That's putting it mildly."

Clint locked the shed back up, and they crossed the gravel driveway, the wind whipping at their coats.

Jerry raised his voice. "We lost money almost immediately, and instead of taking it like a man and figuring out a new plan, I let my pride get the best of me. Took out loans to cover the costs."

"I can relate."

Jerry paused and clapped him on the shoulder. "I lost it all, son."

The emotion pressing against Clint's chest came as a surprise. Felt the hot rush of pain that had stabbed him when he'd found the bank man at his door, telling him he had to move, that they owned the property. Remembered the frantic research he'd done for days, the calls, the need to make sense of it all. The prayers to God not to take away his ranch.

He didn't want Jerry to have lost his dream, too.

"I'm sorry."

"Never felt so ashamed in my life." Jerry braced himself against wind as they strode toward the office. "Thought my wife was going to leave me. I deserved it. She'd told me not to do it, and I hadn't listened."

"But you're still together?"

"Yep. God blessed me with that woman." He continued talking without breaking his stride. "I hadn't told her about the loans. When it all came crashing down and the bank was breathing down my neck, I had to come clean. Worst day of my life."

They reached the door to the ranch office, but Clint didn't open it. "What did she do?"

A lopsided smile lifted the corner of his mouth. "I girded myself for a verbal lashing. And you know what? She gave it to me good. Lit into me for a good hour. I deserved every second of it."

"And then what happened?"

"She slammed out of the house. When she got back later, she told me she'd been praying, and she forgave me."

"Just like that?"

"Just like that."

Clint didn't know much about wives, but Jerry's sounded like one of a kind.

Jerry waggled his glove-encased index finger. "A good woman will forgive you your mistakes. You want to hold onto her when you find her. And take it from me—don't let your yearnings get ahead of your earnings."

It had been almost five years since Clint had allowed himself a yearning. He'd accumulated a lot of earnings in the years since he'd lost it all. Only spent money on rent and his basic needs. The pile of money in the bank was as much as he'd invested into his land originally. But he hadn't thought about spending it. Hadn't dared dream about buying a ranch again. So it sat there and grew.

"Wish I would have known you five years ago. Would have saved me a lot of trouble. I lost it all, too."

Jerry shook his head. "Let it go. It's done. Give it to our good Lord. He forgives everything from a repentant sinner."

"I've repented."

"Then there's nothing holding you back. Now I'm done freezing my toes off out here. You coming in?"

"No, Banjo will be waiting for me."

"It's the ding-dong-iest thing with that dog. Followed RJ around and wouldn't budge. Knew who his master was. Moped along, barely ate in the weeks following RJ's death. And then you show up, and Banjo clings to you like a tick on a deer."

"You're reading into things too much, Jerry." Clint turned to leave.

Jerry chuckled. "And you can't read the signs to save your life, boy."

Clint couldn't argue. It was true.

"Losing the sheep ranch was a real blow. But my pride could have driven away my missus, too. At the end of the day, I didn't lose anything of real value."

Clint frowned, the words not adding up. How could he say he hadn't lost anything of real value? "But the money and your dream…"

"Money comes and goes. Dreams change. I found a job here at Rock Step and met RJ, the best friend I ever had besides my wife. The Lord blessed me right good, and there ain't a day that goes by I don't thank Him for it." Jerry nodded to the door. "There's Banjo."

"I have some errands to run and won't be around until later tonight."

"I hope those errands include Miss Lexi."

"Stop matchmaking and make yourself useful. Tell Logan to keep his eyes open for anything suspicious."

He strode outside with Banjo beside him. Jerry had lost everything years ago, but now he seemed happy and content. He was able to look back and see the blessings from the wreckage. Clint drew his eyebrows together. Were there any blessings from his own mistake?

Did he have to bear the burden of shame about it forever? Or was it time to let it go?

He didn't have time to think about it now. Lexi was waiting for him.

"You're sure you don't mind if I pick out a few gifts?" Lexi glanced over her shoulder at Clint standing behind her in Loraine's Mercantile.

"Nope."

She choked down a laugh at how he was standing, his gaze straight ahead, arms locked down by his sides. He appeared to be trying to mentally transport himself anywhere but here. She, on the other hand, wouldn't mind staying in this cozy shop for hours. With Christmas music playing softly over the loudspeakers and evergreen boughs hung with red ribbons, the store put her in the holiday spirit.

She'd had an ulterior motive for inviting Clint today. Yes, she wanted his advice about the building, but more than that, she needed a few answers before she could think about making a major life change. Unfortunately, the answers couldn't be found by asking direct questions. Not to Clint, anyway.

She needed to spend a little time outside the ranch with him, to see if she was whipping up romantic notions where they didn't exist. Some good conversations, chemistry and mutual interest in the ranch did not equal a lasting love. From what Clint had told her, he wasn't even looking for love.

But what guy was?

If love found him, would he be the kind of man

she'd always hoped to find? Or would he be emotionally closed off? Unwilling to share the deepest parts of himself?

"I remember coming in here a few times in high school. Wasn't it a junk store?" Clint picked up a glass paperweight before setting it back down.

"Pinko's Odds N Ends." Lexi checked the price on a tube of lavender lotion. "I don't remember when it changed hands, but Loraine clearly has the style thing going on. I love the rustic chic feel of this place."

"Rustic what?"

"Chic." She pointed to the vintage wooden hutches and tables used for displays. "Elegant with outdoor elements."

"I'll take your word for it."

"Look at these adorable candles." She held the open Mason jar up for him to smell. He didn't move or take a sniff. She raised an eyebrow, shoving it closer to his face, plastering her sweetest smile on her own. It was fun pushing his buttons. "What do you think?"

He inhaled. "Blueberry pie."

"Exactly. I think the girls at work would love this." She added four more candles to her basket, then meandered over to the jewelry. "Oh, wow. This silver is stunning."

She lifted a chain with a bouquet of silver flowers dangling from it. "I've never seen a necklace like this. The flowers are exquisite." She brought it closer, then checked the tag. "Handmade."

Clint sidled up to her. "Yeah, it's nice."

"Nice? It's amazing. I think it's perfect for Amy. We'd better get over to the building. Shawn will be there any minute. Let me pay for these, and we can go."

After making her purchases, they strolled down the sidewalk on their way to the old department store. Neither spoke, and Lexi's mind wandered. One gift she didn't have to worry about? Clint's. She'd called Dan and Lola Smith, and she still couldn't believe she'd been able to put a deposit down on the one puppy they had left. Apparently someone had bought it, then canceled. The best part? It would be available on Christmas Eve.

She sighed in contentment. So far, the day had been lovely. A relaxing lunch with Clint at the sandwich shop. Browsing the mercantile. And now this. She found herself wanting to get closer to him, to tell him some of the things she'd been mulling over lately.

"Do you read the Bible much?" She glanced up at him.

"You come up with the most random topics." He seemed taller right next to her.

"I know, my mind operates in mysterious ways. I've been reading my Bible more."

"And?"

"I'm not as angry about Daddy not telling me."

"That's good."

"Yeah." She shivered against the cold.

"Prayer has kept me going many times over the years."

Could she say the same? "I used to pray regularly. Used to take everything to God."

"You don't anymore?" He extended his arm for her to cross the road.

"I'm starting to, but there were several years when I didn't. I got busy. And excited. I think I was so passionate about my business taking off that I left God out of the picture. Oh, I still prayed at church and before meals, but let's face it, a prayer before dinner isn't really inviting Him into my life, you know."

"I know. I've had periods where I've gotten wrapped up in my own stuff, too."

"Like when?"

"Off and on throughout my life."

"How did you get back into praying?"

He shrugged. "I just did it."

While she was thankful he was willing to have this conversation, he wasn't opening up much to her. She wanted to know more.

"What do you pray for?" she asked.

"Looks like the Realtor arrived." Clint nodded to where Shawn's truck was parked.

So much for digging deeper. She hurried ahead. "Wait until you see the inside."

Clint let the tape measure slide back into its case with a snap. Lexi had been right about this building. It was a gem. A neglected eyesore, but a prize just the same. He'd checked everything he could—the roof needed work and the heating system needed to be replaced altogether, but the electrical system and wiring were fine— and he was jotting notes for Lexi to ask a contractor. Shawn had left an hour ago, telling them to text him when they'd finished.

Lexi waved to Clint from the second-floor balustrade. He grinned up at her. Couldn't help himself. She had dirt smudged on her cheek and the biggest smile he'd ever seen. She was practically skipping around up there, speaking into her phone. She hadn't stopped talking into it since they arrived. At first he'd thought she was calling someone, but she'd told him she was leaving herself voice memos. He didn't even know you could do that on your phone.

Yeah, she was something.

And, as they'd methodically checked the building, he'd enjoyed listening to her prattle on about refinishing the floors, restoring the staircase, converting the first-floor storage room into a kitchen and moving the office to the second floor.

Even better? He'd caught her vision. He could see the building with shining floors and brides and grooms. He could practically hear the laughter of the wedding guests and smell the roasted chicken Lexi claimed was on every bride's menu.

What a gift—to see the world through Lexi's eyes. Her way of seeing things was so different than his, so filled with hope and beauty. She made things the best they could be.

He accepted things as they were. Messy, difficult and unchangeable.

Just being around her made him feel alive.

Eating lunch with her, trailing her through the girlie store, having real conversations with her—they made him want more. He'd caught himself wondering what it would be like to hang out with her on a daily basis. To cook together and watch goofy movies and chat about the ranch and ride horses around the property.

When had she become his idea of perfect?

From the minute she opened the door the day I arrived.

"I'm about done," Lexi called from upstairs. "I'm texting Shawn."

"Yeah, I'm wrapping up, too." He gathered his notes and slipped the tape measure into his pocket.

"All day I've been imagining this staircase." She stood at the top with her hands up. "Okay, go back in time mentally. Picture me in a gown circa 1900. It's a Christmas wedding, so I'm in long sleeves, and the dress is flowing with lace overlays. Sorry, but you're going to have to be the groom in this scenario. So you're in a dark suit. Very dapper. And the lanterns are glowing, it's getting dark and snowflakes are falling outside the windows. The wedding supper is about to begin, and I'm all set to make my grand entrance."

."Wait, is this a wedding today that's imitating 1900, or is it really 1900?" He couldn't believe he was playing along with this. A month ago, he would have refused. But today...it felt right.

"It's 1900. Okay, someone's playing the piano, and the wedding guests are lined at the bottom of the steps." She tipped her chin up, then lifted an imaginary skirt. He had no idea what he was supposed to do, but he sure couldn't wait to see what happened next.

With one hand on the handrail, she glided down, pretending to hold a skirt. Even with the smudge on her cheek, he envisioned her as a bride back in the day. When she had about two steps to go until the bottom, his hands got a mind of their own. He caught her by the waist, swinging her to the floor.

"My, my, you're one strong cowboy." She batted her eyelashes coyly, still in character.

"Wouldn't want the little lady to slip," he said in a deliberately low voice, still holding her waist.

"That's very chivalrous of you." Her eyes gleamed, challenging him. "What now, tiger?"

"Well, it is a Christmas wedding, right?"

Wide-eyed, she nodded.

"Then I reckon there'd be mistletoe hanging above us."

"I reckon there would."

"And the ceremony *is* over."

"Oh, yes. Any self-respecting bride would have had the wedding in the church." She twined her arms around his neck.

"Then, sugar, the only logical conclusion would be this." His voice grew husky, and he pressed his lips to hers. Warm, soft, tasted as sweet as the candy canes hanging from his Christmas tree. She kissed him back, and he held her tightly, wishing time would stand still. Wishing she could be his imaginary mistletoe bride forever.

But nothing lasted forever, and he knew it all too well.

He broke away, still holding her close, not wanting to let go of her, not wanting her to loosen her hold from his shoulders.

She smiled up at him. "If I'd known you were going to kiss me like that, tiger, I would have married you sooner."

He laughed. Only Lexi could come up with the perfect thing to say in this situation. Maybe they could both pretend the kiss had been harmless, a little make-believe on a winter's day.

"If I'd known you tasted as sweet as your name, sugar, I wouldn't have waited so long to kiss you."

The door clanged open, and Lexi jumped back. Clint turned, patting his pockets, pretending he'd lost something. "I think I left my pen in the other room." And he fled to the back.

This had to stop. Playing pretend wedding wasn't smart. His heart was getting too tied up with Lexi.

Without him, she'd be fine. But what about him? Life without her... He was beginning to think losing his land had been nothing compared to losing Lexi.

If he never had her, he couldn't lose her. One kiss was as far as it could go.

But he knew he'd forever remember the taste of sugar and the closest thing to a wedding he'd ever have.

Chapter Eleven

"I hate to do this so close to Christmas, but I'm driving to Denver right after our meeting." Lexi waved for Clint to take a seat in her office the next morning. Christmas was a week away, and the questions inside her were eating her alive. Buy the building in Sweet Dreams and stay? Or move back to Denver, back to reality and her company?

She knew what she wanted to do. But what if Clint wasn't interested in pursuing a relationship with her?

"For good?" His blue eyes darkened as he frowned.

"No, I'll be back on Monday." She forced a smile, but inside she was a mess. Staying here if he wasn't interested was unthinkable. He'd been in her office for all of three seconds and already her heart was beating out of control. She'd thought about his kiss a gazillion times. Couldn't stop herself from imagining a future here full-time. Horseback rides. Summer picnics. Snowmobiling in the winter. Showing him the mock-ups for the weddings she'd be planning. Running the ranch. Holding hands. Stealing a kiss or two.

Maybe, just maybe, a wedding of her own.

"Madeline Roth, the senator's daughter I told you about, wants a meeting before hiring me, and I have some things to discuss with my assistant and vice president. The new year will be here before I know it, and I have decisions to make."

"I hope you trust me when I say I will always put the ranch's needs first." He looked so earnest, she wanted to round the desk and caress his cheek. Role playing yesterday had been such an exhilarating surprise. She'd had no idea he would play along so well…and so convincingly. But today he appeared to be as conflicted as she was.

"I don't question it, Clint." She didn't question his loyalty to the ranch, but what about his feelings toward her? She'd never planned her future around a man, and she'd be crazy to create one around someone who might not be interested in the same things she wanted.

"Why aren't you staying in Denver for Christmas?"

"I don't want to." She crossed her arms over her chest. Didn't he want her here? "In fact, I was hoping you'd come to church with me on Christmas Eve. You don't have plans, do you?"

"I'm taking care of the herd so the rest of the crew can celebrate with their families."

"The church service isn't until seven at night. The chores will be done by then."

"Are you sure it won't complicate things even more?"

Comments like that were why she didn't know what to do. His kiss yesterday had taken her to another place—one where she felt safe and cherished and, dare she say, loved. But if he only saw her as a complication, well, she'd be a fool to sell her company and pine for someone who didn't care about her.

"It's church, Clint. A Christmas service."

"I'll pick you up at six thirty."

"So I guess we should discuss the ranch. Anything new I need to know about?"

"Yes, actually." Frowning, he opened the file folder he always brought with him. "I heard back from the ranch in Montana I contacted about buying extra feed this winter. Turns out they could have sold to us. The price was right."

She leaned back, her hands on the armrests. "Well, it doesn't matter now. The calves are sold."

"I should have pushed harder to get an answer." His gaze bored into hers.

"Didn't you call them several times?"

"Yes."

"There's only so much you can do. It's over. No big deal. We have pregnant cows and enough food to get them through winter, and we sold the calves. We're in good shape."

If Clint cared half as much for her as he did the ranch and Banjo, she'd be making an offer on the building downtown today. Why was this decision so difficult?

He'd taken a pen out of his pocket and was jotting something on one of the papers. Watching his long fingers gracefully hold the pen and his forehead furrow in that serious way of his, she caught her breath.

When had she fallen in love with him?

"I know it might not be a possibility this winter, but I'm looking for used farm equipment so we can fill the hay barn next fall. I don't want to be at the mercy of other ranches all the time."

He had no idea her heart was bursting with love even as it deflated from reality.

She'd told herself she wouldn't settle for ho-hum. And being around Clint was never dull. The breathless kisses he had down, but what about the other things she wanted—someone who loved her enough to make a grand gesture and who wanted marriage and kids?

If breathless kisses were all she'd get from Clint, maybe she should move back to Denver.

He'd be spending Christmas Eve with Lexi. And he had no idea what to get her for Christmas. Did he buy her a gift an employee would give—something impersonal like a canister of cashews? Or did he follow his heart and buy her chocolates, roses, jewelry—things that shouted *Lexi*?

Neither, you fool.

Clint finished mucking Nugget's stall and moved on to the one next to it. He was on cleanup duty, which suited him fine. Good, hard work might take his mind off the brown-haired, brown-eyed girl who burrowed into his thoughts night and day.

When he'd said goodbye after their meeting, he'd wanted to yank her close to him and kiss her again.

Those kinds of wants were coming at him more and more.

Was this what love felt like? *Love*. He snorted. This wasn't love. It was infatuation. A guy like him would fall for any girl who looked at him twice. It was proximity, loneliness…

It felt like love.

The clink of the pitchfork hitting glass stopped him. *What in the world?*

He dug through the hay and found an empty pint bottle of whiskey. He ground his teeth together as he held up the offending bottle. Same as the ones he'd found in the old cabin.

Whoever had been in the cabin had surely been here, too.

He texted Logan to come to the barn.

His gut told him Jake was to blame, but he didn't have evidence, and in the past, he'd been accused of crimes he didn't commit.

Logan entered the stables.

"Look what I found." Clint held the bottle up.

Logan looked taken aback, then his lips firmed into a thin line.

"Any ideas who it might belong to?" Clint asked.

"I've got an idea, but I don't have proof."

"Name?"

"Jake. Ryder's been reliable." Logan frowned. "He has been hanging out with Jake more, though. I don't think it's him, but to be fair... Well, you know how it is."

"Is Ryder here?"

"Checked in at 6:00 a.m. He wanted extra money for Christmas—I think he's got a girlfriend—so I told him to come in an hour before school this week and next. Hope that's okay. I probably should have mentioned it to you yesterday."

"It's fine. I would have done the same."

They stared at the bottle a minute, the nickering of horses the only sound.

"I'm not sure how to handle this, Logan. I can't tolerate drinking, but without any proof of who did this, my hands are tied."

Logan scratched the stubble on his chin. "I was

thinking the same. Whoever left this is clearly drinking here. And stupid enough to leave the bottle around."

"I have caught Jake here when it wasn't his shift. And he claimed he was mucking stalls. I didn't buy it, but a phone call made me forget to come back and check the area."

"Well, I guess we'll have to have a talk with him tomorrow morning. That's his next shift, right?"

"Yep." Clint leaned against the stall frame. "Send him to my office when he arrives. I'll show him the bottle and ask if it's his."

"Want me to get Ryder in here? Ask him a few questions?"

"No. Let's wait to see what happens with Jake first."

Clint took the bottle back to his office and slipped it inside his file cabinet drawer next to the petty cash. Then he locked the cabinet and headed back out to the stables to finish cleaning. Letting the matter go didn't sit well with him. He wanted to find out who dared drink in the stables. Boot him off the property. Drunks could be a danger to everyone on the ranch, including the animals, but most of all, inebriated men posed a threat to Lexi.

For the first time since she'd left yesterday, he was glad she was in Denver. Safe from harm. He'd do whatever it took to keep her safe. He wished he could keep her safe forever.

"I'm concerned if I hire you, you won't be available for my needs. I'm wary of a wedding planner not being in the same state." Madeline Roth's posture would put a debutante to shame. Wearing a pale gray pantsuit and lavender silk blouse, matching lavender heels and with her blond hair smoothed into an elegant chignon, she projected confidence and sophistication.

Had the previous two hours of pitching wedding themes been for nothing? Lexi forced her smile to stay in place. She wasn't even sure she wanted to plan Madeline's wedding. "That's a valid concern, but let me assure you I do what it takes to keep my clients happy. I have an office in Wyoming, and I'm in constant contact with my staff."

"Oh." The word was loaded with negative implications. "Does this mean you're not planning on returning to Denver?"

Tough question. "I will know after the holidays."

"I'm interested in working with you *if* you decide to move back. I'm not comfortable hiring you if you'll be splitting time between here and Wyoming. Carson and I will be out of the country until January 2. We won't be making a decision until then. I'll call you when we're back." Madeline stood, and Lexi walked her to the door.

"I appreciate your honesty. I hope we'll be working together soon."

As soon as Madeline left, Lexi dropped into her chair, propped her elbows on the desk and let her forehead fall into her hands. Madeline had been her final appointment of the day. Lexi had put a lot of thought and effort into the themes she'd pitched to Madeline, but now that they'd met, she couldn't muster the same excitement as before.

Devoting so much energy to demanding brides never used to bother her.

But now?

The sixty-hour workweeks before Daddy died came

to mind. She was tired. She'd had no life of her own in years.

Her thoughts switched to riding horses with Clint and sipping coffee with Amy. To her pretty office at the ranch and the ideas she'd been toying with to remodel the ranch house and the old department store in Sweet Dreams. Shawn Lesly had called her earlier and told her he'd talked to the listing agent. The owner loved the idea of a reception hall and was willing to negotiate on the price.

She'd hoped coming back to Denver for the weekend would remind her what she'd be giving up, but so far, it had only made her want to return to Wyoming as soon as possible.

Her gaze fell to the phone on her desk. She'd been sitting right here in July when Daddy had called. *I'm thinking about going to Yellowstone next month. Want to join me? It's been years since we hiked Mystic Falls Trail.*

He'd taken her to Yellowstone many times, and Mystic Falls was their favorite spot. She cringed, remembering her reply. *I'd love to, Daddy, but I'll have to wait until next summer. I'm booked for months.*

Booked for months.

Some daughter.

Her throat felt tight, scratchy, and today had been bad enough without adding tears. She took a drink of water from the bottle on her desk.

Nothing was going according to plan.

Oh, who was she kidding? She didn't have a plan. She'd been living on a whim ever since the funeral. And it was time to get back on track.

Today had been rough from the start. Jolene had called off with the flu, so Lexi had been stuck with hours of administrative duties. And while she'd heaved a sigh of relief that the offices were neat this time, the storage room was a mess. Each planner had shelves for their orders, but boxes had been stacked on the floor, making it difficult to move around. And some of the shelves were empty. How hard was it to put a box on a shelf? Not much more difficult than setting it on the floor.

She'd only seen one planner in the office all day, which wasn't unusual if the others had weddings scheduled for the weekend, but Natalie didn't have one on the books. Why wasn't she here?

And every time Lexi had walked past the front desk, her blood boiled. The flowers were still wrong. They were *not* blush-colored blooms. They were red roses. Red! Again. She'd trusted Natalie to handle the problem, but it hadn't been dealt with.

It had taken every ounce of her self-control not to throw them in the trash and order the blush-colored bouquets.

"Lexi, you're back." Natalie Allen, a tall redhead in a black pencil skirt and fitted emerald blouse, entered the room. She took a seat opposite Lexi and placed her cell phone and planner on the desk.

Lexi took a deep breath to calm her agitation. She checked the time. It was after six.

While the cat's away, the mice will play.

"Why are there red roses on the front desk?" Lexi flattened her palms on the desk. "You assured me you would take care of fixing the order. This is the second time I've been here this month, and both times I've seen red roses. What is going on?"

Natalie lifted her chin as her cheeks flushed. "The

other designers and I thought red brought a more festive air to the office. It *is* Christmas."

Lexi's fingers curled into her palms. Was she imagining the challenge in Natalie's tone? And since when did all the designers change the rules? None of them had invested their money in this company, worked sixty-to eighty-hour weeks to build the best reputation possible. She straightened. "Every Christmas the florist adds silver branches and mint-colored greens for a more subdued holiday look. The color scheme is important for our brand."

"Maybe it's time for a change."

Lexi blinked. She counted to three, trying to control her temper. "If a change were to be made, it would be *my* decision. These details matter to me. They're important. And looking around, I see other things being neglected. You told me you would handle them."

"I'll make a note." Not appearing overly concerned, Natalie checked her phone. "How did the meeting with Ms. Roth go? If you think you'll be in Wyoming and unable to accommodate her needs, I'm available. Her wedding is *the* wedding to land. I have so many ideas."

Lexi gaped at her. Didn't Natalie care what the other details being neglected were? And had she really just tried to undercut the Roth wedding from her?

"I don't know where to go with that comment at this moment." Lexi didn't even try to keep the incredulity out of her tone. She sat back in her chair, setting her elbow on the armrest and letting her cheek rest against her index finger. "Am I missing something? When I left in October, this place was running smoothly, and now I'm getting complaints from our clients. I see problems."

Natalie scoffed. "Brides always complain if the day

doesn't go exactly the way they'd hoped. They're impossible to please."

"Maybe so, but these complaints have been valid. Missing invitations, the wrong place settings, no photographer showing up?"

"I haven't had any complaints from my clients."

"But you're the VP. Every client is my responsibility and yours."

"I think we're all adults here, and each planner should be responsible for her own clients. If you hired a purchaser…"

"My name is on every contract. This is my reputation."

Natalie pursed her lips.

Lord, I'm not getting through to her. What happened? We used to be on the same page, but now she acts like I'm insane for having standards. I don't know if I want to do this anymore. Let the flowers be red, and the boxes be shoved anywhere the planners want. Let them figure out their own insurance and come up with their own expense accounts. I'm so tired of managing them. I want a life. What do I do? Show me the way.

Something changed—a wave of peace settled over her like a warm ray of sunshine. She turned her head and studied her office, the hall beyond it and Natalie looking like she'd been sucking on a lemon.

"Natalie, where do you see yourself in five years?"

Natalie jerked to attention. "Sounds like a job interview question."

"Maybe it is."

She tipped her chin up. "I see myself as one of the top designers in Denver. I've landed several influential couples in the past three years, and I've been positioning myself to be the go-to designer for the crème de la crème. Not only here, but throughout the state." She held herself proudly.

Lexi bit her lower lip. Natalie's goals weren't terrible, but they didn't fit with the Weddings by Alexandra philosophy. Lexi had always prided herself on planning weddings for every budget. She enjoyed making the dreams of all her brides come true, not just the ones with the most money or status.

The truth stared her in the face. Her business would not thrive unless she moved back and made changes to her staff.

Lexi studied the office she'd put so much thought into decorating, and for the first time, it felt impersonal. Worse, it stifled her. These four walls contained so much responsibility.

"Have you thought about going off on your own?" Lexi asked.

A flicker of unease lit her eyes. "It's crossed my mind on occasion. Why?"

"I'm thinking about making a change. Like you suggested."

"Look, Lexi," Natalie said quickly, "I'm sorry about the flowers. I should have checked with you before changing the order."

"Don't worry. I'm not firing you." She tidied the papers on her desk. "I'm seriously considering moving to Wyoming for good. If I did, I would keep the Weddings by Alexandra brand, but I would sell this building. You and I have worked together for a long time, and frankly, I don't think we see eye to eye when it comes to the company anymore. If I sell, I'm giving you the first right to make an offer on it. I don't know if you'd want to set up a company the way I did or rent space to other planners. You'd have to figure it out for yourself. If I don't sell, we're going to have to schedule a meeting to get on the same page."

Natalie paled. "You'd sell this to me?"

"Yes."

"I… I never thought…" She blinked a few times. "I'm honored you're giving me the first right."

"Do you have the capital to consider this? I can recommend a financial adviser to help you come up with a business plan."

"I can raise the money. Are you serious? I mean, really serious about possibly selling? I don't want to get my hopes up for nothing."

"I'm not giving you false hope. Get a business plan together. Even if I ultimately don't sell, your work won't be for nothing. Maybe this is what you need. I have a feeling you want more control, and that's why so many details are being ignored around here. Maybe you resent the fact that I make the rules. Or maybe I'm way off base. I don't know. I do know things change, and we have to change with them." Lexi stood, yawning. "Now, if you'll excuse me, I have a date with a burrito platter."

After locking up and picking up takeout from her favorite Mexican restaurant, she admired the city's glittering Christmas lights on her way home to her condo. She'd long loved Denver, but her life here had become all work all the time. She climbed the steps to the front door, turned on the lights, changed into sweats and switched the television on to enjoy her burrito with a Christmas movie.

Thirty minutes later the half-eaten food had been pushed aside, and she turned off the television. There wasn't anything good on, and a restlessness had been building inside her ever since she talked with Natalie.

How could she have gone from living her dream to ready to sell her company in a few short months? What happened?

Clint Romine. He's what had happened.

And worse, she was ready to move back home and live on the ranch when it was too late to spend time with her father. Why couldn't she have gotten this urge last year, when it would have mattered and she could have enjoyed being with her dad?

If he were here now, what would she say to him? *Well, Daddy, it's like this. There's a super-cute cowboy, and he took over the ranch for me. He's reliable, and I trust him, and I like being with him, although I'm pretty sure I drive him nuts sometimes. He's quiet. Gets things done. And he kissed me. It was a good kiss. I can't stop thinking about it.*

And what could her father possibly say in response? *What about the business you sacrificed so much time and money for? I'd hate to see you throw it all away for a guy, especially a cowboy. Didn't I warn you about them? He'll only break your heart, Lexi.*

Oh, what do you know, Daddy? I'm in love!

She yanked a throw off the edge of the couch and spread it over her lap. *Fantastic.* She was having imaginary conversations with her deceased father where she sounded like a silly teenager. And she was arguing with him, no less. Inhaling a long breath, she counted to four then exhaled.

Her brain was useless. What she needed was divine guidance.

Lord, thank You for opening my eyes to the reality of

Weddings by Alexandra. I want to be sad my heart isn't here in Denver anymore and the company You blessed me with doesn't jolt me out of bed with excitement the way it used to. I know changes are coming and they're needed. But I don't know if I should start fresh in Wyoming with a new wedding planning business and a possible future with Clint, or if I should move back here and make hard choices about my current staff.

Lexi opened the Bible app on her phone and scrolled through the topics before stopping on one. She read Philippians chapter two, about being united in Christ. Instead of continuing on, she circled back to verses three and four of the second chapter. *Do nothing out of selfish ambition or vain conceit. Rather, in humility value others above yourselves, not looking to your own interests but each of you to the interests of the others.*

The verses were about how to treat fellow Christians, but they could have been written to describe her father. He always treated his employees as family, anticipating their needs and looking out for them. He'd worked hard his entire life to build the ranch into a large, profitable operation, but not out of selfish ambition. He'd told her time and again to offer first fruits to the Lord, that all they had was from Him alone. He'd drilled it into her that using her talents to the best of her ability was a way to honor God.

She burrowed under the throw. Selfish ambition described her. She could have made the time to spend a weekend hiking in Yellowstone with her dad. No wonder he hadn't told her about the cancer. She'd put her job above him for years.

Lord, forgive me for my selfishness. Help me change. Help me be the person You want me to be.

A few months ago, she'd believed she was exactly where she was supposed to be. And now? So many options. Sell the business. Open a new one. Stay here. And do what with the ranch?

Too much to think about right now. What would be best for Clint? For Natalie? For her other employees, like Jolene? Logan? *Ugh.*

Her lawyer had agreed to a meeting tomorrow morning, even though it was Saturday. Maybe she'd get some answers then. Risking it all had never been her strong suit.

Chapter Twelve

As dusk fell Monday evening, Clint finished his rounds and headed back to the office to lock up. Jake hadn't shown up for work on Saturday or Sunday, and he and Logan figured they'd seen the last of him. And after watching Lexi's car drive up to the main house an hour ago, Clint hoped Jake was the one who'd left the bottle. He didn't like having an unknown threat around the ranch, and he really hadn't liked the way his heart had somersaulted when he'd seen Lexi's car.

Just get through Christmas Eve with her. She's probably moving back to Denver, anyway. Then you can concentrate on the ranch without all these distractions.

Like her pretty eyes, her laugh, her kindness. Her soft hair, the feel of her slim waist in his hands, the way her lips tasted as sweet as syrup. Man, he missed her.

He took his gloves off and slapped them against his thigh, yanked open the office door and stopped in his tracks.

"What do you think you're doing?"

Jake stood over the file cabinet with the petty cash box in his hands and guilt etched into his face. Even if the kid didn't reek of hard liquor, the way he swayed and his bloodshot eyes left no uncertainty he was drunk.

"Just filing some papers, boss." He tried to discreetly drop the petty cash back into the cabinet, but it fell with a thud.

"You're fired."

"What?" He slammed the drawer shut. "Why?"

Fury shot through Clint's veins, but he'd been practicing keeping his temper in check since he was four years old.

"You're drunk. And you're stealing."

"I don't know what you're talking about."

"Call someone to pick you up, or I'll find you a ride in a squad car."

Jake stumbled toward him, getting in his face. "What's your problem, man? I'm not botherin' you."

Clint stood his ground, staring Jake right in the eye. "I know you used illegal drugs and were drinking during work hours. You're only, what, eighteen? You've got your whole life ahead of you. Don't throw it away on this garbage."

"It's not work hours now."

"Then you have no reason to be here."

Jake glared, swaying, then pulled his fist back, but Clint caught it, twisting the kid's arm under him. "That's it. I'm calling the cops."

"No! I'll leave. I'll drive away right now."

"You're not driving, dummy. I can't have you kill anyone out there. You've put enough people in danger." He let go of his arm. "Here, call your friend." He held out his phone, but Jake chopped down on his arm, sending the phone crashing to the floor, and took off.

"Hey, get back here!" Clint ran after him, but the kid

was fast. He chased him past the barns to the parking lot, but Jake didn't turn. He ran toward the main house.

Lexi!

Clint dug deep and channeled every ounce of energy he had, surging forward and tackling Jake. He hauled him to his feet and dragged him by the arm back toward the office. Jake kicked at him and tried to escape, but Clint kept an iron grip on his arm and didn't slow down.

Logan ran toward them as they passed the stables. "What's going on?"

"Call the police. Then join us in the office."

Logan looked taken aback, but he nodded.

Clint shoved Jake into the office chair and blocked his path. His thoughts couldn't keep up with the pounding of his heart.

"Aw, let me go, man. I'll leave. Never come back. Don't get the cops involved. Please!"

He wouldn't feel sorry for him—didn't feel sorry for him. This was for the safety of Rock Step Ranch. And Jake had it coming.

"Hey, I tried to let you go easy. You haven't shown up for work. You come here and use the Harringtons' property as if it was your own personal seedy playground. Why are you messing around with this junk?"

Jake sniffled. "My grandma died a few months ago—"

"And you're honoring her memory by drinking, drugging and stealing? You'll have to come up with something better than that."

He wiped his nose with the back of his hand. "You're heartless."

"I know I am."

"You never liked me. You don't know what I'm going through."

Clint crossed his arms over his chest, his legs wide. "Save the sob story for someone else. I'm your boss. And if I don't make sure you're punished, I'm afraid you won't learn your lesson. You'll hire in at the next ranch and abuse their trust. Keep on with your drinking. Steal to support your habit. And maybe no one will be around to stop you next time, and you'll really hurt someone. You want that on your conscience? I don't want it on yours or mine. When you break the rules, there are consequences. And you broke them. Big-time."

"I won't do it again, I promise."

"Why don't I believe you?"

"I want to talk to Lexi." The slurring returned. "Let her hear my side of the story."

At hearing her name on Jake's lips, Clint balled his hands into fists but kept them down by his sides. "No," he said through clenched teeth.

"Says who? You ain't my boss anymore. Just said so yourself."

Clint flexed his hands and tried to control the anger pulsing through his veins. "If you ever get within a hundred yards of her, I'll rope you like a spring calf and drag you up and down this property for fun. Got it?"

Jake's face turned a greenish hue.

Clint bent to look him in the eye. "Do. You. Understand?"

His Adam's apple worked as he nodded. "Yes."

"Yes, what?"

"Yes, sir."

"Good."

They sat in silence for several minutes until Logan

and two officers entered the office. Clint answered their questions, and ten minutes later, one of the officers led a handcuffed Jake away.

"You pressing charges?" the other officer asked. "He doesn't have any priors, but he sure had plenty of excuses for tonight. Makes me wonder how many times he's sweet-talked his way out of trouble."

"I'll have to talk to my boss first." Clint followed him back to the squad car. "It's her call."

"Well, let's hope this experience scares him into getting his act together." They shook hands, and moments later, the police car was on its way off the ranch.

As much as he dreaded this, Clint had to tell Lexi what was going on, and it couldn't wait. He felt like such a fool. His gut had been telling him Jake was a problem, but he'd ignored it and look what had happened. Lexi could have been hurt. Robbed. Worse.

He put his hands on top of his head and looked up at the stars starting to light the sky. His inaction was unacceptable. Last time, his bad judgment had only hurt him. This time, it could have hurt Lexi.

God, forgive me.

She was doing this! Really doing it! Lexi finished unpacking her suitcase, took her earbuds out and headed back downstairs for a cup of tea and a muffin. She'd stopped in at her favorite bakery in Denver before driving back today. The weekend had given her so much clarity. The meeting with the lawyer had revealed more than what would be involved with selling her business; it had shown her what she truly wanted.

Clint made her feel important, special. He anticipated her needs, cared about her safety and looked at her like she was the most beautiful woman in the world. Sure, he hadn't swept her off her feet or even told her how he felt about her, but that was understandable given his upbringing. If she told him she loved him, he'd then feel safe enough to share his feelings.

She opened the bakery box. Triple chocolate chunk, poppy seed or white-chocolate raspberry? Triple chocolate always won. A knock on the door startled her. Taking a bite of muffin, she hurried to the door.

Clint stood before her, throbbing with pent-up energy and looking disheveled. "Sorry to bother you right now."

"What happened?" She dragged him inside. "You look upset."

He took his hat off and stood there with his jaw clenching in and out.

"Come back to the living room where it's warm." Her nerves began ratcheting. What was going on? She didn't even know where to start guessing. "Sit."

He obliged by lowering his body into the chair, and she sat on the couch. "It's Jake. I…" He raked his fingers through his hair. "I had to fire him. The police were involved."

"Oh, my!" She set the muffin down. "Tell me everything."

Clint explained about finding the empty liquor bottle in the stall and his suspicions about Jake. Then he told her about their encounter tonight. "Initially, I planned on firing him and letting him go, but when he ran to your house, I had Logan call the cops. Your safety is too important. I told the officers it was up to you if you wanted to press charges."

Lexi crossed to where he sat, and she slid her arms

around his shoulders, hugging him. "I'm so sorry you had to deal with all this."

He edged out of her embrace and rose. He walked to the Christmas tree and touched one of the ornaments. "I should have fired him when I first suspected he was the one drinking."

"Without evidence? That's not our way, and it's not yours, either."

"Don't you see?" He spun and rushed back to her side in two strides, clasping her upper arms. "He could have hurt you. I know what drinking does to people. Some only need the thinnest excuse to take whatever they want."

"But he didn't hurt me." She wanted to soothe him. He was so close physically, but so far away emotionally. "You took care of it. You did the right thing."

She reached on her tiptoes and pressed her lips to his cheek. How she wanted to take away the misplaced guilt he carried.

"If I'd followed through with my suspicions earlier, we could have avoided this. Now he might be facing jail time."

"Hey." She placed her hand on his chest. "You did nothing wrong. I'll go into the station tomorrow and talk to the officers. From what you've told me, I think spending the night in jail will do Jake a world of good. I don't have to press charges, and I probably won't."

"I think I scared him."

"I'm sure you did. Now wait here. I'm getting you a muffin and telling you my news." She padded back to the kitchen, then returned with the white-chocolate raspberry pastry. She handed it to him, but he set it on the coffee table.

"Lexi, I don't know. Maybe you should consider pressing charges. What if he's vindictive? He knows his way around here. He's snuck in without us knowing on more than one occasion. I caught him trying to steal the petty cash. And when he's drunk, he's mean."

"Okay." She lifted her hands, palms out, to her chest. "The police have him, so we don't need to worry about it anymore tonight."

The vein in his forehead bulged, but he picked up the muffin. A good sign.

"I have some news." She stayed on her feet, pacing away from him to collect her thoughts. Then she pivoted, feeling happy and light. "I'm selling my business in Denver, putting an offer in on the building downtown and moving back for good!"

The muffin dropped out of Clint's hand and rolled under the coffee table. She was moving back.

Selling her business.

And starting over.

Here.

His chest filled with concrete, and it was hardening by the second.

"I realized I've met my goals in Denver. I built a good reputation, and I planned a lot of beautiful weddings, but I'd let my professional goals completely crowd out my life." She moved over to him, took his hands in hers—her eyes gleaming with excitement—and beckoned him to his feet. He rose out of his chair. "I want a life, Clint. A life here. I realize how much I've been missing. Simple things, like riding around the ranch on horseback and spending time with friends. You. Amy. Feeling like I'm part of a community. You know?"

He looked into her trusting, hopeful brown eyes and knew what he had to say was going to fill those eyes with disgust. Tears. Hatred, even.

"But that's not all," she said. "I could do without the horseback rides and being part of a community, but I've come to care for you. Well, more than care, really. I trust you, and not in a you're-a-great-manager way. I've been falling—"

"Lexi."

"What?" She tilted her head, still staring at him like he was someone worth confiding in. Staring at him as if she loved him.

"Sit down."

"Why?"

"Just sit."

"You're scaring me." She sat on the couch.

"You have the wrong impression of me, and it's my fault you have it. The way you're looking at me is the way every guy dreams a girl will look at him, but I don't deserve it."

"What are you getting at?"

"Let me finish." He swallowed, still standing, trying to figure out how to start. "You remember how I told you I lost my land?"

She nodded.

"I didn't tell you all of it. I left out the most important part."

She clasped her hands, wringing her fingers, consternation dipping her eyebrows.

"All those years at LFR, I saved every penny I made. My dream was to own my own cattle ranch. I didn't care how small. I wanted land that was mine, land no one could take away from me. Five years ago, a property came on the market. It had three run-down out-buildings, a fenced-in pasture and a house so beat-up it could have been demolished and it would have looked better. The house didn't matter to me. But the property came with cattle."

He could still feel the rush of excitement when he'd found out about the ranch. If he could go back in time and tell his younger self to think it through…

Shaking his head, he continued. "The owner had died, and the son wanted no part of ranching. I didn't have enough money for the down payment. The bank needed twice as much as I had. So, defeated, I went to the local bar and grill, thinking there was no way I'd be able to buy it."

Why hadn't he trusted God with the timing? Why had he been in such a rush? He could have worked five more years and raised the money. But he hadn't. His chin dropped to his chest. He dreaded telling her the rest.

"I met a man named Devon Fields. By the end of the night, he was my business partner. We worked it out that he'd buy the property. Then he'd sell it to me on a land contract. He said my down payment was enough for him, and I would be paying him back plus interest in monthly installments instead of the bank. I figured it was more than fair. In the light of morning, I had my doubts, but I ignored them. And everything went smoothly, the way Devon said it would."

Lexi leaned forward, chewing on her fingernail. He girded his shoulders, ready for her reaction to what he had to say next.

"Imagine my surprise six months later when the property was foreclosed on. Devon had purchased the property with a mortgage, and instead of using my money and his own for the down payment, he'd obtained an illegal silent second mortgage. The land contract had been built on a lie. He took all my cash and ran. Made two mortgage payments. Two. Then he just disappeared, leaving me with nothing and the bank with the property."

His chest burned at the memory of that time. The disbelief, the helplessness. He'd hired a lawyer and found out Devon Fields wasn't even the guy's real name. There had been nothing he could do to get his land or money back.

"Oh, Clint. I'm so sorry. That's horrible." She stood, her eyes stricken.

"It was my own fault. Who in the world would ever agree to something as stupid as that? My greed blinded me. I should have told you the day you hired me. I've been so ashamed over losing the land. I thought I would be fine managing your ranch, letting you make the big decisions, but I'm not. I got a lousy price for your calves. I lost the heifer when I should have been here, and now I've let a drunken thief do whatever he wants on your property."

He threw his hands to his forehead and ran them over his hair. He had to let her go, and to do that, he had to leave. "I can't do this anymore. Consider this my two weeks' notice."

"You're quitting?" Lexi could barely take it in. "I don't understand."

"I'm done. Two weeks should give you enough time to find a new manager. I'll pack up and be ready to leave the way I should have left right when you hired me."

All the compassion she'd been holding in dissolved at his clipped words.

"Why? Some jerk cons you out of your dream, and you're suddenly not capable of ranching? That's the stupidest thing I've ever heard."

"Well, guess what? You're right on the mark. I'm the stupidest guy you've ever met."

"I didn't call you stupid." But she sure was thinking it right now. What would make him think he had to quit?

"You might as well have. I certainly call myself that and more on a daily basis."

"You shouldn't. You're not stupid. You were tricked. And you've been the best manager I could have ever hoped for here."

"No, I haven't." He looked at the ceiling. "I couldn't get the extra feed we wanted, couldn't get you better prices, couldn't stop Jake from drinking here constantly, and I couldn't even admit to you who I really am. I'm not the man for this job."

"No one could have gotten better prices or extra feed or stopped a cow from dying."

"Look, you've built me into a guy I'm not. If I don't quit, I'll let you down."

"What do you think you're doing now?"

"Not like this… It will be worse. I can't explain it— it's just how it is."

"You can't explain it?" Her voice rose. "It's how it is, huh? I deserve an explanation. We connected. You felt it, too. I know you feel it."

"You're lonely." He didn't meet her eyes.

"So are you."

"I've been lonely my entire life. I can live with it."

She wasn't getting through to him. It was as if a rock wall had formed behind his eyes. What was he so afraid of?

Me. He's afraid of a relationship with me.

She had to talk some sense into him.

"I don't want you to leave. I don't want you to be lonely, Clint. You're scared. I am, too. What I just told you about moving back and starting fresh? Having me here all the time probably terrifies you. But I've been honest with you from day one, Clint Romine. I want this... Wyoming...and you."

"And I've lied to you from day one."

"You haven't lied to me." She wanted to growl in frustration. "You're lying to yourself."

"About what?" He let out a fake laugh.

"About me. About what's between us."

"There can't be anything between us. I'm your manager—your former manager—just a worthless brat, an orphan, a nobody who never belonged to anyone. You think I could really belong here with you? You're ranch royalty. I'm nothing."

"I can't even respond to that. Does how I feel matter at all to you? I'm an orphan, too. And I'm no royalty. I'm a woman who was so busy chasing her professional dreams, I forgot what was important to me."

"You need someone better."

"The fact you just said that makes me wonder if I made a big mistake."

"Oh, honey, you made a mistake."

"Don't call me honey." If she told him she loved him, he'd toss it back in her face. She couldn't get through to him, and she was done trying. "Why don't you go? Go cut yourself off from everyone. It's easier, isn't it? Then you don't have to take a chance and get your heart broken again."

"I told you I don't have a heart."

"You're right. Because all these weeks when I've been opening up to you and telling you personal things, the secrets I didn't want anyone knowing? I was trusting you. And you didn't trust me back."

"I trust you."

"No, you don't." She gaped at him. "If you trusted me, you would have opened up to me. You would have told me the scary things inside you, the ones you don't want anyone to know. You kept the truest part of yourself from me. And now that you finally tell me your secrets, you're leaving. Running away. Unacceptable."

"I know. That's what I've been trying to tell you."

"I understand protecting yourself. I do. But I'm being real tonight, whether you're willing to join me or not. I know why Daddy didn't tell me he had cancer. He figured I'd blow him off for my job. I only have myself to blame." She spun away from him, hating the tears pressing against her eyes. "When you're sitting by yourself each night, you're going to realize you only have yourself to blame, too."

His hands touched her shoulders, but she flinched.

"Your dad knew you loved him," Clint said gently. "He probably didn't want to burden you. He might have thought he had all the time in the world. That was all. He wasn't punishing you."

"Just leave," she whispered.

The sound of his footsteps grew faint. The click of the front door shutting unleashed her tears. She dropped to her knees and covered her face with her hands.

When would she learn? Every time she got something she really wanted, something she loved was ripped away from her.

Her punishment for wanting it all.

Chapter Thirteen

Clint slammed the front door to his cabin as hard as he could and tossed a bag with a change of clothes into his truck. His lungs burned, were closing in on him, but he peeled out of the drive and sped away from the ranch without a second glance. She wanted him to leave? No problem. He'd leave.

He couldn't spend another second on Rock Step Ranch.

The past half hour flogged him. He'd known she'd been on the brink of telling him she loved him, and he'd snapped. Had laid his own sorry past out for her to see. Had done the honorable thing by putting in his notice. Tomorrow she'd wake up and realize what a mistake it had been to develop feelings for someone who had been so dumb. She'd probably be embarrassed she'd gotten involved with him. He'd avoid her as much as possible the next two weeks.

He thumped his fist on the steering wheel. Thirty years of anger and self-loathing churned inside him. Why couldn't he have been raised in a stable home? Had a parent or two who actually cared about his needs?

In all the foster homes he'd lived in, he'd never—not once—been so much as considered for adoption.

And no matter how hard he tried, he couldn't convince himself he was anything more than the kid who'd been yelled at and neglected by his grandfather, torn from Miss Joanne and her warm home, shifted from one overworked foster family to another until landing at Yearling.

Rock Step Ranch felt like home, but he'd known from day one it wasn't his. Could never be his.

What is wrong with me? Why am I fundamentally different from everyone else?

He let out a cynical laugh. He'd fallen in love with Lexi, and he didn't even know what love looked like. It was more than discussing the ranch and decorating Christmas trees. It was more than a kiss under the mistletoe.

It was bringing a woman flowers and taking her out for dinner. Listening to her talk about her day, driving her to church, helping her with whatever she needed.

He stared through the windshield at the stars dotting the sky as the truck created distance from the ranch. Love was more than all that, too. Lexi had it right back there. She wanted his secrets. She wanted the deepest part of him, but she wouldn't be able to handle it. He'd bricked the vital parts up and mortared them shut long ago.

Maybe he couldn't handle the deepest parts of himself, either.

The miles sped by as memory after memory of his childhood came back. Running from his grandfather, not being fast enough to avoid the slap of his leather belt across his back and legs. Making cookies with Miss

Joanne, sitting on her lap, waiting for her to kiss his hair. Hiding in his bedroom to avoid taking a beating from the kid at the final foster home and taking the beating anyhow. Mucking stalls at Yearling, thankful for a bed and food.

More memories came back. More recent ones. Checking into a dive motel the day he'd been kicked off his property. Curling up on the lumpy bed and crying for hours. A grown man, crying. He should be ashamed of that memory, but he wasn't. Maybe he'd been crying for more than the land. Maybe he'd cried for his entire youth.

Man, he had to stop thinking. Had to cut his losses and move forward. He'd done it so many times, he should be the expert. He switched the radio on, but Christmas songs depressed him. He turned it back off.

The lonely country road enveloped his truck. If only his mind would stay as empty as the blacktop ahead. He couldn't face thoughts of Lexi. Not yet.

A sign appeared stating the next town. He was a few miles from the property he'd lost. How had he ended up here? Funny, he'd thought he'd never want to see it again, but more than anything right now, he did.

After turning down the gravel road where the ranch stood, he drove slowly until he reached the land that had once been his. He drove beyond the pasture and passed the house. Even in the darkness, it looked the same. An old truck was parked in front of it. He reached the edge of the property, pulled over to the side of the road and climbed out, shivering in the cold.

What am I doing? It's the middle of the night, and I can't get this place back.

He trudged through the snow to the fence, and his

eyes adjusted to the night sky. An owl hooted somewhere nearby, and the sound comforted him, reminded
him of the many nights he'd spent checking cattle over
the years.

His heart lurched. He should have been living here,
checking his own cattle, building a life he could be
proud of. He curled his gloved hands around the top
fence wire, staring into the night.

*I was such a fool, trusting that jerk. I should have
gotten a lawyer before I signed a thing.*

Jerry's tale of owning and losing the sheep ranch
came to mind. Clint didn't think less of him for losing his sheep operation. He understood. And Jerry had
come out of it okay. He'd found a place at Rock Step.
Started over with his wife by his side.

From far away he heard the low of a cow. He already
missed Rock Step Ranch. Every day since he'd been
hired there had been soul filling. He'd been content.
Doing what made his soul sing.

*How many times will I be punished, Lord? I'm sorry.
I'm sorry for not waiting to buy this ranch. I wanted it
so badly. If I'd waited a few years, I would have saved
enough to get my own mortgage.*

His chest burned within him, and his throat was tight
as he tried to keep his emotions from erupting.

*And, Lord, I'm sorry I lied to Lexi. She's right. I've
been lying to myself.*

It was time to face the truth. He was never meant
to have it all—parents, a ranch, a wife and family. He
didn't deserve it.

No one deserves it.

Where had that thought come from? He slid to his

knees in the cold snow, the land he'd once owned spread out before him, and he prayed.

No one deserves it? I know I don't. But someone does. They must. Take Lexi, for example. She deserves it all.

The Bible verse he'd memorized came back. *For all have sinned and fall short of the glory of God.*

No one deserved anything but punishment.

Just as quickly, the rest of the verse came to mind. *All are justified freely by His grace through the redemption that came by Christ Jesus.*

The air whooshed out of his lungs.

Justified freely by His grace—undeserved, but given anyway.

You didn't just die for people who have their lives together. You know, the ones raised in loving homes and who are successful in life. You died for me. And I need a Savior more than anyone.

The cold air swirled around him, but he couldn't move. The memories he'd been avoiding—the best ones—all rushed back.

Lexi, so fearless and compassionate, showing him his cabin although she'd been wrecked with exhaustion. Riding out to the pasture with her and listening to her talk about her father. Making Thanksgiving dinner together, decorating his cabin for Christmas, all the Thursday meetings, kissing her under the imaginary mistletoe.

Priceless memories he'd cherish and revisit when his heart didn't throb with pain anymore.

No one but himself to blame. He'd brought this heartache on himself the same as he'd lost the land he knelt on.

Father, I've read the Bible enough to know I'm Your

child. And You love me. So why can't I love myself? Is Lexi right? Do I push people away to make sure I'm alone? I don't want to be alone anymore.

He turned his head and caught his breath. A deer stood not ten feet away, chewing on prairie grass and watching him.

Clint laughed, big gulping guffaws, startling the deer. It leaped away.

God was always with him, and the deer was a reminder of it. Lurching to his feet, he brushed the snow off his knees and returned to the truck.

With God on his side, he could move forward. If he could just figure out a life without Lexi.

He'd left. And Lexi had never felt more alone.

She picked up the half-eaten muffins and threw them at the Christmas tree. A bulb fell to the floor and shattered. *Perfect.* She wanted to smash every ornament on the tree and drag it outside and let the wind blow it to Montana. Erase any sign of goodness and hope in this house.

This empty shell of a house.

She wiped her tears and took a deep breath.

Her parents were gone. Clint was gone. Her passion for Weddings by Alexandra was gone.

What was left?

A whine at the door startled her. She rushed to the door. Maybe Clint had come back. Maybe he hadn't meant what he'd said. Maybe…

She opened it, and Banjo slunk inside. No one else was around.

She choked, kneeling, and wrapped her arms around

the dog. "He left you, too, didn't he? What are we going to do without him?"

Once more, she'd fallen for an emotionally unavailable guy. And it wasn't as if the warning signs hadn't been there all along. She'd told herself he was safe. Just a strong, silent cowboy. Someone she could depend on to manage the ranch and nothing more.

But she'd been wrong. He was more than a dependable ranch manager. He was caring, a great listener. He made time for her whenever she asked, and it wasn't because he was her employee. He cared about her needs. He made her feel safe and warm and loved.

But he didn't love her.

"Come on, Banjo." She padded to the living room. "Let's get you warm. Hop on the couch, and I'll get a blanket for us."

The poor dog tried to get up on the couch, but he couldn't. She heaved him up and he stretched out at one end.

She made her way to the hallway to find a blanket.

As much as she wanted to forget about Clint tonight, she couldn't. All the things she'd shared with him came to mind. Had her secrets meant nothing? Why wouldn't he have confided in her earlier? Surely he knew she wouldn't hold losing his property against him? Especially after being clued in to what his childhood had been like. His dedication to the smallest ranch details proved his integrity and intelligence.

He should have told her. Should have trusted her.

But what about before? Would I have still hired him if he'd told me during the interview? Yes, she still would have hired him. She believed in the best in people, and she'd needed a manager.

She opened the linen closet, but her favorite throw wasn't there. She'd forgotten she'd taken it to Denver.

The fact Clint had walked out was unforgivable. Didn't she have a say in whether he stayed or not? Had their kiss only been a silly game to him? Was she really just *sugar*, a moment of pretend and nothing more?

What had she thought would happen? That he would suddenly become this grand gesture–making, romantic guy who bared his soul and wanted to spend his days with her?

Yes.

A tear slipped down her cheek, and then another.

What was she going to do now? She'd been ready to buy the building downtown, sell Natalie her company and live happily ever after here.

She'd already lost so much. To lose this dream of coming back, of starting a new business venture, was hard. But losing the hope she'd finally found the man to spend her life with—someone who shared her values, who loved the ranch like it was his own—she didn't think she'd recover from this. She just wanted to curl up with Banjo and sleep for days.

Daddy always kept a blanket on the top shelf of his closet. She went into his room and opened the closet door. The navy blanket was folded exactly where she knew it would be. She tried to reach it, but it was too high. She jumped, snagging it so that it fell to the floor. A shoe box crashed down, spilling its contents. Photographs, cards and other papers landed on the carpet.

She crouched, picking up the card closest to her. A birthday card she'd given him. The photo next to it had been taken last year. She and Daddy were grinning like fools with his arm slung over her shoulders and her arm wrapped around his waist. A swanky restaurant in Denver was the backdrop. She clutched it, remembering the way they'd laughed that night. A folded-up square caught her eye. She unfolded the glossy paper and gasped. It was the magazine article that launched Weddings by Alexandra into fame.

Every item she touched was related to her.

A keepsake box.

Full of a father's love.

Oh, Lord, I was wrong. How could I have been so wrong? I was angry at Daddy because I thought I had let him down, that he was mad at me.

Clint's parting words came back. *He probably didn't want to burden you.*

The words rang true. Daddy had loved her. And his death hadn't been a punishment. It had been his time. Nothing she could have done would have changed it. He was in one of those rooms in Heaven, and shouldn't she be happy for him? Living in paradise instead of suffering here?

She tucked everything back into the shoe box, took the blanket back to the living room and sat on the couch next to Banjo, spreading it over them.

Had she unintentionally burdened Clint with taking Daddy's place, not just in ranch operations, but as her friend and confidant? He'd helped her through a difficult time. His quiet understanding, the way he listened had helped her heal from her father's death.

Oh, God, I think from the day Clint walked in, I expected too much from him.

A sob erupted, and she started crying again. For her dead parents. For her own lonely future. For the company she no longer wanted. For the building she wouldn't be buying. But most of all for the man she loved who couldn't see himself as valuable. The one who'd left. The one she doubted she'd ever get over.

And when her eyes were swollen and no tears were left, she stared at the Christmas tree and felt as lost as the day she'd gotten the call Daddy had died.

Chapter Fourteen

"Let me make sure I have this correct." Nash Bolton held a piece of crispy bacon in his hand. Clint sat across the table from him in the kitchen of Wade's ranch house, where he'd driven after his meltdown last night. "Lexi Harrington not only hired you but has feelings for you, and you quit and drove here?"

"Yes." It sounded stupid, but how could Clint explain?

"And you say she's going to sell her successful business in Denver to move back to Wyoming."

"Uh-huh." He wasn't thirsty, but he took a drink of coffee anyway.

"And you told her, 'no, thank you,' yesterday because…? This is the part I'm confused about."

Clint pinched the bridge of his nose. "I told you. The ranch I lost? My fault. I signed a land contract with a man I didn't know, and I lost it all."

"Yeah, yeah, you explained that." Nash's eyes always seemed to hold mischief, and now was no exception. Clint wanted to wipe the smirk right off his face. He drank the rest of his coffee instead. "Listen, man, none of us had a real dad in our lives. Big Bob did his best for us at Yearling, but the way we all survived our childhoods, it's no wonder we had big dreams and no idea how to go about getting them. I did some stupid stuff, too, Clint. You can't beat yourself up over this."

Wade walked in and poured himself a cup of joe. "Looks like I'm missing the good stuff. What exactly are you beating yourself up for, Clint?"

Clint shifted his jaw, glaring at Nash. Nash sat back and opened his arms as if to say, *Tell him.* Clint might as well get it over with. No more secrets. Not from his friends. Not from anyone. He told Wade the basics, and when he'd finished, he ran his hand through his hair. What a morning.

"I've got a lawyer friend. One of the best in the state. She'll find this guy and get your money back."

Clint shook his head. "I talked to a lawyer after I was evicted. Devon skipped town after he stopped paying his loans, and apparently he was using a fake identity. There's nothing I can do. And, to be honest, I want to keep it in my past."

"Doesn't seem to be staying in the past," Nash muttered.

"What's that?" Wade asked.

"Well, it seems our boy Clint here has a thing going on with his boss."

"Lexi?" Wade leaned back, openly interested. "Do tell."

"Nash," Clint warned.

"Yes, she's been planning weddings and gotten quite successful at it in Denver, but it seems she's pretty set on moving back to Wyoming."

"What's this have to do with Clint?" Wade asked.

"Yeah, Clint," Nash said, acting innocent. "What does this have to do with you?"

Clint slammed his mug on the counter. "I'm in love with her." He spun to face them. "There. Are you happy?"

Their shocked expressions would have made him laugh on any other day.

"Does she love you?"

He shrugged. "If she does, it's based on a lie."

Nash raised his finger, leaning toward Wade. "Last night he told her about how he lost the land, and then he quit."

"You don't want a woman who is going to hold every mistake you make against you," Wade said. "Good riddance."

"She didn't hold it against me. *I* hold it against me."

"So you have reason to believe she cares for you, but you quit because of a mistake you made five years ago?"

"Yes." He pressed the heel of his hand into his eyebrow. "No. I don't know. She doesn't know me. Not the real me."

"Oh, ho!" Nash chuckled. "How many Clint Romines are there?"

"Nash," Wade scolded. "Clint, you're the quietest man I know. Always have been. You're kind of a mystery. But you're also the most loyal, honest, hardworking, humble man I know."

Wade thought that about him? Clint had to swallow the emotion building inside him.

"Hey, what about me?" Nash pretended to be hurt.

Wade ignored him and pointed at Clint. "There's only one you. You're genuine. The real deal."

"I want to believe it. As a kid I felt so worthless,

and—" Saying the word *worthless* choked him up. He shook his head, unable to continue.

"Me too." Nash's expression was sober, his eyes stone cold. "That's exactly the word I would use. *Worthless*."

Wade raised his eyebrows, took a sip of coffee and sighed. "I didn't just feel worthless. I *was* worthless."

Understanding knotted them together.

The mortar binding Clint's heart crumbled into dust.

"You were never worthless." Clint stared at Wade. Then he turned his attention to Nash. "And *you* were never worthless."

Nash squirmed in his chair.

"And I'm not worthless, either."

Wade crossed to Clint and pulled him into a side hug. Nash joined them and gave Clint a half embrace and a slap on the back before wiping under his eye with the back of his hand.

"You're my best friends," Clint said. "My brothers."

"You know it, brother." Nash pumped his fist in the air.

"So what are you going to do now?" Wade sat back down, and Nash and Clint followed.

He pictured Lexi, so anguished and angry last night, and he shook his head. "I don't know."

"You love her," Wade reiterated.

"Yep."

"She loves you?" Nash asked.

"I'm not sure."

"Well, tell us everything, and don't leave anything out." Nash crossed his arms over his chest.

What did he have to lose? He'd already turned his back on it all. "Well, it started in November…"

An hour later, they still sat around the table but in

complete silence. Clint had finished telling them everything.

"What makes you think you could have gotten better prices for the calves?" Wade asked. Clint should have figured he'd home in on the business stuff. Wade had built an empire complete with a working dude ranch, thousands of acres of land, a horse-breeding business and anything else that could make him money. The guy was a genius, and he'd done it all on his own. "That's the same price I got for mine."

Clint raised his eyebrows. He hadn't realized that.

"As far as the drunk kid, you couldn't have prevented it." Nash thumped his knuckles on the table. "Trust me. I know. My mother snuck around, stealing, drinking, drugging. No one could stop her. Still can't. I'm sure she's either in jail or smoking crack as we speak. You did the right thing, getting the cops involved."

"Sounds like you have some mighty thin excuses about why you can't be with Lexi." Wade sucked on a toothpick.

What had Lexi said last night? *Go cut yourself off from everyone. It's easier, isn't it? Then you don't have to take a chance and get your heart broken again.*

"I think you're right," Clint said. "I don't know love. I don't know how to do it. I'm scared of messing up."

Nash looked thoughtful. "What makes Lexi happy?"

That was easy. "Weddings. She loves planning them. And the building in Sweet Dreams—she's got all these ideas for it. She loves riding her horse, Nugget. And she gets all sparkly, like she's been dipped in glitter, when she's shopping for candles or jewelry. She loves decorating, and she misses her dad something fierce."

Wade and Nash exchanged shocked looks. "You need to go back. Tell her you love her."

"It's not enough."

"Sure, it is," Nash said.

"No, you don't understand. She deserves more."

"Then give it to her." Wade flourished his hand. "Buy the woman a ring. If you need money, I've got you covered."

"I've got money. Haven't spent more than two nickels since losing my land. It just piled up in the bank." In the past, Wade's offer would have embarrassed Clint, but today it made him grateful. "She's so generous. She makes other people's dreams come true for a living. She deserves to be swept off her feet. Dazzled."

Nash leaned forward. "How are you going to do it?"

"I'm going to need some help."

Lexi steeped a cup of tea and bent to pet Banjo, who looked up at her with what seemed to be hope. "I know you miss him. I do, too."

She'd finally drifted into a restless sleep around three in the morning and hadn't gotten out of bed until after noon. She'd yet to change out of her pajamas. What was the point?

Sitting cross-legged on the couch with the blanket nestled over her, she let the cup of tea warm her hands.

She needed a new life plan.

Did she still want to live on the ranch?

Maybe.

If she never saw Clint again, would she still want to live in Sweet Dreams and buy the building?

Maybe.

If she did see Clint again, would she want to live in Sweet Dreams?

She didn't know if her heart could handle bumping into him the way they'd left things, but if they made up…

Forget it. Not happening.

In any scenario, with Clint or without him, did she want to return to Denver and continue planning weddings there?

No.

Hmm…the suddenness of the no surprised her. Looked like she could cross one option off her list. She'd call Natalie later and fax her the proposal the lawyer had drawn up.

I want it all. I want to buy the building and renovate it into an elegant reception hall and plan weddings here. I want Clint back. I want him to manage the ranch with me as his wife.

Despair weighed on her.

She'd questioned Clint's feelings for her, but the past two months had said it all. Love was making a stranger soup when she was dead tired from grief over her father's death. Love was fixing her faucet and checking her fireplace to make sure she was safe. Love was driving her to church and playing pretend wedding at the building she'd asked him to inspect.

Love didn't have to be grand and sweeping.

Love had stared her in the face, taken care of her ranch, her employees, her horses and even her dog.

And what had she given him in return?

Maybe Clint couldn't see his value, but she did. The Bible passage she'd read the other day came to mind. *Do nothing out of selfish ambition or vain conceit.*

All her thoughts had been centering around her wants. What did Clint want? What did he need?

A ranch of his own.

An idea hit her so suddenly, she almost gasped.

Lord, I don't know. This is extreme. Even for me.

When she thought of all she'd been given over the years, though—parents who loved her, this loving home, not one worry about money—the idea didn't seem so extreme.

Maybe she was always meant to be the maker of grand gestures. No one deserved one more than Clint.

And she was going to give him one. No strings attached.

Really, Lord? I want to do Your will. Not my own.

Pulling up the Bible app on her phone, she typed in Philippians chapter two and read the entire thing. Then she came back to the fourth verse. *Rather, in humility value others above yourselves, not looking to your own interests but each of you to the interests of others.* She jumped up and ran to her bedroom. Threw on jeans and a sweater. Then she hurried downstairs, pulled on a coat and jogged to the ranch office.

"Jerry?" She stopped short in the doorway, trying to catch her breath.

"Miss Lexi? Get in here. You look as spooked as the horses before a lightning storm. What happened?"

"I need some advice."

His wide-eyed expression held fear. "I don't know. I'm not the best person for that."

"Clint left. He told me he was putting in his two weeks and he left."

"I was wonderin' where he went off to. Logan said his truck was gone."

"I want him back."

"Well, I reckon we all want him back. Why'd he quit? Those goings-on the other night?"

"I love him."

Jerry just about fell off his stool.

"I scared him away, Jerry. And he had a terrible childhood, got swindled out of the only thing he ever wanted, and he has all this misplaced guilt about catching Jake drinking on the job."

"Well, seems there's a lot of suds in the bucket, missy." Jerry rubbed his chin. "What makes you think you scared him off?"

"I… Well…" She hunched over like a truant schoolgirl. "I'm me. I'm too intense, and I pushed him into feelings he probably didn't want, and—"

"He might not have wanted those feelings, but he had them, and it wasn't due to you pushing or whatnot. He loves you. It was as clear as the signs a cow's about to give birth."

She grimaced. Love was similar to a cow going into labor? *Ew.* She shook her head. "I ruined it. I got pretty mad, and I yelled some things, and, well, I told him to get out."

"Before or after he quit?" He appeared deep in thought.

"After. Why?"

"Okay. I think we can work with that. Yes, sirree, I think we can."

Work with what?

"See here, Clint's like the moose. He's a loner, but strong, and sometimes moose—"

"Jerry, I'm sorry, but I don't have the brains to figure out the moose analogy today." She took a seat on the stool next to him. "Without Clint, what happens to this ranch?"

He frowned, shaking his head. "I don't know, sweetheart. You'll have to hire someone else, I guess."

"What if I didn't? I got this crazy idea, and I need to know your opinion."

"Shoot."

She explained it as best she could, and for the next twenty minutes she and Jerry volleyed questions and answers back and forth. Then Jerry grinned.

"If you go through with this and that boy doesn't get on his knees and beg you to marry him, I'll kick him straight in the keister, and you can count on that."

"I'm not doing this to get a proposal, Jerry." She hopped off the stool to leave. "I'm doing this because it's right. For Clint. For the ranch. Do you think Daddy would have approved?"

"Yes. I do. He'd want to see the ranch taken care of, and he'd want you to be protected financially. You're a smart 'un, Miss Lexi."

She hugged him tightly. "Thanks, Jerry. I don't know what I'd do without you."

Chapter Fifteen

Christmas Eve morning arrived with a fresh fall of snow and gentle flakes floating in the air. Clint opened the sliding door to the old shed.

"Thanks for helping me, Jerry." Clint clapped him on the shoulder. "We'll have to move out the old hay wagon first."

"Just glad to have you back." His big grin looked like it held a secret. "Miss Lexi is going to like this."

"Well, I'm glad you think so. I've got some apologies to make. I hope she'll hear me out."

"Something tells me she'll be all ears." They moved inside. "She's like a filly. High-strung with a heart of gold. Spirit. And class…"

Clint tuned out the filly talk and dragged the tarp off the sleigh. All day yesterday he and Wade and Nash had planned, shopped and prepped for this. The first hurdle had been driving into Rock Step Ranch undetected this morning. Since he'd arrived at 5:00 a.m., he'd made it without seeing Lexi. He'd called Jerry last night and asked for his help this morning. Thankfully, the man agreed without giving Clint a lecture.

"I'll be right back. Charger can pull these out faster than we can." Jerry pivoted to leave. "In the meantime, you get the sleigh cleaned up. The missus sent some blankets for the ride."

"Okay." As Clint polished the sleigh, he reviewed the plan. He needed to shower and get dressed. The flowers were in his fridge. And the other item was safely tucked away in the cabin. His heartbeat had been tapping out Morse code distress signals for hours, but he figured that was his body resisting the threat of laying his soul bare.

He *would* lay his soul bare.

Soon.

It didn't take long to get the sleigh cleaned up. He ran back to his cabin, his nerves still jittery. After showering, he was buttoning his dress shirt when he heard a knock on the door.

He answered it and stopped breathing. Lexi stood before him with her hair in waves down her shoulders. She wore a black jacket, revealing a red dress that hugged her body. Black heels made her seem taller, more sophisticated than he was used to, and her makeup accented her eyes.

"You're beautiful."

She blinked. "Thank you. Jerry told me you were here. Can I come in?"

She looked nervous, and the way she briefly touched her ear before nodding made him want to reassure her. "Let's go to the living room." He took her jacket and draped it over the back of a chair.

Banjo followed her inside, sat at Clint's feet and let out a yowl.

"I missed you, too, buddy." He patted his head.

Lexi handed him a slim folder. A slither of unease went down his spine. What was this?

"Go ahead. Open it."

Warily, he obliged. He drew his eyebrows together as he realized it was a partnership agreement. His head swam. This couldn't be what he thought it was. He'd read it wrong, or she'd been fooled by an attorney. It didn't make sense.

"No way." He snapped the folder shut, handing it back to her. How could she even think to give up her inheritance? After all he'd confessed…

"I want you to run this ranch, but not as my employee, as part owner. I'll be a silent partner. Rock Step Ranch will be yours to run, to manage, to live on. I'll take a portion of the profit. You would never have to see me." Her brown eyes pleaded with him to understand, but he didn't. He only knew one thing. The woman standing before him was better than anyone he'd ever met. He loved her with an intensity he'd never thought possible.

"I don't want this ranch," he said. "I can't believe you'd even think to do this. This is your inheritance, your home. It belongs to you. I could never let you give it away."

Her eyes filled with tears. He was messing this up. It wasn't what he'd planned. He'd never imagined she would show up and blow him away with this incredible offer.

"I'm sorry, Lexi. The other night—you were right. About everything." Her perfume drifted to him, and it was all he could do not to crush her to him. "I did push you away, and I was stuck in my past. I never thought someone like you would look twice at me. And from the moment you hired me, I was attracted to you. I knew it wasn't smart, but I couldn't help being drawn to you."

"I didn't help with that." She looked at the floor. "I was so lonely. I pushed you into spending time with me."

"You didn't have to push hard. Those times we spent together are precious to me. No matter what happens, I will hold onto them forever."

"What do you think is going to happen?" She wrapped her arms around her waist.

"I don't know. But I know this. I love you. I think it's the coolest thing that you plan weddings for a living. You bless so many people. I feel like you live to make people's dreams come true. When you decorated my cabin for Christmas—I was blown away. You're smart and kind and honest and true. I'm not the romantic guy you deserve, but I want to be your tiger. Do you know what I'm saying?"

Lexi couldn't stop her lips from wobbling. Clint looked like he'd stepped out of a men's magazine. She couldn't stop staring. At first she thought he was turning down her offer because he was set on leaving, but... had he just said he loved her? "I know what you're saying. I'm sorry, too, Clint. I pushed you. Expected you to be everything here—the manager, my confidant, even my handyman—"

"I wanted to be all those things."

"But I never thought about how it affected you."

"It affected me in the best way it could. You showed me what love looks like. Your friendship—you gave it to me freely without questions or strings."

"I needed you." Tears threatened again.

"I've never been needed. Not by anyone. Do you know how great it is to be needed?" He gently clasped her arms. "I'd been trapped in nothingness for years, and working here, meeting you, spending time with you was like breathing fresh air after being locked in prison. Thank you."

"I still need you." She touched his cheek.

His eyes darkened. "You do?"

"Yes. I love you, too, Clint." She blinked. "But I don't want to trap you. You gave me my life back, my smile, my joy. You helped me make peace with Daddy's death. And you never asked for anything in return."

"You'd already given me the world."

"I love you, Clint, and that's why I had these papers drawn up. You deserve your own ranch."

"I don't want any ranch unless you come with it." He hurried to the kitchen, grabbed the roses and came back, handing them to her. "This wasn't how I planned it, but these are for you."

"Blush colored." She inhaled their scent. "My favorite. How did you know?"

"Well, the silky squares in your office are all pink." Clint took her hand in his and dropped to one knee. "Alexandra Harrington, I love you. I don't deserve you, will never deserve you, but I'll do my best to make you happy every day of your life. Will you do me the honor of marrying me?"

He reached into his pocket, took out a square jeweler's box and opened it. The diamond engagement ring she'd swooned over in Sweet Dreams Jewelers winked at her. She covered her mouth with her hand, shaking her head in wonder. "How did you know? It's the exact one I picked out, but I never told anyone."

"I saw it and knew. It was you." He still looked up at her. "Well?"

"Yes!" She drew him to his feet. "A million times, yes!"

He tenderly slipped the ring on her finger and tugged her into his arms. Then he bent his head and claimed her lips. Her knees wobbled as she sank into his kiss.

When he broke away, he smiled, pressing his forehead to hers. Her cell phone rang. Lexi checked it and grinned. She had to take this call.

"I'm at your house with the puppy," Dan Smith said. "Should I come back later?"

"No. Drive to the cabins. I'll meet you out front." She ended the call and spun to face Clint. "I have a surprise for you, too. Come on." She opened the door and stood on his porch.

He followed, a questioning look on his face.

Dan parked his truck and approached them with a border collie puppy in his hands. "Hope I didn't come too early. Lola's got a ham in the oven, and she'll have my head if I don't deliver this before our guests arrive for supper."

"Thank you so much, Dan. Please tell Lola merry Christmas for me."

"Will do. Merry Christmas, Lexi. Sure is nice to have you back."

Lexi held the wiggly black-and-white fluff ball and turned, almost crashing into Clint.

"This is for you, tiger." She grinned, holding the puppy out to him. "Your first puppy. All yours. Merry Christmas."

To her surprise, his eyes welled up. He took the dog in his arms and cradled it. "I can't believe you got me a dog. My own dog. No one has ever gotten me a gift like this."

"You needed a dog."

"I don't know what to say. Thank you." He drew her into his embrace, the puppy between them, and kissed her. "I love you, sugar."

"I couldn't love you more, tiger."

He looked like he was going to kiss her again, but he checked his watch. "Wait here. Get your jacket on. I'll be back in a few minutes." He handed her the dog, yanked a coat out of the closet and ran up the drive.

What was that all about? Not knowing what to think, she set the puppy down. He and Banjo sniffed each other as she eased into her jacket. The sound of bells reached her ears, and she peeked out the window.

Clint drove the horse-drawn sleigh. She scooped up the puppy and raced outside. He stopped the horses, jumped down and kissed her. Thoroughly.

"Your ride, my lady." He gestured to the sleigh.

"Oh, Clint, I used to love riding around with Daddy and Mama."

"You don't mind riding around with me? I don't want you to be sad." He helped her onto the bench next to him and covered her, Banjo and the puppy with blankets.

"I want nothing more than to ride around with you." She stared into his eyes. "Thank you, Clint."

He grinned. "That's tiger to you."

She laughed. "Well, the tiger I know would have some mistletoe ready for this moment."

Clint lifted a sprig of mistletoe above her head.

"Way ahead of you, sugar."

Epilogue

He'd been engaged just shy of a year, but married life beckoned. Clint reached for Lexi's hand, squeezed it and reached for the handle of the church door.

"We're married." His gaze swept from the white veil and tiara on top of her shiny dark hair down her beautiful wedding gown until stopping at their joined hands, two rings sparkling on their fingers.

"We are. We're finally married." She looked up at him with a massive smile. He opened the door and helped her down the church steps.

Fat snowflakes drifted to the ground, and at the end of the sidewalk, Coco and Charger stamped their feet, waiting to pull the sleigh with the Just Married sign attached to the back. Wedding guests congratulated them as they hurried down the sidewalk.

He helped her up, still in shock that she was actually his. Jerry had done the honors of escorting her down the aisle. *Thank You, Lord. I lost a run-down piece of property, but I gained a wife and the best ranch in Wyoming. My wildest dreams couldn't have come up with this.*

Clint drove the sleigh past snow-covered pines on the country lane that led into town.

"When we get back from our honeymoon," Lexi said, settling under the blankets, "we'll have to call the ranch in Idaho and tell them we have the hay they need for their horses."

"No ranch business today, Mrs. Romine." He grinned at her. "We agreed."

"But Daddy's dream—we did it." She hooked her arm under his and leaned against his shoulder.

"He'd be proud of you." Clint smiled at her. "For the ranch and for moving your business here."

Lexi had bought the building downtown earlier this year. She insisted on keeping the name of the building the Department Store, but she had a Weddings by Alexandra sign made for the door. Their wedding reception would be the debut of the Department Store's new role as the go-to reception hall in Sweet Dreams. Together, he and Lexi had hired contractors and planned the space. All the construction and refinishing had been worth it.

The horses turned onto the side street, thankfully still snow-covered, that led to the reception.

"Are you ready to christen your building?" he asked.

"I am. Let's go!"

As soon as they arrived, Clint jumped down from the sleigh and carried Lexi into the building to a round of applause. He placed her back on her feet and whispered, "Don't be long, sugar."

She flashed him a grin and winked. Amy hustled Lexi up the stairs and out of sight. Clint couldn't stop watching her the entire time.

People were milling around on the main floor, soft music filled the air, and his best friends Wade and Marshall clapped him on the back. The only one missing was Nash, who had called Clint two days ago sounding devastated, explaining he had an emergency and couldn't come to the wedding.

"I couldn't be happier for you, tiger." Dottie dabbed her eyes and gave him a long hug.

"Let the boy up for air." Big Bob pulled her back then shook Clint's hand. "Congratulations, son."

"Ladies and gentlemen, direct your attention to the stairs." Wade held the microphone.

Clint took his spot—the same spot he'd stood in almost a year ago—and held his breath as Lexi descended. She'd never been prettier, and the mischievous smile on her face told him she was remembering their moment, too. She lifted her skirt as she came down, her other hand trailing the railing.

When she reached the second step from the bottom, Clint swung her off her feet, twirling her until she stood before him. Everyone cheered.

"You mesmerize me, sugar."

"You're pretty easy on the eyes yourself, tiger." She wound her arms around his neck. "What are you going to do now?"

"Well, there is mistletoe."

She looked up. A branch of mistletoe hung from the ceiling.

"You're pretty sly, tiger," she whispered. "Why don't you show me what you've got?"

He didn't need to be asked twice. He kissed her, the first in a lifetime of mistletoe kisses.

"Anything for you, sugar."

* * * * *

THE RANCHER'S
CHRISTMAS BRIDE

Brenda Minton

And we know that God causes everything to work together for the good of those who love God and are called according to His purpose for them.
—*Romans* 8:28

Chapter One

When memories crashed in on Alex Palermo, he drove. He never thought about a destination. He only knew that if he rolled down his truck windows, played some cowboy country on the radio and prayed, the memories would fade and so would the guilt. The praying part happened to be a new addition to the process. Pastor Matthews of the Bluebonnet Community Church had insisted he try it.

They'd joked that real men can eat quiche. Real men can pray. They can even cry every once in a while. As long as it didn't become habit. They'd fist-bumped and joked over that.

On a cool day in December, Texas Hill Country wasn't at its warmest. But the breeze coming through the open windows of his truck helped to clear his mind. He'd been doing really well, but tonight, maybe because it was almost ten years to the day since he'd killed his father, the memories had resurfaced with a vengeance.

No, he hadn't really killed his father. Deep down he knew that he hadn't. But for years he'd told himself he was responsible for the death of Jesse Palermo. In reality, alcohol and a mean bull had killed Alex's father.

Earlier, standing in the arena where his father had drawn a bull rope   and his last breath—Alex had been hard put to remember that it hadn't been his fault his dad had gotten on that bull.

The tires of his truck hummed on the pavement. He took a deep breath and turned up the radio. As if he could outrun the pain.

A few miles out of Bluebonnet Springs, he hit the brakes. Because either he'd gone crazy, or ahead of him, on the shoulder of the road, was a woman in a wedding dress. The last thing he wanted was a bride, even someone else's bride. His common sense told him to keep on driving.

Common sense told him that he had enough problems of his own without getting tied up in someone else's hard times. He'd taken off driving in the hopes of outrunning some of those problems.

Unfortunately he'd never been good at listening. His twin, Marcus, always accused him of being the good twin. He didn't know if he'd agree with that, but he supposed he must have a chivalrous side. He pulled to the shoulder just ahead and got out of his truck. The woman was definitely real. And wearing a wedding dress. As if on cue, it started to rain. Steady, big drops. The kind of rain that danced across the pavement and soaked a person's clothing.

"Need a lift?" he asked, hoping they could get back in the dry warmth of his truck soon.

Better yet, she could tell him she had a ride already on the way to pick her up. But a bride without a groom?

That didn't exactly spell wedding bells and happily-ever-after.

"I'm fine." She said it with her chin raised a notch, even as the rain picked up pace. He was losing objectivity because that little lift of her chin showed some pride and big eyes that rivaled the stormy sky.

"Ri-i-i-ght." He said it slowly. Did he point out to her that she was miles from anywhere, wearing a wedding dress and standing in the rain?

"You can go on. I know where I'm going."

He looked around, at the open fields, pastures full of cattle and nothing else. He glanced back at her and grinned, because they both knew she was bluffing.

"I know we're taught from the time we're little not to get in the car with a stranger. But I think even your mama would want you to get in out of the rain."

Hands up so she could see them, he took a step toward her.

She reached for the bag slung over her shoulder. "Don't come any closer. I'm armed."

He glanced at the bag and the object pointing through the thin cotton. "With a high-heeled shoe?"

"I'm warning you." She issued the command with a startling amount of conviction as rain poured down from the steel-gray sky. She was a tiny thing with a pixie face and a massive amount of brown hair piled on top of her head.

Rain dripped down her face and she swiped it away with her shoulder. That chivalrous side of him kicked into gear. He jerked off his jean jacket and held it out to her. She eyed it the way a stray kitten eyed a bowl of milk, but didn't take it.

"Well, I'm not really worried you'll shoot me with

a shoe." He grinned as he said it, hoping to put her at ease. "But I do think we're both in trouble if we don't get out of this rain. I'm not going to hurt you, I just want to get you off the road."

The rain picked up and he saw her shiver. Her feet were bare. So were her arms. She took another swipe at the water dripping down her face. She eyed the jacket and his truck.

"Listen, we could stand here all night or I can just literally pick you up and put you in my truck." He did not want to do that. She looked like the kind of female that once a man had her in his arms, he'd want to hold her forever.

He didn't do forever.

For a full minute she stood there facing him, then she nodded, giving in. He hurried ahead of her to open the passenger door of the truck. As she struggled to get her skirts under control, he took her hand and helped her in.

That hand was like a frail bird's, cold and fine-boned. He held it gently, afraid he'd hurt her.

"Are we on the way to the church? Or do you have somewhere else you'd like me to take you?" he asked as he climbed behind the wheel of his truck.

Huddled in the seat, her teeth chattered. He turned up the heat.

"Do you know Dan Wilson?" she asked, hugging herself for warmth.

"Yeah, I know Dan."

"Could you take me to his house?"

He tried again to give her his jacket. This time she took it, sniffing at the collar before settling it over her bare arms.

"It's clean," he said, a little defensively.

"I know, I just…" She shrugged a bit and looked sheepish. "I'm sorry. It's been a long day. If you could take me to Dan's…"

"I can, but do you know what you're getting yourself into?"

She gave him a puzzled look. "No, I guess not."

"Dan isn't the most pleasant guy in the world. He's been sick and that's made him extra cranky."

"I'm his granddaughter."

He had pulled onto the road so he shot her a quick look. "Seriously? I mean, not that you can't be. But I didn't know Dan even had a granddaughter."

"He hasn't seen my mom since she was a little girl. I tried to get him to come to the wedding…" She let the words trail off as her gaze slid to the window. A delicate finger brushed across her cheek.

Tears. He'd never been good with tears. He had two sisters and fortunately neither of them was the type to cry. The Palermo siblings had learned the hard way that tears didn't help. In fact, sometimes tears made it worse.

His dad hadn't invented the warning "Do you want me to give you something to cry about?" but he'd definitely put action to the words. He'd put the words into action the night he'd locked Lucy in the tack room of their barn. He had put the words into action the night he'd punched Marcus in the throat. They'd all learned not to cry and they'd learned not to tell.

But that had nothing to do with now and the lady sitting beside him wanting a ride to Dan's.

"None of my business, but does Dan know you're coming? I don't think he'd take kindly to a surprise family reunion."

From the look on her face, a grim mixture of worry

and sadness, she wasn't amused by his poor attempt at humor. Some things just weren't that funny. And a bride that was walking down a back road, still in her wedding dress, pretending a shoe was a weapon? He guessed she'd had a pretty rough day.

The road was bumpy, but as they bounced along he managed to open the glove compartment and pull out a box of tissues.

"I'm not going to cry," she insisted. But a few tears trickled down her cheeks.

"I guess I don't have a right to ask what happened. But if you need to talk, I'm all ears." He glanced in the mirror. "Seriously, have you ever seen ears this big?"

She glanced at him and burst into watery laughter, shaking her head as she surveyed his ears.

"They aren't *that* big," she countered. At least he'd made her laugh. He'd always been good for a laugh. And not much more.

"He picked the caterer," she said quietly into the darkened interior of the truck. Her voice was soft, kind of sweet.

The windshield wipers clicked as they swept back and forth, and Chris LeDoux was singing "Cadillac Ranch." Alex cleared his throat and shot her another quick look.

"Who picked the caterer? You mean you let him decide what to feed the guests and you're upset about that? I think you'd need a bigger reason to walk out on a wedding."

She shook her head vehemently. "No, he picked the caterer."

He pulled to the side of the road because he couldn't focus on the road and a conversation that seemed important. She fingered the sleeve of the jean jacket and her gaze slid to the window.

"He picked the caterer," she said with meaning. "Not the chicken or the beef—the caterer. He picked her. Over me."

She pinched the bridge of her nose, closed her eyes and breathed. The tears disappeared but they'd left streaks down her cheeks. They'd left marks, the way this wedding would leave marks, he knew with certainty.

Another reason he was single and planned to stay that way. People had a tendency to hurt one another. His dad had hurt everyone in his path. His mom had walked out on her own children.

He shifted and pulled back onto the road, trying to find the right thing to say. A few minutes later he drove into Dan Wilson's driveway.

"I'm sorry," he told her, knowing his apology wasn't the one that mattered. She'd been left at the altar by the man she had planned to spend her life with. He could tell her hard lessons about being let down by people who should have cared, but she didn't need to hear it from him.

He'd let down people, too. He'd let down his siblings. He'd let down his best friend. He guessed he'd let down himself a few times, too. That made him the last person who could really help the woman sitting next to him in the dim light of his truck. He reached to turn down the radio and told himself it didn't mean a thing. This moment would pass, like so many moments in his life. For these few minutes, though, maybe he could be her hero, the person she could count on.

"He was a fool. If he picked the caterer, he didn't deserve you." He parked next to Dan's old farm truck.

She leaned across the truck in a rustle of white satin

and lace and kissed his cheek. "Thank you. I don't even know your name, but thank you."

He held out his hand. "Alex Palermo, at your service."

She took his hand and again he was surprised by the way it felt, as if he should cherish the moment a little longer. "Marissa Walker."

The rain was steady now and the light of early evening had given way to darkness. She peered through the windshield and frowned. "Is that my grandfather's home?"

Alex glanced away from the bride sitting next to him and nodded as he looked at the little camper, hay bales stacked underneath to keep out the winter wind. "That's Dan's place."

"He lives in a camper?"

"For as long as I've known him. He's always been ornery and he's always lived in this camper. Don't let it fool you. He's one of the best horse trainers in the country and he raises some mighty fine Angus cattle."

A gunshot split the night, ending the conversation. The woman sitting next to him screamed. "He's shooting at us!"

"Nah," he said with a grin. "He's just warning us to get off his land."

Marissa couldn't help it; she cowered in the seat, close to the cowboy. He was a stranger, but at the moment he was the only thing she had to hold on to. The day was catching up with her. She'd been awake since sunrise, because it was her wedding day and there'd been so much to get done. And then she'd stood in the dressing room of the wedding venue waiting for Aidan. And waiting. Until he sent the text that he was on his way to Hawaii. With Linda, the caterer. Unable to face her family and friends, she'd taken off with the limousine, leaving her mom a note that she needed time.

The limousine had broken down and the driver had told her he was done. The tow truck would take him back to the city and she was on her own unless she wanted to go to Austin.

And now this. Her grandfather was a madman with a gun.

The cowboy sitting next to her rolled down his window and leaned out. "Dan, stop shooting. You're a little shaky these days and you might accidentally shoot someone."

"Is that you, Alex?"

"Yeah, it's me. And you don't usually shoot at me when I pull up."

"Cattle thieves have hauled off three of my best heifers, Alex. I ain't taking no chances."

"Yeah, but I'm your neighbor, not a cattle thief. And I've got your granddaughter in the truck with me. This isn't the best way to introduce yourself."

That was her cue. Marissa got out and walked tentatively through the dark and the mud to the front of the truck, where headlights illuminated the trailer and the man standing on the rickety porch. She glanced around, looking for the cowboy, and he was there, joining her. He grinned and winked and she felt as if he was her lifeline for the time being. A stranger with dark flashing eyes, dimpled cheeks and a flirty smile. A black cowboy hat covered his head but she thought she saw dark curls peek out from beneath.

His hand touched her back, between her shoulder blades, giving her strength to move forward.

"I'm Marissa. I'm your granddaughter."

Her grandfather leaned against the porch as a fit of coughing hit. She wanted to tell him they'd be better off inside, but she wasn't sure yet that it was true. Or even that he'd let her inside. Her grandmother had walked out on him, taking his only child, Marissa's mom. He probably wasn't going to feel too charitable to his only grandchild.

"I thought you were getting married today," he said, surprising her. "What are you doing here?"

"I wanted to meet you." She couldn't very well tell him that she was twenty-six and she'd basically run away from home. That she'd run from a wedding that would have been the social embarrassment of the decade.

"You wanted to meet me?" He barked out a harsh laugh. "On your wedding day? Where's your groom?"

"Hawaii."

"Shouldn't you be with him?" he asked, his voice softening a bit.

"I would have been if he hadn't left with the caterer."

He sighed. "That's too bad. But that doesn't explain why you're here."

She bit down on her lip, unsure of what she should say. "I need a place to stay."

"I'm sure you have a home and parents to go to."

"Dan, it's just for a night," Alex Palermo said with a confident tone as he winked at Marissa.

She hadn't said a thing about it being for just one night.

Dan's hand was on the doorknob of the camper. "I don't have an extra bed. And I don't think a princess like her, in a dress that cost more than this camper, is going to want to stay here."

"I *do* want to stay." She took a few cautious steps forward.

"You don't have to," Alex said out of the corner of his mouth. "We can find somewhere else for you to stay."

"Didn't you hear the girl, Alex? She's my granddaughter. She's welcome to sleep on the couch. Tonight." Her grandfather started to take a step inside but he wobbled a bit.

Alex hurried up the steps and steadied the older man. Marissa watched, unsure.

"Dan, are you okay?" Alex asked.

"I'm fine." Marissa's grandfather shook loose from the hand that steadied him. "A little light-headed from this cold. Get on in out of the rain, girl."

"You're sure about this?" Alex asked again.

"I'm sure," she answered. Nervous or not, she was staying.

"Nobody's asking if *I'm* sure," her grandfather grumbled but he pushed the door open and motioned her inside. "Go on, Alex. We're fine. You can come by tomorrow and check on her."

Alex gave her one last look and left, walking down the rickety steps and across the muddy yard to his truck. She watched him go and then she stepped inside the camper and the door closed them in.

She heard the truck start, and her last chance to escape was driving off into the rain-soaked night, leaving her with a less-than-welcoming stranger. She peeked out the window, saw brake lights on the truck and smiled, because, unlike her groom, he wasn't leaving without a second thought. And it felt good to know that a stranger, someone who didn't have to care, did.

Chapter Two

Something heavy stretched out on Marissa's legs. She tried to move and it growled long and low. She froze, peeking up at the bloodhound that stretched across her. The movement brought another soft noise from the animal—it wasn't quite threatening, but was more of a warning growl. She looked up at the ceiling as another wave of something that felt like grief washed over her.

Today she should have woken up in Hawaii. She should be Mrs. Aidan Dean. Instead she was on her grandfather's couch somewhere outside Bluebonnet Springs, Texas. Sometime in the night she'd decided she would never again play the fool. She would be stronger. More independent. She wouldn't back down or give up. Aidan had hurt her badly. But he hadn't broken her.

At least her grandfather had given her a place to stay the night. Last night, after Alex Palermo had left, they'd eaten bologna sandwiches in silence as he watched a game show. After the show ended he'd declared it bedtime. He'd tossed her a quilt and a pillow before he headed to his room. At the door he'd warned her about Bub, without telling her who Bub might be.

She guessed that Bub was the dog stretched out next to her.

"Get down," she insisted. Bub just sprawled a little more and rested his head on her belly. "No, really, I don't like dogs. Go," she muttered, moving her legs. Bub growled again but nestled in closer.

She closed her eyes to regroup and must have dozed off again. A rooster crowed, something banged loudly against the roof and she jumped. Bub rolled off the sofa. He landed with a thud, shook his entire body and stared at her with meaningful contempt in his sad eyes. Marissa ignored him as she got to her feet and looked around.

In the light of day, the camper was small and cluttered. Magazines were stacked on tables. The kitchen was just a tiny corner with a minifridge and stove, a single sink and a few cabinets. A mirror hung on a closet door. She took a cautious peek at the woman in the reflection. The woman looking back at her had long hair that hung in a tangled knot. The wedding dress, a monstrous creation with too many sequins and ruffles, was wrinkled and stained. She didn't know herself. Maybe once, a long time ago, she'd known what she wanted. She might have had her own dreams. But over the years she'd lost sight of the dreamer, the achiever, and she'd fought hard to become the person her parents wanted her to be. She'd lost herself.

When she left the wedding venue and headed for Bluebonnet Springs yesterday, that might have been an awakening. A rediscovery of the girl she'd left behind.

Looking back, she realized nothing about this wedding had been her choice, her style. The wedding venue, the dress, the flowers and the cake had all been picked by her mother. Guilt had robbed her of the ability to speak up for herself. She was her mother's only child. This would have been her mom's only wedding to plan. And on every last thing, Marissa had conceded to her mother's desires.

Because of guilt.

Looking at her hair, she realized that she'd been giving up pieces of herself for a very long time. And now, because of Aidan, it was time to start taking back some of her independence.

She headed for the kitchen and rummaged through drawers until she found what she was looking for. She pulled out the clips and pins from her hair, then grabbed it up, leaned forward and cut it with scissors she'd found in a junk drawer.

The sound of scissors slicing through hair brought her back to reality. She looked at the long chunk of hair in her hand and straightened to look in the mirror at the ghastly sight.

"What have I done?"

Next to her the dog whined. She glanced down at the beast stretched out at her feet. He looked up at her with soulful eyes and six inches of drool hanging from his mouth.

"Did I really do that?" she asked him. In answer he put his head on his paws and closed his eyes. Of course he didn't have an opinion. She returned her attention to the rather uneven layers of hair.

She snipped away the longer pieces, shortening her hair by another two inches. She looked in the mirror and winced. Her hair was now just above her shoulders. It wasn't the best cut in the world but it felt good to be rid of the weight. She brushed it out with her fingers and then tossed the long locks she'd cut in the trash and dropped the scissors back in the drawer.

Now to find her grandfather. She opened the front door and was greeted by a sunny December day. There was a hint of chill in the air and the smell of wet earth. And no sign of Dan. She stepped back inside, leaving the door open a crack.

The camper wasn't big, maybe thirty feet in length. She walked to the hallway and peered into the empty bathroom.

"Dan? Are you here?" She took another cautious step. "Dan?"

And then she heard the coughing, the same as the previous evening, almost as if he couldn't catch his breath. She knocked on the closed bedroom door.

"Dan? Are you okay?"

The coughing fit lasted a few more seconds. "I'm fine. Can't you leave a man in peace?"

"Not if he sounds like he might need help," she said through the closed door. "Do you need help?"

"No, I don't need help. Not unless you plan to feed livestock for me." Through the thin door she heard a raspy chuckle.

"Okay. I think I can do that."

"You don't know a cow from a bull." He began coughing again.

"Do you need a doctor?"

"Call your folks and tell them to come get you," he said at the end of the spell, his breathing sounding off, even through the door.

"I texted them yesterday but my phone didn't charge last night."

"Deliver me from nosy relatives and do-gooders,"

he grumbled. But she thought he sounded pleased. Or maybe she wanted him to be pleased.

"You rest. I'll figure out the difference between a cow and a bull."

"Don't get too close to that bull or you'll be on the business end of his horns. City gals. Land sakes, they drive a man nuts."

"I'll yell if I need help." She looked down at the wedding dress. She guessed it wouldn't do any good to ask for clothes.

As she headed out the front door and down the steps, careful to avoid loose boards, something red and winged came flying at her. She jumped off the porch and ran but it kept up the chase. The dog began barking and joined the fray. Chickens scattered, squawking in protest.

The crazy thing jumped at her, claws ripping at her dress, and a vicious beak tried to grab hold. She headed for the beat-up old truck parked to the side of the driveway, and when the doors wouldn't open, she climbed in the back, the dress tangling around her legs. She fell in a heap of white, but then she scrambled to her feet, grabbing a rake that had been left in the bed of the truck.

A truck eased down the drive and stopped a dozen feet from where she stood. Through the window, even with the glare of early morning sun, she could see the cowboy from the previous evening. His wide grin was unmistakable.

The rooster must have known she'd been distracted. He flew at her again. She was ready this time and gave him a good smack with the rake. He made a stupid chicken noise as he fell to the ground, squawking and fluttering his wings.

Alex Palermo got out of his truck, shaking his head

and smirking just a little. She probably looked a sight, standing there in the bed of a truck wearing her wedding dress. He didn't look like he'd slept on a sofa. No, he looked rested. As he took off his cowboy hat, she saw his hair was dark and curly. His ears really were a little too big. It was good to know he wasn't perfect. He was compact with broad shoulders, wore jeans that fit easy on his trim waist and had a grin that would melt a girl's heart. Any girl but her.

Her heart was off-limits. Out of order. No longer available.

"It looks like you've killed Dan's rooster," Alex glanced at the rooster and then raised his gaze to hers. "Want down from there?"

She peeked over the side of the truck, where the rooster had regained his footing. "The rooster looks very much alive to me."

He flashed a smile, revealing those dimples again. "Yeah, I was teasing. He's a little stunned. I doubt he's ever been knocked out with a rake."

"Stop," she warned. "That rooster had it coming. And the dog is going down next."

"What did Bub ever do to you?" He held out a hand for her. "Come on down now, you'll be fine. I'll protect you."

But who would protect her from all of that cowboy charm? He was cute and he knew how to make a girl feel rescued without making her feel weak. She took his hand and managed to climb over the tailgate of the truck without getting tangled up in the massive white skirts. If she'd had her choice she would have picked a slim-fitting dress that didn't overwhelm her five-foot frame.

"My grandfather is sick," she told him once she was on the ground.

"Dan has emphysema," Alex explained and then he held out a bag. "I guess someone will be here to get you today, but I borrowed some clothes from my sister. They'll be a little bit big on you but I'd imagine you'd like to get out of that dress."

"Thank you." She held the bag and looked back at the camper. "I told him I'd feed his livestock."

His eyes twinkled. "Did you now? And do you know how to feed livestock?"

"I'll figure it out."

"I don't doubt that a bit. But I'll help you. I usually try to check on Dan every few days, since he hasn't had anyone else."

Her grandfather didn't have anyone. Of course he didn't. She hadn't even known about him until her grandmother passed away the previous summer. There were family secrets and hurt feelings. She got all of that. But Dan deserved family. He needed family.

"Oh, city girl, I wouldn't get that look in my eyes if I were you."

She glanced up at the man standing in front of her, watching her with his steady gaze. "What look?"

"The look that says you think Old Dan needs rescuing. He won't take kindly to that."

"But he…"

Alex held up a hand. "You just showed up and he has pride. He isn't going to let you come in here and start prodding him into submission because you're a granddaughter with a need to make up for lost time."

"But he's sick," she sputtered. "And I *am* his granddaughter."

"Right, I get that. I'll give you some advice, before you ride in there on a white horse. Let Dan think he's helping you."

Her indignation died a quick death. "Oh."

He pointed to the bag of clothes. "Go change and I'll wait for you."

For the first time she took a good look at the place her grandfather called home. The land was flat to a point and then it met rolling, tree-covered hills. The fences sagged and the barn looked as if it was at least a century old. The camper sat in the middle of it all, a relic from decades past. Behind that was a chicken pen, the door open and the rooster now inside getting himself a drink of water but still watching her with serious intent.

"Go on," he said, and patted her shoulder. "I've learned that life has these little moments. I guess we learn from them when we can and we survive."

She saw something in him she hadn't noticed before. There was laughter on the surface, but in his dark eyes she saw pain. For a moment it was so intense, that flash of sadness, she wanted to comfort him. She shook free and stepped back. His easy smile was back in place and he winked, making her think she'd imagined it all.

Alex scrounged around in the shed, found the chicken feed and scooped out a can. As he exited the building, Marissa came out of the camper. She was dressed in his older sister's—Lucy's—jeans and a T-shirt she'd tied at the waist. Probably to keep it from hanging to her knees. The jeans were tucked into the boots he'd borrowed from his little sister, Maria.

He wondered if he should comment on her hair. Having been raised with two sisters, he kind of doubted it. Even though it was a little short and uneven, he liked it.

"So, you might not be a country girl, but dressed like that you could fool some people."

"Because I put on jeans and boots?" She shook her head and kept walking.

If he had to guess, that fast walk of hers was intended to help her outrun an argument with her grandfather. He paused for a few seconds, and sure enough the door of the camper flew open and Dan, in overalls, muck boots and a straw hat, appeared. His gray hair stuck out from beneath the hat and his face was scruffy with a few days' growth of gray whiskers.

"I don't need no pity from long lost relatives," Dan squawked, sounding a lot like that bad-tempered rooster of his. "Now call your folks and tell them to come get you. After all these years…"

He had a coughing fit and didn't finish. And even with the tongue lashing, his granddaughter hightailed it back to his side and told him to take it easy. She might be a city girl but she had a determined side.

Alex didn't want to like her too much. In his experience, women like her didn't last in his world. And they were too expensive for his bank account. It didn't matter what he told himself about her being a city girl, or his bank account or any of the other mental objections he might have; he liked her.

A woman like her, if she stayed around long enough, could make a guy start thinking about forever. Even if he hadn't planned on having those thoughts. Ever. "I'm asking you to let me stay because I need a little time before I go back and face the embarrassment." She looked at her grandfather as determined as that old rooster had been. "Just a week or two. Please."

Dan reached into his pocket for an inhaler. After a few puffs, he shoved it in the front pocket of his bibs and gave his granddaughter a once-over.

"Nope." He went on down the steps, holding tight to the rail. "You call your folks and you go on back to Dallas. I don't need a keeper. And you don't need to hide from what happened."

"But…" She followed him. "I could help you out around here."

Dan shook his head as he took the can of chicken feed from Alex. "I don't need help. I'm just fine."

"Dan, just let us feed for you today," Alex offered. But at this point, if he had any sense, he'd hightail it back to his place and take care of his own life instead of wading knee-deep into Dan's. "Give your granddaughter the chance to be a farm girl for a few days. She's all dressed up for the part. Might as well introduce her to country life. Maybe we'll even take a ride over to Essie's for lunch. My treat."

Dan looked skeptical, but even he seemed to know when to give in. He handed over the feed can and gave his granddaughter a sharp look. "Don't be abusing my rooster. He'll remember that and he'll be waiting to get back at you."

"He's a rooster," she said. "I doubt roosters plot vengeance."

"Just you wait," was his grumbled response as he headed back to the trailer. "I'm holding you to lunch, Palermo. You're buying."

"What do we do now?" the woman at his side asked Alex as they headed for Dan's old farm truck.

Alex unlocked her door and opened it. "Well, we feed Dan's cattle. In the summer he had plenty of grass, but this time of year we feed hay and grain. In years past that would have been more of a job than it is now. Dan's been selling off some cattle recently. I've actually been a little worried about him."

"Do you think he's okay? I mean…" She hesitated and then got in the truck. "Dementia?"

He got in and turned the key, knowing it would take a few attempts to get the old truck started. Dan had a sedan he kept parked in a carport behind the camper, but he claimed it didn't have a battery.

"No, I don't think he has dementia," he answered as the truck roared to life. "His health isn't the best but I think it's more. Something seems off and he won't say much about it."

"If he'll let me stay, maybe I can figure it out."

Alex thought the best thing she could do was head on back to Dallas. Dan's old camper suited him but it wasn't the life she was used to. Not that he knew about her life or what she was used to. But he guessed she didn't know what it was like to live in an old piece of metal when the wind blew hard from the north.

"I don't think he's going to let you stay," Alex told her as they drove toward the barn.

"Have you always known him?" she asked after he'd opened the gate and they'd driven through.

"All my life. He's always been here."

"So you grew up in Bluebonnet?"

He stopped the truck at the feed trough and got out. She followed, watching him, then watching the cattle heading their way. She moved to his side and stayed close as he tossed a feed sack over his shoulder, pulled the string to unseal the bag and poured it out, starting at one end of the trough.

"Did you?" she asked as he went back for the second bag of grain.

"Yeah, I grew up here."

"You don't sound happy about that."

"Because I'm busy and you're asking a lot of questions." Questions about growing up were his least favorite. There were too many bad memories attached to his childhood in Bluebonnet. Not because of the town but because his father had tarnished childhood for Alex and his siblings in a way that should have been against the law. It probably was against the law.

"Do you have siblings other than your sister?" she asked.

He pulled off his hat, swiped a hand across his brow and shook his head. "You know a guy for five seconds and suddenly you need his life story."

She started to protest but he stopped her. Holding his hand up to quiet her, he studied the cattle that were heading across the field. His attention shifted to the slightly damp ground. And tire tracks.

"What's wrong?" Marissa asked as she moved to stand next to him.

He pointed to the tracks in the soft earth. "Someone has been out here. On four-wheelers. And I might be wrong but there seems to be a couple of cows missing. I wouldn't usually notice that about Dan's herd, but he had two black baldies that looked ready to drop their calves any day. And they're gone. I'll ask Dan if I need to go look for them. It's possible they're off having their calves. But I don't know who would have been out here with an ATV."

"Black baldy?" she asked with narrowed eyes and her nose scrunched up.

"A black cow with a white face."

Her mouth formed an O. "Maybe he sold them?"

"Yeah, maybe."

He tossed the empty sacks and headed for the truck. "We'll ask him when we get back. And then I'll head to my place. I've got to get some work done before more rain hits."

"Work? Do you have another job, other than ranching?"

Another question. He motioned her into the truck. "I used to be a bull rider. Now I ranch and I'm starting a tractor-and-equipment-repair business. I also own bucking bulls." He got in the truck and cranked the engine. "What about you?"

"I teach kindergarten." She said it with a soft smile but also with a little bit of sadness that he didn't like. She looked like the type of person who walked on sunshine and never had a bad day. But that's what he got for judging a book by its pretty cover.

Everyone had bad days. Most people had secrets or a past they didn't want to talk about. Those were the hard facts of life. He tried to stay out of other people's business and leave them to their own past, their own secrets.

Marissa Walker caused a man to forget those simple rules for an uninvolved life. Rule 1: don't ask personal questions.

They were nearing the gate and he slowed. "Why don't you open that gate for me?"

She climbed out of the truck and pulled on the gate until she had it open. A couple of times she had to stop and tug up on the jeans Lucy had loaned her. He swallowed a grin as she got back in the truck.

"I hope you enjoyed that," she muttered.

"I did." He leaned over to brush her cheek. "You had something on your face."

And just like that the humor died, and he was face-to-face with the greatest temptation of his life, a woman who just last night had sat in his truck and cried. A woman who wouldn't be around long enough to know left from right when it came to Bluebonnet.

He leaned back in the seat and put his hands on the steering wheel of the old truck. The clutch was sticky and the gears grinded a bit. It was familiar, and right now he needed familiar.

As they pulled up to Dan's camper, his passenger let out a soft gasp and reached for the door handle before he could get the truck stopped.

"Hey, at least let me stop before you…"

She was already out of the truck, the door wide-open. He hit the emergency brake and jumped out because Dan was leaning against the side of the camper and he didn't look too good. Alex remembered those praying lessons the pastor had been giving him, because this looked like a moment to pray for some help, to pray for an old man to take another breath.

"Dan, are you okay? Here, let me help you sit down." Marissa had an arm around him but he was fighting her off.

"I can get myself to the house." He leaned, wheezing as he tried to draw in a breath. "Lungs don't work like…"

"Dan, stop talking and let us help you. We'll go see Doc Parker." Alex put Dan's arm over his shoulder.

The older man was taller than him by a few inches and he was still solid. He leaned heavily on Alex as they headed across the dusty yard to Alex's truck.

"I don't need the doc." Dan gave one last attempt. "Trouble. I knew when she knocked on my door that she'd be trouble."

Dan's granddaughter bristled at that. "Listen to me—"

"You old coot," Dan said, finishing her sentence, in a somewhat mocking tone.

"I wouldn't call you that." She opened the truck door. "We're taking you to the doctor, and like it or not, I'm not going anywhere."

"Dad-burn-it." Dan collapsed as they managed to maneuver him into the truck.

Alex gave her points for courage. She'd shown up on Dan's doorstep like a rain-soaked kitten tossed to the curb. Today the kitten had claws and she wasn't walking out on a grandfather who wasn't going to make her visit easy.

Alex had to admit, if he wasn't so tangled up in his bucking-bulls business, and in his past, a woman with her kind of spunk would be the woman to have in his life.

But he wasn't anything close to solvent and she wasn't the kind of woman who looked twice at a cowboy like him.

Chapter Three

The doctor's office was in an old convenience-store building on the south edge of Bluebonnet Springs. Alex drove them there in less than five minutes, with Marissa's grandfather arguing the entire time that he was fine and didn't need that "quack doctor." Alex had merely grinned during the rant. Marissa had tried to get Dan to calm down because his lips were turning blue from lack of oxygen.

They pulled up to the clinic, and Alex parked next to the front door. Thanks to a brief phone call, the physician waited outside for them. He had an oxygen tank on wheels, and as Dan argued, the doctor placed the tubing in his nose.

"Don't fight me, Dan Wilson," Doc Parker said, as they helped Marissa's grandfather out of the truck. "I told you to keep oxygen at your house. Now you're going to have to do what I say and maybe you'll live a few more years."

"Don't talk like that," Dan said, inhaling deeply. "You'll scare the kids."

Doc shot them a look, his eyes narrowed. "They're

young but they can handle reality. Where did you get this pretty young lady?"

"I reckon that's my granddaughter. She showed up on my doorstep like a stray puppy and now I can't get rid of her."

Once they were inside, Doc got Dan to sit down.

"Did you feed her?" Doc asked, giving her a swift smile as he examined her grandfather. "If you feed them, they won't go back where they came from."

"I reckon I fed her a sandwich last night and she had a cup of coffee this morning. To repay me, she nearly killed my best rooster."

Doc laughed. "That rooster had it coming, Dan. He tried to flog me when I was out there checking on you last week."

The physician put a stethoscope to her grandfather's chest, telling him to breathe, then moved it to the next spot. Dan obeyed, but he shivered from time to time, and Marissa could hear the wheezing even without the stethoscope. A movement out of the corner of her eye caught her attention. Alex moved to stand behind her. Briefly his hand touched her shoulder.

The comfort took her by surprise. Brief as it was, it untangled the emotions of the past twenty-four hours and brought an unexpected tightness to her throat.

Doc sat back and gave her grandfather a long look. "Now listen to me, you old coot, I'm sending you to the hospital. I called the ambulance before you got here because I figured that cold you've had finally knocked you down."

"I don't need the hospital." Dan paused to take a breath. "And I've got animals to take care of."

"You've got neighbors who will help." Doc Parker

looked at Marissa, his gray eyes kind. "Can you talk some sense into him?"

How did she talk sense into someone she'd just met? She looked at the gruff man who was her grandfather and she wished she'd had twenty-six years of knowing him. He was salty and rough but already she loved him.

"Granddad…" she began. He looked up, his eyes narrowing. She couldn't back down. Not when it was something this serious. "I'm not going anywhere. I'll stay and take care of the animals. You go to the hospital and get better."

"He's trying to send me off to a nursing home," her grandfather said quietly. "I'm not doing that."

"No, he's sending you to the hospital. And then you're going back to your own place to tend to that worthless rooster." Marissa put a hand on his arm. It seemed a natural gesture, but she was surprised by how easy it was to reach out to him.

"I'll help her keep an eye on things." Alex inserted himself into the conversation.

"Keep an eye on her, too. She doesn't know a thing about cows." Her grandfather paused again to breathe. The color was slowly seeping back into his cheeks. "Don't you kill that rooster while I'm in the hospital." And then he raised his gaze to Alex. "And no fox better get in the henhouse, either." He took another long breath of the oxygen.

Doc rolled his eyes. "Dan, I'm sending you in for some IV antibiotics and a few tests. That's all. You'll be home in a few days at the latest."

"You're sure?" Dan asked.

"Pretty close to sure. And the ambulance is pulling in. Alex and your granddaughter can follow unless they want to ride with me." Doc Parker helped her grandfather to his feet, then he gave Marissa his attention. "Do you need to call your family?"

It was a normal question, but this wasn't a normal situation. Before she could answer, her grandfather waved his hand and stopped her.

"No, she won't be calling family. She's my family. My *only* family."

Doc raised a questioning brow. "Is that so?"

Again, Dan answered. "It is if I say so."

"Dan, you have to let her answer." Doc glanced at her as he continued to examine his patient.

"Yes, I'm his family. But Granddad, I will tell my mother what is going on."

"Bah," he said, waving her away. As if she would go.

Suddenly, the paramedics entered. Alex stood with her as they readied her grandfather. Memories crashed in, and she closed her eyes against the pain that the images brought. It had been so long, but seeing her grandfather on that gurney, it seemed more like yesterday.

In an instant she was ten again. Her mom was screaming. There were police cars. And she was alone, standing on the sidewalk, unable to scream, unable to cry. That day had changed her life. Since then, she had felt alone.

The paramedics were moving. Her grandfather was cursing them. She tried to shake off the pain of the past. A hand briefly touched hers, giving a slight squeeze.

She wasn't alone.

"Are you all right?" Alex asked in a husky whisper.

She nodded, her attention glued to the scene taking place in front of her. She was okay. But she wasn't. She was about to fall apart.

"Sit down," he ordered. He led her to a chair.

She sat, then lifted her gaze to meet his. He squatted in front of her, putting him at eye level.

"I'm fine," she insisted.

"I don't believe you. I know what it looks like when a woman is about to come unglued. But trust me, he's going to be okay. He's too ornery for anything else."

"I know. It isn't…" She swallowed and met his gaze again. "I'm fine. It was just a memory. But I'm okay."

"Do you want to talk about it?"

She managed a shaky laugh because he didn't look like a man who really wanted to talk. "No, not really. I should go. Maybe I can ride with the doctor."

He put a hand out and helped her to her feet. "I'm driving you."

"I'm sure you have other things to do. You aren't responsible for me."

"I know I'm not, but I found you. Finders keepers and all of that childish stuff. And besides, you don't want to ride with Doc Parker." He leaned close as he said it. "He's had so many speeding tickets, they're about to take his license."

"Thank you," she said, smiling at his warning. No matter how she felt at this moment, she wasn't alone.

Alex walked with Marissa to his truck. A breeze kicked up, blowing dust across the parking lot. In the distance the ambulance turned on its siren, and he could see the flash of blue lights on the horizon. The woman standing next to him shivered violently as if a cold arctic wind had just blown through her. He reached into his truck, grabbed his jacket off the seat and placed it around her shoulders.

He didn't think it was the breeze that had chilled her.

He'd watched her in Doc's office. He'd seen the moment that past met present—her eyes had darkened and the color had drained from her cheeks. He recognized a person getting hit head-on by a painful memory. It had happened to him more than once.

There were days he could still hear his teenage self tell his father he wouldn't last five seconds on the bull he was straddling. His father had laughed and said, *From your lips to God's ears*.

Thirty seconds later his father was gone. His last words, a whispered, *You were right*.

He had his past. It appeared Marissa might have her own.

He wouldn't pry because he didn't let anyone pry into his memories. He helped her in the truck and then he got in and started it up. She was still stoic, still dry-eyed.

"Did you charge your phone?" he asked as they pulled onto the road.

"I'll have to buy a charger." She averted her gaze and concentrated on the passing scenery.

There wasn't much to Bluebonnet Springs. Main Street with its few business, the feed store and his aunt Essie's café. On the edge of town there was a convenience store and a strip mall with a couple of businesses. The rest of the town was made up of a few churches and a couple of streets lined with houses that had been built a few decades ago. There was a new subdivision being built in the east end of town. That had caused quite a stir and given the lunch crowd at Essie's something to talk about for a good month.

A city utilities truck was parked on the side of the road.

"They're putting up the Christmas lights," he told

her, because the silence was deafening and he didn't know what else to say.

"Christmas isn't my favorite holiday." She cleared her throat. "I didn't mean it like that. Christmas is difficult for my family."

"I'm sorry." He sped up as they left town. "It's a big deal here in Bluebonnet."

She gave him a questioning look.

"Christmas," he responded. "They love Christmas in this town. They have a big community service. There are four churches in the area and they all come together and each one has a play or music. The whole month of December the shops are open late each Friday. They serve cookies and hot cocoa."

"That does sound nice," she answered. "Maybe I'll be around for that. If not, I might come back. We typically don't do a lot at Christmastime."

He wanted to ask her about her family, maybe even wanted to know why her blue eyes clouded with emotion as she told him that bit of insight into her life. But he knew better than to dig into someone else's life. He knew from his own past that families all had their private stories. After his dad died, his entire family had avoided attending church. Specifically, they'd avoided the Church of the Redeemed, the church their father had pastored with an abusive hand.

Maria, the youngest Palermo, hadn't lived through much of Jesse Palermo's craziness, so she hadn't struggled with her faith. The oldest, Lucy, had found it a little more difficult. Alex had found his way to a church service after a bull-riding event. He believed that service probably changed his life and set him on a new course. His twin brother, Marcus... That was a whole other set of problems.

The woman sitting next to him had shut down a little after the topic of Christmas so he wasn't going to push.

He usually had something to say, a joke to crack, anything to ease the tension. But he couldn't find that old ease, not with her. What could he say to a woman he didn't really know? All he knew was that she'd been jilted on her wedding day. She was Dan's granddaughter. And she didn't really care for Christmas and he didn't know why.

Somewhere out there she had people who did know her. She had people who would have the right words. And they had the right to say the words she needed to hear.

"Do you want to use my phone?" he offered in the silence of the truck. "To call family?"

"That would be good. Thank you."

He handed her his cell phone. And then he listened as she spoke to her mother, explaining where she was and how she'd come to be there. At the end of the conversation she told her mom she would keep her posted on her grandfather's condition.

She ended the call, then ran a shaky hand through her now short hair. The brown layers were chunky and framed her face, making her eyes large and luminous. He took the phone from her, their fingers touching in the process. Blue eyes met his and she smiled.

"Thank you."

"Anytime."

He reached to turn up the radio. The classic country station was playing George Jones. A typical song about heartache.

"So, you're a teacher?" Suddenly he felt the need to

fill the silence. He shot her a quick look. "Good thing you aren't a beautician."

Her laughter was soft but genuine. She glanced in the mirror on the visor. "Not my best work. After this, I'll stick to teaching the alphabet."

He gave her another a quick look. Yeah, she looked like a teacher. The kind that wiped faces, hugged kids when they fell and made math seem fun. He'd had one or two teachers like her. The teachers who looked past the rough-and-tumble little boy and told him they thought he mattered.

Those teachers had inspired him. He'd managed to achieve a few goals thanks to their tutoring and encouragement.

Soon they were nearing Killeen and the hospital. Marissa appeared lost in her own thoughts and he doubted he wanted to go where she'd gone.

It didn't take a genius to realize he was knee-deep in this woman's life. For some reason he kept wading in deeper. For a guy who prided himself on keeping to his goals and priorities, that came as a surprise.

The last thing he wanted was the worry that he wouldn't be able to help her. He didn't like the feeling of letting someone down. Or, worse, the moment when someone looked him in the eyes and told him not to worry about it, he couldn't have done anything to help.

Chapter Four

"You don't need to sit at my bedside," her grandfather mumbled. Something about the growling words seemed half-hearted to Marissa. Or maybe it was wishful thinking on her part. Maybe she wanted him to need her. Or she wanted to try to make up to him whatever it was he'd lost when her grandmother left.

"I know I don't need to be here." She moved the chair closer to his bed. "I *want* to be here."

He shook his head. "Do-gooders, always trying to make up for what other people did wrong. Like Alex over there. He's trying to make up for that crook of a father he had. You're trying to make up for your grandmother walking out on me. What the two of you need to do is take yourselves off and live your own lives. Not together, mind you. That would be another mistake."

Heat climbed into Marissa's cheeks and she avoided looking at the man standing near the wall. But he moved, forcing her gaze to shift toward him. He pushed away from the wall he'd been leaning against and approached her grandfather's bed.

"Dan, you're just being grouchy. And your grand-daughter is the wrong person to take it out on," he said.

The last thing she needed was for him to defend her. She shot him a warning look that he disregarded with that cool, cowboy way he had. As if nothing ever got under this skin.

"I'm not taking it out on her." Her grandfather patted the hand she'd rested on the rail of the bed. "I'm giving some advice. Go on about your life. I don't know why any man would dump you. Maybe it's the grandfather in me talking, but I think any man in his right mind would want you. And don't be looking at her like that, Alex Palermo. We all know you're not in your right mind. Marissa, you need to go back home to your folks and to your life. I imagine there's some pieces you need to pick up. Things you need to deal with."

"I already told you I'm staying," she said softly, hop-ing he wouldn't disagree.

He opened his mouth to say something and coughed instead. The cough lingered, turning his face dark red as he fought to catch his breath. When she offered a glass of water, he raised his hand and shook his head.

"I'm fine. Water's good for nothing but washing dishes. And making coffee. Get me some coffee and you'll be my favorite granddaughter."

"As far as I know, I'm your only granddaughter."

His hand over hers tightened and his gaze caught and held hers. "I know."

Those two words shook her. She saw in his eyes that he did know. She saw sympathy and sadness. She saw understanding. How did he know? But she couldn't ask. Not yet.

"What if that fiancé of yours comes to his senses?" her grandfather asked.

"I don't think I'd be willing to revisit that relationship."

"I'll get you a cup of coffee, Dan," Alex offered, and quietly slipped from the room.

Silence hung between them. Marissa tried to turn away but her grandfather kept his hand on hers.

"I know about your sister." He patted her hand. "I can't imagine how that hurt you. It hurt me and I didn't know her. But you were young. How old?"

"Ten."

"Yes, ten. Your grandmother sent me the newspaper clipping. She was heartbroken."

The information unsettled Marissa. "You talked to my grandmother?"

"Yes, we talked. No, it was more like yipping. We yipped at each other. Like the coyotes you hear at sunset. We never did get along. She was city and I was country. We were oil and water. The two don't mix. She wanted shopping malls. I wanted cattle. We bought the camper and planned to build a house later. At first she loved the idea. It was romantic, the two of us making our own way. And then along came your mom and it was crowded. To make matters worse, it upset her wealthy daddy that we were living like that."

"So she left you."

"Yes, she left. For good reasons, mind you. But after a while she called and apologized. She sent me letters. I mailed her checks. She decided I wasn't fit to be a father and I agreed. I understood horses and cattle but not little girls. I guess from the mess I made of my marriage, I didn't understand women any better. And that's why you should go on home. It was nice meeting you and I hope you'll stay in touch, but you belong in Dallas, not Bluebonnet."

"How do you know where I belong?" Even she didn't know where she belonged.

"That's what your grandmother said when I told her she shouldn't marry a cowboy from Bluebonnet Springs. And I was right."

"You're not right about me."

Footsteps announced Alex's return. She stepped away from the bed, moving to the window to look out at the city landscape.

"Did I need to give you more time?" Alex asked as he handed the coffee to her grandfather. He pushed the button to raise the back of the bed so that Dan could sit up a little higher.

"You can take my granddaughter on back to my place. I think her folks should be able to find their way down here to pick her up."

Marissa picked up her purse. "Don't tell me what to do. I'm not that easy to get rid of. I'm going back to your place because someone has to feed the dog. And that stupid rooster."

"Don't be picking on my rooster," Dan grumbled.

"I won't. And I'm also not going anywhere."

Alex chuckled. "Dan, I wasn't sure if she was really your granddaughter until just now. She's definitely stubborn enough to be a Wilson. You may have met your match."

"Go away. I need my rest. Didn't you hear the doctor?"

"I heard him." Marissa leaned in to kiss her grandfather's scruffy cheek. "Don't worry about a thing. I'll take care of your animals."

He patted her shoulder. "That's what I'm worried about."

He smiled, a twinkle in his faded blue eyes. Eyes she realized were the same as hers. She'd always wondered where she got her blue eyes. And her stubborn streak. Now she knew. For the first time in a very long time she felt connected. He might not want her, but in her grandfather she'd found someone who might understand who she was and how she felt.

It was late afternoon when they pulled up to Dan's camper. Marissa felt a strange sense of coming home. It was a world away from her home. It was completely out of her comfort zone. And yet there was something about this place...the fields, the cattle, even the rooster.

It was change. Maybe that's what she'd needed.

"You're actually going to stay here alone?" Alex asked as he moved to get out of the truck.

"Of course I am. Why wouldn't I?"

Alex shrugged as he headed for the barn. She hurried to keep up.

"Maybe you didn't hear Dan, but I did. Your grandmother was a city girl who broke his heart." He shot her a look. "She told him she wanted this life with him but when it came down to it, she couldn't hack it."

"I'm his granddaughter, not his wife. And I want to be here to help him."

"Suit yourself."

"So you don't think I can do this, either, do you?"

He headed through the barn, stopping to give her a

look before scooping grain into a bucket. "I make it a habit not to get involved."

"Then you should go. I'll feed and do whatever needs to be done here."

He headed out a side door, whistling shrilly. She heard an answering whinny and then hooves beating across the hard-packed earth.

"You'll do whatever needs to be done?" He grinned as he poured feed in a trough. "There's a couple of cows about to calve. Do you know what to do with a downed cow that's been laboring too long?"

"I can look it up on the internet."

He grabbed her by the wrist, his hand strong and warm, and they moved back a few steps as a couple of horses headed for the trough. The animals didn't seem to want to share. Ears were pinned back and one turned to kick at the other. Marissa didn't need to be told twice to get out of the way of those flying hooves.

"Should you feed them separately?" she asked.

"Nah, they'll get over it once they get to the business of eating. They've been fighting that way for years. That's what Dan gets for buying mules."

"They're horses, aren't they?"

He pointed to the heads of the big, golden red animals.

"Those are not the ears of a horse. Dan sold his horses when he stopped training and he bought mules. They're sure-footed and he uses them for trail rides and hunting. But I'm sure you can look that up on the internet," he teased, punctuating his words with a wink.

"Stop making fun of me. When I decide to do something, I do it. I'm staying and I'm going to help my grandfather."

"Calm down, I'm not making fun of you."

Of course he wasn't. But she'd gotten used to Aidan and his brand of teasing, which she now realized had been more. He'd smiled as he pointed out her shortcomings, then he'd told her he was teasing. Now she could look back on the last two years and a relationship that had been chipping away at her hard-earned self-confidence.

She briefly closed her eyes. When she opened them he had stepped a little closer. His expression, soft and concerned, eased the tension building inside her.

"I'm calm," she said.

"I admire that you want to help Dan, even if you don't know a thing about ranching. But don't you have a job you need to get back to?"

A few days ago she would have said that she did have a job. She had an apartment, a job and even a fiancé, who would now have been her husband.

"I have a new job but I don't start until mid-January. I have plenty of time to stay and help my grandfather."

The job now seemed like another area of her life she'd given over to her parents. It was a job they'd wanted for her and approved of. And she'd agreed to the private school even though she'd wanted something else. She'd been looking at a small rural school when her father told her he'd gotten her an interview with a friend.

"Suit yourself." He headed for the barn with the empty bucket. "I have to get home and get my own chores taken care of. Tomorrow morning you'll need to move a round bale to the cattle. They'll eat about two of those fifty-pound bags of grain. And then you'll need to feed the chickens and gather eggs. Don't forget Bub."

The list of chores made her take a step back and reevaluate the plan. She quickly swallowed past the lump that lodged in her throat. She could do this. The other thing she could do was ignore the humorous glint in his dark eyes and the dimple in his left cheek.

He was the complete opposite of Aidan. He was the opposite of what she knew about life and men. He laughed too easily and smiled too much. He was too carefree.

But her grandfather had commented on his life, making her think everything hadn't been so easy for Alex Palermo.

"I can do all of that," she informed him because he seemed to be waiting for confirmation.

"I think you probably can," he said, suddenly serious. "Don't forget to lock the doors tonight."

"Lock the doors. Of course."

The humor evaporated. "I'm serious. I know you want to stay here. And I know you can handle things, but these cattle rustlers are real and I don't want you to think you have to go out and tangle with them."

Her earlier ease with the situation dissolved with that warning. "What should I do if I see or hear something?"

"Call 911 and then call me. I'll write my number down for you. And let Bub sleep in the house with you. He looks like a drooling mess, but he's got a pretty vicious bark."

"Okay, I've got this."

He winked, then he kissed her cheek, taking her completely by surprise. "Of course you do. I believe you can do this."

Alex heard a truck door slam. He walked out of the stall he'd been cleaning and spotted his sister Lucy getting out of her truck. She waved and headed his way. Lucy was proof that the Palermo family could overcome the past.

An abusive cult leader for a father. A mother who'd abandoned them. Some folks around town still gave them the stink eye, as if they were waiting for one of the Palermo kids to turn out like their father.

Years ago, Lucy had escaped, joining the army and then returning to start a protection business with her former army buddies. Last spring she'd finally come home to Bluebonnet and ended up marrying their neighbor, Dane Scott. And Lucy had adopted Maria's baby girl, Jewel.

The only problem with all of this was that Lucy suddenly was into everyone's business and thought all her siblings needed to be fixed. She'd turned into a mother.

"How's Dan doing?" she asked as she entered the barn.

Alex put the pitchfork back in the storage room. He closed the door of that room. Long ago it was the room their father had locked Lucy in when he'd learned of her teen relationship with Dane.

"He's good. Word travels fast in a small town."

"Yeah, it does. I was at Essie's." The café their aunt owned. "She said Doc came in after he'd gotten back from Killeen."

He knew that hopeful look in Lucy's eyes, she was thinking maybe there was something between him and Dan's granddaughter. He headed out the front door of the stable. The sun was setting and the air had cooled ten degrees with a wind coming out of the north. He figured there'd be frost on the ground when he woke up in the morning.

"I guess Dan's granddaughter is sticking around?" Lucy asked as she walked next to him.

"Is there a point to this visit?" He opened the door to the garage he'd had built since he returned home last spring. Inside were a couple of tractors and a farm truck. The equipment belonged to neighbors. The tools belonged to him.

"How's business?"

He pushed a rolling toolbox in the direction of the John Deere tractor. "Business is good. And I'm not interested in Dan's granddaughter, not as anything more than a neighbor in need. I'll remind you that it wasn't too long ago that you weren't interested in dating. Just because you've gone to the other side doesn't mean I'm going to."

Lucy sat on a rolling stool and watched him. Studied him, more like. The way a scientist studied an insect. "One of these days there will be a woman who makes you forget. Or at least helps you let go of the past."

"It isn't going to be this woman." By the past Lucy meant the women who couldn't be seen with him because their daddies didn't want them dating a Palermo. As a teenager it had hurt. As an adult, he guessed he didn't blame them.

His dad had been a cult leader who abused his family. And most people would have said the apple didn't fall far from the tree. For a long time he'd almost believed it, thinking that he had no choice but to grow up in the shadow of Jesse Palermo.

He slid under the tractor and ignored his sister. Time was limited and Jerry Masters expected his tractor fixed in the next week. "I'm looking at buying some used equipment to sell."

"Can you do that and get those bulls ready to buck?"

"I can. Marcus is going to come home and help with the bulls. It works for us both. I invested my earnings. He blew through his like water." He scooted out and picked a different tool. Lucy was watching him, her dark eyes serious. "Stop worrying, Luce. I've got this."

"I always worry. It's my job."

"You don't have to worry."

"Yes, I do. I worry that Marcus is going to hurt himself or someone else. I worry that Maria has been talking to Jaxson Williams. And I worry that you still think it was all your fault. Everything."

"It was." He scooted back under the tractor, hoping she'd take the hint and leave. He knew better, but it was worth a try.

"You were a teenager and not responsible for our father's actions. Ever."

He gave up on the tractor, slid out and sat up, knees bent and arms resting on them. He gave his sister a long look. "Are you finished?"

The look in her eyes told him she wasn't. "No. I have a lot to say. You didn't lock me in that room. Our father did. You couldn't have busted me out. He wouldn't have allowed it. You didn't kill him. He made a choice to get on a bull that was rank and couldn't be ridden."

"I'm pretty sure I wished him a less-than-heavenly reward."

"You've regretted those words a thousand times."

"Are we done?" Because she hadn't yet brought up his best friend, Daniel, who had died under a bull. It had been Alex's job as a bullfighter to protect him but he hadn't. He had a long history of not being able to protect the people he cared about.

Lucy shook her head and he knew the worst was yet to come.

"What is it?" he asked when she didn't spit it out.

"Mom."

Great. This was going downhill fast. Deloris Palermo had a habit of putting her kids last. She'd skated in and out of their lives for the last dozen years.

Lucy sighed. "She took out a mortgage on the farm."

It took him a minute to make sense of those words. "And?"

"And she hasn't been making the payments."

He wanted to punch something. Instead he sat there with a wrench in his hand, waiting, hoping she'd tell him it was all good somehow.

"Please give me some good news."

Lucy shook her head. "I'd love to but there isn't any. She hasn't made the payments in six months. I wouldn't have known if I hadn't seen a man at the end of the drive taking pictures. The place is going to be auctioned off."

"What do we do? I've invested most of my savings in this business and the bulls. I know Marcus doesn't have two dimes to rub together."

"I don't know if you're right about Marcus. He's been winning lately. Mom said she'll sell her half to us if we want. She's being generous, she says. Because she won't make us buy the whole ranch. She said Dad wanted her to have half and the rest split between his four kids. So in order to get her name off the land we have to pay her half the appraised value."

"The appraised value of five hundred acres and a house." He hung his head, wishing he could start this day over. "If we do that, she has to pay the second mortgage. That or we pay her, less the amount she owes. But do you really want to go in on this? Now that you're married, it doesn't seem like this should be your problem."

"We stick together, Alex. All of our lives we've only had each other. That doesn't change just because I'm married."

He tossed the wrench to the ground and did something he rarely did: he gave his sister a quick hug. "Thanks."

She hugged him back, the gesture awkward. "You're welcome."

He headed back to his tools. "So now I just have to figure out how to scrounge up a down payment. And face the reality that our own mother has put us in debt."

"Yeah."

"And you ask me why I'm not interested in a relationship. From what I can see, people who say they care tend to just rip each other to pieces."

"There's a difference between people who care and people who *say* they care. You've never let me down. I don't know if I've ever said it, but I love you, Alex."

He blinked to clear his blurry vision. Because he wouldn't let her make him cry. "I have to get up early," he said as he wiped his hands on a towel. "And you have kids to take care of and a husband probably wondering where you are."

"I'm sorry. I shouldn't have brought this up."

He managed a grin. "Remember when you used to stay out of our business and just let us all live our lives?"

"I seem to remember that person. I was a little bit broken, too."

"I'm not broken. I'm not even fragile. I'm cautious."

"And you're not *cautiously* interested in Dan's granddaughter?" she asked as she stood at the door, preparing to leave.

"No. I'm not interested. I found her on the side of the road in her wedding dress. If that doesn't scream trouble, I don't know what does."

Lucy's eyes widened. "A wedding dress? That's a part of the story no one is talking about. Including you."

He was filled with some kind of strange loyalty and protectiveness. Hadn't he just said he wasn't getting tangled up in Marissa Walker's life?

"It's a part of the story that doesn't need to be talked about. No one ought to be walking down a back road on their wedding day, in the dress and without the groom."

Lucy gave him a long look. "You're right. But when you said she needed extra clothes, you didn't mention the dress."

"I didn't think it was anyone's business but hers."

"It's a good thing you're the one who found her."

"I guess it is. I'll see you later, sis." He reached to open the door for her. With a quick hug, she left.

He watched her truck head down the drive and then he went back inside the garage. Focusing on the tractor helped him keep his mind busy and kept him from worrying too much about the mortgage and buying the ranch he'd always considered his home. Fixing that tractor also kept him from thinking about Marissa.

Kind of.

He didn't want to think about blue eyes that rivaled the bluebonnets his hometown was named for. Or the blue of the sky on a clear winter day. He didn't want to think about how she'd managed to pull herself together, even though she had to be pretty close to devastated.

He couldn't help but think she needed family. Or a friend. Someone to help her through what had to be a pretty difficult time.

Someone who was not him.

Chapter Five

The gray light of early dawn peeked through a crack in the curtains. Marissa tried to roll over on the lumpy sofa but a bigger lump kept her from moving. She pushed at the drooling dog that had climbed up and was stretched out next to her.

"Down, Bub."

The dog groaned, then made a noise that was followed by a foul smell. She pushed him off the sofa and sat up, holding a hand over her nose.

"You are the most disgusting animal."

Bub just looked at her with his soulful eyes, his skin sagging downward, ears slightly perked. His tail thumped the faded carpet. Then he got up and lumbered to the door.

She followed, pushing the door open to the cool air. The rooster was sitting on the porch rail. As if on cue, he bristled his feathers and starting crowing.

"Good morning to you, too." She closed the door, shutting out the rooster and the noxious dog.

Blurry-eyed from lack of sleep, she headed for the coffeepot. She found coffee in a canister and filters in the cabinet. The refrigerator, as she'd learned the previous evening, didn't contain much in the way of food. Her grandfather seemed to live on eggs, skim milk and bologna.

She didn't know how he ever got to sleep. The quiet country seemed so loud compared to the sounds of the city. All night long she could hear the wind whistling through windows, the creaking of the camper settling, an occasional coyote howling and cattle mooing in the distance.

She put eggs on to boil and sat down at the table with a pad and a pen. She needed a list. Her life was about lists. It was important to her that she stay organized and stay on schedule. As she put pen to paper, she placed a fishing magazine on the pad to keep her penmanship level.

Tricks of the trade, she told herself. Before being diagnosed with dyslexia she had learned to compensate for her disability on her own. She'd learned to block off sections of reading material and use rulers to make her writing stay on one line—she'd never understood how these difficult tasks seemed to come easy for everyone else.

As she wrote out a list that included feeding livestock, cleaning, picking up groceries and visiting her grandfather, her phone rang. Her mom. It was too early for a lecture. She let it go to voice mail.

A text came through a few minutes later.

You have responsibilities, a job and a family. When will you be home?

She stared at the text for a full minute. Then she got up to pour herself a cup of coffee. Why couldn't her mother say something comforting? Why couldn't she tell Marissa that it wasn't her fault? That yes, Aidan had hurt her, but she would get past this. There were so many things a mother could say to comfort a child. But her mother had ceased being that person when Lisa died. She'd burrowed into her own pain, forgetting the daughter who still lived. A girl who had lost a sister and been overcome with guilt.

What they never talked about, what no one ever said, was that it had been her fault. Because of her, they'd all lost the thing they treasured most—her sister. Her parents' first child. And they never talked about it. Ever.

She'd spent sixteen years trying to make it up to her parents, always following the rules, always working twice as hard. She'd done whatever she could to make life easier for them, to cause less trouble.

Through it all, Marissa had felt guilty. Because she was alive and Lisa wasn't. She'd felt guilty each time she'd saw a glimpse of sadness in her parents' eyes or caught one of them looking at a picture of Lisa.

And every single day she'd missed the sister she should have grown up with.

Blinking back tears, she poured the coffee down the drain and turned off the burner under the eggs. She typed out a text to her mom, telling her she was sorry that she never seemed to be enough for them. But the words were too honest. Instead she deleted the message and texted her mom she was sorry and would come home soon. Maybe after Dan got out of the hospital. Without waiting for a reply, she walked out of the camper.

Cool air greeted her. She shoved her hands into the pockets of her jacket and walked a little faster.

Cattle mooed at her approach. Red, the rooster, hurried across the lawn, wings flapping. She grabbed a stick and turned to face her attacker. The rooster jumped at her, and when she shook the stick, he squawked as it brushed against him.

"Oh, come on, I didn't even hit you."

The rooster flew at her again, but when he saw the raised stick he changed course and settled on the ground, feathers ruffled and a lot of rooster indignation in evidence. As she continued to the barn he followed, still making agitated noises and ruffling his feathers as he marched along behind her. He didn't trust her. She wasn't feeling a lot of trust for him, either. Occasionally she shot a look back to make sure he kept his distance.

As she entered the barn, a phone rang. She followed the sound to the feed room. An old rotary phone hung from the wall. She picked it up and answered.

The caller stuttered at her hello, and when Marissa asked who was calling, there was a long pause.

"This is Sheila from the IRS calling to speak to Mr. Wilson," the woman said, her tone hesitant.

"I'm sorry, he isn't here. Can I help you?"

"No, you can't. It's a matter of some importance. Could you please give him a message that I called?"

"I'll tell him." She hung up, staring at the avocado-green phone that hung on the rough wood-plank wall.

She wasn't about to give her grandfather that message while he was hospitalized. But maybe the call explained the cattle that Alex had insisted were missing and had been sold off, and the run-down conditions of the property. How much could Dan possibly owe?

She stood there in the quiet, musty barn and replayed the call in her mind. Did the IRS actually make phone calls asking for money? A cat mewed. She glanced around and saw it sitting on the door that led to an empty stall. It licked a paw and surveyed her, then turned its attention to the rooster.

"Do you get fed, too?" she asked the cat. It looked at her with amber-colored eyes.

Inside the feed room she searched cabinets and buckets until she found a bag of cat food. She poured some in a metal dish she found in the aisle of the barn.

Marissa returned to the feed room, where she poured a few cans of grain into a bucket, the way Alex had done when he'd fed the mules the previous day.

Outside the air was still cool and a trace of frost remained on the grass. She had found leather work gloves in the feed room. They were loose on her hands but at least offered some warmth. The mules grazed a short distance away. When they spotted her pouring feed in the metal trough their heads went up. They watched curiously for a moment before heading her way. She emptied the bucket and then moved away. Having witnessed those hooves yesterday she had no desire to be too close.

She leaned against the side of the barn, breathing in the cool air. In the distance a bird swooped low over the field. She watched as the hawk grabbed at something, then ascended, carrying its prey as it flew away.

Closing her eyes, she thought about her childhood and the Sunday morning services they had attended. It had been different then, when there had been four of them and they'd been happy. After Lisa's death it all changed. They didn't attend church. Holidays became quiet affairs with dinners at restaurants and limited decorations. The mourning should have faded and life should have returned to their home. She knew that now. As an adult she knew that something had been very broken in their home.

As a child she hadn't comprehended, she'd only guessed that she was to blame. Maybe if they had healed, maybe if things had returned to normal, she wouldn't have been attracted to Aidan, to his laughter and to his promises. She'd seen him as an escape.

A horse whinnied. She opened her eyes and surveyed the horizon until she spotted horse and rider coming across the field. The rider wore his hat low over his eyes, but even on their short acquaintance, she recognized Alex. He rode the horse with the same easy confidence that seemed to be his trademark.

But now that easy confidence got under her skin. She'd never possessed that personality trait. Instead she'd fought hard to feel somewhat accomplished. She'd had tutors in college, studied on her computer when possible and occasionally she'd paid someone to read assignments out loud for her so that she could process them easier. She was an auditory learner. Reading too much, trying to decipher words that jumped around the page, sometimes brought on a migraine.

She went inside the barn, avoiding him, avoiding the strange need to talk to him. That urge to talk to him got under her skin as much as his brazen confidence on the back of that horse.

Of course she couldn't escape him. He came in through the front double doors of the barn, leading the big gray horse behind him. The animal snorted and shook its head. Alex patted the horse's neck and spoke in a soothing voice, as if the horse was a small child in need of calming.

"He doesn't like new places," Alex explained as he

approached. The horse, as if to prove him right, side-stepped like it had been spooked at something. Alex held tight to the reins, drawing the animal back to his side with a firm hand.

"I see. What are you doing here so early?"

He glanced at his watch. "Is it early?"

"You know it is."

He shrugged it off. "I've been up for a while. I thought I'd check and see how your night went."

"Good."

"You look tired." He stepped closer, bringing the horse with him. With his free hand he brushed at her cheek. "And you have something right there."

"You shouldn't point out that a woman looks tired." She paused, then went on, "I'm not sure why people talk about how quiet it is in the country. It's loud. Coyotes. Cattle. Wind."

"Those sounds are like a lullaby, you just have to get used to them."

"I won't be here long enough."

He led his horse to a stall, removed the saddle and bridle and then gave the animal a flake of hay from the nearby stack of square bales. Marissa watched, waiting for him to say something, anything. The silence was getting to her. This was what came from watching the old programs picked up on the broadcast antenna and then switching to her grandfather's hunting magazines.

With the horse happily munching on hay, Alex stepped out and latched the stall door. The cat prowled past him. Alex watched it for a few seconds, then looked up, grinning at Marissa.

"I'm assuming you won't be here for much longer, but Sunday after this one we're having a community dinner at church for anyone who wants to join us, and for the families who live in the shelter. My sister wanted to make sure I invited you and Dan to join us."

"There's a shelter in Bluebonnet?"

"For abused women trying to start new lives. Several have children."

"I'll talk to my grandfather. If we come, what should I bring?"

"I'm not sure. If you'd like to help me bake pies, you're more than welcome."

"You bake pies?"

"Best pies in the state. And no, I won't give you my recipe. But I will let you slice the apples."

"I don't know how I could refuse such an offer. But I'm sure I'll be gone by then." Because this wasn't her life. It was a distraction. This was the adult version of a child running away, but only making it to the end of the driveway with a favorite doll and a pillow.

This wasn't her life. This dusty barn with the rooster eating cat food, a horse munching on hay and a cowboy offering to let her help make apple pie. None of it was hers.

What did she have left? Not even the ring on her finger was legit. She hadn't thought about the ring. Not until she looked down and saw the glimmering gold and the sparkling diamond. She yanked it off her finger and contemplated throwing it.

"Don't," Alex said quietly, the way he'd spoken to the jittery horse.

She held it tightly in her hand. The ring was one more thing she'd have to deal with when she got home. She'd return it the same way she would return the flatware, the china and the blender.

"Marissa?"

She shook her head to ward off any questions that might undo the fragile hold she had on her emotions.

Before she could stop him he'd closed the distance between them and wrapped strong arms around her. He held her against him.

"It's wrong, what they say about not crying over spilled milk." He whispered the words against her temple. "If it's your milk and you wanted the milk, you should be able to cry about it."

"I don't want to cry," she insisted.

Unfortunately the tears did come. Standing there in the circle of his arms, she couldn't stop them from rolling down her cheeks. What she couldn't tell him was that she cried more for the loss of her family than she did for the man who had walked out on her.

Alex hadn't meant to hold her. It had just happened. She'd looked at him with those sky blue eyes and he hadn't been able to stop himself from stepping forward and pulling her close. After a few minutes, she pulled free and backed away from him. With a hand that trembled, she brushed away the tears.

"I'm sorry," he said. He took off his hat and swiped a hand through his hair, wishing he could think of something better to say.

"No, I'm sorry." She pointed to his shirt. "I might have soaked your shoulder."

With her tears.

He felt his mouth kick up because she made it easy to smile. "No problem, it'll dry. I usually waterproof my shirts when I'm planning to bring a woman to tears."

"You didn't," she said, then sighed. "It was a long night. I haven't had a lot of sleep."

"All that silence," he teased.

Her eyes flashed with relieved humor. "Yes, it was loud."

"I thought I'd help you feed. I know you have the internet to look up how to do it, but it might be quicker if I start the tractor and hook a bale for you."

"It might be. Especially since I don't know what you're talking about." She pulled on the gloves she'd probably found in a drawer somewhere. They were leather and too big for those tiny hands of hers.

He nodded his head toward the side door of the barn. "The tractor is this way."

They were outside in the cool air when she spoke again. "My grandfather got a call this morning. From the IRS."

He grabbed the handle and climbed the two steps to the door of the tractor. "They called this morning?"

She stood a few feet below him, looking up, the sun kissing her face. Looking at her, he kind of wished he wasn't the son of Jesse Palermo, and that he wasn't still scraping and clawing to earn respect. He wished he hadn't learned that he was going to have to go waist-deep into debt to keep his ranch.

And she had her own baggage, which included a rain-soaked wedding dress and the ring she'd slipped into her pocket not fifteen minutes earlier.

He'd had a lifetime of living with people's suspicious looks. Kids he'd gone to school with had been warned not to hang out with the Palermo kids. He'd learned a lot of hard lessons in his life, but the hardest had been about women. They liked bad boys. They liked the boys their fathers told them to stay away from. But they didn't marry those boys.

Not that he planned on getting married. This woman was the type that might look twice at a cowboy like him, but she sure wouldn't take him home to meet her parents.

"Alex?" Her voice brought him back to the present.

"Right, the IRS." Something wasn't adding up. The IRS and stolen cattle.

"Yeah, they called this morning. I'm worried it wasn't legit."

"I'm not sure, but I do know that Dan wouldn't want you involved. He's pretty private."

"He's my grandfather."

"Yeah, he is. But this is his private business."

"I'm still going to ask him."

"I thought you might. Do you want to climb up here and I'll help you get a bale of hay?" He reached down and she took his hand, allowing him to pull her up. The cab of the tractor wasn't meant for two but he squeezed her in next to him.

She smelled of spring flowers and soap. It was a sweet combination.

"What do we do?" she asked. "I mean, about the hay, not the IRS."

"We spike a bale and move it to the field for the cattle. I noticed the mules are grazing the grass down to the dirt. I'll get them a bale, too, so you don't have to worry about handling the square bales."

"Where is the hay?"

"Dan bought a truckload in the fall. The bales are against the fence row," he told her as he started the tractor. "Hands on the wheel. I'll handle the gears this time and you watch what I do so you can do it next time."

He bit back a grin as she took the wheel in her hands and focused.

"By myself?" She said it softly.

"Of course. If you're going to take care of things for Dan, you have to know how to drive the tractor."

She worried her bottom lip but she nodded. "Of course."

The tractor jumped as she hit the accelerator. To compensate she hit the brake. It reminded him of teaching his little sister to drive. Alex steadied himself and swallowed a chuckle when she shot him a questioning look. He raised a hand and nodded, indicating she should keep driving. She hit the accelerator again, this time a little more smoothly, and he relaxed.

When it came to backing the tractor in the direction of a bale of hay, he had to call it quits. He didn't think he or the tractor could take much more.

"I thought I was doing great," she said with amusement glimmering in those blue eyes of hers.

"Oh, you were amazing, but I'd feel like a slacker if I didn't do something."

"I doubt you're ever a slacker."

He chuckled. "And now she compliments me."

"I mean it."

"You don't know me well enough. I promise, I'm very good at messing up."

He wished he'd said anything but that because she got that look in her eyes. She wasn't the first or last woman that would look at him as a project, a man in need of a woman's soft touch.

She was the first to make him believe she might actually stand a chance. She didn't look strong enough to stand up against a stiff breeze. And yet, he almost believed she could stand up against his past. He always wondered what that woman would be like, the one he thought would be able to handle it.

He got his wayward thoughts back on track because it wasn't real. She had enough on her plate without hearing about his life or the baggage he'd been dragging around for most of his twenty-seven years.

"Let's get this hay to the cattle and I'll take you to town for breakfast."

There went common sense and logic. Out the window.

Fortunately she shook her head. "I need to go see my grandfather."

"How are you getting there?"

"I'm driving his truck. The keys were hanging by the door."

He dropped the bale and for a minute he didn't comment on the idea of her driving Dan's farm truck to Killeen. He positioned the spikes and got the bale rolling. Behind them the cattle were moving in on the hay he'd spread across the ground.

She watched, clearly thinking farmwork was a lot of fun and not the hard work it really was. He knew her kind. She'd enjoy it for a few days, then head on back to Dallas.

"You can't drive the truck," he told her as he headed the tractor back to the equipment barn. The three-sided building had an open front. Dan parked his baler, the tractor and the ATV inside. There was also an old tractor he'd retired but couldn't part with. The tractor had rolled with Dan on it once, about fifteen years ago. Still, he held on to the rusted-out piece of junk.

"Why can't I drive the truck?"

"Because it doesn't have tags. And I doubt you know how to drive a stick shift. Those are two pretty good reasons."

"His truck doesn't have tags?"

"Nope. It's a farm truck. Not that it's legal for him to drive it that way, but everyone kind of turns the other way when they see Dan driving through town. He doesn't leave Bluebonnet Springs and he does have insurance. But you can't drive it."

"Can I drive it to town to get groceries?"

Hadn't he just told her she couldn't? He shook his head.

"I can drive you to the store or the hospital."

He helped her down from the tractor, her small hand in his. He let go as soon as her feet hit the ground because her hand in his made him want to hold on a little longer.

But he didn't have time for chauffeuring her all over the state.

"You don't have to do that," she told him, letting him off the hook.

He repositioned his hat on his head as he studied her determined face. "Suit yourself. If you run into trouble, give me a call."

Then he left, telling himself he should feel as if he dodged a bullet. Instead he felt more like he'd just left a defenseless kitten on the side of the road. He wanted to go back, but he couldn't. He guessed he'd have to look at her the way he would look at that kitten. If he didn't help her, someone else would.

Chapter Six

It took Marissa a whole day to work up the courage to
drive the truck. After she'd fed the livestock the next
morning she grabbed the keys and headed out the door,
glad that Alex hadn't shown up and wouldn't see her
poor attempts at driving a stick shift. The last thing she
wanted him to know was that she had watched a video
showing her how to drive a stick-shift car.

Bub the bloodhound followed her across the yard to
the truck. He plopped down under a tree, a big rawhide
chew bone held beneath his paws. She thought he might
be as skeptical as Alex. He chewed on the bone but occasionally he'd lift his head and watch her.

She could do this. She'd show them all. She shoved
the key in the ignition and turned. The truck jumped
forward and died. Bub picked up his bone and moved
a safe distance away.

Aggravated, she ran through the instructions from the
video she'd watched. The clutch. She'd forgotten to use
the clutch. She tried again. This time she got the thing
started, eased off the clutch and moved forward about
twenty feet. The truck shuddered to a halt and died.

It took ten minutes for her to figure out the nuances of the gearshift, the clutch, the gas and brake. It took another five minutes to make it down the driveway to the road. Hunger gnawed at her stomach, pushing her to keep trying. She also didn't like to give up. One way or another she would learn to drive this truck.

She was tenacious. That's what her grandmother had told her. And from her grandmother, it had been a compliment. She'd told Marissa it took a strong woman to overcome difficult situations and survive in this world.

She wondered why her grandmother hadn't been more tenacious in her relationship with Dan Wilson.

Once she got to the main road she sort of had the hang of things. There were a few jerky starts, but she got the truck headed in the right direction. She also found that it wasn't so easy to drive. It constantly pulled toward the left and she had to fight to keep it in the lane.

When she reached the Bluebonnet city limits she took a deep breath and let her shoulders relax. She'd made it. She had driven the old truck all the way to town.

A siren split the air and she jerked her attention to the rearview mirror. The police car behind her definitely wasn't there to give her a friendly escort. She pulled over to the shoulder, the truck shaking at her quick maneuvering and downshifting. It spluttered to a stop and she sat there, hands on the wheel, breathing past the tightness in her chest. She glanced in the mirror again.

The officer got out of his car, his hand on his sidearm. As if dangerous criminals drove old farm trucks. He glanced at the back of the truck and then at her. She closed her eyes briefly and opened them to smile at the officer when he walked up to the window.

"Driver's license and registration. And could you tell me what you're doing in Dan Wilson's truck?"

"I'm his granddaughter, Marissa Walker." She reached for her purse.

"Slow and easy, keep your hands where I can see them."

Yes, she would keep her shaking hands where the officer, named Jones, could see them. "Dan is in the hospital. I needed to pick up groceries."

"I know where Dan is. I also know he's had some cattle disappear. So why don't you go ahead and show me your license and we'll figure this out."

A truck drove past. A familiar dark red truck.

"Great," she muttered to herself.

"Problem?" Officer Jones asked. He momentarily shifted his attention to the truck that slowed as it moved to the shoulder of the road just in front of them.

"No."

Other than being pulled over. Humiliated. Jilted. She could go on, but he didn't want the list. He didn't want to know that it had been a horrible few days. He didn't care that until he'd pulled her over, she'd actually been feeling very proud of herself because she was not only surviving, but she'd also managed to drive the stupid truck.

Although she tried to fight the urge to glance at the truck on the shoulder just fifty or so feet ahead of her, she couldn't help but look. Alex was just getting out. He adjusted his black cowboy hat, shook his head and started their way. Officer Jones let out an exasperated sigh.

"I'm going to have to call this in," he told her. "Take the keys out of the ignition and hand them to me. And don't get out of the truck."

"I'm not going to drive off."

The officer looked skeptical and held out his hand for the key.

"Tim, is there a problem?" Alex asked as he finally reached them.

"I know Dan is in the hospital, so I was surprised to see his truck heading down the road. I'm checking it out now."

"This is his granddaughter. If you'll let her go, I'll make sure she gets it parked before she runs someone off the road."

"I'm right here and I resent that," she informed the too-confident cowboy. He leaned against the side of the truck, then shot her a grin and winked.

She resented that wink. That smile. As if he was there to get her out of trouble. She could get herself out of trouble. She also resented the way she suddenly felt better, as if his presence changed things for her.

He was the last thing she needed.

The police officer glanced at her driver's license and then he handed it back to her. "I'm not sure why you think I should take your word for this, Alex."

"I wouldn't lie to you, Tim." He said it casually. But she noticed the way his mouth tightened and his eyes lost their humor.

"No?" Officer Jones asked. This time neither man smiled.

"No." Alex moved away from his casual position against the side of the truck. "I help Dan at his place. I'm not the person who would take from an old man."

The officer handed her back the keys she'd given him. "Get it off the road. I've turned a blind eye to Dan driving back and forth to town, but I have to draw the line somewhere."

"Of course," she murmured. "I understand."

"We'll park at the café and I'll have it towed back to Dan's place." Alex stepped a little closer and she could see how tense he was.

"Good plan." Officer Jones nodded in her direction. "Give Dan my best."

"I can just drive back to my grandfather's place," Marissa offered after the policeman had walked away.

Alex leaned against the door, and she pretended not to notice that he smelled good. Not expensive-cologne good, but soap-and-country-air good.

"Can you get this thing started and follow me to Essie's?" he asked.

"Of course. I got it to town, didn't I?"

He laughed a little. "Yeah, you sure did. And got yourself pulled over. If you'd called me, I would have given you a ride to town."

"You have your own stuff to take care of. And I need to learn to drive this thing. I talked to my grandfather. They're going to send him home today and I'll need to be able to pick him up."

"Not in this truck you won't. Not only is it not licensed, but it wouldn't make it to Killeen."

"What about the old sedan behind the trailer?"

"No battery and I doubt it's in any better shape."

"I'll call a taxi," she insisted.

"Let's just get something to eat and we'll discuss this later."

Because she was hungry, she gave in. "I'll follow you."

"Good thinking."

She watched him walk away, then she started the old farm truck, pumping the gas when it tried to cut out on her. As Alex pulled back onto the road, she eased off the clutch and prayed the stupid thing wouldn't die. It didn't. She smiled as she turned down Main Street, victorious over the old Ford.

Essie's café was a tan, metal-sided building attached to the local farm-supply store. Farm trucks, sedans and SUVs alike were parked in front of the café. In a nearby parking lot cattle mooed from inside a livestock trailer hooked up to a truck.

Alex got out of the truck and motioned her to join him. She grabbed her purse and followed. As they headed for the diner she heard a rustling sound and turned just as a pig ran down the street, a small dog running along next to it.

"Please tell me that wasn't a pig?" She shook her head. "And a three-legged poodle?"

He chuckled as his hand went around her arm and he guided her toward the steps. "That was indeed a potbellied pig. And his buddy, Patch. They belong to Homer Wilkins. Homer can't seem to keep the two of them inside. Or they wear him down and he lets them out. No one is sure which and the city council has a heck of a time dealing with it."

She followed him inside the café and it seemed that all conversations ceased at their arrival. The silence lasted only seconds, then the steady hum of voices picked back up.

"Hey, Alex, have a seat and I'll be with you in a few," the dark-haired waitress called out as she rushed to a table with several plates. "Aunt Essie is in the kitchen. She's fixing the sprayer on the sink."

"Does she need help, Libby?" Alex asked the waitress. She was probably in her late twenties, with her long hair in a ponytail and an obvious baby bump.

"I don't think I'd go in there if I was you." Libby headed toward the table Alex had guided Marissa to. On her way she picked up a coffeepot. "You won't believe what Bea has done. She tried to make tea by taking off the sprayer and shoving tea bags in the faucet. She said it just made sense to her that if you turned on the hot water that would work. You could spray tea into glasses and never have to make a pot of tea again."

"She didn't really do that, did she?" Marissa blurted out before she could stop herself. "I'm sorry."

Libby grinned. "Oh, she did. Bea is a sweetie and she can cook just about anything, but she can get herself in trouble if you don't keep watch over her. You must be Dan's granddaughter! I bet he is just tickled pink to have you in town."

"I don't think *tickled* would be the word," Alex said. "And I think I'll take your advice and stay away from the kitchen."

The door to the kitchen pushed open and a middle-aged woman shuffled out. Tears were streaming down her rounded cheeks. She wore a bright, floral-patterned dress, brown shoes and blue socks. She brushed the tears away and yanked the hairnet off her head.

"I'm quitting because she's mean," she sobbed as she looked back at the kitchen door. "You're just angry because it didn't work."

"And that is Bea, the woman who should be cooking everyone's breakfast." Alex got up from the table. "I'm going to see if I can't put this fire out."

"Alex, your aunt is mean." Bea grabbed a napkin from a table. "And she doesn't like me anymore."

Alex took hold of the older woman's arm and led her to their table. She sat, giving Marissa a suspicious glare. "Is she your sweetheart?"

Alex turned a little red around the ears. "No. She's Dan Wilson's granddaughter."

"That don't mean she isn't your sweetheart. You can't account for taste. Have you seen that silly dog and that pig? What the good Lord joins together let no man put asunder. I think that's how God works. He puts together the most unlikely. If you get married, can I bake the cake?"

Alex groaned. "Bea, we aren't getting married. I'm taking Marissa to see her grandfather. I'm just being neighborly."

"Hmm. That isn't nice. Shame on you. My mama told me once about Mr. Carson being neighborly and I seen his car parked in front of Nora Jeffries's house…"

Marissa burst into laughter and that earned her a glare from Bea and a warning look from Alex. Before either could comment, the door to the kitchen opened again and this time an older woman with long, graying dark hair hanging in a single braid walked out. She didn't look at all pleased as she headed toward their table.

"Bea, I got the tea bags out of the faucet. Don't ever do that again. I know you have some very good ideas, but next time will you please tell me your good ideas so I can tell you if it will work."

Bea nodded. "Yes, Miss Essie, I'm sorry. Now I'll go cook. If you don't mean to fire me. And you can explain to Alex, because he is your nephew, that being neighborly is a sin. My mama said so."

As Bea left, Marissa felt heat crawl up her neck and her stomach chose that moment to growl loudly.

"I should go after her and correct her, but I'm just too tired." Essie smiled at Marissa. "Don't let her bother you. She's just Bea and we all love her and take what she says with a grain of salt."

"Of course," Marissa responded.

Essie's gaze slid to Marissa. "How long are you planning on staying in town?"

With her coffee cup midway to her mouth, Marissa paused. How long? She hadn't really thought it through. She'd left the wedding knowing that she had to go somewhere else and for some reason it had seemed like a good idea to come here, to see her grandfather. And the longer she stayed, the less she wanted to leave.

This town. These people. They might be exactly what she needed to get over the humiliation of her failed wedding.

She spied a Christmas tree in the window of the café, and in the distance she thought she heard church bells. For the first time in a long time, she felt at peace.

Alex watched the expressions that flitted over Marissa's face. First she'd been embarrassed and then maybe a little bit cornered. Now she looked like a woman contemplating a life change. Not that he blamed her. He knew how it felt to come home and face people his family had hurt. He knew how it felt to be whispered about.

He guessed that's what she had to look forward to when she returned home. Fortunately she'd have an easier time getting lost in the crowd in Dallas. In a town the size of Bluebonnet, everyone knew everything about everybody.

"I'm just staying a week. Or maybe two," Marissa

finally answered. "I want to make sure my grandfather is well enough to take care of himself."

"Dan's been taking care of himself as long as I can remember," Essie replied without censure. She turned her attention to Alex. "And you. Friday is the carnival fund-raiser for the children at the shelter. I think there are six little ones we'll be buying gifts for. And the rest of the money we raise will go in the shelter fund. You said you'd help."

"I will. I'm bringing the pony. We'll give rides and also let the kids pet him." Alex glanced at the menu. "Could we order before Marissa passes out from hunger?"

His aunt laughed. "I heard her stomach rumbling. Yes, give Libby your order. I need to make some phone calls. I have about half a dozen people setting up craft booths for the festival. I need to return phone calls and arrange for Walt Smith and his friends to play music."

"I know you'll let me know what I need to do," Alex said as he poured sugar in his coffee.

"Yes, I will. And you can start by calling your twin brother and asking him to come home soon. I know he is having a good year and making a lot of money, but he hasn't been home for a long time."

"I can't control him." Alex hoped she would leave it alone. He didn't want to have uncomfortable family conversations in front of a woman who didn't need to know all of their secrets.

If she stayed in town and listened to gossip, she'd find out soon enough. She'd learn that his father had been nothing but a con man who bilked money from the good men and woman of Bluebonnet. Soon Marissa and the rest of the folks in town would also learn that if he couldn't find the money, the Palermo ranch would be auctioned on the county courthouse steps.

Essie patted his arm. "You can't fix it by worrying about it."

Alex nodded and hoped she'd let it go. Fortunately Libby appeared, order pad in hand. As his aunt departed, she sat down and propped her feet up on a chair he scooted close for her.

"When are you going to have that baby?" he asked.

"From the way I feel right now, could be any second." She reached for the glass of water Alex wouldn't drink. "I'm so glad you always let me give you a glass of water. You're my favorite Palermo."

"You know that isn't true."

She gave him a serious look and then turned her attention to Marissa. "He fixed our tractor and didn't charge us. No way could we have gotten our hay crop in last fall without his help."

Alex tugged at his collar. "Stop."

"But he doesn't like for people to know what a decent guy he is."

"Yeah, that's me. So, could I have biscuits, gravy and a couple of fried eggs?" Alex looked over at Marissa. "What would you like?"

"The same. And more stories about Alex."

"Stop," he ordered.

Libby got up and laughed as she walked away from the table. "I'll refill your coffee in a minute."

"The carnival and fund-raiser are to buy Christmas presents for kids at the shelter and around the community. This time of year it seems there is more need. The community likes to make sure the children are taken care of at Christmas," Alex explained.

"That's wonderful. I'd like to be involved if I'm here. I love that Christmas is important to the people in town."

"You won't have plans of your own with your family?"

"No. Not since…" She stopped herself. "It isn't. There are just the three of us. Some years we visit my father's family and other years we go away on a vacation."

It sounded lonely but he didn't say that. "What did you start to say? Since what?"

She shook her head. "Nothing. We used to attend church on Christmas. Things were different when I was younger."

He was left wondering what she'd meant to say and why things had changed for her family. He knew he should leave it alone. Knowing her stories put him much more firmly into her life. And that was the last place either of them needed him to be.

They were almost finished eating when Marissa's phone rang. She glanced at the caller ID, silenced the ringer and finished her last bite of food. It rang again almost immediately.

"You should probably answer it," he offered.

"I'd rather not."

"Why is that?" he asked.

"Because I don't want to be lectured. I don't want to hear that I've let them down. I try very hard to always do what is expected and what makes them happy and I had no control…" She stopped talking. "I'm sorry, I didn't mean to do that."

He was sorry, too, because of the hurt he saw in her eyes. And because he couldn't find a way to distance himself.

"You don't have to apologize," he told her.

Her words had tumbled out as if she hadn't expected to say them and he got the feeling she'd never said them to another living soul. Not exactly a helpful realization for a guy who didn't want to get this involved.

"No," she answered with hesitation. "I guess I don't have to apologize. Not to you. But I do need to apologize to my parents. If you don't mind, I'll step outside and call them back."

"Go ahead. I'll pay the bill and be out there in a minute. If you want, we can take Dan's truck back to his place and then I'll drive you to the hospital to see him. I'll even drive Dan's truck back to the farm and you can drive mine if you want."

That offer elicited a smile from her. But still she shook her head.

"You have a life and I'm sure things you need to do."

He did. But he couldn't very well leave her on her own.

"Make your call and then we'll go see Dan."

Alex was pouring himself another cup of coffee when Duncan Matthews, the pastor of the Bluebonnet Community Church, arrived. Alex motioned him to his table.

It had taken a lot of years for Alex to trust anyone associated with ministry. He guessed a lot of people in the area felt that way after having been victims of Jesse Palermo's brand of religion. The Church of the Redeemed had been a cult with Jesse as the leader, controlling lives, controlling finances and abusing his family. Duncan Matthews had shown up in town a couple of years ago and he'd slowly but surely started the process of renovating the church and helping people heal.

"Is that Dan's granddaughter out there on the phone?" Pastor Matthews asked as Alex filled his coffee cup.

"Yeah, it is."

"She's crying."

Alex started to swear but an amused look from the pastor caused him to swallow the words. Instead he carried the coffeepot back to the warmer and returned to the table, where he sat down, stretching his legs in front of him as he nursed his third, or maybe fourth, cup of coffee.

He wasn't going to her rescue.

"You're not going to check on her?" Pastor Matthews asked.

"It's a private conversation." And none of his business. He didn't want it to be his business.

Libby approached, her hand supporting her back as she looked less than happy. She sat down and pulled a pen out from behind her ear. "Pastor?"

"Libby, you look like you might want to go home and put your feet up."

"I think you might be right."

Alex happened to glance toward the front of the café, and when he did, he saw Marissa at the corner of the building wiping at her cheeks.

"I have to go."

Pastor Matthews stirred creamer into his coffee. "I thought you might."

He let the comment slide. He'd known this woman less than a week and it seemed like a lot of people had let her down. He knew how that felt. And he didn't want to be another person who let her down.

It didn't make sense but there was no way would he say it out loud.

Chapter Seven

Wednesday afternoon, Alex drove the twenty miles to his bank. He stood on the sidewalk of the business he'd used since he'd been old enough to save money. He didn't usually take the time to think about what he'd wear or even what he'd say. He went in, deposited money, ordered checks—whatever needed to be done. Things were different today. There was a lot riding on this meeting.

A lot had changed since his conversation with Lucy. He'd found out that the ranch would be auctioned off if they didn't come up with some money soon. Lucy's husband, Dane, had offered to bail them out. Alex wasn't crazy about that idea. Dane hadn't gotten them into this mess, their mother had.

He stepped into the bank. The tellers, the same women he would see each time he came to the bank, waved greetings to him. He nodded and headed past them.

"Alex, come into my office." Blake Adams motioned him into the glass-walled office at the back of the small bank.

Alex followed, feeling less than comfortable with

the situation. First, he knew how much money it would take to buy their half of the ranch. Second, he knew the amount their mother had borrowed and he couldn't get over how she'd blown through that much cash.

He sat down across from the middle-aged man, who always seemed genuinely interested in their lives. He'd probably lose that interest when he learned what was needed.

"So, tell me what's going on and how I can help."

Alex spilled the story, knowing it was no use holding back. Blake listened, took notes, nodded his head frequently and groaned as the details unfolded.

When Alex was done, the older man steepled his hands and leaned back in his chair. He drew in a long breath and exhaled.

"I hate this for you all," he began. "That doesn't mean we can't do something. But it's going to take cash on your part. I know you've invested in cattle, bucking bulls and your business. I'm not telling you to sell off any of that, but I am telling you to make some careful decisions. Also, make sure this is what your siblings want. Don't take on a big mortgage if you're going to be stuck doing this alone."

"And if we do nothing?"

They both knew the answer to that question. If he did nothing, the ranch would be gone.

"I don't like the idea of you having to buy your mother's half of the ranch, but if that's what it takes to get you out of this mess, then I would probably do the same."

Alex rubbed a hand over his face. Cash. Something he didn't have a lot of.

"I appreciate your advice, Blake." Alex stood and reached for the other man's hand.

"Alex, I'm here to help. I've watched you grow up a lot in the past ten years. You've done well for yourself, and you've thought about your future. I know you're going to make the right decision and get through this. Here's a loan packet. Fill this out. Get me the documents I've listed in there."

Alex took the envelope and left. It was a warm day and the sun beat down on him as he crossed the parking lot to his truck. A truck parked next to his looked familiar. He pushed his hat back to get a better look and then he shook his head.

"Marcus," he said as he walked up to the passenger-side door.

"Alex," Marcus whispered, his voice hoarse.

"How'd you know where to find me?"

"Lucy told me." He shook his head. "I can't believe Mom did this."

"I'm not sure why we're surprised."

"I don't think I want the ranch," Marcus said. "Or anything to do with it."

Alex shouldn't have been surprised. Marcus had been running since he turned eighteen. Even when he was in town he stayed with a friend on the opposite side of Bluebonnet Springs. But Alex hadn't thought Marcus would turn his back on them. Or on the ranch.

"I can't do this on my own."

"Lucy will help," Marcus whispered.

"It's our home."

"It's *your* home," Marcus countered.

Alex pulled off his hat and swiped his arm across his brow. "Where are you headed?"

"I'm on my way to Kansas. But if you want to go to Killeen, I'll buy you lunch."

"Sure, why not." He placed his hat back on his head. "I'm picking the restaurant."

One side of his twin's mouth kicked up. "Sure."

Alex headed for his truck. As glad as he was to see his twin, he couldn't help but feel like things were going from bad to worse.

On the drive to Killeen he had a talk with himself and the good Lord. Because he had to believe that this would work out. He had to believe that God had a plan.

He decided to call his sister. It was new, this relationship where he turned to Lucy. He'd avoided her for a long time after that night his dad had locked her in the barn. He'd felt as if he let her down and he hadn't been able to look her in the eyes for a long, long time.

He put his phone on speaker and placed it on the console. "Marcus isn't interested in helping."

"I talked to him earlier. I told him to cowboy up and tell you to your face. Did he?"

"Yeah, he did."

"We'll do this, Alex. Don't let it get to you. You can't force Marcus to choose the path you're choosing."

"I know. I still kind of feel gut-stomped."

"I know. This whole thing has been a bit of a shock. We'll figure something out. I promise."

"Right. So I guess Mom isn't coming to Christmas dinner."

Lucy laughed a little at his poor attempt at a joke. "No. I guess she isn't. I saw Dan in town. I guess you busted him out of the hospital yesterday."

"Yeah, we did." No. He and Marissa weren't a *we*. Or a *they*. Yesterday Dan had told her she could stay a few more days.

And then she'd be gone. Back to Dallas. Back to her

life. She would be a kindergarten teacher. She'd meet a subdivision kind of guy who drove a big sedan. Or maybe one of those electric cars that had to be plugged in.

"Alex?"

"Sorry. Just thinking." He cleared his throat. "I'll sell the bulls."

"What?"

"The bulls. I invested a lot in them, and I can use that money to pay off the second mortgage. That'll buy me time to get a loan to buy out our mother. I'm afraid if we don't, she'll do something else to get us further into debt."

"Calm down. Don't rush into anything."

"I guess we don't have time to sit on our hands." He approached a steak house. "I've got to go. Marcus is buying me lunch."

She hung up and he made the turn into the parking lot of the restaurant. His brain had taken a serious left turn and was stuck on Marissa. He'd never been the person who saw himself as part of a couple. He'd never relied on anyone other than his siblings.

That's why it didn't make sense that he didn't want to be at this restaurant with his twin. He wanted to be in Bluebonnet Springs sitting at the tiny table in Dan's camper, having a cup of coffee with Marissa. As much as he wanted to be with her, he had to be the last thing she needed or wanted in her life.

Marissa held tight to the kitten she'd found in the barn. It didn't really seem to want to be held. She deduced that from the way it was clawing and biting at her gloved hands. But she wouldn't let go. The other grown cat she'd seen stalking a mouse the previous day had cornered the kitten in the feed room and Marissa had been positive the cat meant to tear the kitten to pieces.

Using her teeth, she pulled the glove off her left hand and held the kitten tight with her right hand. She opened the door of the camper and stepped inside. Her grandfather looked up from his recliner, his eyes narrowing in on the gray kitten. He'd been home for a day, but already he was telling her to go on back to Dallas. She'd told him she needed to be here to help him. And besides, she was getting pretty good at driving a tractor and she finally knew the difference between a cow and a bull.

"No," he said as he pointed to the front door. "Barn cats stay in the barn."

He'd been acting what Alex called "cantankerous" since they brought him home. He'd complained about the wreath she'd put on the front door. He'd told her he wasn't going to let her put up any kind of Christmas tree. There wasn't room for one, he insisted. And he was probably right, but she couldn't imagine not having a tree. Even if she wasn't staying, she wanted him to have one.

"The old tomcat was after him," she explained. She took the kitten to the kitchen and poured it a small bowl of milk.

"I don't care if he was using that kitten to bait a mousetrap. It goes back to the barn."

She gave him a warning look. "You'll have yourself coughing if you don't stop."

"Bah." He waved a dismissive hand. "You'll have me coughing if you don't stop testing my patience."

"I'm not sure what you mean. I hadn't noticed you have any patience."

He pushed himself up out of the chair and headed for the kitchen, a frown firmly in place, but she'd seen the hint of a grin. "I don't. And that's why your grandmother left me. I was a drunk with a short fuse."

The revelation shocked her.

He poured himself a glass of juice. "And you remind me of her. You don't have any quit in you."

She smiled at the compliment. Even if he hadn't meant for it to be one. "I couldn't find that cow you told me to look for."

He set down his glass on the counter. "Well, maybe you should have said that the minute you walked through the door instead of worrying about that kitten."

"I'm sorry. I'll go back out and look again. I just wanted to get a heavier coat."

"I'll go." He was already heading for the tiny closet by the front door.

"No, Granddad. You have to stay inside."

"I have to find that cow. You don't understand her value. And the value of her calf. I can't afford to leave them out there to die."

"Granddad, Alex said you have cattle disappearing. We noticed four-wheeler tracks. And the IRS called. I'm worried about you."

"It isn't any of your dad-burned business."

"It is my business. You're my grandfather."

He pointed a shaking finger at her. "You didn't seem to care about that until your groom walked out on you."

"I would have cared had I known. And stop trying to badger me. This is serious. We need to call the police."

"Don't you dare call the police. I'll take care of this. Once I get the IRS paid off, they'll go back to bothering other taxpayers."

Except she wasn't convinced it was the IRS. How did she tell him she thought he was being duped?

"I have to go get that cow." He pulled open the door of the tiny closet.

"I'll go get Alex," she said quickly, before he could head out the front door. As much as she didn't want to lean on their neighbor so much, he was really the only person she knew to go to for help.

"Alex has his own set of troubles." He gave her a pointed look. "And don't be thinking that's the direction you need to be turning. I know how you young people are. You get hurt and you immediately rebound to whoever you can find. Alex is the last person a girl like you needs to take up with."

"I'm not looking for a rebound relationship," she informed him as she watched the kitten lap up the milk. "I'm trying to help you, and Alex seems to have the same goal. And he's really the only person I know in town, so I thought I would go get him."

"Uh-huh," he said. "I know what it's like, you city gals and the lure of a cowboy. I wasn't always this old."

"I'm not interested in a cowboy. I'm not interested in anyone. A little under a week ago I thought I was getting married and he walked out on me. There is no instant rebound from that."

The expression on his face softened. He hung his jacket back in the closet and returned to the juice he'd left on the counter.

"No, I reckon there isn't an easy rebound from that. And I'm sorry. Sorry as anything that you thought you had to come here to me and not to your parents, or whatever friends you have in Dallas. It doesn't seem natural that you'd want to be here with someone you've never met before."

"It seemed natural to me," she said.

Awkwardly he patted her arm. "I can't see how I et me give you some advice anyway."

"Okay."

"Don't shut yourself off. Now, that doesn't mean I want to see you chasing after Alex Palermo. He isn't right for you. But I wouldn't want you to be anything like me. After your grandmother left, I decided there wasn't much about me that anyone else would want. Oh, I quit drinking, because I thought she might come back someday. But she didn't. And after some years went by I decided I was just meant to be alone. But being alone, it can be lonely."

Sage advice from a man who had lived with much regret. She stood on tiptoe to kiss his weathered cheek. "Thank you."

"Go on now. Don't thank me. I still don't want you here, underfoot and bringing barn cats in my house."

"Of course you don't. If you'll watch the kitten, I'll see if I can get us some help to find your cow and calf."

"That would be good. I need to take a few head to auction next week." He picked up the kitten. "Take it back to the barn. Not enough room in here for Bub and a cat."

She took the kitten.

"I'll go get Alex."

She was heading for the door when he stopped her. "How'd you learn to drive that truck?"

"Looked it up on the internet," she answered. She left smiling, because she heard him chuckling and saying something about her backbone.

* * *

The bull in the chute bucked, kicking at the metal enclosure, and then rattled the gate with his horns. Alex grabbed the horns and brought the bull's head back around. The teenager standing on the catwalk backed up a bit, his eyes widening as he watched the animal try to come out of the chute.

"Second thoughts?" Alex asked.

"No, of course not."

Alex laughed. The other boys leaned against the arena wall and looked as if they were about to run for their mamas. They were neighbor kids who wanted to bull ride and their parents had given permission for them to buck bulls with Alex. His bulls needed the experience. The boys needed experience and instruction. It was a win-win situation.

Unfortunately the boys also needed courage, which they hadn't gotten on steers that were used in the earlier stages of bull-riding training.

"Okay, I'm going to ride this bull and show you all how it's done. And then we'll try again on Hazardous Duty." As if he heard his name, the bull pushed against the metal of the pen.

He motioned the boys close. "Come on over and help me out. Jason, you get down there and be ready to open the gate. Dusty and Kyle, stand here with me and help me get settled."

The last thing he would admit to these boys was that he had no desire to get on the back of a bull. Not now. Not ever. Especially not in this arena. But if he was going to let these kids do it, he had to be willing to pull his rope on one of the rankest of the six bulls he owned.

For now. He didn't want to let go of this dream, to

own bucking bulls. But every now and then he wondered why it was his dream.

He pushed his hat down tight and climbed over the side of the chute to settle on the back of the bull. The minute he got his seat, the bull started to shift and buck, trying to unseat him. He wished the eight seconds could start inside the gate because sometimes this was the toughest part, and could even be the most dangerous. He'd seen men broken and knocked out just trying to get their bull rope tied.

He pounded the resin-covered rope over his gloved hand. The bull went up but Dusty pushed him down and Kyle held Alex's shoulders. He heard a truck and he groaned. That sounded like Dan's truck. He hadn't seen Marissa since he helped her get Dan home the previous day. "Ready, Alex? He's just going to get more rowdy," Jason called from the dirt floor of the arena.

"Ready." He nodded once. The gate flew open.

He breathed past the first jolt and the left-hand turn he knew was coming. He blinked away the image of his father's prone figure on the arena floor. The bull bucked right twice and then he took a flying leap and belly rolled. As Alex flew through the air he caught a glimpse of a woman with short dark hair and heard her scream.

He hit the ground, rolled, covered his head with his arms and then felt the bull slam against him. White-hot pain slashed through his leg and his side. The bull came at him again.

He caught his breath and scrambled to get on his feet. Someone was there, distracting the bull. Jason. The kid grabbed at the bull and then ran for the gate. Dusty had the gate open for the bull.

Alex leaned forward, winded. When he straightened, Marissa was there. She looked small in Dan's straw hat and denim jacket.

He swiped at his face to clear his vision. "I lost my hat. And you should not be in this arena."

"Your hat? You're worried about losing a hat when you might have lost your life?" she yelled at him.

"I wouldn't lose my life." He took a cautious step forward and bit back a groan.

"Who would help me if you weren't here?"

He managed to chuckle. "People. There are plenty of people who can help you."

"I like you." She helped him walk out of the arena. "So I would be very offended if you got yourself killed by a bull."

He pulled free from her arms, and he admitted it took some doing. Not because he couldn't walk on his own, but because he liked being in her arms. They were slim but strong. They felt like a safe haven. He couldn't say that he'd ever felt that before.

And it frightened him more than being on the back of that bull. Because a safe haven was a place where a person took refuge. She couldn't be his. Ever.

But her words were ricocheting around in his brain. He could have been killed by that bull. She wasn't far off the mark.

"My dad died in that arena," he said softly, then moved ahead of her. She came after him. Though admittedly she didn't have to move too fast. He collapsed on the closest bench and put his head between his hands. She sat down next to him. Her shoulder brushed against his.

"I'm sorry," she whispered. She sat close to his side,

her presence undoing something inside him. Something he'd kept boxed up and off-limits for years.

It might have been the hit to his head, but he was having a hard time understanding how she had managed, in such a short amount of time, to make him think things he'd never thought and feel things he'd never felt.

"Don't worry about," he replied.

"It has to be difficult, being here, knowing that you lost him here."

The truth happened to be pretty ugly and he didn't want to see the reaction on her face when he told her. But maybe if she knew the truth, she'd walk away from him and he wouldn't have to keep fighting his feelings for her every time they got close.

"I wanted him to die. I was a kid, just seventeen, and more than once I'd thought how much better life would be if he…"

"You were just a kid," she said, moving closer.

"Yes, a kid. And he was as mean as a snake. My sister has her own stories. We all do. But that's not why you're here."

"I'm sorry." Her hand settled on his cheek. He briefly closed his eyes and her hand slipped away.

"Childhood shouldn't be so difficult." She said it in a way that made him think she had experience with troubled childhoods. It made him want to ask questions of his own.

As if she knew what he was thinking, she walked away from him.

He swiped at his face and saw blood on his hand. He needed to clean himself up and get back to work. As he stood, he saw Marissa at the entrance to the arena talking to Jason, Dusty and Kyle. The three teenagers were listening intently, as if she was somehow in charge. He headed their way but they didn't wait. Jason did give him a salute as he turned and left.

"They're leaving but they put the bulls back in their pen first," Marissa said as she returned to his side.

"You don't have to stay, either."

"I think someone does have to stay. Plus, I can't go until you tell me what to do about a missing cow. Dan is beside himself and I'm afraid he'll try to go look for her." She moved his hand away to look at the cut on his head.

"It's fine."

"Of course it is."

"So you're here about one of Dan's cows?" he asked, trying to deflect her attention from him.

Her blue eyes flashed with humor. "Well, I certainly wasn't here to see you get knocked unconscious. It just worked out that way."

"Don't be dramatic. I was never unconscious," he argued as he pushed her hand away from the cut. "Ouch."

"Sorry. I don't think this is too deep. Do you have a first-aid kit?"

"In the tack room."

She glanced around. "And where would that be?"

"This way," he told her, not pulling away when she took his hand.

"You're limping."

"Yeah, he went after me pretty good."

"Do you need me to drive you to the ER? Or to Doc?"

He opened the door to the tack room. "I can doctor myself. A bandage on my head and maybe some ice on my knee and I'll be good to go."

"Where is the first-aid kit?" she asked.

"The cabinet. Maybe the second shelf."

"Okay, sit down and I'll get you fixed up." She maneuvered him to the seat in the corner of the room.

"We need to get that cow found," he told her.

"I'm sure she's fine." She wiped the wound clean and used a butterfly bandage. Her fingers were gentle, cool. He closed his eyes as she worked. Because if he looked into her eyes, he might lose himself.

"There." She finished. "What about your knee?"

He opened his eyes. "I'm good. I can walk it off."

"Really? You'll just walk it off?"

"Isn't that what you've been doing since I found you walking down the road?"

"Yes, I guess I have. And surprisingly, it doesn't hurt much."

"There you go. I'll walk it off and it won't hurt much." With a grimace he managed to stand. "But we should take care of that cow. Dan won't thank us if he's lost one of his good heifers."

"Will he be upset if I put up a Christmas tree, do you think?"

He took advantage of her nearness and slipped an arm around her waist. Just to steady himself, he told himself. And because she smelled good.

"I don't know if I remember Dan ever putting up a tree. But I don't think that's going to stop you."

"No, it won't." She allowed him to lean against her and he felt a little guilty. Not guilty enough to admit he didn't really need her help.

They left the barn walking side by side, her steps slow, in order to match his. When they got to the old farm truck, he leaned a little closer, tempted. He wanted to know what made this woman tick. What made her strong as steel and yet tender. She taught kindergarten. She cared about a grandfather she hadn't known until recently.

"I know I shouldn't. So let's just blame this on the head injury," he murmured low, close to her ear. He pulled off the straw hat she wore and pulled her closer, hoping she wouldn't back away.

Once upon a time he'd told Aunt Essie he would never get married because he would never fall in love. Essie had laughed and told him that the right woman would come along and no matter how hard he fought, he wouldn't be able to keep from loving her.

Marissa was everything he shouldn't want. And he was the last thing she needed.

He reminded himself of the mortgage on the ranch, hoping it would bring him back to his senses. He told himself this woman deserved better than he could ever give her. But then the breeze kicked up and blew soft tendrils of hair around her face and a tropical scent filled the air.

He moved close enough to feel her breath against his neck. And then he kissed her. His lips brushed hers. With that kiss, his whole world spun a little bit out of control. And he couldn't blame it on the blow to his head. Not really.

It took him by surprise, the way it felt to hold her, to kiss her. It took him by surprise because she kissed him back and her hands fluttered on his shoulders until they settled.

Then suddenly, it was over.

"No," she whispered, pulling away from him. "This isn't why I'm here. I'm not here to jump from a failed relationship to a relationship that can't be anything more than temporary."

"It was a kiss, not a proposal," he assured her with humor he was nowhere close to feeling. "Temporary is the only kind of relationship I've ever had."

"Yes, me, too." With that she got in the truck and cranked the engine to life. He stepped back, letting her go.

It was better that way. She'd hold on to that iron will of hers and he would learn to stay on his side of the fence. But then he remembered she had a cow to find, so he headed to his truck.

Out of the frying pan and into the fire.

Chapter Eight

She shouldn't have kissed him. Marissa parked the truck and then rested her forehead on the steering wheel. What had she been thinking, kissing Alex? How stinking cute he was in his jeans and faded T-shirt. She'd thought about how he'd fallen off that bull and managed to walk away. And then his arms had been around her. And she'd wanted to know that a man found her attractive.

Fortunately she'd come to her senses. Or maybe unfortunately. Because she'd loved being in his arms. She'd loved the way he'd held her as if she was precious to him. But he liked temporary. He'd said it himself.

She didn't want to be anyone's temporary romance, ever again.

She leaned back in the seat and sat there for a minute in that old truck of her grandfather's. It smelled of cattle, oil and age. The seat had a rip that he'd fixed with gray duct tape. Why was she here? Driving this old truck? Searching for cattle? Feeding barn cats?

Kissing cowboys.

This wasn't her life.

But she couldn't leave. Her grandfather wasn't healthy and he needed her help. If someone was taking advantage of him, she needed to figure it out. Headlights flashed through the cab of the truck. She knew who it would be. A moment later Alex was climbing in the passenger seat. He tossed her the hat he'd pulled off her head when he'd kissed her.

"Thought I should return this."

"Thank you." She shoved it back on her head.

"I'm sorry," he said.

She glanced at him and couldn't help but smile. He was cute. Even with his big ears. She thought about telling him, but why add to that ego of his.

"Please don't apologize," she said instead. "Just help me find that cow."

"That's the other reason that I'm here."

"I thought I heard her earlier. Maybe down by that pond. But it was getting dark and I knew if I found her, I wouldn't know what to do with her."

"Don't worry, we have everything we need in the back of the truck."

She started the truck and headed for the field. She noticed he didn't grimace too much at her driving.

"I'm getting better at this," she informed him.

"I agree. By the time you leave, you'll be an old hand on the farm. When you get back to the city you won't know how to drive your car anymore, or remember how to handle that city traffic."

"I sure don't miss that traffic."

"Oh, you will miss it." He said it with authority. "The same way I kind of like the city for a little while, but then I'm ready to get back here. No stoplights. No traffic jams."

She didn't argue with him, but what if she went back to the city and she wasn't happy there? What would she do then? Come back here to her grandfather's camper? And no job.

The conversation trailed off. Marissa drove around the pond, searching for any sign of the missing cow. Finally the headlights found her. She was on her side in a brushy area near the pond.

"There she is. Be sure to set the emergency brake. I wouldn't want Dan's truck to roll into the pond." Alex jumped out of the truck. Marissa did as he'd told her, then she followed him.

When the cow saw them, she let out a plaintive cry and made a strong attempt to push. Alex examined her and shook his head.

"I'm only seeing one hoof."

"Do we call a doctor?"

He laughed. "No, we don't call a vet. There are times when that's necessary but usually we can handle it ourselves. I'm going to see if I can get that other hoof and then we'll see if she can't do this on her own. If not, we'll pull the calf. There's a chain and pulley in the truck."

Chains? Pulleys? She cringed, thinking how difficult and painful this sounded.

Alex took over. It took some time but eventually the calf slid out. The mama was exhausted but she cleaned her baby, then managed to get to her feet.

Marissa watched, completely enthralled by the process. She'd never seen a birth. Not even kittens. Alex stepped to her side, wiping his hands on a rag he'd found in the back of the truck. Side by side they watched as the calf found his legs and stood, wobbly but healthy. The cow nudged him, her long tongue taking swipes down his back. Eventually he found his way to her belly and was able to get his first meal.

"Will they be okay now?" Marissa asked as they walked away.

"They'll be fine. She'll feed him and then she'll find the rest of the herd."

"But it's cold."

"She'll keep him warm," Alex reassured her. He opened the passenger door of the truck. "Climb in. I'm driving."

"I can drive."

"I'm driving because you behind the wheel of this truck is more frightening than eight seconds on the back of a bull and thirty seconds under its hooves."

"You said I was doing better."

He winked. "You are, but I'm just not sure I can handle the return trip right now."

"I made sloppy joes for dinner and I was going to invite you to join us. Now, maybe not."

"I take it back. Really. For sloppy joes, I'll even let you drive." He bumped his shoulder against hers.

A few minutes later they walked through the front door of the camper. Bub got off the couch to greet them, but before Marissa would pet him, she grabbed the towel she'd left on the coatrack. She wiped the drool from the dog's face and he thanked her with a soft woof.

Marissa's grandfather was on the phone. He held up a finger to keep them quiet. Marissa nodded and leaned to pull off her shoes. Next to her, Alex did the same.

Dan hung up, saying a few things he shouldn't have said.

"Who was that?" Marissa asked as she headed for

the kitchen and the slow cooker she'd filled with sloppy-joe ingredients.

"That was the lady from the IRS. They think I owe them another payment."

"Dan, you have to let me look at your paperwork and anything they've sent you. Please."

He shook his head. "I've been taking care of myself for a good long time, young lady."

"There's nothing wrong with letting someone else help."

He switched off the television. "I know there isn't. But this is my business."

"Right. You're right." She stirred the hamburger and then turned off the cooker. "Are you hungry?"

"Of course I am. It's pretty near bedtime."

She glanced at the clock on the stove. "It's seven o'clock."

Alex had stepped to the sink and was washing his hands and arms. "Dan, you have a bull calf."

"You found the cow? I'm glad. She's one I wouldn't want to lose. They're both healthy?"

"They're both healthy," Alex assured him. "Dan, let her look at the papers."

"Since when do you get in my business, Alex?"

"I'm getting in your business because you're losing livestock and now you're paying out money you might not have to pay. Someone needs to figure this out. And you probably need to call the police."

"You should worry about your own affairs. The county paper came out and there's an interesting list of properties up for auction."

Alex didn't respond, he just shook his head. Her grandfather had gotten up and made it to the kitchen, stopping once to catch his breath. He had an oxygen tank nearby but she knew he wouldn't use it until he absolutely had to.

"The only reason you're getting in my business," Dan said to Alex as he poured himself a cup of tea, "is because I have a pretty granddaughter living here."

"And you're getting in my business because I'm a Palermo," Alex muttered.

"You said it, not me," her grandfather responded.

"Stop. Both of you," Marissa yelled. "Sit at the table and I'll get you a plate."

Her grandfather sat down. Alex helped her get the plates and food on the table. And then they all sat. The table was small, more of a miniature booth than a dining room table. When her grandfather wouldn't budge from his seat, she sat next to Alex. They fixed their plates, then Alex cleared his throat.

"What?" Dan grumbled.

"I'd like to ask for the blessing." Alex grinned at Dan.

"Suddenly he gets religious and makes a nuisance of himself." Dan bowed his head. "Make it quick, Palermo."

Marissa bowed her head. Her breath caught when Alex slipped his hand over hers. His fingers were warm and strong. His prayer was sweet. Her heart tripped over the moment, getting tangled up in something she knew could be dangerous.

Dangerous in a sweet, tempting way that made it hard to resist.

Alex lifted the fence-post driver and slammed it down on the metal post. It vibrated through his arm and his back, reminding him of the spill he'd taken from the bull the previous day. He raised it and brought it down on the post again.

Today he was repairing fences. But he was also taking his frustrations out on those posts. It was a good thing they needed some serious pounding to get them in the ground. He raised the driver one more time on the post and then he stepped back, pulling a handkerchief from his pocket to wipe his brow.

A truck pulled up the drive and parked by the fence. Pastor Matthews got out. He eyed the fence and the post driver, and started to get back in his truck. Through the windshield Alex could see his grin.

"Oh, no, you're already here." Alex motioned him out of the truck. "Showing up is the same as volunteering. Wasn't that the sermon a few weeks ago?"

Pastor Matthews adjusted his ball cap and gave the fence a good look. "No. I think what I said is complaining is the same as volunteering."

"Then I guess I should call Dane to help because he complained about my fence." Alex lifted the post driver again and positioned another metal fence post. "What brings you out here?"

"I don't know." He waited until Alex was finished with the post before finishing. "I guess I thought you might need to talk."

"Did you get that in a text or an email?"

Pastor Matthews laughed. "God mail."

"I guess you and about everyone else in town has seen the county paper."

Alex headed for his truck and the thermos of water he'd left on the tailgate. His gaze shifted to the bulls he'd bought. They were on a five-acre field with fences that were strong enough to hold them. They hadn't been cheap. And there was a lot of risk involved.

He should sell them. They were a dream, but not a necessity. He told Pastor Matthews as much, expecting he'd probably agree.

"Why would you want to do that? You're just getting started. Don't you want to give it more time?" Pastor Matthews asked as he sat on the tailgate of the truck. Alex joined him.

"I don't know. It feels like I'm being shut out of the bigger events. And I can't make money if my bulls don't qualify." He shrugged it off.

"I guess that's a decision you'll have to make. And one I'd put a lot of prayer into. It's hard to trust when things aren't going the way we thought they would, or the way we planned."

"Ain't that the truth?"

Alex's gaze skimmed the ranch that his dad had bought thirty years ago. "I wish I could just walk away from this place. I have a lot of bad memories and most of them are attached to this land."

"Put it on the market and do something different."

He laughed. "What would I do, Pastor? I'm a rancher. I've spent some time in the city and I can't say I liked it much."

"What if there is something else and you're so focused on this one aspect of your life, you can't see the other path?"

"I guess I'll have to hope there's some road signs so I don't get lost. I'd just like for things to go smoothly for a change. I kind of thought this was the easy part of my life. I'm home, business is going well, I have my bulls, rebuilding the livestock on this place. And then out of the blue…"

Out of the blue came a bride standing on the side of the road looking for all the world like she'd been meant for him. But she wasn't for him. Her kind never was.

"Out of the blue?" Pastor Matthews had hopped off the end of the truck and picked up the post driver, as if he really did plan on helping with the fence.

"Out of the blue you find out your mother has put a big old mortgage on the ranch and you might lose it all."

"Don't let it get you down, Alex. It'll work out. Even if it doesn't work out the way you thought it might."

"Growing up, my dad liked to tell me to stop dreaming. He told me I'd never make it to the pros in bull riding. He told me I wouldn't amount to anything. Worthless. That was his pet name for me and Marcus."

Duncan Matthews had heard the story more than once but he still shook his head and sighed. "His voice is still in your head. But the difference is, God is in your heart and His plan is what matters. He's given you a hope and a future. So whose voice do you trust the most?"

"Good sermon, Pastor."

The sarcasm rolled off the other man and he just laughed. "Thank you, Alex. I might use that next Sunday."

"Then you won't mind if I'm not at church. Since I helped write the sermon and all."

"Oh, you should be there. I'll mention your name in the final credits." He pulled on a pair of work gloves. "Let me help you with this fence before I go."

"Thanks, I'd appreciate that."

An hour later they were pulling the fence when Duncan stepped back and wiped at the perspiration dripping down his face. "This is not easy work and I'm out of shape."

"Stick with me. I'll keep you working and get you back in shape."

"That's good of you, but I think I'll stick to my day job. Hey, by the way, how's Dan doing?"

They fastened the last section of the fence and Alex pulled off his gloves.

"He's better. Marissa is still here, helping him out."

"That's good of her. I'm sure he appreciates it."

"I don't think I'd call it appreciation. And if he does appreciate it, he isn't going to tell her or anyone else."

"She seems like a nice girl."

At the seemingly innocent statement, Alex laughed. "I see where this is going."

Pastor Matthews looked innocent. "I'm not sure what you mean?"

"Single woman comes to town. Single man obviously needs a wife."

"I didn't know you were looking for a wife."

"I'm single and I plan on staying that way."

"Time has a way of changing things."

Alex tossed the post driver and two remaining posts in the back of the truck before answering. "That isn't changing. I know how to ride bulls. I can raise some cattle. I can train a horse. But I'm not about to follow in the footsteps of my father and ruin the lives of a woman or children."

"Alex, you aren't your father."

"No, I'm not. And I don't plan on becoming my father. Ever." Alex glanced at his watch, needing to end this conversation before it went from uncomfortable to downright aggravating. "I'm bringing the pony tomorrow and I'll be there to help with the Christmas lists."

"Again, I'd say you aren't your father. You're the real deal, Alex."

Alex reached for the jug of water in the back of his truck. "Bringing a pony to a fund-raiser for some kids to ride doesn't change much. I'm just doing what I can."

"That's all any of us can do. I'll see you tomorrow."

"Sure thing."

He watched the pastor drive away. He could admit he was pretty thankful for Duncan Matthews. The man had done a lot for the community. He'd done a lot for Alex.

Now if Alex could only make himself believe that there was a silver lining in this cloud of a situation with the ranch.

He could live without this place. He could start over on a smaller spread of his own. No matter what, he knew he'd survive the loss of the ranch.

But he wasn't sure about Marcus. Or even Maria. He couldn't let go of the ranch. Bad memories and all, it was one of the few constants in their lives.

He had a lot of plans for this place, and for the future. Marissa Walker didn't figure into those plans.

At least, that was what he told himself, even if it wasn't close to the truth.

Chapter Nine

"I don't see why I have to go to town with you," Dan grumbled as they headed for the truck late Friday afternoon. "When are you going to head back to Dallas? Or are you going to stay and nag at me for another couple of weeks?"

Marissa kept her lips pressed in a firm and disapproving line, the better to deal with her grandfather. He was right, she should be going home. With Christmas coming up and a new job to start in January, she needed to get back to life. Her life.

But lately she wondered if it had ever truly been *her* life.

"Dan, get in the truck." She opened the passenger-side door and he stood there looking at her. He scratched his grizzled chin and shook his head.

"This is my truck. Why am I getting in on the passenger side?"

"Because you haven't been cleared to drive." And because she obviously loved getting pulled over by the local cop.

Her grandfather glowered at her. But then his expression softened. "It hasn't been all bad. Having you here."

"It hasn't been all bad being here."

"It wasn't like I had a choice," her grandfather said a few minutes later, as they were driving down the road toward Bluebonnet.

Marissa gave him a quick look. "What?"

"Letting you stay. I didn't have much choice in the matter, now did I?" He cleared his throat and she waited, wondering if he could give her a final ultimatum on leaving. "Still, I'm glad we had a chance to get to know each other."

"Me, too." She drove another mile, then slowed to pull into the church parking lot. "I'm going to buy us a Christmas tree."

He brushed a hand over his unshaven face. "Now listen here, just because I said something nice doesn't mean you have the right to start hauling in your stuff. I don't want a tree. I don't have room for a tree. End of story."

"It's almost Christmas. We need a tree."

"You're going back to Dallas and then I'll have to deal with taking it down. And the mess. No, ma'am, no tree."

"The money goes to the shelter. And besides, you'll thank me when it's decorated and has lights."

"I doubt that," he grumbled. "But go ahead. Do what you want."

She got out of the truck and headed for the trees that were in a sectioned-off area of the churchyard. She didn't look back to see if Dan had followed. The sound of children laughing drew her attention to an area at the back of the church. In a round pen a man walked a gray pony carrying a little girl.

"Dad-burn-it," Dan growled. "I nearly ran into you. What in the world are you thinking, stopping like that?"

"Sorry, Granddad, I got distracted."

"Uh-huh, by Alex Palermo. No wonder you're still hanging around."

"I'm here because you're my grandfather."

"I know who I am. My lungs are bad, not my memory. Now let's get a tree. Mind you, keep it small. I don't have a lot of room."

She hooked her arm through his and he shook his head. But he also didn't pull away from her.

The trees were all sizes and shapes, already set up in tree stands. Marissa led her grandfather to a tree that stood about three feet tall. It wasn't overly round and it had a nice shape.

"This one," she told him.

"If that's the one you want." He pulled out his bill-fold.

"I'll buy it."

"Don't argue with me. It's my tree and my house." He pulled away from her. "Dane Scott, I'm here to buy a tree."

The man her grandfather approached was in his early thirties. He was tall and had a genuine smile as he greeted Dan.

"Having a woman around will make a man change his ways, Dan."

"Don't I know it." Her grandfather shot her an amused look. "One week almost and she's had me in the hospital and now cluttering the place up with a Christmas tree."

Dane laughed. "But you love it and don't deny it."

Her grandfather didn't deny it. Granddad grumbled

that Dane could help put the tree in the back of the truck.

"Come on," her grandfather said as he walked past her. "I guess we might as well see what else is going on. You're a little old but I reckon I can take you to the pony rides. Seems that's what a grandfather should do."

"I'm a little too big for pony rides but you can buy me a burger." She pointed to the concession stand.

"That'll make my cholesterol go up."

"It's for a good cause. The money is for the women's shelter. The money they earn today will help buy Christmas gifts for these children and other needy families."

"I know what the money is for." Dan headed for the pony rides. "Come on. We have twenty-six years of lost time to make up for."

She followed her grandfather, her feet dragging. He'd somehow managed to turn the tables on her. When she reached the pony ride, there were only a few children waiting. Her grandfather got in line.

The children and the two moms present gave them curious looks and then whispered behind their hands. The little girl in front of Dan reached for his hand and gave it a tug.

"Hey, aren't you too big to ride a pony?" The little girl wrinkled her nose at Marissa's grandfather and then squinted as she looked at Marissa.

"My granddaughter has never ridden a pony," Dan told the child in a much kinder tone than he'd ever used with Marissa. "And if you're nice, I'll pay for you to ride that pony twice."

"Really? Twice?" The child beamed with happiness.

Dan nodded and handed her the money. "Merry Christmas."

The child pulled on his hand and motioned him to

her level. When Dan leaned down, the little girl gave him a quick hug. "Thank you."

"You're welcome," he said in a voice thick with emotion. "It's not like it's a big deal."

"To her it is," Marissa countered. "You're a big softy. But I won't tell."

They waited ten minutes in line. Marissa kept her gaze averted so that she didn't make eye contact with Alex. She talked to her grandfather. She talked to the child, whose name was Joy, and then to the mom, Hanna, and her daughter, Amy, who got in line behind them.

She allowed the children to move ahead of her in the line.

Finally they were at the front of the line. She had no intention of getting on the tiny pony that Alex held as he looked at them. His hand went to the gray neck of the pony. He studied them with his hat pulled low. Ever so slowly he shook his head, and white teeth flashed as the corners of his mouth tugged up.

"Dan, the pony ride is for kids."

Dan looked from the pony to Marissa and back to the pony. Marissa put a hand on his arm. She'd gone along with the silliness. Now she felt even more.

"Dan, really, we both know I can't ride that pony."

"I know but I liked the idea of it." He looked away but not before she saw a shimmer of moisture in his eyes. "It's what I would have done…"

"Yes, I know."

Alex patted her grandfather on the back. "Give me five minutes, Dan. I think I can solve this problem."

Marissa wanted to walk away. The last thing she wanted to do was stand there looking conspicuous while her grandfather smiled as if he'd just scored a major victory.

When her grandfather chuckled she shot him a questioning look. "What's so funny?"

"You," he replied. "That is not a happy look on your face. I got you a pony ride. I don't see why you're so upset."

"I didn't want a pony ride," she told him. "I'm doing this for you."

"And I'm doing this for you. You'll either thank me. Or you'll thank me to stay out of your business."

She was being taught a lesson. On meddling. And for some reason, rather than being put out, she was amused. Her grandfather's blue eyes twinkled as he watched her. When he winked, she laughed.

"You're impossible."

He laughed a little harder. "That's what your grandmother told me the entire twelve years of our marriage."

"I wish…" she began. But she didn't know how to continue. He must have known because he shifted uncomfortably and let out a long sigh.

"She had good reasons for leaving, so don't wish for something that wouldn't have done anyone any good."

"But she could have let my mother see you," she said.

"I wasn't much of a husband. Or much of a father. I drank too much. I cared too little. Until they were gone. Later on I cared a lot, but it was too late. Your mother was better off without me."

"I'm sorry," she told him. Briefly she leaned her head against his shoulder and she wondered what life might have been like had he been in their world. He would have been gruff but he would have spoken the truth. Maybe he would have prodded them all into living their lives and not wallowing in the grief after the loss of her sister.

"I've never been more sorry than now," he answered. "And I mean that, Marissa. I really do wish I'd been there for you all."

She wiped at tears rolling down her cheeks. She wished he'd been there, too. Because at times it had seemed that everyone had someone to lean on. And she'd been left with no one. Her parents had leaned on each other. Her grandmother had leaned on friends. Marissa had been a child alone.

After the near miss of a wedding, she realized she would have continued to have no one if she'd married Aidan. Not once in the entire time they'd been dating had she ever shared with him how much it had hurt to lose her sister. She hadn't confided how she'd always felt guilty. She hadn't shared anything of her struggles with him.

Alex was lifting a child off the pony and talking to her about the little horse he called Cobalt. The mother thanked him. He watched them walk away and then focused his attention on Dan and Marissa. She wondered what he thought of them.

Because she wanted to confide in him. She wanted to tell him things about herself and about her new job that she didn't really want.

She pushed away the thoughts because this wasn't home and could never be home. She knew that.

Still, it never hurt to dream, did it?

Alex checked himself before he tied Cobalt and headed for Dan and Marissa. She had that hurt expression on her face. As much as he wanted to ask her what was wrong, he knew he couldn't. She wasn't his problem. If he knew what had put that look on her face, he'd want to know more. To help her. He was already all kinds of involved, he didn't want to get even more involved. The sooner she hightailed it back to Dallas, the better.

"Well, Palermo, tell us why we've been standing here waiting for you," Old Dan grouched in his customary tone. Most people were put off by Dan. Alex wasn't. He'd seen the older man take in too many strays. He'd also seen the kindness in his eyes when he asked questions.

More than once in Alex's life, Dan had given him a stern talking-to about living in the past and how it did a man no good to dwell on mistakes made. Better to make wiser choices in the future and keep moving forward, Dan had told him.

"I have a pony more Marissa's size." Alex took her by the hand, the gesture a little too easy, and led her to his truck and trailer. He'd put up a few panels and penned his horse, Bolt. "I brought him with me today because he needs to hang out with crowds."

Bolt was a pale cream, almost white. He had crazy eyes but a good disposition. Alex had learned not to judge a horse by the eyes.

"That horse isn't going to throw my granddaughter, is he?" Dan asked, stepping close to take a good look at Bolt.

"I wouldn't let her on him if I thought he would throw her," Alex answered as he stepped inside the pen with the horse.

Bolt stood still as Alex slid the bridle on and then saddled him. He adjusted the stirrups, tightened the cinch and led the horse out. All this time he'd been avoiding eye contact with Marissa. Now he could no longer avoid it. She had backed a few steps away from the horse and her blue eyes were wide.

"Don't tell me you're afraid of this one, too?"

"Has she seen any other?" Dan asked, his eyes narrowing as he looked from one to the other of them.

"Yeah, the other day I rode over to your place." Alex had tossed out the comment with a casual shrug. Dan didn't look happy.

It seemed wise to move on. "You ready for your pony ride?"

She stepped forward.

Alex stepped around the front of the horse. "You're on the wrong side."

"Oh." She eased around the front of the horse.

He circled her wrist with his hand. It was a small wrist. She gave him a look and he cleared his throat and remembered that he was letting her have a belated pony ride. He glanced at Dan. "This is going to cost you five dollars for the shelter fund."

"I'll write the preacher a check," Dan said with a twinkle in his faded blue eyes.

"Left foot in the stirrup."

She lifted her left foot.

"Grab hold of the saddle horn and pull yourself up."

She did, but with a struggle. He smiled as she settled on the saddle, looking a little apprehensive as she bit down on her bottom lip. He handed her the reins and she took them in hands that appeared to shake. And then, before he could take hold of the bridle, she gave Bolt a nudge with her heel and shot forward.

"Hey," he yelled as she took off.

She glanced back, laughing. "Summer camp. Every year since I was five."

Dan slapped his leg and chortled. "I guess she showed you."

Alex glared at the older man. "This is going to cost you more than five bucks, Dan."

"I kind of figured. But in my defense, I didn't know she could ride."

Alex went after the woman and his horse. She had slowed to a walk. He whistled. Bolt immediately stopped. Four hooves planted in the dusty yard of the church as the horse looked back at him.

"I'm guessing summer camp didn't teach her that." Alex walked fast, not convinced the horse would really stay.

"That wasn't fair," Marissa called out. She was beaming, though, and her blue eyes flashed with humor.

"Neither was pretending you needed a pony ride." Alex caught hold of the reins. "Move your foot."

She eased her left foot from the stirrup. He claimed it and swung up behind her, letting her keep the seat. His arms were around her as he guided the horse in the direction of an open field across the dirt road at the back of the church.

"We shouldn't do this," she said over her shoulder.

"Probably not. There are probably dozens of reasons this is a bad idea. But you started it."

Her dark hair was in his face, the scent something tropical and sweet. He leaned in a little, so that his chin was on her shoulder and his arms were around her as he held the reins. She was dangerous. She was beautiful. There were so many reasons he shouldn't want to be around this woman.

He tried to list them off for himself, hoping it would help him keep perspective.

She could ride a horse but she was still a city girl.

She'd go back to Dallas and he'd still be in Bluebonnet, living his dreams that were nothing like what a woman in her world dreamed of.

She had been let down by the man she was supposed to spend her life with, and he didn't want to be another man who let her down.

But there was one big, fat, undeniable truth. When he held her in his arms, it felt like a promise.

"Where are we going?" Her voice was soft when she asked the question.

They were riding along a line of trees, the shade cool. In the distance he could hear children laughing and a car honk. When he glanced back, he saw Dan still standing by the horse trailer.

"We won't go far," he assured her.

She shivered and he held her a little closer.

"We shouldn't do this." Hers was the voice of reason, soft and sweet and way too tempting to be reasonable.

It took him a minute to decide what she meant. They shouldn't ride away from the church? Or they shouldn't be tempted? He realized she meant riding away, together, alone.

"No, we shouldn't," he agreed.

But her hair blew against his cheek and he came a bit closer. His lips grazed her cheek. When she turned to say something, he kissed the corner of her mouth. Her eyes closed and she whispered his name. She should have told him to stop. She didn't.

He pulled back on the reins and Bolt stopped. He slid off the back of the horse and walked around to take hold of the reins. He reached up and Marissa took his hand, wary, as she should be. Watching him, she brought her leg over the horse's neck, slid her left foot from the stirrup and jumped. He caught her, holding her loosely with one arm.

"We shouldn't," he whispered against the soft skin of her cheek. His hand had moved to her hair, finding it soft and silky in his fingers.

"No," she agreed. But she stood on tiptoe and her mouth captured his.

Slow down, he told himself. *Think things through.* Slow and steady, no one gets hurt. But she tasted sweet, like coffee and sugar and everything wonderful.

She tasted like forever. Someone else's forever. She was subdivisions, picket fences and a husband in a suit. He was one month away from losing the family ranch if he didn't make quick decisions and find cash.

He pulled back. Her eyes were closed, her dark lashes brushing her ivory skin. He kissed each cheek, feeling the flutter of those lashes on his lips.

"I can't imagine…" he began, but cut himself off. He couldn't imagine a man walking away from her.

"What?" Her head was on his shoulder. She took a deep breath, her shoulders rising and falling.

"Nothing. We should go."

She stepped away from him in silent agreement and remounted the horse. He handed her the reins and then, with one hand on the horn and the other on the back of the saddle, he swung his right leg over Bolt's back and settled behind her.

As they rode back to the church he told himself he'd made a mistake that he wouldn't make again. And then he disagreed with himself. The man who had walked away from her had made a mistake.

She wasn't a mistake. She was just out of his league. And he was nowhere near the ballpark.

Chapter Ten

Marissa fought the urge to lean back into Alex's arms. That would be a mistake. But these days she seemed to be an expert at making mistakes. She closed her eyes just briefly. What she needed was to go home, back to Dallas.

To what? Humiliation? Disappointed parents?

She opened her eyes and saw her grandfather sitting in the passenger side of Alex's truck. He stepped out as they got closer and she could see the worry on his expression. He looked protective. The look took her by surprise.

"I'm sorry," Alex whispered as they got closer.

She couldn't let him take the blame. "I'm the one that took off on your horse. I…"

And she had initiated the kiss, hadn't she?

"Don't overthink it," Alex said. His hand was warm on hers.

"Right. Of course." She didn't wait for his help. She slipped her right leg over the horse's neck and slid to the ground. Bolt gave her a curious look but didn't seem too offended by the awkward dismount.

Her grandfather joined them. The glare he gave Alex was long and hard. She was sure a lesser man would have been shaking in his boots. "The preacher asked me to bring her on in. He'd like to show her around the shelter."

Alex rested a hand on Bolt's neck. He nodded but he didn't say anything as she walked away with Dan. They entered the church through a back entrance into the large kitchen and fellowship hall. There were women in the kitchen and children gathered around a tree that reached the ceiling of the dining room.

Pastor Matthews approached, his face split in a friendly greeting. "Hey, good to see the two of you. I saw you picking a tree and when you didn't come inside I thought you'd left. And, Dan, I know you don't want to miss this chili or the pies. All of this is a fundraiser for the shelter as well as helping families in the community."

"I guess I'm already owing you money for the tree and pony ride."

"Well, come on in and we'll see what else you might want," the pastor said. "Marissa, good to see you again. I'm not sure if you'd be interested but the kids are looking for someone to help them decorate the tree."

There were half a dozen small children and a plastic tub full of decorations. Marissa nodded and headed for the Christmas tree. Pastor Matthews followed.

"Kids, this is Marissa. She's going to help you with the tree. All of you remember your manners and be respectful."

"Yes, sir," one little boy said, and saluted. "She can't reach the top of the tree, though."

The pastor chuckled. "Well, she can reach most

of the tree. I'll send someone to help with the higher branches."

He left and she was alone with the children. They were immediately curious. But she was in her element; she knew how to talk to them.

They showed her the popcorn and cranberries they were stringing. Together they sat in a circle sharing stories about favorite pets, what they wanted for Christmas and things they missed.

And that was the part that hurt. A little girl named Julie poked the needle through a cranberry, then popcorn. She had sad brown eyes and she told Marissa she missed her cat, Zippy. Zippy used to sleep with her but that was a long time ago, when her mom and dad still lived together.

"I haven't seen Zippy since we left." Julie drew in a breath but she didn't cry.

"We had to give our pets away," Amy from the pony ride told Marissa. "We didn't have electricity for a long time and my mom said we couldn't have our puppy because food was too expensive and we needed electricity for heat. But then we moved here."

The stories went on and on. There shouldn't be so many children with such heartbreaking stories.

When the cranberries and popcorn were finally strung, they lifted the strings and together wrapped them around the tree. The children played and laughed as they worked and Marissa smiled easier than she'd smiled in days.

"We should hang the rest of the decorations on the tree and then we'll plug in the lights." Marissa pulled the tub of decorations to the center of the children.

Amy pulled out a manger scene painted on a bulb

shaped like a star. "I like this one the best. It's the story of Christmas."

A little boy named Timmy leaned close and then looked up with a sweet expression on his face. "Pastor Matthews says it's the story of hope."

"What does hope mean?" Marissa knelt down in front of the child.

"Hope is the evidence of things unseen. We learned that in Sunday school," Julie said brightly. "And I think that must be about trusting God even when we can't see Him."

Amy tugged on Marissa's arm. "Because God always has a plan. That's what Pastor Matthews said. He said we aren't supposed to worry. We're supposed to let God and the grown-ups handle the problems."

Marissa hadn't been to church in years, but sitting here with these children, her own hope was renewed. Timmy handed her the star ornament. "Do you believe in Christmas?"

She nodded, but her heart ached at the question because these children had been through so much and yet they were still smiling. They were finding faith. And hope.

No child should ever be without hope.

Marissa couldn't help but be touched by the children, their stories, their joy. She hadn't experienced anything like this in a long time. Maybe ever.

"How's it going over here?" Alex appeared at her side. He'd taken off his hat and his dark curls were flattened against his head. With a glance he took in the children, the tree and the decoration in her hand.

Timmy reached into the tub of decorations. "We're doing great. And the tree is beautiful."

The little boy pulled out a book and handed it to Marissa.

"Will you read it?" he asked.

She took the book. Of course they would want a story. She touched the cover before opening it to look at the beautiful illustrations inside. Alex was watching. He would wonder why she hesitated. He wouldn't understand.

Worse, what would he say if he knew her secret? Would he make a joke of it as Aidan had, and then pretend the teasing was in good fun? Would he be embarrassed for her?

The children were looking on with expectant faces. Hopeful. And she wouldn't let them down. She couldn't let her own insecurities dampen what they had found. Hope.

They all believed so strongly in the story of Christmas and the hope of things unseen.

"'Joseph took Mary, who was great with child.'" She smiled at the children and then her eyes misted as she touched the words, the pictures. She told the story as she remembered it. "And went to Bethlehem. And while they were there, the time came for the baby to be born. She wrapped him in warm cloths and lay him in the manger. There was no room in the inn.

"'At the same time there were shepherds in a field.'" She smiled at the children. They'd moved closer. "'Watching over their sheep.'

"'And there appeared in the sky an Angel of the Lord saying, "For unto you is born this day in the city of David, a Savior who is Christ the Lord. And this will be a sign unto you. You will find the baby wrapped in swaddling clothes and lying in a manger."'"

She took a deep breath and looked up, catching Alex's gaze on her. His eyes were warm chocolate and his lips tilted up as he winked at her. If Aidan hadn't left, she never would have known this about herself, that she wanted a man who made her feel strong. And special. And Aidan hadn't ever been that man.

"It isn't over, is it?" Julie asked. She was six, she'd told Marissa. And her mommy was having a baby.

"No, it isn't over." Pastor Matthews appeared. "The story continues through us and through our faith. But right now, it's time for you all to eat. And maybe Miss Marissa can come back again."

"I would love to come back. I loved spending time with you all."

"Be careful," Alex warned. "Pastor Matthews is always looking for volunteers."

"I won't be here long," she told him. "But I'd love to help when I can."

The children hugged her and then they were gone, laughing and telling how they'd decorated the tree and talked about hope. Pastor Matthews's voice rose above theirs as he told them only one person could talk at a time. And then they disappeared into the kitchen. Marissa stood by the tree, alone with Alex.

"I'm dyslexic," she said before he could ask. "So no, I wasn't reading all of the words. I can read. But at times the words seem to bounce. Or they're jumbled."

"I wondered. My twin brother is dyslexic." He studied her face. "You're a teacher. That couldn't have been easy."

"It wasn't." She wanted to hug him. She wanted to grab him and thank him. She couldn't put into words how his statement, making it an accomplishment, making it matter, made her feel.

It hadn't been easy, to put aside her fears and pursue a career she had wanted and that she loved. It still wasn't always easy to pursue what she wanted. Not when there might be rejection at the end of the chase.

Several days after the fund-raiser, Alex walked through the house, the very empty house. He couldn't wait for Maria to arrive. At least she would make a mess or play her music too loud. Even Marcus would be preferable to the silence. Maria wouldn't be home for another week or so. He wasn't sure about Marcus.

It hadn't always been this way. Growing up it had been a full house. Alex, his twin brother, their sisters and parents. Their dad had been loud and rarely peaceful. The house hadn't been a place any of them ever wanted to be, but it had been their home. Sometimes there had even been laughter.

Alex had no intentions of making it a home again. His goal was to build his own place, just big enough for him. He didn't need more. Marcus or Maria could have this house and do what they wanted with it. He needed no reminders of their past.

But first, he had to get the loan. He needed cash.

The light on the kitchen phone blinked, letting him know someone had left a message. He pushed the button and put the phone on speaker before playing the messages. The third one made him stop. He had to replay it. Twice.

His bulls had been accepted for a charity bull ride. He glanced at the calendar. Not a lot of money to be made but it would add to his points. And he desperately needed to make points in order to get the bulls into the bigger events. He said a quiet thank-you because he had needed something good to happen.

Not only would the money be good, but it would also be time away from Bluebonnet. He scrubbed a hand over his face as he contemplated the contents of his fridge. Nothing looked decent. Most of it probably needed to be tossed out.

He wondered what Marissa and Dan were having for dinner. Yeah, that's why he needed to get away from Bluebonnet for a few days. He didn't have time to be distracted. He grabbed a package of ham out of the fridge and a loaf of bread that wasn't so stale he couldn't eat it.

The phone rang. He let it go to voice mail.

It rang again. He picked it up.

"Hello," he said as he put ham on a slice of bread.

"Alex, its Marissa. I need help over here."

"Another cow down?" He glanced out the window. It was starting to rain and the thermometer read fifty degrees. He was a good neighbor but he sure didn't want to go pull a calf in this weather.

"There's someone here with a stock trailer. They're claiming they're from the IRS and Dan said that because he didn't have the money to pay back taxes, they can have half a dozen head of cattle. You and I both know that the IRS doesn't work that way."

"I'll call 911. And don't argue with them. They're cattle thieves, plain and simple, and you don't know what they might do." As he gave the warning, he realized just how true it was and how much danger she was in. But he also knew she wouldn't sit back and do nothing.

Dread settled in the pit of his stomach as he ended the call and dialed 911. He gave the details and Dan's address. They tried to tell him to stay clear and let them handle the situation. He couldn't do that.

He couldn't sit at his house eating a ham sandwich while Dan and his granddaughter faced off with what were probably armed cattle thieves who had found a new way to rob an old man blind.

He tossed the sandwich to his sister's poodle and headed out the door, jamming his hat on his head as he went. Leave it to Dan to fall for something as crazy as an IRS scam. What made a normally intelligent person think that something such as this was legit?

When he got to Dan's, Marissa, wearing a rain parka, stood in the muddy yard hugging herself tight and staring out toward the field. Dusk had fallen and the gray sky was going to be dark soon. He jumped out of his truck. She shifted to look at him, shaking her head. Drops of rain sprayed from the parka.

"They insisted on Granddad getting in the truck with them. I told him to stay but he wouldn't. That's when he told me to call you. I hope they didn't hear him."

"I hope so, too." He put an arm around her and she shivered, tucking herself close to his side. When she leaned into him like that, he wanted to be the man who didn't let her down. He wanted to make things right for her.

He shook off those dangerous thoughts. "Go inside the camper. When the deputies get here, tell them I'm down there pretending to help load cattle. I want to make sure Dan is okay."

"You shouldn't."

"I know. But I can't leave Dan down there alone.

They probably didn't count on you being here so they're probably a little on the nervous side. Hopefully the deputies don't come in here with sirens blaring." He gave her a gentle nudge toward the camper. "Go."

She nodded and walked away from him, but her gaze kept traveling back to the field and to headlights in the distance. Cattle mooed and he could hear men shouting. He wished he'd done something sooner, like the first time Dan mentioned the IRS. But at the time Dan hadn't mentioned the details, just that he owed money.

The door to the camper closed with a click. He headed back to his truck.

He found Dan and the cattle thieves at the back of the property. They'd brought four-wheelers and they were loading cattle. Dan stood off to the side with one of the men. He looked a little gray and even from a distance it appeared he was trying to catch his breath.

Alex parked his truck and got out. He gave the men a friendly, helpful smile and waved. "Hey, I thought I might come out and help you all. This rain is getting worse."

"Sir, I'm going to ask you to stand back." The fake agent in his fake black jacket pulled a handgun from his pocket.

Alex had never thought himself a fool and he wasn't going to be one today. He raised his hands. "Hey, I'm not here to cause any trouble. I just wanted to help. It would be a shame if you all got that truck stuck out here, and the way this rain is coming down, that's a possibility."

The men—there were four of them—looked at each other. The one who still had his handgun fixed on Alex shook his head. "No, I think we can manage. Go ahead and get back in your truck."

"How about if I take Dan off your hands. It looks like he's about to pass out on you. He's got some heart problems. Dan, do you have your heart medicine on you?"

Dan looked a little confused and shook his head. "No."

"You're a little pale. Why don't you go sit in the truck?" Alex kept his hands up and a smile on his face. Maybe he was a fool because the more he pushed, the more the thug with the gun looked as if he might like to unload some lead in him.

As if on cue, Dan weaved a little and he reached for the man next to him to steady himself.

"Get off me, old man."

No way would an IRS agent talk like that. Alex thought about mentioning it but kept his mouth shut. All those people who said he didn't know when to shut up would have been surprised.

"Dan, you okay?"

The guy with the gun pointed the weapon at Alex. "Get back in your truck and take him with you. But don't try to leave. Just sit there and stay out of the way."

Dan headed his way at a snail's pace.

"Dan, why don't you try to hurry and we'll get out of the rain?"

"I'm going as fast as I can, Alex. I don't know why you're over here getting in my business. I owe the IRS and I'm taking care of my debt."

Alex opened the passenger seat of the truck.

"I hope you know these men aren't IRS," he whispered.

"Well, I kind of figured that out. And that's why I didn't offer them what I have in my safe."

Alex swallowed a chuckle and closed the door. As he went around to the driver's side he heard cars in the distance. He moved a little quicker. He was behind the wheel and closing the door when the first shot rang out.

"They're shooting at my truck. Now that just makes a guy mad. Dan, stay down." He floored it and headed for the nearest four-wheeler, making the guy spin the thing and almost go sideways in the mud. With that one close to disabled, Alex turned and headed back toward the gate.

He pulled to the side as deputies in SUVs headed through the gate. As they slowed, he rolled down the window. The first vehicle stopped.

"They're armed. They have a truck and trailer and a couple of ATVs."

After that he headed back to the camper with Dan, who was having a hard time catching his breath. "You know you're supposed to use that oxygen. You're just being stubborn. Imagine how much better you'd feel if you used it."

"Oh, stop. Now you sound like Marissa. What I'd really like is if she'd go back to Dallas and you'd go back to minding your own business."

"And leave you to lose your life savings to fake IRS agents?"

"Well, I do appreciate your help. But not your advice on my health. I'm seventy-five and the last thing I want is to have a couple of kids telling me how to live. She's making me eat oatmeal in the mornings. And juice. 'Drink water,' she says. 'Cut back on coffee,' she says."

Alex laughed as he pulled his truck up to the steps of the camper. "You know you love her."

"I know I do." Dan gave him a meaningful look.

"Don't look at me like that, Dan. She's your grand daughter, not mine. And I don't have any intention of getting tangled up with a city girl on the rebound who won't be here long enough for me to know her favorite color."

"Come on in. She'll make us a cup of that herbal tea she's so dad-burned fond of."

Alex followed Dan up the stairs. The door opened as they got to the top and Marissa was waiting. She hugged her grandfather as she pulled him inside. Before Dan could protest, she had a towel around him and she was drying his hair. The older man grumbled but he put up with her ministrations. He even turned a little pink when she kissed his cheek.

"Sit down and I'll get you something warm to drink."

"I guess it's too much to hope for a cup of coffee?" Dan asked with a hopeful tone.

"No coffee this late at night. But I made some ginger tea."

Dan groaned but he took a seat in his old recliner and put his feet up. Alex grabbed the oxygen tank and pulled it to Dan.

"Use this thing."

Dan took the tubing, adjusted the knobs and gave Alex a look that didn't need much interpretation. When Alex moved back a step, Marissa was there with a towel.

"Dry off," she said, handing it to him. Her eyes searched his face. He didn't know what she was looking for, but he hoped she didn't look too deep.

He took the towel, dried his face and hair and handed

it back to her. "I'll wait until the police are finished. Do you need anything done while I'm here?"

"No. The chores are all done."

"Good grief, this is enough to make a man feel a little sick," Dan grumbled, capturing both of their attention.

"What?" Marissa asked. Alex could have told her asking was a mistake.

Dan pointed from her to Alex and back to her. He wrinkled up his nose. "This. The cooing. And the looks. He's a confirmed bachelor. He just told me a month ago that he thinks women are more trouble than they're worth. And you, you just got jilted by your fiancé. Why would you even think of trusting another man?"

"I'm just being nice to a neighbor who helped us out." Marissa wagged her finger at her grandfather. "You're just being testy because I've cut you back on coffee and sugar. And because we're having baked chicken for dinner and not fried."

"I like baked chicken," Alex said to no one in particular. After all, he'd tossed his sandwich to a dog when he'd left the house.

"You can have mine," Dan told him. "I'm having bologna. And I think in a month or two, you'll both be eating crow."

"I'm not a fan of crow," Alex said. Fortunately the police chose that moment to knock on the door.

Marissa peeked through the window, then opened the door to let in a couple of rain-soaked deputies. They had a few questions for Dan and Alex, but the thieves were in custody and there would be several charges filed against them.

Alex stepped into the small kitchen area as they questioned Dan. Marissa joined him. She avoided looking at him and he guessed he might have been avoiding her. She pulled the chicken from the oven and took the lid off a pan with some kind of cheesy potatoes.

"You'll stay for dinner?" she asked.

"I wouldn't mind." He moved close—close enough to smell the soft floral scent of her perfume, close enough to hear her quickly indrawn breath. He touched his fingers to her, just briefly. "You're okay?"

"I'm okay."

"You know he was just teasing." He'd felt compelled to say it.

"I know."

She looked at him then and he felt a tightness in his chest. The vulnerable softness in her blue eyes begged him not to hurt her.

He wanted more than anything to be the man who wouldn't let her down.

Chapter Eleven

By Saturday morning Marissa thought things were settling down nicely. Including her grandfather, and her nerves. They were in a groove, she and Dan. They'd dealt with several visits by the police. They'd had a lot of questions about the past six months, how much had been taken and how many head of cattle Dan had turned over to the men. Because of the police report, Dan would be able to file insurance claims and be reimbursed for his loss. In all he'd given up over twenty head of cattle without ever questioning the men or their motives.

The police had taken Marissa aside and told her that it was a new scam, but not surprising that they targeted her grandfather. Dan lived alone, with no family that checked in on him, and he was older, therefore the crooks figured he was an easy mark. Fortunately Marissa had come along when she did.

She could have told them it had been fortunate for her, too.

With the church potluck taking place the next day, Marissa had plans to make deviled eggs. And she also needed to plan her exit from Bluebonnet Springs.

She peeked in the nesting box in the dimly lit hen-house, pulled out an egg and placed it in the basket. She reached in the next box and a sharp beak pecked at her hand. The hen squawked a warning a little too late. A nester. Her grandfather had warned her that a few of the hens were determined to sit on their nests and to just leave them be.

At least she hadn't dropped the basket of eggs.

"Fine, have your eggs." She counted the green and brown eggs in the basket. Almost a dozen. That was perfect. With the dozen in the house she could make a couple dozen deviled eggs for the potluck.

She left the chicken coop and headed across the yard, avoiding puddles that had formed from the rain the previous day. As she walked up the steps the rooster flew to the rail. He lowered his head and rounded his back.

"Now aren't you sweet." She gave him a couple of pats to his softly feathered back.

In the distance she heard a vehicle and then saw Alex's truck come up the drive. She waited for him to park. It took him a minute to get out. When he did he had two brown paper bags in his hands. He grinned and inclined his head in greeting. Even from a distance she knew his eyes would flash with humor and dimples would crease his cheeks.

"What are you doing?" she asked as he headed her way.

"Baking pies. Remember?"

He had mentioned that. She thought in jest. She should have known he wasn't joking.

"I see. You're baking them here?"

"Yep." He came up the stairs. The rooster flew off the rail and glided to a safe spot a short distance away.

"Come on in. But hopefully you really do know what you're doing. Because I don't."

He gave her a long look and then he winked. "I know what I'm doing."

Without warning he kissed her cheek.

As if that kiss hadn't mattered, he stomped the mud off his shoes and followed her inside. Marissa hurried to put the eggs away. Or to escape his nearness. He followed at a slower pace. Her grandfather was making himself a peanut butter sandwich. He turned as they entered the camper.

"Stop making a pet out of my rooster," he grumbled as he put the lid on the peanut butter. "Did you see her out there, petting Red?"

"I did, Dan. I don't know if I would put up with that."

"Don't see as I have much choice in the matter. She doesn't seem to be going anywhere anytime soon."

Marissa gave her grandfather a quick hug. "You'd miss me if I left."

"I might at that." He kissed the top of her head.

Every day that she stayed was a day she got closer to her grandfather, and she regretted that she'd missed out on so many years. With each passing day, her desire to go home dwindled. She didn't know what awaited her back in Dallas. But she also didn't know what a future in Bluebonnet Springs would hold for her, either.

In the tiny kitchen she became aware of the other reason she wasn't excited about going home. Alex. He moved past her, their arms barely touching as he set his baking supplies on the tiny table. When he turned she swallowed because they were face-to-face, and with her grandfather in the kitchen, there was no room to move.

She and Aidan had never done anything quite as intimate as sharing space in a kitchen, cooking together. Or even doing chores together. They'd dated. Dinners. Work functions. Movies. She had thought about it often in the past weeks. They hadn't really known each other. She hadn't known his friends. He hadn't known that she didn't want to live in an apartment. She wanted a small house in a neighborhood where they would have a fenced yard and children.

Now she'd expanded that to house in a small town and maybe some land. Because this time with her grandfather had opened her eyes to some new experiences, and to a part of herself she hadn't known.

"Nice tree," Alex said, dragging her back to the present.

She glanced at the scraggly tree they'd hauled home from the church fund-raiser. "It needs more ornaments. I found one box at the thrift store in town. It was all she had."

"Before you start on those pies, why don't you go to the barn and get what I have out there?" Dan suggested as he sat down in his recliner, a plate in his lap and a glass of milk on the table next to him. He reached for the remote. "I'm going to watch sports for a bit and maybe take a nap. If the rats haven't eaten everything, the decorations are in the attic over the feed room of the barn."

Alex glanced at her and lifted a shoulder. "I don't mind helping."

"Are you sure?"

"Come on. Get a jacket and let's get that poor tree decorated before it gets repossessed by Charlie Brown."

"It isn't that bad."

"It's worse." He grabbed her jacket off the coatrack and held it out for her.

The rain started as they headed across the yard to the barn. It was a light rain but cold. Marissa huddled into her jacket and Alex's arm went around her. The rain picked up. They ran the rest of the way, laughing as they hurried through the door.

The barn was dark and dusty, and smelled of hay, horses and cattle. Marissa found she liked the quiet and the smell. It was comforting and peaceful.

"Where is the attic?"

"This way." Alex took her hand and led her to the feed room. Inside was a ladder. He opened it beneath a square door in the ceiling.

"We have to go up there?" She eyed the opening and shook her head at the idea of climbing through and into the dark attic space.

"Yeah. Up there. Follow me."

"What if there are bugs?"

"And mice?" he asked.

"Stop."

He was already up the ladder and pushing the square door open. She watched from below as he disappeared into the dark hole. A light came on and he peeked down at her.

"No bugs. No mice. Come on up."

She eased up the ladder, trying to keep her eyes on the man above her and not the floor below. He reached and she gave him her hand. With his help she climbed through the opening and landed safely on the floor of the attic. Tubs lined the wall. Each was labeled. There were Christmas ornaments. Photographs. Important papers. There was even a fireproof box.

"He's kept everything." Marissa stood, the ceiling

just inches above her head. Alex had to duck in the confined space.

"Well, where do you want to start?"

"Christmas decorations. But I want to look in the other boxes." She reached for one of the tubs that had been taped to seal the lid. "It's funny that these boxes contain the history of my family, of people I didn't know existed."

"So we aren't getting the Christmas decorations and leaving, are we?" He gave her a hopeful smile.

"No, we aren't."

"Why would he keep this up here?" he asked, pushing the fireproof box with his foot.

"Because he's Dan and it makes sense that if he's going to get robbed, they wouldn't look in the attic of the barn. Or even think that a barn would have an attic."

"I guess you're right."

She pulled the tape and removed the lid of the first tub. Inside were family photos. Some appeared to be from when her mother was a child. Some were older than that. She picked up one of a little girl with dark hair. On the back in faded ink were the words *Mary, age five. Kindergarten.*

"My mother," she told Alex.

The next photograph was of her grandparents on their wedding day. Alex peered over her shoulder.

"Dan was a charmer."

"Yes," she agreed. "He still is."

Alex laughed. "If cranky is the new charming."

Alex reached for a newspaper clipping. Marissa leaned to see what the article was about and suddenly she couldn't breathe. She shook her head, reaching for the aged piece of paper.

"Marissa?" Alex sat down next to her.

Her fingers shook as she held the bit of paper. Alex leaned close to read the story as she blinked to make sense of the words. Seeing it in print, it all came back to her. A twelve-year-old girl was killed. Witnesses said the two children tried to cross a busy intersection. One was hit by an oncoming car. She shook her head, trying to block the image, the pain.

The loss.

Alex reached for her but she couldn't let him hold her. She'd fall apart if he touched her. She'd shatter. She could already feel the pieces coming apart as she stood there holding the article. He took it from her hands.

"You?"

She nodded at the question.

And then, without asking, he held her. And the pieces that had been shattered for so long seemed to shift. Instead of scattering she felt something else, something she hadn't expected. In the arms of this man she felt more whole than she'd felt in years. Her heart still ached with loss, with memories, but his arms around her were strong and she felt strong because of them.

She remembered all of those years ago, standing on the sidewalk, alone. It had become a trend. She'd stood to the side at the funeral. Alone. Her parents had held each other. She'd wrapped arms around herself and cried.

Her grandfather had kept the article from the paper. It had gone in the tub with pictures of a wife who had left him, a daughter he didn't really know and grandchildren he'd never met. He'd been alone, too. She wiped at her eyes and removed herself from the comfort of Alex's arms.

She wondered if her grandfather had cried over that newspaper clipping. Did he sometimes come up here and go through these memories, piece by piece.

"You're okay," he said.

The way he said it, it wasn't a question. It was a statement. She was okay.

"I'm okay." She looked at the picture of a smiling Lisa, just twelve years old. "I miss her. My family hasn't been whole since…"

She shook her head.

"Since she died." He'd supplied the difficult words and she realized his arm was still around her. She still leaned against him. How was it possible that she'd miss this man she'd known only weeks, and she didn't really miss the fiancé who had left her?

"Yes. My parents haven't been the same. It's as if life stopped. Happiness and laughter ended. Remember when we talked about Christmas for my family? It's as if we avoided the holiday because it brought back memories of that first Christmas after we lost her."

"You weren't responsible." He said the words that a few friends had tried to impress upon her. Even a counselor she'd talked to had tried to make her see that it had been a horrible accident. That she hadn't been responsible.

But how could she accept that?

"I talked her into crossing the road. Our parents gave us strict orders to stay on the sidewalk but I wanted to go to the park."

"You were ten at the time."

"I should have known better."

They sat in silence for several minutes. He continued

to hold her. She should move. She knew better than to sit in the comfort of his arms, but it felt like a safe haven.

"I'm sure your parents don't blame you," he said softly.

"They do blame me. They always have. And I've spent years trying to make it up to them. I've tried to be the best daughter I could be. I've made every decision based on what would please them. My sister was amazing. She was smart and funny. She wouldn't have crossed that street but she wouldn't allow me to go alone."

"It only seemed that way because you were ten and she was your big sister," he said after a while. "Things happen that change us. What matters is how we move forward. Or don't."

She eased from his warm embrace. "You're speaking from experience?"

He smiled but she wasn't fooled by the gesture. There was no warmth in his eyes. It was a gesture, nothing more.

"I killed my father," he said simply, then got up and moved away from her.

Alex grabbed the plastic tub that was labeled Ornaments and slid it toward the opening in the floor. Marissa continued to watch him, her expression thoughtful. Of course she would have a ton of questions for him.

"Why do you think that?" she asked.

"I was an angry teenager. He'd abused us. He'd taken advantage of people in the community. I just wanted him gone. And that day, when he got on that bull because he had to show me how it was done, I told him I hoped it took him down. And it did."

"But you didn't kill him."

"No. I didn't. But for a long time, I thought I did."

"We're a mess," she finally said.

He sat down with his back against the container of decorations. "Yeah, I guess. I like to think I'm a survivor. I've been trying to get my head on straight and working on realizing that I didn't write my father's destiny. He made choices. He wasn't a good person. And when he got on that bull, my thoughts didn't control what happened."

"No, they didn't."

He was close enough to touch her, but didn't. "I do control the choices I make and how I deal with the things that have happened in my life. I'm not perfect. I'm definitely flawed. But I like to think I'm in a better place than I was a few years ago."

For instance, if he'd been a little braver, he would have told her that he was starting to believe he could be the man who wouldn't let her down. She needed someone like that. But he knew better than to say the words.

Sitting there on the dusty wood floor of that attic, even in the light of a single bulb hanging from the ceiling, she looked like someone's princess. Even in jeans, an old denim jacket and her hair framing her face in chunky layers. She didn't look like a woman a cowboy like him should be thinking about.

It was hard to connect this woman who wore Dan's old jacket and did her best to drive his truck to the woman she was in Dallas, before she landed on the side of the road in Bluebonnet.

"We should get these decorations back to the house before Dan comes looking for us," he suggested. Mainly because he needed to get her back before his heart started playing tricks on him. He stood and then reached for her hand.

He knew it was mistake immediately, reaching for her hand. But he held it, pulling her to her feet. Then she was in front of him. He touched her hair, curling the soft strands around his finger. His knuckle brushed her cheek and she closed her eyes.

He took his time as he brushed his lips over hers. Kissing her was a gift. He'd never felt that away about a woman before, as if she should be treasured. This woman made him feel that. And more.

Truth be told, what she really made him feel was scared to death.

He slowly broke contact. She slid her fingers from his.

"Hey. Did you two get lost up there?" Dan yelled from the tack room beneath them.

"No, Dan, just going through all of this stuff you've packed away up here. Who knew you were a hoarder? You should be on a reality show." Alex peeked through the door. "Hey, what do you have in this locked box up here?"

"Stay out of there. That's my retirement."

Marissa was restacking boxes and wouldn't look at him. Alex walked up behind her, smoothed her hair and kissed her cheek.

"I'm sorry," he whispered. "Not for kissing you. But because you've been hurt. I don't want to be another person who hurts you."

"You won't," she said with confidence.

He wished he could believe that.

"I'll carry the decorations to the house. Is there anything else you want from up here?"

"No. I think that's all we need." She reached for the chain on the light but she didn't pull. She stared at him for a few seconds.

"You okay?" he asked.

"I'm good." She managed a smile. "We should go."

He went first, carrying the decorations on his shoulder as he went down the ladder. Almost to the bottom, Dan took it from him. Alex waited for Marissa to climb down. She didn't need his help but he waited, just in case. When she reached the bottom, she grinned.

"Let's go decorate that tree," she said brightly, as if a short time ago she hadn't fallen apart, and as if the kiss had meant nothing.

The sun had come out and the clouds were breaking up, showing patches of blue in the sky. The three of them trudged across the lawn with Bub following along. They were almost to the camper when the dog started howling, the ear-splitting noise piercing the quiet. In response to the dog's warning, the rooster flew across the yard and landed on the porch.

"Car coming," Dan said as they headed up the stairs of the camper. "He does that when he hears unfamiliar tires on the road."

Alex kind of doubted the dog was that smart. But sure enough a car had turned off the main road and was easing down Dan's driveway. Next to him, Marissa drew in a breath and whispered something he couldn't hear.

"Who is it?" he asked.

She stood on the rickety front porch of Dan's camper and with a shake of her head walked back down the steps. "My parents."

They parked next to his truck and sat for a full minute. Alex remained on the porch next to Dan, because he thought Dan might need a friend. But he was torn between Dan and Marissa, who was standing in the yard waiting to greet her parents. He guessed she needed a friend, too.

Not thirty minutes ago she'd felt like a lot more than a friend. She'd felt like the best thing to ever happen to him.

The car doors finally opened and she took a few, hesitant steps forward. He wanted to go to her, to stand next to her. It wasn't his place, to be at her side. These were her parents. He guessed there was a lot of distance between them but they were still her family.

He was just the cowboy who had picked up a bride on the side of the road. She wasn't even his bride.

"Let's go inside and have coffee," Dan said as he turned away from the scene playing out in the yard.

"I should probably head on home."

Dan shook his head but he shot a look back at Marissa and her family. "I wouldn't go if I was you. She's probably going to want a couple of allies."

Marissa joined her parents as they got out of the car. They were talking quietly, hugging each other. Yeah, Dan had the right of it. She was going to need a couple of allies. To an outsider, it looked like a normal scene, but there was something a bit off.

"You think you might need an ally, too?" he asked Dan.

The older man gave him a sheepish grin. "I might. I taught that woman to ride a horse and drive a tractor. She was a little bitty thing back then. And I also watched her mom load her up in a car and drive her away from here. Guess I'll have to watch another little girl get loaded up in a car and dragged away from this ranch."

"I'm sorry, Dan." Alex patted him on the shoulder. "If it helps, I think even if she leaves today, she'll be back."

"Nice of you to think so. Don't get your hopes up, cowboy." With that, Dan opened the camper door and walked inside.

Alex followed him in but he couldn't help but think that Dan should be involved in the family reunion. After all, it was his daughter and his granddaughter out there. Instead he was fixing himself a cup of coffee as if it didn't matter. As if it had nothing to do with him.

"Stop staring out the window," Dan muttered as he kicked back in the recliner. "Ain't nothing you or me can do about it. She has to make her own decisions. Don't you have enough on your plate without worrying over what she's doing to do?"

The ranch. Alex had to agree. He stepped away from the window and allowed Marissa her privacy because he had creditors nipping at his heels and not a lot of time to solve his own problems.

Chapter Twelve

Marissa hugged her mom and then her dad. It didn't matter that she was an adult or that there was distance between them, they were still her parents and she still wanted their hugs. But in their embrace she still felt like the child they resented, the one who had let them down, the one who hadn't lived up to their dreams.

"I'm sorry," she whispered as her mom hugged her a second time.

"Stop," her mother said, surprising her. "You aren't the one who should apologize. Aidan should have talked to you. He should have had the decency to end things sooner."

"And he shouldn't have hurt you," her father said. "I can't imagine how any man would walk out on you."

It took a minute for the words to sink in.

The words were healing. Her parents were here for her. She swiped at the tears that rolled down her cheeks. Her mom brushed a hand against the dampness, then her fingers sifted through the strands of her now shoulder-length hair.

"Don't ever become a beautician."

"Don't worry. I realize I have no skills in that department," Marissa assured her. "I have found I'm decent with a tractor and I'm something of a rooster whisperer."

"Also not skills I'd want to encourage."

Her mom froze, as if suddenly realizing where she was. She glanced around. "It's been so long. I'd almost forgotten this place."

"Come inside." Marissa took her by the hand.

"I'm not sure if I want to."

Marissa's dad moved to her mother's side. Marissa had seen it all of her life but had somehow missed it. Her parents supported each other. They leaned on one another. She should have wanted that in her relationship with Aidan. Instead she'd only ever thought of him as an escape route. She'd wanted someone—anyone—to be her person. And she hadn't allowed herself to really see what they had, which had been less than friendship.

"We really just came to take you home," her mother assured her.

Back to Dallas. Marissa glanced from her parents to the camper. "I'm not quite ready yet. There's a potluck at church. And a Christmas program. I'd like to be here for those things."

"This isn't your home," her mother insisted.

"No, it isn't. But I have family here. I have a grandfather. We were getting ready to decorate his Christmas tree. I think he hasn't had one in a while."

A family or a tree.

"Marissa, please." Her mom reached for her but her hand dropped short of contact. "We want you to come home."

"I will. I promise. But I need to be here right now

Why don't you come inside, just for a minute? There's coffee." She looked from her father to her mother. She called on all of that backbone that had gotten her through life. "And there's a man in there who is your father."

Her mom drew in a deep breath, then she nodded. "Okay, a cup of coffee and then we have to go. But you'll come home before Christmas?"

"I'll come home before Christmas."

They walked up the steps of the camper and she opened the door, now more nervous than she had thought she'd be. Alex was inside with her grandfather. What would her parents think of the man who had picked her up on the side of the road?

The three of them made the cramped confines of the camper seem even smaller. Marissa took her mom by the hand. She led her the few feet to where Dan sat in his recliner watching them, his eyes misty as he pretended to sip his coffee.

"It hasn't changed much," he said gruffly. "But I guess I have. You certainly have. It's good to see you, Mary."

Then he waited, and Marissa knew his heart would break if her mother turned away from him. She knew, because on the day Lisa had died, her mom had turned away from her. She'd closed herself off and she hadn't realized that Marissa's heart was breaking, too.

For a long time Marissa thought it would always be that way, that they would exist in this world separately. They would look like a family, do the things families did, but there would be invisible walls.

Dan put the footstool of the recliner down and pushed

himself to his feet. He stood there looking down at his daughter, now a grown woman.

"You look a lot like your mother," he said. "And I've missed you every single day for these forty odd years. Every day. Your mom sent me pictures and occasionally we talked."

"She talked to you?" Marissa's mom shook her head. "I thought we left and never looked back."

He scratched his chin. "I guess in a way you did. But your mom and I, we talked. You know, we never got a divorce. I always kind of thought she'd come back eventually. Maybe she'd get you raised and remember she had a husband."

"I'm so sorry," Mary said. "I didn't know."

Marissa caught movement out of the corner of her eye. She glanced back as Alex headed for the door, pushing his hat down on his head as he went.

"Don't you dare leave," she ordered. "We have a tree to decorate and pies to make."

He paused at the door. Face shadowed by the brim of the hat, he looked from her mom to her dad and back to her. "I should go."

No, he shouldn't. She wanted him there. No, she *needed* him. And she had never really needed anyone. No, that wasn't true. She'd needed her parents.

"We're going to decorate the tree," she reminded him. The tree was important to her. It was her way of belonging here, in her grandfather's life.

"Oh, sit back down, Alex. It isn't like they'll stay long." Her grandfather had moved to the kitchen and he was pouring another cup of coffee. "Here, have a cup."

He held the cup out to Alex. "Mary and what's your

name? Joe? This is my neighbor, Alex Palermo. He helps me out from time to time."

Marissa's dad stepped forward to shake Alex's hand. "Good to meet you, Alex. I'm Joe Walker. And thank you. For everything."

For rescuing his daughter off the side of the road, he meant. Her mom looked uncomfortable, her attention focusing on the floor and not the people around her. She finally lifted her gaze to meet Alex's.

"We are glad to meet you." She looked at her watch. "But we really should go now. Marissa, do you want to get your stuff?"

Marissa should have expected that. Her parents had shown up with a purpose. To take her home. And they weren't taking no for an answer. "Mom, I just told you. I'm not going. Not yet. I'll be home in time for Christmas. And I plan on starting my job in January. But I need to stay here a little longer."

Her mom's eyes widened and she looked past Marissa to Dan. And to Alex. "You're staying *here*?"

Mary Walker glanced around the tiny camper. Her gaze landed on Bub, the bloodhound. The dog picked that moment to stretch and yawn. Marissa chuckled at the dog, because he really didn't care who had come to visit.

"I see," her mom finally said.

"Stay and help us decorate the tree?" Marissa invited.

Her mom looked from Bub to the tiny tree in front of the window. "No, we should go. It's a long drive back. We have plans this evening. Will you walk us out?"

"Of course." Marissa glanced at her grandfather, coffee still in hand.

"Well, I guess I'll be seeing you around." He said it with a casual tone, as if they were neighbors who had met up at the local café.

Marissa watched her mother's expression change, soften. She stepped forward to hug Dan. "Yes, we'll be back."

Dan patted her on the back, awkwardly, with the cup of coffee. Alex stepped forward and took the cup from his hand.

"Mary, you've done well. And this little girl is one to be proud of." He leaned close. "Don't live in the past. Time to live the life you've got."

Marissa's mom brushed at tears and nodded. "Thank you, Dan. Dad." She laughed a little. "Thank you."

She hurried out the door and Marissa followed. When they reached the car, Marissa's mom stopped. She ran a shaking hand down her face, and, with tears still shimmering in her eyes, she hugged Marissa tight.

"Don't fall in love with a cowboy. Let your heart heal and come home to figure out what you'll do next."

Marissa laughed at the advice. "I'm not going to fall in love with a cowboy and I will be home. I take that back. I have fallen in love with a cowboy. He's my grandfather. He's gruff and says what he thinks, but I do love him."

Mary nodded as she let go of Marissa's hands and moved toward the car. "Yes, and he loves you, too."

"Daddy, goodbye." She hurried to give her father a hug. "I'll call and you'll come get me?"

"I'll come get you no matter where you are."

She watched her parents drive back down the dusty dirt driveway. When she turned to go back inside, Alex was there. He waited for her at the porch, concern narrowing his eyes as he looked from her to the car in the distance.

"You're okay?" he asked.

"I'm good. Really, probably better than I've been in years. And I just bought myself a little more time in Bluebonnet."

His smile faded. "I'm glad. Dan is less cantankerous with you here."

"I'm not sure about that," she answered. "I know I'll have to go back eventually. I have a job and responsibilities."

"Of course."

"We should decorate the tree and make those pies." She looped her arm through his and together they walked back inside. "But I insist on knowing the recipe."

"I'm not about to tell you how I make my pies. What kind of woman are you, going after a man's secrets?"

She pulled him close. "I want all of your secrets."

"There are some things you just can't have, Marissa Walker. And my secret pie recipe is one of them."

She could have corrected him. She wanted his secrets, not his pie recipe. She wanted more time with him, too.

But she guessed he was right about this: there were some things she couldn't have.

The camper smelled of apples and cinnamon. Alex opened the tub of ornaments while Marissa wrapped the little tree in lights. He guessed he shouldn't poke fun at their tree. He'd bought one for his house that came already decorated.

"That pie sure smells good," Dan said from his chair. He'd watched as they made the pies. The process had taken longer than usual because Marissa hadn't been much of a hand peeling and slicing apples. And she'd kept trying to watch as he measured out the ingredients to mix with the apples. He'd moved to block her view and she'd tried to put her hands on his shoulders and peek around him.

"Do I get a piece of that pie tonight?" Dan asked as he got up to mess with his old portable record player he'd pulled out of the closet. Soon Bing Crosby was singing Christmas songs.

"You stay out of the pie, Dan." Alex picked a small box of ornaments. When he opened it, it was like opening a time vault.

Marissa plugged in the lights and the tree lit up. He had to admit, lights made it better. He handed her the box of ornaments. She sifted through the homemade decorations, most of which had her mother's name on them. Who would have guessed Dan to be sentimental? Not in all of the years Alex had known him had he thought Dan cared about anything other than this piece of land he had and the bloodhound that emitted more noxious odors than a defective septic tank.

"Don't start thinking I'm sappy or something," Dan said as he hooked himself up to his oxygen. "I'm cheap. That's all. When my wife left she took what mattered. She took Mary. She left the rest for me. The camper. The bills. The ornaments. A few pictures."

"Of course, and you kept them all." Marissa pulled out a star made with yarn wrapped around sticks. And then a glitter-covered manger scene. She handed Alex back the box and she started to hang decorations. He didn't say anything, just watched as she placed the decorations on branches that sagged a bit from the weight.

After she'd finished with the homemade ornaments, she moved onto old bulbs that were brightly painted but chipped and faded in spots. She hung each and every one of those decorations. When she finished she stepped back and the tree had been transformed, thanks to glitter and twinkling lights. The red bulbs that had originally been hung twinkled amongst the older decorations.

"Not bad," Dan said. "That's not bad at all. Now why don't the two of you head to town for dinner? I'm going to take a nap but you can bring me back a cheeseburger."

Alex glanced at his watch. "I'd love to do that but I've got a meeting at the church."

"You aren't becoming your dad, are you? That's the last thing this town needs, another Palermo fleecing the flock."

Alex somehow managed a tight smile. "No, Dan, I'm not Jesse Palermo. And you know Pastor Matthews is nothing like my father."

"I know but I'm just making sure. I wouldn't want you caught up in something you couldn't get out of."

"I'm not. I'm going to the church to help Lucy with her self-defense class."

"What are you going to do at a self-defense class?" Curiosity gleamed in Dan's eyes.

"Oh, you'd be surprised," Alex answered without really answering. He knew if he gave too many details, he'd never hear the end of it.

"So you're not going to tell me…" Dan paused and finally shrugged. "How's those bucking bulls and the tractor repair?"

"I guess I won't starve," Alex answered as he headed for the kitchen and the pies. He didn't add that he had bigger concerns. But since Dan had seen the foreclosure notice in the paper, he guessed it wasn't a secret.

"Is Marcus not willing to help you out?" Dan asked, his tone suggesting he was truly concerned.

Alex shrugged. "I'm not sure he wants to keep the place. I'm going to get a loan or sell off cattle. It'll work out."

"Cattle prices are down." Dan cleared his throat. "Drought makes people nervous, even though we've been getting rain. But you're right, it'll work out. If they have something to eat at the church, would you bring me back some supper?"

Marissa shot her grandfather a warning look. "I'm making pasta and salad."

"Green stuff." Dan made a face and waved them away. "Go on, then. I guess we'll see you at church tomorrow. Green food and Jesus. She's taking over my life."

"I guess I could take her off your hands." Alex winked at Marissa. "For the right price. I'll even bring you back a few tacos from the dinner they're serving at church."

"You take her off my hands and I'll double your wages for helping out around here." Dan cackled as he made the offer.

"Dan, double of nothing is still nothing. And even if I take her, I bet she'll still make you eat some vegetables with those tacos."

"For a few hours of peace and quiet, it'll be worth it. Sometimes a man just wants to nap and watch a car race without a woman squawking that there's a good movie she's missing."

"She might not want to go." Alex chanced a look at

the woman in question. She was standing quietly, looking at the tree.

"*She* might have an opinion of her own," Marissa answered at long last.

"Marissa, would you like to go to town with me?"

Her hand dropped from the ornament she'd been touching. It was a horse made of baked dough and on the back her mother had written "I love you, Daddy."

He wondered about a family that had mementos that spoke of love, and yet they'd been split apart at the seams and never put back together.

Dan noticed what had caught her attention. "She was horse-crazy, your mom was. She had this little spotted pony she'd ride around on. She said she was a rodeo queen."

"That must be why she always sent me to a summer camp with horses. Every summer."

"I'm glad she did that for you," Dan said in a gruff tone that might have meant he didn't care. Alex knew he cared a lot.

"So am I." Marissa grabbed her jacket off the hook by the door. "Are we going?"

Alex glanced back at Dan. The older man was pretending he no longer cared. "Yes, we're going."

"Okay, but this isn't a date."

"Definitely not a date," he assured her.

Dan flipped on the TV. "Would the two of you just go? And don't be a cheap date, Alex. You can't keep a woman if you're cheap. That's why you're twenty-seven and still single. You're cheap."

"Dan, you're knocking on the door of eighty and you're single."

"And I was cheap," he grumbled and turned up the

volume on the TV. "Go on now. Have her home at a decent hour and don't go down any back roads."

"Thanks, Granddad. I feel like I'm sixteen and going to the prom."

"Well, I missed out on a lot. I have to make up for all of those little moments." He tapped his cheek but he didn't smile. Marissa understood and hurried to his side to kiss his cheek.

"You're a mess."

"Yes, I am. Be careful. Don't fall for a cowboy. All lines, but no follow-through."

Alex opened the front door for the woman who wasn't his date, but he leaned back in to tell Dan goodbye. "And for your information, I don't have lines. Or follow-through."

"You're the worst kind," Dan called out as the door closed.

Alex led Marissa across the yard to his truck. He opened the door for her and helped her in. Was it just a few weeks ago that she'd appeared in his life? It seemed as if he'd known her forever.

Chapter Thirteen

Alex stood in front of Lucy in the church fellowship hall. The women from the shelter and a few ladies from the community usually attended the self-defense classes. Today Marissa stood amongst the women. He tried to avoid looking her way but that was easier said than done.

Occasionally his gaze strayed, the same way his thoughts strayed. She wouldn't be here much longer. He guessed that was probably for the best. Since she'd shown up, he'd been distracted. He'd managed to get his own work done but he'd also spent a lot more time at Dan's than he normally would have.

Vaguely he heard Lucy tell him to come at her from behind. She said something to the crowd of women that made them all giggle. He put his hands up and before he could prepare, Lucy had him by the arm and flying through the air. His back hit the floor.

He groaned and tried to take a breath. Lucy looked down, grinning at him. "That's what you get for being distracted. Ladies, being aware of your surroundings will help to keep you safe. As you can see from my brother's position, flat on his back, being distracted is dangerous."

"Find yourself a new victim," he groaned as he sat up.

"Oh, but that's where you're mistaken. We are not victims. We are empowered because we know how to protect ourselves. And you are not the victim, you're the attacker."

He sat for a minute with his arms resting across his bent knees. "Yeah, well, you seemed to have forgotten that I'm not really attacking you."

"When did you get so soft?" she asked.

"I'm not soft."

She held a hand out and pulled him to his feet.

"Let's go over some basics. If you're in a parking lot, walking down the street or even in your own home, do you know what to do? I want you to remember, it is always better to fight, to call attention to yourself and to run. If you go with an attacker, your odds of escape decrease." Lucy positioned him in the center of the mat.

Alex made his best scared face to get a giggle out of the women watching the demonstration. Many of them had escaped abusive relationships, and smiling was something they didn't do a lot of. Not yet. The hope was that as time went on, they would smile more.

No one understood that better than Alex and Lucy. Lucy had left home at eighteen, intent on escaping the abusive home they'd grown up in. Alex had done his best to stay on the edge of his father's radar. He'd gained the most attention when he tried to protect his siblings, or distract their father.

He hadn't always been successful.

Lucy snapped her fingers to get his attention. "Cowboy up and pay attention, Alex. What has you so distracted tonight?"

Heat crawled up his neck. "Just tell me what you want me to do."

"Come at me from the front."

He did his best, knowing he wouldn't win. No one went up against Lucy and won. She was trained in hand-to-hand combat. She was a bodyguard and she'd been an MP in the army. She could outshoot, outrun and outfight him. He was okay with that. She would never again be anyone's victim.

Lucy explained that even if a woman had her hands blocked or the attacker held her, she still had a foot, a knee, a head. Alex raised his hands and backed away. Lucy grinned at his cowardice.

"Come on, Alex, come at me."

"I think I'm done."

She motioned him on, so he moved to grab her. She showed the women a variety of techniques to block his attempts and also to bring him to his knees.

"Lucy Palermo, that isn't nice," Bea said. He gave her a quick grin as Aunt Essie tried to quiet her. "I sure don't think she should hit her brother that way."

"It's okay, Bea, she won't hurt me." Alex stepped away from his sister. "She wants to show you how to defend yourself if anyone ever tries to hurt you."

Bea's face took on a soft, kind of sad look. Alex didn't know what to do or say when she started to cry. He walked off the mat and gathered the older woman in a hug.

"Bea, did someone hurt you?"

She leaned against him, sobbing until she hiccupped. "Yes, and it wasn't neighborly."

"No, Bea, it probably wasn't. I'm sorry." Alex gave

his aunt an imploring look because tears were not part of his job description.

Bea didn't seem to care. "I had a baby, Alex. She was a pretty little girl and they took her away and said I wasn't able to raise her. I heard the nurse say I wasn't in my right mind. But I was."

"Honey, let's go home now." Essie took Bea by the hand. "We'll work on self-defense another day."

"But I wanted to help decorate for the Christmas program." Bea wiped away her tears.

Out of the corner of his eye, Alex saw Marissa leave with a couple of the women from the shelter. He'd catch up with her later. At the moment, Essie more than likely needed his help with Bea.

"Bea, would you like to help me put the finishing touches on the manger that we've set up on the stage. It needs some shingles on the roof. If you're good with a hammer."

"I am good with a hammer." Bea smiled brightly, stories of neighbors and babies forgotten. But he wouldn't forget. Somewhere out there, Bea had a little girl.

"Let's go hammer then." He led her through the church to the sanctuary.

Pastor Matthews and a couple of men from the church were working on the stable that would be the center for any nativity dramas performed at the Christmas program. One of the men stood on a ladder attaching a star to the highest peak of the ceiling.

Alex spotted Marissa sitting on the piano bench. Her hands began to move across the keys and he stopped to listen as she played "Silent Night." The women she'd been talking to now sat on a nearby pew listening. She played the piano. He guessed he shouldn't be surprised. She could ride a horse, drive Dan's tractor and play the piano. If he had to guess, he thought she could probably do anything she set her mind to. He guessed she did whatever she thought would make her parents happy. With one exception.

She'd stayed in Bluebonnet. For Dan.

As his mind had wandered, he'd lost Bea. She had moved to the piano bench and was in the process of scooting Marissa over so that she could sit next to her.

Marissa glanced at the other woman and gave her a sweet smile, but kept playing. They were quite a pair, Marissa in her blue jeans and oversize flannel shirt; Bea in her floral house dress, still wearing her hairnet from work. But Bea's feet were bouncing in time to the music and, without warning, she started singing the chorus of "Silent Night."

She blew the roof off that little old church with the sweetest rendition of that song Alex had ever heard. From the looks of things, the music was having a similar effect on everyone. The hammers stopped. Pastor Matthews and the men sat down. The ladies stood silently in the background. Bea and Marissa entered a world of their own.

Alex desperately wanted to be in that world with them, because from the expressions on their faces, it was a good place to be.

As "Silent Night" ended, it became clear that Bea was on a roll. She flipped the pages to another song. Marissa nodded and began to play. This time she joined Bea and the two of them sang "Carol of the Bells." It was clear that Bea was directing things. She would sing and occasionally point at the music and Marissa would chime in.

When they finished, Bea turned red and hung her head. Emotion hung heavy in the air and no one spoke.

They were all too stunned. Alex sat back, watching as Marissa hugged the other woman tight and told her something that encouraged her to smile and look up. Marissa took her hand and stood with her. That's when everyone stood and applauded the duo.

Alex's gaze connected with Marissa's and he was almost knocked over from the strength of emotion that stretched between them. It was more than the song. He tried to tell himself it was the moment or the music, but he knew better. And he knew he had to do something to break this connection.

He walked away—he'd think up an excuse later.

Marissa knew a person couldn't really forget how to breathe but that's how she felt when she looked up and met Alex's gaze. His dark eyes had been full of emotion. And then he'd simply turned and walked away.

It hurt that he would walk away from her. She got that it didn't make sense, this imagined connection between the two of them. She shouldn't give it more credence than it deserved. She had always dealt in hard facts. She had managed for a very long time to keep her emotions in firm check. For her sake. For her mother's.

Stop crying, her mother had told her all of those years ago. *Just stop.* She couldn't undo what had happened with tears. She couldn't make it all okay again.

But she'd tried. She'd tried so hard. With every tear she blinked away. With every test she aced. With every award she earned. She had tried.

What had it gotten her?

Lonely. It had gotten her loneliness. It had brought her to the doorstep of a grandfather she hadn't known existed and into the life of a man who didn't want to be troubled by her.

Further thoughts were interrupted by the approach of Pastor Matthews. He looked from Marissa to Bea and back before shaking his head and grinning. She didn't know what to say to that, because she had been just as astounded by Bea's voice.

"That was amazing. Will the two of you perform for the Christmas program?"

The invitation took her by surprise. She glanced past him to Alex, who had taken up a hammer and was helping the men put shingles on the makeshift stable. Someone plugged in the cord attached to the star and it lit up, glowing bright with Christmas lights.

Alex shifted just a bit, his dark eyes boring into her. She shook off the lingering feelings of losing something important.

Next to her, Bea didn't hesitate. "We would love to, Preacher. I do love to sing. Mama always told me not to go around town bragging about my singing. She said it was a sin. That's what Pastor Palermo told her. She sure liked the pastor. But I like you better." She glanced at Alex. "I'm sorry about that, Alex."

"I'm not sure if I'll be here," Marissa answered when Pastor Matthews directed his attention to her.

"But you have to," Bea interjected. She gave Marissa and then Alex a reproachful look before leaning toward Pastor Matthews. "Alex has been neighborly and my mama said that's a sin."

"Being neighborly is a sin, Bea? How is that?" Pastor Matthews looked truly confused.

"Don't. Ask," Alex shouted, getting everyone's attention. He swung the hammer at a nail and then jerked his hand back. "Ouch."

"That's what a temper will get you Alex Palermo." Bea shook her head. "He needs to repent. He also needs to repent because he looks at Marissa like he wants to kiss her."

"Bea, I think it's about time I take you home." Aunt Essie to the rescue.

Bea grumbled as she grabbed her enormous purse and swung it over her shoulder. "You're the one who said it, Essie. You told Libby that Alex is in big trouble and he can't look at—"

"Stop," Essie whispered a little too loudly.

Marissa was stuck somewhere between humor and wanting the floor to open and swallow her up. Essie offered a sheepish smile.

"I'm going to take Bea home. But I do hope you can be here for the Christmas program, Marissa. That music was beautiful."

"Thank you," she answered. Turning to Bea, she said, "Bea, I'm not sure how a beautiful voice like yours could ever be a sin and I hope you sing often."

"And I concur," Pastor Matthews added.

Bea gave him a narrow-eyed look. "If I wasn't getting in trouble by Miss Essie, I'd ask what *concur* means."

"It means I agree, Bea. Having your beautiful voice and singing those songs for God is not a sin." Pastor Matthews hugged Bea. "I'm looking forward to hearing you sing more."

Marissa excused herself and went in search of Alex. He was no longer working on the stable. The other men were packing up tools and the star had been unplugged. She walked through the church and didn't find him anywhere. She wondered if he might have left, forgetting that she needed a ride. Or maybe not caring.

He hadn't left her, though. She found him outside, a short distance from the church, sitting on a bench near the playground. As she approached, he looked up, un-smiling.

"I'm sorry." She didn't know what else to say.

"For what?"

She sat down next to him. "I'm not sure. It would help if *you* would tell *me* what I'm apologizing for."

One side of his mouth tugged upward, easing the tension in his expression. "I'm not mad at you, so you don't have to apologize."

"Bea?"

He shook his head. "No, I would never be angry with Bea. She says whatever is on her mind. She can't help that. I'm angry because my father told her she shouldn't sing. That voice, tonight when she sang and you played, that was amazing. It made me feel maybe a little bit of the awe those shepherds felt when they approached the stable, knowing they'd find their savior inside."

He managed to put into words what she'd felt sitting next to Bea. As she'd played, the men had ceased working on the stable, but one of them had continued to work on the star. The lights would twinkle and go out and they would try again. It had brought that long-ago night to life in her imagination. Silent night, holy night.

"A gift like Bea's shouldn't be wasted," Alex said. "But my father, for whatever reason, had tried to silence that voice. Maybe because of what happened to Bea. Or he might have been jealous. Logic never mattered to Jesse Palermo."

"I'm sorry." Somehow his hand ended up in hers.

"Thank you." He gave her hand a light squeeze. "We should go. Pastor Matthews would be upset if he thought we were being neighborly in front of the church."

She giggled. "Bea does have a way with words."

"Yes, she does." He stood, still holding her hand, and led her to his truck.

The night was cool and crystal clear with millions of stars twinkling overhead in the inky darkness of the sky. The world seemed so much bigger here, with no buildings to mar the skyline, no lights to compete with the brightness of the moon or the stars. She'd always thought the city, with all of the people, the cars, the buildings, was big. But this quiet, country night changed that for her.

When a person could stand in the yard and see the sun come up in the east, the colors as brilliant as spilled paint across the morning sky, and then in the evening watch the sun set on the opposite horizon, there was a hugeness in that.

She drew in a deep breath of the cold December air, closing her eyes as she waited for Alex to unlock and open the truck door.

"There's nothing like this air," she told him.

"No, there isn't. And a night like this, when the moon is that bright."

She looked up, nodding her agreement. "It almost looks as if you could reach out and touch it."

"Yes, it does."

She became aware of the man standing in front of her. His hand was touching her cheek and there was a sweetness in his expression.

"Bea would be appalled," he whispered. "But I'm about to kiss you."

"We shouldn't."

"Yeah, I've never been the best at should and shouldn't."

He kissed her as his fingers stroked a sweet line along her jaw. The kiss was everything. It made her feel treasured and beautiful. It made her feel like the woman she wanted to be. His woman.

No. She wasn't his. She didn't know how to trust what she felt, not after Aidan. She had tried to be who Aidan wanted her to be, too. She'd tried to fit into his world. The same way she'd always tried to please her parents, she realized. And here she was, feeding chickens and driving a tractor.

Kissing a cowboy and wanting to be the person who fit in his life.

The sounds of people talking and laughing, a car starting, helped to bring her back to reality. She moved a step back from Alex, and from emotions that were jumbled up.

It made sense that they shouldn't talk just yet, so she was glad when wordlessly he opened the door for her. She climbed inside the warm, confining space of the truck cab. Alex got in and started to speak.

"I'm going to miss you."

She would miss him, too. "I'll be back from time to time."

"Right. Of course."

That wasn't the answer he wanted but she didn't know what else to say. The kiss had been a revelation. It had also revealed some things about her life and how she'd been living it. Pleasing others, trying to be who they wanted her to be.

She had obligations, responsibilities, back in Dallas. Most of all she knew that it was time for her to figure out what she really wanted out of life and who she really wanted to be.

Chapter Fourteen

Marissa bit back the grin she knew her grandfather wouldn't appreciate. He was sitting next to her in the church pew wearing his Sunday best, which happened to be new bib overalls and a button-up shirt with his good boots.

"Church," he grumbled. "I can't believe I let you talk me into going to church."

"It isn't going to hurt you," she said calmly.

"You don't know that it isn't. And don't sass me."

"I'm not sassing, I'm telling you that this won't hurt you."

A few rows of ahead of them, Alex sat with his family. Aunt Essie, his sister Lucy and her husband, Dane, and his younger sister, Maria. Alex glanced back at them, teeth flashing as he grinned. Next to him, Essie gave him a pointed look. A warning, if Marissa had to guess.

The warnings should have come sooner. Someone should have warned Marissa that a too-charming cowboy with funny ears would make it difficult for her to leave Bluebonnet Springs behind. Even when she knew she did have to go. She'd signed a contract for a teaching position. She wasn't the country girl she'd been pretending to be.

"Stop looking at the boy that way. People are going to wonder." Her grandfather spoke in a too-loud whisper, and the people around them giggled.

"Shh," Marissa warned her grandfather.

He chuckled as if it happened to be great fun. Her heart filled up. With love for him, for this town and for a God who was as real to her today as He had been all of those years ago when she'd been a child in Sunday school.

The service started. She'd never been so thankful for anything. She could sit there in relative peace, sing songs she hadn't forgotten, listen to a message of hope and stare at the back of Alex's head.

The service ended and people started making their way to the fellowship hall. Dan and Marissa joined the crowd, somehow falling in with Alex and his family as they made their way down the short hallway to the kitchen area.

"That wasn't so bad, was it, Dan?" Alex asked as they entered the big, fluorescent-lit room with the many tables and chairs set up with pretty evergreen centerpieces.

"No, not bad at all." But he pulled on his collar and shivered. "There sure are a bunch of people here."

Marissa took her took her grandfather by the hand. "Yes, there are. And you need to sit down."

He bristled a bit. "I think I know when I need to sit down."

"Of course you do." She paused and waited.

"Now I need to sit down." His blue eyes twinkled. "I just like to decide these things for myself."

Essie walked past. "Dan, you look pretty spiffy today."

"Charm me all you want, Essie, you're not getting my money."

"You might smell kind of good, but you don't have that much money."

He took a seat and looked around. "Now what is the plan? I thought you were going to feed us."

"We have to get the food set out and then we'll start a line," Essie informed him with a pat on his shoulder. "You won't be sorry, Dan."

"I know I won't."

"What can I do to help?" Marissa asked as Essie started to hurry off.

Essie glanced toward the kitchen and then looked around. "I don't really know. There are already too many women in the kitchen. There are some smaller children that are starting to look restless. Would you corral them while their mothers finish getting the food ready?"

Children, she knew how to handle. "Of course. Can I take them outside?"

Essie lifted a shoulder. "Suits me. In the closet by the door there are bubbles, balls and other outdoor toys."

Alex had disappeared. He'd mentioned helping the pastor put something in the attic. Marissa wouldn't wait for him. She could handle a few children on her own. She gathered up the kids, who seemed restless, and headed them out the door, stopping on her way to get bubbles, Frisbees and a ball.

"What are we going to do?" Amy, the little girl she'd met on her previous trips to the church, asked.

"Whatever you want, as long as it is safe." Marissa led them to the playground and she laid out the items she'd procured from the closet. "What do you all want to do?"

"Tag!" one of the boys yelled.

A chant of, "Tag, tag!" went up from the group of half a dozen children.

"Okay, tag it is. Who is going to be 'it' first?"

The biggest boy touched her arm. "You're 'it.'"

That didn't seem fair. But before she could protest, they ran, scattering across the lawn. She chased after one of the bigger boys but he quickly outran her. She went after another and he laughed as he slid past her and kept going. She could see that this wasn't going to go very well for her. If she had any hope of catching any of them, it was one of the little girls. They'd managed to get farther away as the boys kept Marissa distracted.

She went after little Julie. The dark-haired child was laughing and running backward. "Not too close to the parking lot," Marissa called out.

The little girl stopped for a moment, laughing a real belly laugh. A truck suddenly pulled into the parking lot.

"Stay where you're at until the truck stops," Marissa warned.

The little girl peered around the cars to see the truck, then she screamed. Marissa ran forward. Had a bee or a wasp stung her?

"What's wrong?" she asked as she knelt in front of the child. She noticed the other children had congregated at the picnic table and were blowing bubbles.

"My daddy," she whispered through her tears. "I have to go. He can't be here." And then the child ran off.

Marissa stood up. When she turned around, someone caught her from behind. "Go inside," she screamed.

The children all ran away.

"I'm just here to get my kid." The man held her tight and she heard the flick as he moved his hand. A knife. He had a knife.

"I'm sorry," she said quietly. "I'm new to the area. I didn't know which child was yours."

"I think you did. And I think you're going to help me get her back. You're going to keep walking toward the church. Nice and steady. You're going to tell my wife to hand over my daughter and then you're going to walk me back to the truck."

"They won't give her to you."

"That's why my day got a little better when you showed up," he told her. His breath smelled of onions. His clothes were dirty. She was aware of the rough stubble of his unshaven face as he leaned close.

She wanted away from him. First she wanted the children safe. The older ones had herded the younger children inside. Pastor Matthews stepped outside, Alex and a few other men close behind him.

For some reason she thought about the food getting cold. She laughed at the thought.

"Are you crazy?" the man holding her tightly against his body asked. She felt the knife thump against her arm. She tried to move and he dug it into her forearm. The sting of pain across her arm took her by surprise.

Why had she thought he wouldn't really hurt her? But he wasn't playing. This wasn't a game to him.

As she contemplated her next move, she saw that a woman had joined the men. Lucy.

Seeing the other woman brought back the previous evening's lesson. She focused on Alex's sister and Lucy nodded, as if she knew.

Blood was dripping down Marissa's arm. She tried to move, testing just how he was holding her. He squeezed her wrist and yanked it behind her back.

"Don't try anything funny."

"What would I try? I'm a teacher. It isn't like I'm armed. You have the knife. And I have the cut to prove it."

Get mad, Lucy had said the previous evening. Get mad but don't lose focus. Don't get stupid. Always have a plan. It's one thing they do in their protection business, Lucy had told the ladies. They always knew were the exits were located. They always had an exit plan.

Julie's dad stopped walking. He twisted her arm until she felt her wrist twist. Exit strategy. She couldn't use that arm to hit him. He had a knife. She'd taken a drama class in college.

"I think I'm going to faint."

"Don't you dare," he warned. "Stand up straight."

"I can't." She took a deep breath. "My arm, the blood."

She went limp, hoping beyond hope that it was the right move and praying God had a moment to spare. As she went down it seemed to throw him off balance. He struggled to hold her dead weight and the knife. She took her opportunity and drew her arm back and into his nose, then she knocked him under the chin with her head. He reached for her but she slid to the side and ran.

Alex caught her up against him. "Shh, you're okay. Calm down."

"I can't," she sobbed against him. "I can't be calm now."

"Good job," Lucy said, appearing at her side. "Let's get that arm cleaned up."

"Did he leave?"

"Pastor Matthews is talking to him. The police are on their way."

"Julie and her mom?" Marissa asked as she leaned against Alex.

"Both safe." Lucy nodded at her brother. Without warning he scooped up Marissa in his arms and carried her inside.

"People should go ahead and eat," she told Lucy as they hurried through the fellowship hall. "And tell my grandfather that I'm fine. It's just a scratch."

"Lucy will tell him. And stop talking." Alex sounded gruff. And angry.

"Why are you mad?" she whispered against his shoulder.

They were in a hallway and he headed for the living area at the back of the shelter.

"You have to ask?"

She did have to ask. And she should also tell him that she could walk just fine. Her arm had been cut, not her legs.

She should have told him to put her down. But she didn't. Because his arms felt strong and safe.

Alex held Marissa a little closer. He could hear the sirens in the distance. He knew how sirens affected her. He also knew that she didn't have a clue how deep the gash on her arm was, or she wouldn't have been so nonchalant about serving lunch.

She'd asked him why he was angry. He was angry because he'd been helping Pastor Matthews and she'd been outside. He hadn't been there. If he'd been with her, he could have kept her safe. As it was, he'd been unable to do anything. He'd had to stand there while that idiot sliced her arm. He'd watched as she went limp and fought to get away.

He'd been pretty proud of her and he guessed it had something to do with Lucy's self-defense class.

Marissa had rescued herself.

He carried her through the door of the family room of the shelter and placed her on the daybed. Marissa curled up on her side, grimacing as she tried to reach for her arm. It was then that he realized Lucy had followed. She put a towel against the wound and held it tight.

"Doc is getting his bag out of the car. He'll be here in a minute," Lucy said softly. "Marissa, are you feeling okay?"

Marissa opened her eyes. "By okay, do you mean horrible?"

Lucy laughed. "I was hoping for better, but I'll take it."

"I didn't realize how bad it hurt until just now."

Alex stepped away for a moment. He needed to take a deep breath and get control of his temper. Lucy shot him a look over her shoulder. "Get a grip, bro."

"I'm not twelve."

"Children," Marissa said in a whisper. "I'll call the principal."

"I should have been there," Alex said as he scooted a chair close to the bed. "I'm sorry."

"When did you become responsible for me? Or for keeping the whole world safe?" Marissa asked, her eyes a little hazy as she looked down at her arm and then at the wrist that was swelling.

"He's always had this complex," Lucy revealed. And she really shouldn't have. "He wants to keep everyone safe. But even the best of us can't always be there to stop tragedy."

"If I'd been there..." he began.

His sister gave him that scathing look she had. "Stop. If you'd been there, you could have what? Gotten hurt, too? Stopped our dad from locking me up? Stopped the bull from barreling down on one of your best friends?"

"There's nothing wrong with wanting to protect the people you care about."

Marissa lifted her head a few inches. "I'm so glad you care, but really, I did this. I also took care of myself. So stop. You did rescue me off the side of the road. That doesn't mean you took me home to raise."

"You're already raised." The tension drained from his body. "And I'm glad you're okay."

"How's our patient?" Doc hurried through the door. "Looks like she's going to be fine. That's a dandy of a cut, though."

"Did they get him?" Alex asked.

"Still trying to talk to him."

"Is everyone eating lunch?" Marissa asked as Doc pulled the towel off the cut. She grimaced, closing her eyes as he poked around at the wound.

"They're eating. At least it's a good clean cut. I'll have to sew it up. You're not going to like this part. I'm going to give you some shots to deaden that and then..."

"Here? Now?" she asked, her eyes opened wide.

"Unless you want to drive down to my office. I'm not like those fine doctors in Dallas. I take my office with me."

"But stitches?"

Alex pulled another chair close. "He's the best."

"You're going to have to sing to me," Marissa said with a teasing glint in her eyes.

"Sing to her, Doc," Alex said.

"I think she meant for you to sing, Alex." Doc pulled a needle and a small vial out of his bag. "We're going to numb you up a bit. Just be glad this isn't the old days and I'm not giving you a stick to bite."

"Thanks. I think." She closed her eyes again. "Sing, Palermo."

"Silent night, holy night…"

"Stop," she whispered as the needle entered her arm.

"Stop?"

"You're horrible."

Doc laughed. "The woman is honest. Okay, can you rest your arm on your side? I'm going to clean this up a bit and make sure we're all sterile. Sterile as we can be."

Marissa opened her eyes. "It's going to hurt, isn't it?"

"You'll feel a sting."

She closed her eyes again. Alex thought she was magnificent and strong. He guessed maybe he'd been wrong about city girls. Some of them could hold their own.

Doc stitched her up and then he turned his attention to her wrist. Alex got mad all over again. Her wrist, small and fine-boned, was bruised and swollen.

"It's going to be sore for a few days," Doc told her as he wrapped it. "But I don't think anything is broken."

"Thank you. And I have insurance," Marissa offered.

Doc patted her shoulder. "This is on the house."

"Doc, you say that about ninety percent of the time."

"Yeah, well, I'm old and I can do what I want." Doc stood and gave his patient another good look. "You'll be okay, just sore and maybe a little jumpy for a week or so. But you did a good thing getting that little girl to safety."

"I didn't think."

"Maybe not, but you did a good thing. Now try to rest. I'll have someone bring you a plate."

Doc left and Alex moved a little closer to Marissa. She was watching him, studying his face, and she looked concerned. He didn't want her to worry about him.

Before he could tell her that, someone rapped on the door. He called for them to enter and a head peeked in. Dan looked a little bit pale and his eyes were wild beneath the shaggy eyebrows.

"Where's my granddaughter?"

"Come in, Granddad. I'm fine. I promise." Marissa winked at Alex as she called out to her grandfather.

"You have visitors," Dan said as he pushed the door open. Alex wasn't sure about visitors. But little Julie and her mom, Trish, entered behind Dan.

"I wanted to thank you," Trish said as she got closer to the bed. "I don't know what would have happened if…"

Alex watched as Marissa held a hand out to the woman, but she made a very pointed look at Julie, and he agreed. The child didn't need to hear what might have happened.

"I'm just real grateful," Trish said as she pulled her daughter close. "Julie is really glad you were there, too."

"Me, too." Then Marissa held her arms open to the child.

Julie took cautious steps forward, eyeing the bandaged arm and the wrist that had been wrapped. "You'll be okay?"

"Of course I will. And you will, too. I promise."

"We won't keep you. We just wanted to say thank you." Trish took Julie by the hand and led her from the room.

"I had them make your plate to go," Dan said in a less gruff than usual manner. Alex had to take a second look to make sure it was the real Dan.

"I can drive you home," Alex offered.

"Trying to get rid of me?" Marissa asked, her expression soft.

That was a question he didn't want to answer. Not at the moment. It wasn't simple. He needed her to leave, before he couldn't let her go. He needed her to stay, but he knew she wouldn't.

Alex was in big trouble.

Chapter Fifteen

Sun was streaming through the window and Bub moved, pushing and trying to hog the couch Marissa slept on. She moved and an aching back and arm greeted her. After a few minutes she rolled to her side and Bub slid in a boneless heap to the floor.

The clock on the wall chimed eight times. Marissa shot off the couch, her legs shaking as she righted herself. It was long past time to feed the animals. How had she missed her alarm? And Red the rooster? Surely nothing had gotten the rooster. What if a coyote had found the nuisance bird?

She reached for her shoes and a sharp, stinging pain in her arm reminded her of the stitches. One sprained wrist and a stitched-up arm. Somehow she hadn't thought about what a detriment that would be to getting ready in the morning. Actually, it would be a hindrance to the many things she needed to get done today. Not to mention playing the piano. The Christmas performance was a week away.

With great care she managed to slide on her shoes. As she stood back up, the door of the camper opened.

Her grandfather gave her a look. He had the fireproof box in his hands and he sat it on the table.

"What are you doing up?" he asked.

"I overslept and I was going to go feed. What have you been doing?"

He reached for his oxygen tank and gave her a gloating look. "I'm taking care of my livestock the way I've been doing it for nigh on sixty years. And you should be resting after the day you had yesterday."

"I feel much better." Which wasn't really the truth. She had an arm in a sling and one wrist wrapped up.

"Sit down and I'll get you a cup of coffee. You've been taking care of me. Time I took care of you." He gave her a look and she sat.

"Why did you bring the box in?" she asked as he moved around the kitchen. She shivered a bit thinking of him climbing around alone in the barn.

"I'll show you in a bit." He pulled eggs from the fridge and set to cracking them in a bowl. "I know you thought I needed to be taken care of, but I'm pretty handy in the kitchen. And I have to admit that I feel better since I've started taking Doc's advice with the oxygen and your advice on eating healthier."

"You've complained a lot."

He shot her a grin. "Yeah, well, I've been complaining for a long time. It's habit."

"Why are we having this conversation?"

He poured eggs into a buttered skillet. "Well, I've been thinking that it's probably about time for you to head back to Dallas and I don't want you worrying, thinking I can't take care of myself. I know you have a job and friends. You have your parents. I don't want you staying here thinking that if you leave, something bad is going to happen. It won't."

"I know that." Or she hoped she did. But that didn't mean she wouldn't worry.

"You've got to get back to your life, honey." He stirred the eggs and then reached for the coffeepot. "I'm going to be blunt. I know I'm just an old man but I can see that a young woman like you would like Alex. He's a good kid, works hard, I guess he's not too ugly even if he does have those ears."

She laughed.

"But I've been down this road before. Your grandmother thought the same things about me. She liked the idea of a cowboy and a ranch, until we was hitched and she had to move to Bluebonnet."

"I'm not planning on hitching myself to anyone, Granddad," she informed him. But saying the words out loud, she felt a sense of loss. If she left here, she'd leave so much behind. She would leave behind people and things she never would have known or missed if she hadn't come.

She wouldn't regret.

If she didn't go home, she'd let down her parents. She'd also let down the school that had hired her. She had a contract to fulfill.

Her grandfather turned off the stove and brought her a cup of coffee. A minute later he returned with eggs and toast.

"I'm going to miss you," he admitted in a softer voice than she'd heard from him before.

He scratched his chin, looked at her and walked off. His back was to her as he headed to the stove, but his hand came up and he swiped at his face.

"I'll be back. I promise," she assured him.

"I'm counting on that." He returned to his chair with

a plate of eggs and toast. "And that's what the box is about."

"What's in the box?"

"Don't get yourself all worked up. I'll show you when I'm good and ready."

He turned on the news, as if he was enjoying dragging this out, making her wait. After he'd finished he took both plates to the sink and did the dishes. Marissa sat cross-legged on the couch, waiting for him to finish. She smiled and pretended it didn't bother her to be kept waiting. To illustrate that point, she picked up her phone and scrolled through emails and social media.

Eventually he returned to his chair, picking up the box on his way. He pulled a key out of his pocket and lifted the lid of the box. She couldn't see what it was that he sifted through, but his eyes had narrowed as he looked it all over.

"Well, I'll be. I'd forgotten some of this was in here."

"What is in the box?" she groaned, beyond tired of waiting.

Holding the box with one hand, he used the other to empty the contents, and he placed it all on the table next to his chair. Stacks of money, envelopes and papers.

"What is all of that?" She leaned to get a better look.

"My life savings. It isn't much, but enough to build a house with a couple of bedrooms and a nest egg for the future." He held up several official-looking documents. "I'd forgotten all about these stocks."

"What are they for?"

"Oh, some crazy idea of your grandmother's. She told me to invest in technology. That was twenty or thirty years ago. I guess it might be worth something now."

With a groan, Marissa fell back on the couch. "You think?"

His blue eyes twinkled merrily. "Yeah, I imagine. I'll have to check that out. Maybe the two of us can take a trip to Hawaii."

She sat up again, brushing her hair back from her face. "Not Hawaii. Maybe the Bahamas?"

"A cruise?"

"Yes," she said. "A cruise would be good."

Her phone rang. She gave her grandfather an apologetic look. "It's my mom."

"You go ahead and talk. I'm going to take care of a few things in the barn. I'm putting this box under my bed. I guess I should trust a bank with that cash and figure out what those stocks are worth."

"Hi, Mom," Marissa answered as her grandfather left the room. "How are you?"

"The question would be, how are you? Your grandfather called us this morning."

The traitor. "Oh, I see. I've been meaning to call. I'm going to be in the community Christmas program. I'd love for you all to come."

A long pause followed. Her mom cleared her throat. "Yes, okay. And then can we bring you home?"

"Yes, of course." After all, she couldn't hide in Bluebonnet Springs forever.

They talked for several minutes. Afterward Marissa couldn't remember all that they'd talked about. Her brain was trying to wrap itself around the thought of leaving Bluebonnet...her grandfather.

And Alex.

Alex stood in the center of the arena and watched the filly at the end of the lunge line. She started to move in on him and he picked up the whip. That's all he had to do, show her. Her ears pricked forward and she moved back to the end of the line, keeping it tight.

"Walk," he said firmly.

She acted a bit like an impetuous toddler but she did what he asked. The early afternoon sun brushed her coat with gold. He couldn't help but feel a little proud of her. She was the offspring of his best mare and the sire belonged to a friend outside of Austin.

A truck pulled up to the barn. She did a startled little dance but he spoke to her and she settled. Her ears continued to twitch, though, as she sniffed for a hint of the newcomer.

"Easy," he said quietly. "Halt."

She stopped with her hooves squared up and her neck long. Yeah, she was going to be a champion.

"She's beautiful," Marissa called out from the side of the arena. "I thought you were mainly a fan of getting trampled by bulls."

He walked up to the filly, ran a hand down her golden-red neck, then whispered that she was still his favorite female. But he'd be parting with this four-legged favorite very soon. He had wanted to keep her but he was going to need to start liquidating assets so he could pay the mortgage before the auction could take place. He had a buyer looking at his bulls, too.

"I heard that," Marissa called out as she came through the gate. "A horse is your favorite female?"

Did the woman know nothing about boundaries? He led the filly across the arena. She kept an even pace, staying at his shoulder. A month ago she enjoyed nipping at him. Today she kept her teeth to herself.

"How are you doing today?" Alex asked.

"Better. Sore but I'm going to be fine. I wanted to thank you for yesterday."

"Thank me for what? If anything, I should have been there sooner."

"Don't," she warned. "Really, you couldn't have done anything. And I obviously did just fine."

He knew she was teasing but it didn't help. Not really. He felt responsible. Her hand touched his arm, stopping him from walking away. He glanced down at her and she looked up at him with eyes the color of a winter sky. Dark lashes fringed those amazing orbs and he couldn't help but get a little bit lost.

"I'm not sure why you feel as if you let me down. I think you might need to deal with that, with the idea that you should be able to rescue everyone in your life. We can't always rescue people. Sometimes they have to rescue themselves. And sometimes the circumstances are just so dire that we don't have the tools to do what is needed. I'm trying really hard to come to terms with the truth, that I didn't cause my sister's death. I made a bad decision. She made a bad choice to follow. But we were children. Were you ever a child, Alex?"

They were in the barn and he cross-tied the filly so he could brush her out. When she was secure he took Marissa by the hand and led her to the storage room. He opened the door and flipped on a light. He didn't go in.

"What?" she asked, clearly puzzled.

"This is the room my dad locked my sister in. For two days he kept her in there. He played Johnny Cash on a CD and ignored when she cried for him to let her out. After a while she stopped crying. I tried to bust her out but he must have known and he dragged me back to the house."

"I'm so sorry."

"My father was about the meanest man I've ever known. And that isn't something to be proud of. It isn't a legacy to keep going."

"You aren't like him, Alex," she said as she rubbed her hand down his arm. "You're nothing like him."

She pulled his head down and he rested his cheek against the top of her head. Her hand rubbed circles on his back and for the longest time he let her just hold him. He'd never told anyone outside the family, other than Pastor Matthews, about the storage room. He'd always worried what type of reaction he'd get if he shared.

This woman had a quiet strength. It seeped into him and he drank it up. He regretted that he'd met her, because now he would have to know what it felt like to lose her.

"Why are you here?" he asked as he held her close. He had a good idea what had brought her by. But he wanted to hear it from her.

"I wanted to visit."

"That's all?"

"And I wanted to tell you in person that I'll be leaving after the community Christmas program Sunday."

"I see." He pulled back from her. Her gaze drifted from his.

"Dan is going to build a house."

"It's about time. Why is he going to build it now?"

"He said he needs an extra bedroom so I can visit from time to time. And I assured him I will be back. I'm also going to see if he'll come to Dallas for Christmas."

"I'm glad. He needs his family."

"We need him," she responded. "I should go so you can get back to work."

"Yeah, I have a tractor I need to get repaired before tomorrow."

Then everything was suddenly awkward and she backed away from him. "I'll see you soon?"

"Yes, soon. I don't know how much I'll see you between now and when you leave, but I'll definitely see you at the Christmas program and craft fair."

She stood on tiptoe and kissed his cheek. "I'm so glad you stopped and picked me up on the road."

He managed a half-hearted grin but couldn't agree. She had complicated his life. For the first time ever, he found himself wishing he could walk a woman down the aisle. He found himself wanting little girls with dark hair and blue eyes. But thinking those thoughts wouldn't get him anywhere.

She left and he went back to the filly, giving her a good brushing that had her nipping at his shoulder. Her way of pleading for him to stop already. He got the hint, so he tossed the brush in a bucket and untied her to lead her to the stall.

"Was that Dan's granddaughter leaving?" Maria asked as she entered the barn. He glanced her way and did a double take.

He couldn't quite put her in the box of annoying little sister when she looked like a college girl. Her hair was straight and not a tangled curly mess. She wasn't wearing jeans, boots and a T-shirt.

"What in the world are they doing to you down in Houston?"

Her hazel eyes narrowed at that question. "What is that supposed to mean? And don't think I'm forgetting about Dan's granddaughter being here with my brother."

"She came by to let me know she's leaving. So, back to you. Where are you going all dressed up like that?"

She spun in a slow circle, showing off the flowery dress. She was eighteen and his little sister. He wasn't exactly a father figure but she had been a little girl of eight when their dad died. He'd been looking out for her for a long time.

"I'm going on a date," she informed him with a secret smile.

"Are you? Is he picking you up here?"

"No, he isn't. I'm meeting him." She walked closer to him, smiling shyly, but he knew it was a ruse to get him off balance. "And I thought you should know, Marcus is home. He pulled in a few minutes ago and he's unloading his truck, like he plans to stay awhile."

"I'm not sure if that's good or bad. But about this date, why is he not picking you up here? Don't guys do that anymore?"

"No way would I let a guy come here. You're a ferocious pit bull when it comes to protecting your sisters. And you have such a bad opinion of marriage, you can't imagine why anyone would want to date or get serious."

"I don't have a bad opinion of…" He gave her a long look. "Are you thinking of getting marr—"

She cut him off. "Of course not. I have a lot of college ahead of me. I'm saying that because Marissa Walker just left and I'm guessing you're going to let her just walk away."

"Since it would be considered kidnapping if I kept her here against her will. Yes, I guess I am going to let her walk away. She has a job in Dallas. I have a life here. She came here to meet her grandfather. She met him. Now she's going back to her home and her life."

"I love you, Alex, but you're as dense as Marcus when it comes to relationships."

"I heard that, and I resent it." Marcus stood in the doorway of the barn, looking a bit worse for wear.

"I'm being honest. Both of you are a mess. It's a good

thing you all have me." She kissed Alex on the cheek and then danced out of his way and headed for the door.

"Go. And have fun. But be safe," Alex called out after her. "And don't fall for any sappy lines."

"Maybe you should learn some new lines," she said as she stopped just outside the door. He should have let her go. Instead he followed.

"You think?"

"Yeah, I think." She was all serious now. "It does wonders. We women like to think we're all strong and independent. But we still like to be told we're beautiful. We like surprises and flowers. We even like candlelight dinners."

He let her go without trying to get the last word. Besides, he had Marcus to contend with. As identical twins, he didn't think they shared any of that I-feel-what-you-feel bond. But Marcus was there. And hadn't he been thinking it would be good if his brother came home?

"Dan's granddaughter?" Marcus asked as he headed for the barn.

"What?" Alex grabbed a lead rope. He had a young gelding he wanted to green break before he sold him. If he could get the horse under saddle, he'd bring more money than he would barely halter broke. And he could use all the money he could make right now.

"Maria is giving you advice. I guessed it had something to do with Dan's granddaughter." Marcus stepped closer, making it easier to hear his words.

Alex didn't miss how his twin cast a nervous look around the barn, almost as if he expected their father to come roaring from a stall, prepared to beat him half to death. Rather than make Marcus talk, Alex filled the uneasy silence that hung between them.

"Yeah, Maria is convinced I'm in love. She's young. She doesn't get that we have other things on our minds."

"Such as?" Marcus asked.

"Saving this ranch. Whether we like it or not, it's ours."

"Put it on the market. I'll give you the money for the second mortgage if you'll sell the whole place."

"I don't want to put it up for sale. I want to live here."

Marcus shrugged. "Suit yourself. Get a loan. Borrow from Dane and Lucy, but my offer stands."

"It's a piece of land, Marcus. It isn't him. And I heard back from the bank. They won't give me a loan until the second mortgage is paid off and our mother signs the place over to us."

"I can't be here without hearing his voice. I can't listen to Johnny Cash without thinking about Lucy in that room. I don't want to save this ranch."

Alex wanted to be angry at his brother, but he got it. He understood. And he also realized Marcus wasn't as bad off financially as they all thought.

"I understand," he said, finally managing to get the words out.

Marcus nodded. "I know."

"How long are you staying?"

"Christmas." Marcus moved away from him but he stopped at the door. "I'll help you out. But then I'm done with this place."

Alex stood in the doorway of the barn watching his brother's stiff-legged walk as he headed to the house. Because when Alex had tried to humor and charm their father, Marcus had gone against him physically. And lost.

They were all on the losing end of this situation.

Chapter Sixteen

Marissa watched her mother as she helped her grand-father out of the back of her car. He didn't object the way he typically would. Instead he thanked her, then he turned to Marissa and winked.

"What should we do first?" she asked as she stepped to his side.

Her parents had shown up earlier in the day. To break the ice, her grandfather had gotten her dad talking about the house he wanted to build. That had kept the two men busy all day.

Her grandfather nodded in the direction of the craft booths. "I reckon I'd start over there with the crafts, baked goods and doodads you women seem to like. Me and Joe will head on over to the funnel cakes. I've got a hankering for something fried."

Her grandfather gave her a triumphant look as he headed for the funnel cakes. She couldn't help but smile. He seemed a different man from the one she'd met when she'd first shown up.

As they walked, her dad matched his steps to her

grandfather's and the two men talked as if they'd known each other for years, not days.

"This suits you," her mom said as they walked toward the craft booths.

Marissa looked up surprised. "Suits me?"

Her mom touched her hair. "Well, other than the hair. This town. Your grandfather. You seem happy."

Marissa glanced around, at the tents where tables were set up to sell crafts, desserts and other items. Children were playing in a bounce house. In less than an hour the churches would start the program. Two plays, several songs and the nativity story read by Pastor Matthews. The booth rentals, as well as money from the funnel cakes, would go to the shelter.

"I can't deny that I like it here," she admitted after some thought.

"I can see that," her mom acknowledged, pulling her close to hug her. "It's a comfortable place. I hadn't really thought about it a lot since I was a little girl. But I remember being happy here."

"It's a shame you never got to come back."

Her mom lifted one shoulder in an elegant but casual gesture. "Yes, I guess it was a shame. I never thought too much about it. We left. I don't know why we left, but it happened. My mother came in one day and told me to pack a bag and hug my father goodbye. It must have been traumatic because I didn't think much about it until I came here to get you. That's when the memories rolled over me."

"I do love Granddad," she told her mother. "He took me in and even though he grumbled a bit, I knew from the start that he wouldn't want me gone."

"No, I can't suppose he would." Her mom reached

for her hand. "And I owe you an apology. I've not been a good mother."

"We all did our best." But she really didn't want to talk about what had happened. Fortunately her mother seemed of the same mind and the conversation ended.

Marissa's gaze drifted over the crowd and landed on one person. Alex stood near his truck. He had the gray pony tied to the post of a round pen. A crowd of children had gathered for pony rides.

"You're not going to give everything up for a cowboy? Are you?" her mother asked as they walked to a craft booth with beaded jewelry.

She glanced past her mom and saw that Alex was watching. Would it really be giving everything up? "Mom, I don't want to discuss this."

Discussing it would be pointless. Because she did have to leave, but she was leaving behind more than she'd ever expected. Her grandfather, Bea, Essie, Alex, even the animals. She'd come here to get over a failed attempt at a wedding and now she was going to have to get over being here.

But this she could come back to.

"I'm sorry," her mom said as the two of them looked over the jewelry. "I know that you have your own choices to make. I would just hate for you to give up everything on a whim."

She wanted to tell her mom that nothing she did was on a whim. If her mom knew her better, she would know that Marissa planned everything. She wouldn't walk away from those plans for fear of letting her parents down.

They were paying for their purchases when Pastor Matthews approached with a woman Marissa had seen at church but hadn't met. She smiled a greeting at the two as she and her mother started to move onto the next booth.

"Marissa, wait, if you don't mind." Pastor Matthews spoke quickly before Marissa could leave. "I have someone I want you to meet."

"I'm Theresa Wilkins, I'm the superintendent of the district school. I've heard so much about you and I was hoping, if you're planning on staying in the community, that we could sit down and talk."

"Talk?" Marissa gave her mom a worried glance, because this was probably the last thing her mom wanted to hear.

"About a job," Theresa continued. "We're a small school and we lose a lot of younger teachers to bigger schools, where there are more opportunities and better pay. We're looking for teachers who will be committed to our community and stay with us."

A job. Marissa couldn't help it, her gaze slid to where Alex led the pony, Cobalt, around the pen. A little boy was riding the pony and even from a distance appeared to be having the time of his life.

"I'm sorry, I already have a job."

"Well, if those circumstances should change, please call us."

"I will. Thank you."

Pastor Matthews and Theresa Wilkins left and Marissa returned to her mother's side. Neither of them mentioned the job opportunity. They made a few more purchases, then found their way to the music, where Marissa's father and grandfather waited. The two men had found chairs near the band and they were listening to music and finishing off a funnel cake.

"I have to go inside soon," Marissa said after a few minutes of uncomfortable silence. "I have to find Bea."

What she needed was a moment alone to think, and to maybe grieve the job offer she couldn't take. It was the job she had always wanted. As she made her excuses and walked away from the others, she thought about the fact that it wasn't forever. There would be other job openings in the future. Maybe someday she could return to Bluebonnet to live and to build a life for herself.

The halls of the church were quiet and as she walked, she prayed, something she hadn't done much of in her life. It felt foreign, to take those few moments and her worries and give them to God. It felt like whispering secrets into the dark as a child, hoping someone could hear.

"Marissa," a voice, strong and familiar, called to her from the end of the hall.

She spun around and faced Alex, plastering a shaky smile on her face. "Hey. I was afraid I wouldn't get a chance to tell you goodbye."

"It is goodbye then," he said as he drew closer, stepping out of the shadows. "I was hoping you would take Theresa's offer."

"You knew?"

"Well, yes. I told her you might be interested in a job. I wasn't sure."

She blinked away silly tears. For a few minutes she'd thought that she'd done this on her own. Someone had wanted her for her abilities and not her connections. It didn't really matter now. It wasn't as if she could take the job anyway.

"Of course," she said hesitantly because she didn't know what should come next. Her thoughts tumbled through her mind. She was hurt that the job hadn't really

been about her skills, but hopeful because he wanted
her to stay. Or maybe not. Maybe he'd just been helping her get what he thought she wanted.

"Marissa?"

She wanted to stay close to him. Even there, in the
hallway, she didn't want to walk away. She wanted him
to say something that mattered. But she was afraid of
what he might, or might not say.

"I have to go find Bea," she said. "But thank you. I
can't take the job. I already have one."

"Yes, I know."

As she walked away she thought he whispered that
he would miss her.

Alex sat on the opposite side of the church from Marissa and her family. Lucy sat on one side of him. Maria
sat on the other. As if they thought he needed their
protection. To top it off, they kept giving him cautious
looks, as if they thought he was falling apart.

He wasn't. He was pretty close to frantic, though.
That wasn't what he'd expected to feel. It was the crazed
feeling a person gets when they see someone about to
drive away, and there was no way to stop them. He'd felt
this way before, when their mother left the first time.
She said she couldn't take it anymore and she'd gotten
in a car and left.

From time to time she breezed back into their lives
as if she hadn't crushed them as children. As if she
hadn't let them down. Each time she'd left he'd wanted
to chase after her and bring her back, because Maria
had needed more than a maniac father and siblings who
couldn't be a mother to her.

He hated the feeling.

He wanted to run from it, but not after the person leaving. Because he guessed if he ran after her, he would always be running after her, trying to convince her to stay. He started to get up but Maria put a hand on his arm.

He sat back down.

Bea had moved from the audience to the stage. A movement on the other side of the sanctuary caught his attention. He glanced at Marissa taking her seat at the piano. A hush fell over the crowd. Marissa began to play and then Bea's voice joined.

Throughout the sanctuary were surprised murmurs. People who hadn't seen Bea's last performance were in awe. He sat in awe of the woman at the piano. He couldn't help but remember the bedraggled bride, rain pouring down her face, threatening him with her high-heeled shoe. He grinned a little.

Maria elbowed him in the side.

"Don't be a moron," she whispered.

"Hush," he said.

"Don't let her go."

"Quiet," Lucy whispered. "But she's right."

"Not. My. Choice," he murmured.

Bea caught his attention again. She had moved to Marissa's side. They joined together singing "Carol of the Bells." He closed his eyes and drew in a steadying breath. Tonight the woman at that piano was going to leave town, walk out of his life, and he would miss her.

He didn't quite know what to do about it. Chase her car down the road like a scared kid? Beg her to stay?

No, he wouldn't do either of those. She had to make her own decisions about staying or leaving. She had to want to be in Bluebonnet. For now she'd made her decision. She'd chosen Dallas.

He had things to focus on. He had his own stuff to take care of. The auction was a week away. He was running out of time.

What could he offer Marissa? Not much, he guessed.

After the program ended he spotted her talking to a group of people. She saw him and he told himself it was happiness that lit up her face and that he had something to do with that happiness. She excused herself and headed his way.

"I wanted another chance to say goodbye," he told her.

"I'm glad." She took his hand in hers. "I'm so glad you found me on the side of the road that day."

"Would it be wrong to say that I'm glad Aidan picked the caterer instead of you?"

She laughed at that. "I think I'm kind of glad, too."

"I'm trying to do more than say goodbye."

"Don't." She leaned close to him. "It'll hurt too much. I have to go. My parents… I feel like I've spent a lifetime letting them down and if I don't go home, I'll be letting them down again."

"I'm not going to beg you to stay, but I would like to see you again. I'll drive to Dallas. Or if you're here visiting Dan."

"I would like that." She kissed his cheek. "I have to go now."

It sounded like goodbye in more ways than one. More of a "we'll do lunch" than an "I really want you in my life."

Her hand pulled free from his and he stood there watching her walk away. Who knew a city girl in a wedding dress could change his life and everything he'd thought he wanted? But she had and he knew if she didn't come back, he would miss her forever.

Chapter Seventeen

A pounding on his door woke Alex. He rubbed at his face and crawled off the couch he'd slept on. The pounding continued.

"I'm coming," he yelled.

He yanked the door opened and there stood Dan. "It took you long enough."

"It's six in the morning." Alex opened the door a little wider and motioned the older man inside.

"I figured you'd be up early selling off some livestock."

It was late January and he had gotten an extension. The ranch would be auctioned off on the first of February unless he could come up with all of the money. He'd already sold his bucking bulls. It had been easy, hadn't felt at all like letting go of a dream.

"Yes, I'm selling livestock. Later." He headed for the kitchen and the coffeepot and let Dan trail along behind. "What has you out of bed so early?"

He poured water in the coffee maker. Marcus entered the kitchen looking like a long-haired bear that had come out of hibernation.

Dan glanced at Alex's twin. "Good grief, you don't wear that hair in one of them man-buns, do you?"

Marcus gave Dan a narrow-eyed look and practically growled. He went to the fridge and poured himself a glass of juice. "What's he doing here?"

"I'm here to do what you haven't done. Help your brother." Dan pulled a checkbook out of his back pocket.

"I helped," Marcus grumbled.

"Dan, I don't want your money."

Dan didn't respond. He wrote out a check and slid it across the table. "Don't be prideful. You didn't get yourself into this mess. If you had, I wouldn't help. You've helped me a lot over the years. Not once have you asked to be paid, you just helped. I got to figuring up what I should have paid you and it came to quite a sum."

"Dan, you can't do this."

Dan held up a hand. "I found some good stuff in that old lockbox. Let's just say, I'm not going to worry too much about my future. And neither is my granddaughter. You remember her, don't you? Pretty little thing with dark hair and blue eyes."

From the kitchen table, Marcus snickered. Alex shot him a warning look.

"I remember your granddaughter, Dan." Alex lifted the coffeepot. "Want some?"

"Nah, I don't have time for that. Go pay off the mortgage and buy this ranch before your mother pulls another stunt."

Marcus picked up the check and whistled. He handed the check to Alex.

"I can't take that."

Dan slid it back to him. "You can. And you will. I'm

making an investment. In your future. And I hope in the future of my granddaughter."

"How will this money help her future?" Alex asked, but then he got it. And obviously Marcus got it because his rusty-sounding laugh echoed as he left the room.

"School gets out early today," Dan said with meaning.

"Okay?"

"That gives you time to do your chores, clean up and get on the road." Dan patted the check. "Investment in the future. I wouldn't want you going through life deep in debt. I'd rather give you a gift than an inheritance."

"Dan, you don't have to do this."

Dan pushed to his feet. "Follow me. I have to show you something."

Out of curiosity, Alex followed Dan outside. He was surprised to see his sister Maria standing by his truck.

"What are you doing here?" he asked.

"Dan called and asked if I would help him out." She opened the passenger door of this truck. "Everything you need."

"Because you don't seem to be able to do this on your own," Dan said in his typical gruff tone.

Inside his truck was a box with a necklace, a book of poetry and a bouquet of flowers. "What do you want me to do with all of this?" he asked his sister.

"Go to Dallas and get a girlfriend," Maria said. "I know you thought she'd leave and after a while you'd forget her, but you're not. Forgetting her, that is. And so I'm helping you with romance. Because women do like it. Even strong, independent women. It's how we're made. And so you need to do something romantic."

"I'm not going to Dallas."

"Think about it. Please. I'll take all of this stuff to the house and then it's up to you."

"You can take it inside or take it back to the store. It doesn't matter to me."

She punched his arm. "Why are you being so stubborn?"

He stopped, let out a sigh and thought about how he'd almost believed she was no longer his annoying little sister. "I'm stubborn because it's how we've always survived. I haven't heard from her since she left. So what I'm assuming is she came here, had fun with a cowboy and went back to her real life."

"Idiot. Have you contacted her since she left?"

No, but he wasn't going to admit that.

She punched him again.

"Stop doing that." He rubbed his arm.

"I just wanted to make sure I had your attention."

"You have it. Now I have to feed livestock. If you want to help, get out of those city clothes and put on your work clothes."

"I'd love to help, but I'm going to lunch with Lucy." She headed for the house with the flowers, necklace and book of poetry.

"You're still a nuisance," he shouted after her.

Dan cleared his throat, reminding Alex of his presence and his part in this whole plot. "She's trying to help. So am I. I saw Marissa at Christmas. She didn't miss that idiot that walked out on her. She does miss you. And if I'm guessing correctly, you miss her. I know I made a lot of comments about tying yourself to a city girl, but I was wrong. And you were wrong to let her go."

"It isn't just because she's from the city, Dan. What

am I supposed to offer her? A ranch in debt. A past that makes me question what kind of husband and father I'll be? I can give her all the flowers in the world but it isn't going to make up for all that."

Dan rolled his eyes to heaven. "I can't believe you're going to make me say this. You're not Jesse Palermo. You're not even a close second. You've been like a grandson to me. If you were anything like your father, I would have run you off years ago."

"Thanks, Dan."

"Don't thank me. And I guess don't let me make you do something you don't want to do."

Alex nodded in agreement and Dan left, heading back to his place in his old farm truck. Alex thought about the check on his table and he thought about that old farm truck that Dan would drive until it fell apart.

But then his thoughts shifted to Marissa.

He wasn't taking a woman a book of poetry.

But he might take her flowers and a necklace. Because he might give himself one last chance. Stubbornness might not be the best trait to have in a relationship. And if a relationship was what he wanted with Marissa, he guessed he might need to work on that. Some women were worth chasing after. Especially if they need a little help realizing a man really loved them.

He loved her.

He shook his head at the thought because it wasn't what he'd expected that day he helped a rain-soaked bride into his truck. But it had happened.

Marissa watched the last of her students get on the bus. Her friend and co-teacher, Laura, stood next to her. Laura let out a sigh.

"I'm so glad this week is over. Is it spring break yet?"
Marissa shook her head. "No, but I wish it was."

"Big plans?" Laura asked as they headed back inside.

"Not really. I think I might go visit my grandfather."

At the thought of returning to Bluebonnet Springs, her heart kicked up a notch. She'd missed being there. She missed her grandfather. She missed Essie's café, the church and, most of all, she missed Alex.

There were days she thought she'd call, and then she thought maybe he was happy with the way things had ended. She wanted to tell him that she wasn't renewing her contract at this school. She'd already explained to her parents that it was time she made a few decisions for herself. And she couldn't teach here. Didn't want to teach here. She wanted a school like the one at Bluebonnet because she wanted to teach children like the ones who lived at the shelter. She wanted to inspire them to dream and to believe they could make a difference.

Thinking about Bluebonnet made her want to go sooner than spring break. Maybe today. She could be there in a few hours, spend the long weekend at her grandfather's and be back Monday night in time for school Tuesday.

"You've gone all gooey," Laura said.

"What?"

Laura laughed. "We were talking about spring break and you suddenly had this dreamy look on your face. And I don't think it was your grandfather you were thinking about."

"No, I wasn't." She glanced at her watch. "I'm going to Bluebonnet. I'll be back Tuesday."

"Have a good weekend," Laura said as Marissa hurried off.

She grabbed her purse and book bag from her office as she called her mom to let her know she wouldn't be coming home. She prepared herself for something less than understanding and was surprised when her mom told her it was about time.

She was pulling onto the main road when a truck came up behind her, headlights flashing. She glanced at the tailgater but kept driving. Soon the truck began to honk and the lights flashed again. She took another look in the rearview mirror and her heart collided with her ribs. She pulled to the shoulder of the road and got out of her car.

The truck pulled in right behind her. Alex took his time getting out. She stood near the back of her car. Traffic slowed to watch.

Finally he got out of the truck, his arms full. Flowers, a book, a box. She took a few steps toward him, toward his familiar presence. She'd missed him so much it had hurt, and now, seeing him, the hurt magnified because she didn't want him to go away.

"You almost missed me." She said it out of the blue. "I was leaving town."

"Were you?" he asked, awkward with his arms full. She should help him out but she didn't. He was too cute, too boyish, standing there with his gifts and that awkward, unsure look on his face.

"Yes, I was going to Bluebonnet Springs. I have friends there. I've missed them."

"Have you?" He moved his arms, trying to arrange things. "You could help a guy out. Maria insisted I should come prepared to romance you back into my life. Your grandfather helped her."

"Is that what this is?" She took the flowers. He managed then to get a hold of the box and the book. "What else do you have? Because I do like gestures. Grand gestures."

"I have a necklace." He managed to get it out of the box. "I'd like to say I had the forethought to pick it out. But Maria gets the credit."

He put the single teardrop diamond around her neck.

"Maria has good taste," Marissa told him.

"Yes, she does. She likes you." He opened the book of poetry.

She had to stop him. "Please, no poetry. I don't think I can handle that."

"Good, because I didn't really want to read poetry."

"I've missed you," she said as he stepped close, his nearness making it difficult to breathe.

"I know."

"You're supposed to say you missed me, too."

He took the flowers and held them to his side, and then he kissed her. It was a sweet, searching kiss. Cars driving past honked. Marissa didn't care. She kissed him back and then she rested her head on his shoulder.

"Are you sniffing me?" he asked.

"I am," she admitted. "I've missed every bit of you, even your scent."

"Will you please come back to Bluebonnet?" he asked with a voice that shook.

She was glad he wasn't altogether calm. She wanted to know that she wasn't in this alone.

"I told you, I was on my way there. I have a long weekend."

"I don't want you in Bluebonnet for a weekend. I want you there for good. In my life."

"O-o-h-hh," she said, drawing out the word.

He stepped back, returning the flowers to her hands. "Don't make me have to read poetry."

"Never," she promised.

"I'm not good at this. I'm not a man who ever thought he'd find someone he wanted to spend his life with. But I'd chase after you, Marissa. I'd do my best to never disappoint you."

"I'm coming back to Bluebonnet," she told him. "I'm taking a job at the local school. I'm also going to date a cowboy."

"Really? A cowboy?" He grinned, then lifted her off her feet and spun her around. "You are talking about me, right?"

When he set her back on her feet, she kissed him. "Yes, you're the only cowboy in my life."

"I plan on keeping it that way," he promised.

He followed her back to Bluebonnet Springs and as she drove into town it felt like a homecoming in more ways than one. The man she loved was behind her and their future was ahead of them.

Epilogue

It seemed fitting that Alex and Marissa would wait a year and have a Christmas wedding in Bluebonnet Springs. Marissa stood in the fellowship hall of the church as her mom made the last adjustments to her hair and veil.

"You look beautiful," her mom told her as she kissed Marissa on the cheek. "You were right, this dress is perfect."

Marissa looked in the mirror, pleased with what she saw. She kept her hair shoulder-length now but it had been pinned up with tendrils curling loosely around her face. The veil hung just to her neck. The dress was slim-fitting white velvet and with few adornments.

"Mom, thank you. For loving me. And for being here today."

"I think I'm more here than I've been in a very long time," Mary told her daughter. "I'm sorry that it took so long."

Marissa hugged her mom. "No regrets. Let's just live the best life we can from this day forward."

"Yes, from this day forward." Her mom dabbed at

her eyes. "From this day forward you will be Marissa Palermo. No longer my little girl, but a wife. And someday a mother."

"Stop. You'll make me cry."

"That'll make three of us," Maria said as she sashayed close in her dark red velvet bridesmaid's dress. "Your dad is at the door. It's almost time. Lucy is ready, too."

Her bridesmaid and her matron of honor. It was a simple wedding and Marissa couldn't have been happier. She kissed her mother's cheek one last time before she left to go find her seat in the church. And then Marissa walked out the door and took hold of her father's arm.

They walked around the building to the front of the church. Christmas lights twinkled in the shrubs on either side of the door. From inside she could hear Bea singing a song about forever. Marissa's dad patted her arm and then he led her up the steps and through the doors. She watched as her bridesmaids and groomsmen made their way down the aisle. And then her flower girl, Dane and Lucy's daughter, Lily, followed. She tossed flower petals in the air with gleeful giggles that Marissa had informed everyone was perfect. The child couldn't see, but she knew the number of steps to the front of the church and then Lucy would be there to guide her.

Bea's song ended. She laughed and said that she was so happy that Alex had been so neighborly to her friend Marissa, because now they were going to be a husband and wife. And wasn't that just the cat's meow. Soft laughter rippled through the congregation.

The wedding march began and Marissa's dad walked her down the aisle to the man of her dreams. A man she might have missed out on if her last groom hadn't left her for the caterer.

She knew that sometimes things happened for the very best reasons. The man standing at the front of this church was God's plan for her life.

Alex was her forever groom. And she was his Christmas bride.

* * * * *